THE LOST ARE THE LAST TO DIE

OTHER TITLES BY LARRY D. SWEAZY

SONNY BURTON NOVELS

A Thousand Falling Crows

JOSIAH WOLFE, TEXAS RANGER

The Rattlesnake Season
The Scorpion Trail
The Badger's Revenge
The Cougar's Prey
The Coyote Tracker
The Gila Wars

LUCAS FUME WESTERNS

Vengeance at Sundown
Escape from Hangtown

NOVELS

The Devil's Bones

A SONNY BURTON NOVEL

THE LOST ARE THE LAST TO DIE

LARRY D. SWEAZY

*(Based on the short story
"Point Blank, Texas")*

FIVE STAR
A part of Gale, a Cengage Company

A Cengage Company

Farmington Hills, Mich • San Francisco • New York • Waterville, Maine
Meriden, Conn • Mason, Ohio • Chicago

LIBRARY OF CONGRESS CATALOGING-IN-PUBLICATION DATA

Names: Sweazy, Larry D., author.
Title: The lost are the last to die / Larry D. Sweazy.
Description: Large print edition. | Farmington Hills, Mich : Five Star, a part of Gale, a Cengage Company, [2019] | Series: A Sonny Burton novel | Based on the short story: Point Blank, Texas.
Identifiers: LCCN 2019009605 (print) | ISBN 9781432857233 (hardcover : alk. paper)
Subjects: | GSAFD: Adventure fiction.
Classification: LCC PS3619.W438 L37 2019 (print) | DDC 813/.6—dc23
LC record available at https://lccn.loc.gov/2019009605

First Edition. First Printing: November 2019
Find us on Facebook—https://www.facebook.com/FiveStarCengage
Visit our website—http://www.gale.cengage.com/fivestar/
Contact Five Star Publishing at FiveStar@cengage.com

Printed in Mexico
1 2 3 4 5 6 7 23 22 21 20 19

In memory of Kevin Wayne Byrne (1952–2018)
First cousin, friend, one of my first readers, my best man,
and one of my earliest sources of encouragement.
I will always miss you.

ACKNOWLEDGMENTS

The idea for *The Lost Are the Last to Die* came along after I had written the original Sonny Burton novel, *A Thousand Falling Crows,* as somewhat of a surprise. I originally thought the first novel was going to be a stand-alone, but Sonny Burton had something more to say about that. So, when Scott Montgomery, mystery fan, writer, and bookseller extraordinaire at the Austin, Texas, bookstore, Mystery People, asked me if I would be interested in writing a crime story set in Texas for an anthology for the Austin Mystery Writers, I thought that would be a fitting venue for the next Sonny Burton story. The anthology, *Lone Star Lawless* (Wildside Press), was a success, and I'm happy, considering that I am not a born-and-bred Texan, to have had my story included in it with so many other wonderful Texas writers. A special mention should go to Gale Albright, who was the original editor of the anthology. Gale died in the middle of the production of the project. Gale loved Texas stories, and her enthusiasm was sorely missed. The work done on the short story, "Point Blank, Texas," made it a better story. The *Lost Are the Last to Die* has gone on to become an even more in-depth look at Sonny's life before his encounter with Bonnie and Clyde, as the story evolved into this novel. Thank you, Scott Montgomery, Gale Albright, Ramona Long, Kathy Waller, and everyone who contributed to the anthology for accepting Sonny's story and making it better.

Thanks also goes to Sean Sutcliffe, the historian and reference librarian at the Waco-McLennan County Library in Waco, Texas, for his help with understanding Waco in the mid-1930s, and to Don Mitchell for sharing his knowledge of Model A Fords. Your input was invaluable, and much appreciated. Any research mistakes are my own.

Special thanks also go to Tiffany Schofield and Hazel Rumney. Your enthusiasm and support of my writing is greatly appreciated. As always, thanks to my longtime agent, Cherry Weiner. We've worked on a lot of projects together, each one special, each one a surprise, and a learning experience. Your dedication and belief in my work means more to me than you know.

My wife, Rose, has been at my side while I wrote this book and every other, spending countless hours reading, offering encouragement, criticism, proofreading, with a smile and no complaints. She didn't ask to be a writer's wife, but she has accepted her fate with devotion and enthusiasm. I'm a lucky man and I know it. Thank you for all that you do.

"No man in the wrong can stand up against a fellow that's in the right and keeps on a-comin'."

—Captain Bill McDonald

"No man in the world can . . . make a bell, . . .
that is, he that has no sound or jangle."

—*Samuel Butler 1612-1680*

CHAPTER ONE

October 1934
Wellington, Texas

Sonny Burton downshifted the Model A Ford pickup truck and pulled it over to the side of the road. Dry Texas Panhandle dirt, hard as stone and thirsty as an injured buzzard, crunched underneath the truck's thin rubber tires. A vaporless cloud of dust agreed with the squeak of the brakes and wafted away slowly. The air was unusually still; an invisible breath held in anticipation, or dread, Sonny wasn't sure which. A crowd had gathered outside of town in a fallow field. Something was going on and he was curious to find out what it was that had so many people out this way, at this time of the day.

Bringing the truck to a stop was a lot easier than it once had been for Sonny, considering his right arm had been amputated, replaced with a prosthetic limb carved of maple. He tried not to think about the loss these days, but he hadn't settled to it completely. The entire incident, starting with the shootout between him and Bonnie and Clyde, seemed like ages ago, when he was another man, whole and on the verge of winding down his lifelong career as a Texas Ranger. Losing his arm had changed his view of the world, of everything really. More in a bad way than good. He was no longer a Ranger, but he was still alive. If breathing and walking could be called that.

Doc told him that a gray period was to be expected, but things would get better. The medical man had been right; some things had taken less time to adjust to, no doubt, like putting the wood contraption on in place of his missing arm and driving the truck. But it had been the middle of the night that was the hardest, when Sonny would wake up and swear he could feel a tingle in the fingers of his missing hand. Phantom pains they were called. A cruel trick nature played on his heart and mind. Sleep never came easy after that happened. Nothing really came easy these days. Not to Sonny Burton. Not to anyone.

"Hey there, friend," Sonny called out, the truck sputtering, all the while keeping his foot on the brake. "What's going on here?"

The man looked to be about twenty-five years younger than Sonny, about the age of his only boy, Jesse. This fella was dressed in dirty overalls and carried a three-foot club carved from an old oak tree. He was on a mission. There were a lot of clubs to be seen. A staggered line of people walked alongside the road heading south.

"Rabbit roundup," the man said with a sneer. "You wanna join in?"

Sonny didn't offer an answer. He stared at the man, then looked over his shoulder into the bed of the truck. Blue, his hound dog, stood on the wheel well watching the people go by. The dog wouldn't jump out, but he'd think about it. Blue had a bad leg, a limp from being hit by the very truck he stood in.

"Thanks, but I've got to be getting home," Sonny said.

"We need every man we can get."

"I suppose you do."

There were more rabbits in the world than Sonny could ever remember seeing. Ever since the drought had set in a few years back the jackrabbit population had exploded. The larger predators had either moved on or died of thirst and starvation. Rabbits were a plague, like locusts in the Bible, descending on a weak field of alfalfa, if one could be found. They'd strip it down to the roots so fast a farmer's tears wouldn't have time to hit the ground.

Some people called the rabbits Hoover Hogs since they'd come on at the start of the Depression. That's what they called it. A Depression. To Sonny, it seemed like the world was dying, all dusty and dry, where nothing would grow and nobody had nothin' to hold on to. Sonny figured the people that called rabbits Hoover Hogs had to have someone to blame for their troubles, but the way he saw it, even the men in Washington didn't have control of the weather and nature's ways. They were all in a bad spot, that's the way it was. Rabbits were taking advantage. It's what animals did. They were trying to survive like everything else.

"Last one before the county stops payin' a penny a pelt," the man said. "Won't be nothin' doin' with 'em after that. Got to kill them since they got the fever. Man over in Kansas come down with it after he ate one of 'em and died. Damn shame to see a waste of meat, but it was an ugly death from what I heared. I'd rather eat bone soup for the rest of my life than die like that."

Sonny nodded. "I heard tell of the same thing."

"You sure you won't change your mind?"

"No, I'd be no good to you. No good at all." Sonny didn't want to explain to the man that he didn't have a good arm to swing a club with, but that wasn't the reason. He could've used his left hand easy enough, but he didn't want to. He couldn't bear the thought of killing anything. Not even a little rabbit, when the rabbit didn't do nothin' to deserve it except be a rabbit.

Sonny eased the throttle back and started to let go of the brake. Driving the truck was an orchestrated movement that took a concentrated thought where it once wasn't needed. Thinking about what he had to do to move one way or the other still made him angry.

"Suit yourself, then," the man said over his shoulder as he scurried away with a quick step, catching the rest of the crowd.

Sonny didn't answer. He tipped his hat. An old brown felt Stetson. He'd hung up the white one that he wore with the Rangers after he'd lost his arm. He had no plans to wear that hat again. His law enforcement days were over after being forced to retire. No use reminding the world, or himself, what he once was.

After glancing over his shoulder, Sonny decided to let the crowd pass. A loose group of townspeople walked along the road behind the truck. It seemed more like a line to a revival tent, to him, than to a slaughtering. No sense in covering folks in more dust than was coming at them anyway.

After a few long minutes the way behind him was clear. The wind remained in retreat, a rarity of recent months, and it seemed like every little sound amplified in the stillness. Footsteps crunched on pebbles ahead of him. Blue sat down in the bed of the truck and scratched at a flea. A little finch popped onto a dead stalk of buffalo grass, whistled twice, then flittered away, adding a couple of notes of song to the overwhelming percussive bubble that seemed to surround Sonny. Beyond the immediate noise came a more pronounced thud. Or thudding. Sonny knew that it was a thousand tiny feet scurrying, being driven into a special escape-proof fence. A cloud of dust appeared ahead, drawing closer. A group of men were driving the rabbits into the trap.

"Hang on, Blue," Sonny said. "Time to go."

The dog's long ears perked up and he found his way to the back of the bed and laid down. Smart one, that dog. Sonny'd only had to show him what to do twice before he figured out for himself that that was the safest place to be when the truck was on the move.

Sonny drove slowly, his eyes straight ahead, but once he crested the rise, he saw the crowd gathered off to his right, all clustered around a closed-in four-sided fence. It looked like an arena, the Colosseum without the stone, where lions and men went to die. Death and crowds seemed to go hand in hand. That kind of entertainment didn't make an ounce of sense to Sonny.

Even above the clatter of the Model A's engine, he heard the first piece of wood strike a rabbit. Wood against flesh. Strength against weakness. The air was suddenly full of squeals from the frightened animals, then was joined by the shouts of men, women, and children, mostly boys, rushing in and clubbing anything that moved. It was no song of glory, but one of fear, rage, and madness that was a fever all to itself. The cloud of dust that rose from the scuffle dripped red with countless drops of blood. It was an ugly color against the gray, moody sky.

Sonny pressed down on the accelerator, but he couldn't look away, not once he saw the little boy. He was no more than four or five, standing alone outside the fence, crying for his mother, screaming as if he had been bludgeoned himself. There wasn't a white speck of skin left on him to be seen. The boy was covered from head to toe with blood, screaming at the top of his lungs, wiping the red rain from his eyes as he did.

The sight sent a shiver down Sonny's spine. He wondered what the boy would remember about this day when he became a man. He wondered what kind of a man the boy would become. Would he see the world covered in blood? Or would he run away at the first scream? Only time would tell.

A familiar car was parked next to Sonny's house. It was Jonesy's car. Jonesy was the Collingsworth County sheriff. Nobody called the sheriff by his given name, Layton Jones. He was known as Jonesy to most folks, like his father before him, and most likely his father before that, too. The Joneses had worn a star on their chest in the county for as long as anyone could remember. Sonny and Jonesy had that in common. The law was the family business. Sonny's father had been a Texas Ranger, and now his son was, too. Jesse had taken Sonny's place in the company after the shootout with Bonnie and Clyde.

Sonny parked the truck, got out, and walked to the sheriff. "Figured I'd see you down at the roundup. Lot of folks down there."

Jonesy was nearly a head shorter than Sonny, and a little bit rounder. His hat was squared on his head and his uniform was fresh and ironed. He looked like he was ready to walk in a parade. "If there's call for me to go, I'll find out," Jonesy said.

"Suppose you will." Sonny could tell by the way Jonesy fidgeted that he was as uncomfortable as he was with the kind of killing that was taking place down the road. "You out this way and stop by for a cup of coffee, or is something else on your mind?"

Jonesy leaned down to pet Blue, who had limped over to the two men. "That leg's never gonna get better is it, boy?"

Blue wagged his tail and sat at Jonesy's feet. The dog was agreeable, liked most people, but didn't have any use for other dogs. He wanted to fight for his place even though he didn't have use of all his parts. Blue was a good match for Sonny. They understood each other. Sonny still felt a tinge of guilt about running over the dog with the truck, but in the end, he'd brought him home with him, and he was glad of that.

"Blue gets around pretty well," Sonny said, uncomfortable that Jonesy had ignored his question.

"I imagine he does." Jonesy stood, squared his shoulders, and looked down the road. Sonny followed Jonesy's gaze. He saw a dust cloud produced by a car heading his way.

"Looks like I need to put the coffeepot on." Sonny stiffened.

He knew for certain by the sight of the cloud that Jonesy's visit was no social call. "Or are you going to tell me what's going on?"

"I was waitin' on Jesse to get here."

"So this is Ranger business?"

"You could say that."

"Ain't got nothin' to do with me. Not now. Those days are over for me, you know that, Jonesy. I'm hardly any use to that dog, much less to the Rangers. You tell Jesse to go on about his business and I'll go on with mine. He wants to spend time with me, he can stop by for a visit any time he likes. He knows that." Sonny headed for the front of the house. "But I ain't up for no Ranger business. He's keen to that, too."

"You remember a fella named Billy Bunson?" Jonesy said.

The name hung in the still air for a second longer than it should have. It stopped Sonny in his tracks. "Last I heard he was in Huntsville for life. Put him there myself. I'd have thrown away the key if they woulda let me or pulled the switch on Old Sparky if the good people of Texas would have seen fit to put an end to that boy's madness."

The car pulled in behind Jonesy's and came to a stop. Tires slid on the hard dirt. Another puff of dust adding to the storm that was sure to come soon.

"You ever knowed a prison cell that could hold Billy Bunson?" Jonesy said with a hard set of eyes fixed on Sonny.

"Only if he was in the hole." Sonny waivered, shifted his weight, and watched his son get out of a new model Plymouth and put on his white Stetson. "Got out, didn't he?"

"Worse than that," Jonesy said. "His girlfriend busted him out, but the warden's men got her pretty quick."

"But he got away," Sonny said. His left hand started to sweat. The air had gone out of his lungs at the first mention of Billy

Bunson. He felt like a sickness was coming on. An old, familiar sickness.

"That's right, he did," Jonesy answered. "But his girl's in the county jail. Donna Del Rey's her name, or so she says."

"Name doesn't ring a bell."

"Didn't figure it would."

Jesse Burton walked over to the two men. Jesse favored his dead mother, Martha, and her side of the family. Germans they were, first into Texas by way of New Braunfels. He was stocky, about the same height as Jonesy, and had the sense of humor of an aged skunk. "Pa," he said.

Jesse didn't acknowledge Blue, who was still planted next to Jonesy's ankle, and Blue didn't acknowledge him, either. Jesse was the exception to the dog's agreeable nature toward humans.

"This ain't got nothing to do with me," Sonny said. "You best get back in that shiny car of yours, head back into town, and tell the captain I don't want nothing to do with this Billy Bunson mess. You hear me? It has nothing to do with me."

"You tell him everything?" Jesse said to Jonesy.

"I was gettin' to it."

Sonny glared at both of the men. "If I had my scattergun handy, I'd run you both off here right now. I can still use it. I've practiced pullin' both triggers with my left hand. Now, go. Right now, I tell you. Both of you go on and get. Go on, get!" Sonny yelled.

"Billy Bunson's gone and kidnapped the warden's wife, Pa," Jesse said calmly. "He wants a trade. His girl for the warden's wife. Simple as that."

"It's not that simple. It's never that simple with Billy Bunson."

Jesse stepped in front of Jonesy so he was only a few inches from Sonny's face. Sonny could smell the bacon and eggs the boy'd eaten for breakfast on his breath. "He sent us her pinky finger, Pa, to let us know he was serious. You know what's next. You, of all people, know what's next. We need to find Billy Bunson, Pa. You know we have to find him, and we have to find him real fast, or that woman's gonna face a horror that none of us want to think about. He'll kill her slow, piece by piece. You know he will, Pa. Billy Bunson will kill that woman if you don't help us find her, Pa. You hear me?"

Sonny lowered his head and sighed. "You sure it's her finger?"

"As sure as we can be," Jesse said. He kicked the dirt and watched the dust disappear. "She's pregnant," he said slowly. "The warden's wife is pregnant, Pa, and that ain't gonna matter a bit to Billy Bunson. He'll kill her if he has to. Her and that baby. You know he will."

Sonny stared past Jesse, out to the road, out into the openness. There wasn't a house to be seen in any direction. All he could see were unproductive fields that grew nothing but dust storms, snake holes, and angry crowds who wanted something to take out their anger on. At night, he was so alone it was like he was the only person alive on the planet.

"He knows you all'll come to me for help," Sonny said. "You know that, right? He knows that I'm the only one who can help you find him."

"That's why I'm here, Pa. That's why I'm here," Jesse answered.

CHAPTER TWO

After Jonesy and Jesse had gone on their way, Sonny was left to face the inevitable; a coming to terms with something he wasn't eager to accept. He knew he had to go to Huntsville. There was no way around making the trip. If anybody could figure out what Billy Bunson was going to do next and stop the boy before it was too late, it was him. As odd as it was, and much to Sonny's dismay, something deep inside had begun to rouse, something he'd thought was lost to him: A reason to use his brain and body. The Rangers needed him. *Him.* Not anyone else to go after Billy Bunson. But him. They needed him. He supposed that desire could be enough of a reason for him to make the long trip south. He wished he didn't have to think about any of it at all. Somebody should have locked Billy Bunson in a hole and thrown away the key.

It'd been a long time since Sonny had made such a demanding trip. Long before he'd lost his right arm. The certainty of that thought staggered him, drained all of the newfound gumption and hope right out of him. He had to hold onto the kitchen sink with his good hand and fix his gaze out the dusty window to steady himself. The familiar foe of doubt, followed by its greedy friend, fear, struck him harder than he expected. Neither lived too deep under his skin.

Dark emotions had made companionable use of themselves since the amputation. He wasn't unaccustomed to their presence, and was relieved that they'd been overcome by a sense of purpose. Nobody but him knew what he was up against, especially after age and Bonnie and Clyde had taken his spirit from him, exposed a weakness that Sonny never knew existed. Doubt was ever present. Fear lurked around every corner. Some days he could barely warm a pan of beans for supper.

Billy Bunson was more than a match for most men, strong, healthy, and in their prime, but him? Sonny? Now? Bringing in a seasoned criminal like Billy seemed impossible, foolhardy, a suicide mission. But what choice did he have?

Hell, Sonny thought, *even the prison couldn't hold that boy in, not with all of the guns, good men, and cold steel bars owned by the great state of Texas. What do you think you can do?* Then he stopped himself, and asked the real question: *What are you afraid of, old man? Dying?*

Blue whimpered slightly at his feet, but Sonny ignored the dog. The landscape beyond the window had his full attention. He was staring into the past, then calculating his demise in the near future, concocting a stew made of dread. The stew's base was settled—he had to go back to work. Now all he had to do was add the meat to have a meal, that reason, that purpose to pull himself out of his boring routine and stop a cold-blooded criminal once and for all. It was no easy task, no easy recipe to create; that was for sure. But this was about more than stopping Billy Bunson.

Evening had settled in fast. Dust swirled in the field across the road, a harmless cyclone that had become as common as jackrabbits. Sonny's daily view was of a lifeless world, one that had lost hope and the will to grow anything worth cultivating. Flowers were rare. Birdsong came as an alarm. It was like a virus had attacked every ounce of goodness with a rusty cancer that could never be cured. Death was inevitable. It surrounded him. The world moaned and trudged forth in a Great Depression. There was something more in the air than dust. Truth be told, Sonny had been waiting for death to come after him for a long time. He didn't figure it would be in the form of Billy Bunson.

The inside of the house was no different than the outside world; dusty, overcome with the poverty of purpose, a woman's nag, and the loss of self-respect. The air was stale; oppressive. If he remained standing where he was, either the dust would cover him, smother him, and take his life in slow gulps, or Billy Bunson would come looking for him, slip into the house in the middle of the night, and put a quick end to Sonny Burton once and for all. If death was what he wanted, then all he'd have to do was do nothing. He didn't have to move an inch, and he knew it. Billy Bunson would come after him.

And it was that thought that stirred Sonny awake. He'd never been the kind of man to let a fight come to him. Never. And this time wasn't going to be any different. It couldn't be. There was a pregnant woman in trouble, an unborn baby counting on him to do the right thing. This wasn't about saving himself. It was about saving that baby. Flesh and bone and joy and sweetness that deserved to breathe and enter the world with the hope of making it a better place—if that was possible.

Sonny exhaled, looked away from the window, down to the dog. "What in tarnation am I going to do with you, Blue? I can't leave you here to fend for yourself. I'd worry about you every mile I traveled. I could see if I could leave you at Pete Jorgenson's with him bein' a vet and all. You like them, don't you, those Jorgensons?"

Blue wagged his tail nervously and remained sitting obediently at Sonny's ankle, not offering an answer one way or the other. The dog was pasted to Sonny's pant leg day and night.

"I could do that, leave you behind, in someone else's care," Sonny continued. "Or, I could take you with me. Have some company on the trip. How about that, Blue? How about you come with me? Would you like that?"

May 1911
Vinton, Texas

The house stood at the base of an imposing hill. Shadows covered the simple roof, protected and threatened by a jagged and lifeless brown cliff. Even on a pleasant day the structure looked more like a shack built to give shelter to rattlesnakes and scorpions than a place to settle a family. There were no trees nearby, nothing green in sight to offer a hint of hope or promise. Sonny Burton could tell by the look on Martha's face that she was none too happy to have arrived at another low station that would be their new home.

He halted the single mule that pulled their wagon, and let the dust settle around him before he dared to speak. "I know it doesn't look like much, but you and the boy will be safe here. El Paso's half a day's ride. Any trouble that's brewin' won't reach this far."

"Says you," Martha said. Her arms were crossed tight against her chest. A hint of German spit off the tip of her tongue, making the emphasis of her disdain unmistakable. Her words and mood would not change for the foreseeable future. Sonny knew that as sure as it was daytime. The two of them had been married for fifteen years. Martha was an open book, held no surprises to him, though she'd been quieter of late, more unsettled about this trip, more than any other he could remember. She didn't like South Texas, the heat and uncertainty of it. She preferred the north where it was green and wholesome. Sonny didn't blame her, but duty had brought him to El Paso. He hoped the barrenness of the south was the cause for her distance and not something else.

"There's neighbors nearby, across the ridge, settled around town. This spot has always been a stopping place as long as anyone can remember. The Camino Real ran through here, and the Butterfield line later on. Not many folks stayed around, but some did. The town's nothing more than a post office where the marshal resides, and a general store. We'll make some acquaintances before I leave," Sonny said.

"When I get settled, you will uproot me again?" Moving was an old wound, one that should have scarred over long ago, but Martha was prone to holding grudges. Sonny knew she thought he was lazy, lacked ambition, had settled for his fifty dollar a month sergeant's salary, and she was mostly right. He had settled. He wasn't ambitious. Sonny Burton held no desire to become a captain of a Ranger company like his father had been. He knew that life all too well. Being a captain was a thankless, dangerous job. Even more so than being a sergeant. Something Sonny could never convince Martha of—so he had stopped trying.

"I'm sorry, you could have stayed in Austin. But you insisted." Sonny didn't need to remind her that her presence was her choice, and he regretted saying so out loud.

A red rage swept across Martha's puffy face and settled there. "I am a married woman, not a lonely widow left to raise her only son. At least, not yet."

Sonny waved his hand to ward off a tongue lashing. "The boy," he said, casting a glance over his shoulder.

Martha pursed her lips and let out a loud exhale. If there was one thing the two of them agreed on it was not to argue in front of Jesse, their twelve-year-old son. They couldn't save him from the tension, from the underlying discomfort that had existed between them long before the boy had been born. They did their best not to scream or throw things at each other when Jesse was around.

Anger did not vanish from Martha's face—it lived in her early wrinkled face like a squatter who refused to leave—but she exhaled, and retreated from the battle again. "This is it, then? This is where we are to live this time?"

"Yes," Sonny said.

"For how long?"

"As long as it takes."

It took a few days to settle in, to get a feel for the ground Sonny stood on. With everything inside the house in its place, the time had come to pay a call on the neighbors and introduce himself and his family. Socializing was not a task Sonny Burton took to naturally, but no matter the uneasiness, he knew the chore had to be done. Martha and the boy couldn't be left alone not knowing anyone, where they were, or who to call on if need for help came upon them. The duty ahead of him could take Sonny away for days or weeks; he wasn't sure how long he would be gone this time.

"So, you're the Texas Ranger I hear tell of that's settled in the old Winslow place," the man, Hiram Pete, said. He was thin as pokeweed and his skin as brown and dry as the dirt he stood on.

"Yes, Mr. Pete, I am." Sonny looked past the man, and eyed Martha making small talk with the man's wife, a fellow woman of German descent. The two of them seemed comfortable with each other right away, which helped Sonny relax. Jesse was off with a few of the Petes' six boys, wandering around the hardscrabble ranch they called home.

"You can call me Hi," Mr. Pete said. "And most folks call my wife, Hon. Tell 'em you spoke with Hi and Hon, and that's all you'll need to say. Everybody in the valley knows us. Heck, most of 'em are kin one way or the other. I sure was relieved to hear that a Ranger had come to stay among us. That's never happened before, and it'll bring some comfort to the missus knowin' you're close by."

Sonny flicked as gentle a smile as he could. He towered over Hiram Pete, but tried not to intimidate the man with his height. "Hi and Hon. Well, I don't think I'll forget those names too soon. I'm sorry to say I won't be around much, at least for the time being."

"I 'spect you'll be headin' into El Paso before long then," Hi said.

"Well, that trouble's not news, is it?"

"That's why you're here."

"Is there something else?"

"No, not that I know of," Hi said with a shake of his head. "I been worried about a fight spillin' over from Juárez ever since Francisco Madero revolted against Porfirio Díaz. Bein' this close to a border town is a blessin' and a curse. There's a lot to be had in a city the size of El Paso, but it draws all kinds of folks, now doesn't it? I figured it was only a matter of time before those Mexicans got tired of Díaz. He didn't do that country, or ours, no favors, I'll tell you."

"No, I don't think he did. Díaz has ruled with unrelenting power for a long time."

"Thirty some years."

"Something was bound to give," Sonny said. "It didn't take El Paso long to become a sanctuary for the revolutionaries. They've been free to plot and plan against the Mexican government without worry. They've collected ammunition, stockpiled guns, and helped themselves to all of the needs of making war. El Paso's a powder keg with a short fuse, and we got a real problem on our hands when they start battling for control of Juárez."

"Well," Hi said, "I figured there'd be more Rangers comin' down there."

"Not many of us these days." Sonny regretted the words as soon as he said them. They could've been interpreted as bait to provoke a conversation about politics. And if there was one thing Sonny was certain of, every man in Texas had a strong opinion about politics. Being new in the valley, he wasn't quite sure which way the wind blew, and he surely wasn't going to take sides. That wasn't his job. He'd been a Ranger for nearly twenty years, and during that time, the political pendulum in the statehouse had swung from one side to the other and then back a few times. Staying neutral and quiet, no matter what his own views were, had proven to be a solid strategy when it came to dealing with the subject of voting and keeping friends.

"Doesn't take that many of you, now does it?" Hi said.

Sonny smiled at the recognition. It was good to see a positive view of the Rangers. Not everyone held the organization in high esteem. Reputations, good and bad, followed all of the Rangers, but there was no question that the presence of one Ranger could quell a crowd if need be. It had been proven more than once.

"There'll be five of us, along with Captain Hughes, the sheriff's deputies, and government soldiers to make sure none of the trouble gets out of hand," Sonny said.

"A small force for a town of eighty thousand."

Sonny didn't flinch. "It's our job to keep the citizens safe, and we will. Any encroachments onto U.S. territory by the Mexican government would require a swift response by Governor Colquitt. He's determined to use the sovereign powers of the state against the revolutionaries, too."

"I hear tell that's contrary to the desires and demands in Washington," Hi said.

"Adjunct General Hastings had no choice but to send all available men down here, now did he?" Sonny said, then let out a sigh, stood back, and took in another view of the man's house and the view beyond it. In a way, he envied Hi and Hon Pete. They seemed to have a stable life, planted in place every day, not uprooted like he was by troubles and wars. It seemed to Sonny that mankind had an insatiable thirst for fighting, and for some reason, day after day, he found himself in the middle of one battle or the other.

CHAPTER THREE

July 1909
Velasco, Texas

Five-year-old Billy Bunson stood at the end of the dock, stoic and unafraid. Distant clouds roiled in black swirls, engorged with hurricane-force wind and pelting rain. The surf crashed against the shore with unrestrained fury, hammering the rocks and haphazard seawall like a constantly swinging hammer. The boy was wet from head to toe from the spray, but he didn't mind. Any movement at all would have drawn undue attention to his presence, caused concern about his safety. People ignored him, worried about their own lives. They fled inland like frightened seabirds, buffeted and betrayed by nature. A little boy standing unattended was the least of their worries.

Boats and ships crowded the docks desperate to unload their cargo and get it to high ground as quickly as possible. The incoming storm halted all commerce, all navigation—the only escape was by foot, if there was time for that. Thirty ships waited in the bay, their time to dock growing shorter by the minute. This hurricane was rumored to be huge, stronger, and deadlier than all of those before it. People had heard that cry before, but there was a wariness, an unnatural fear in the air that gave credence to the claim. Rumors of death and destruction bubbled on every laborer's lips.

The coastal town of Velasco was notorious for taking the brunt of gulf storms. What was destroyed was rebuilt. What was killed was replaced, humans, animals, and plants alike, by a fresh onslaught of opportunity seekers. Nothing stayed the same in Velasco for long.

Weary and weak-legged travelers unloaded from a nearby ship and hurried down the gangplank with restrained relief on their pale, seasick faces. They gripped the leader rope tightly, most casting quick glances over their shoulders to the angry clouds, then looking to the town, eyeing a quick ride to safety. There was none. All of the wagons had been hired out, every available teamster and their mules had fled the storm with heavier-than-normal loads. Dogs barked. Horses whinnied. The wind raged and pushed at the passengers and the boy in twists and turns, deafening some men, and terrifying well-dressed women. Hats flew into the sky like birds happy to be free. Skirts whipped upwards with the threat of exposure, shame, and embarrassment. Through it all, Billy Bunson stood watching the crowd, waiting like an unseen snake, preparing to strike at the right time. This wasn't his first storm. He knew what to expect. His only fear was going home empty-handed. He'd outrun the last storm and he figured he could outrun this one, too. The weather was the least of his fears.

It didn't take long. A woman stopped in front of him, her well-dressed husband at her side. He wore a double-breasted suit, a bowler hat, carried a cane, and had a nice pocket watch stuffed in his trousers tethered by a strong gold chain. Billy Bunson refrained a smile. He stood still. Didn't make a move.

"Are you lost, little boy?" the woman asked, leaning down so she was face to face with Billy. She was older than his mother, her hair graying at the edges, piled high, protected by a stylish hat. Ragged white feathers fluttered in the wind, threatening to break off, or pull the woman into the air, Billy wasn't sure which. The woman had soft, caring blue eyes. The kind he liked. They could be milked of trust and pity.

"My pa told me to stand right here and not move an inch," Billy said. He raised his voice to a yell so the woman would understand every word.

"Bad storm's coming," the man said. "Do you live near here?"

"We was on the last boat. We lived in New Orleans. Our house burned down," Billy said.

"That's awful," the woman said, holding her position so she could look Billy in the eye.

"Ma died in it. Now it's me and my pa."

The woman gasped and recoiled. She grabbed her hat with one hand, and pushed down her dress with the other. "Oh, Herbert, we must do something."

The man, Herbert, looked more interested in the sky and the fury of the clouds than Billy's plight. "We really must go, Matilda."

Billy watched obedience cross the woman's kind face. "I don't need anything," he said, then looked to the ground.

"You're sure your father's close by?" she said.

"Yes, he's right there," Billy said, pointing to the crowd. "He was right there. Now he's gone."

A strong gust of wind slapped all three of them at once. People continued to push by in a hurry, their panic impossible to restrain. Billy felt the first drop of rain hit his bare skin. It was cold and desperate.

"We must go now, Matilda," Herbert demanded, grabbing her elbow.

"We can't leave him."

"I'll be okay," Billy said. "Pa always comes back."

"You're a brave lad," Matilda said. She examined Billy like she was looking at him for the first time.

Billy Bunson was tall and thin for his age. His clothes were worn, dirty at the knees, the threads on his oversized shirt thin and threatening to fray. He was barefoot, but that wasn't

31

unusual on the seashore. He looked like a blond-haired waif in need of a bath, a good meal, and a proper mother to care for him.

"Matilda, we must go now," Herbert insisted, looking to the sky. A raindrop thudded against his hat, then bounced to the ground in a hurry to get there.

"All right, Herbert." She followed her husband's gaze to the raging sky, then looked back to Billy. "Here," she said as she dug into her waistcoat and pulled out a simple black leather coin purse, "I have something for you."

Billy didn't move. He waited until the right moment, waited until the purse was within reach, then jumped at Matilda like a starving gull on a negligent fish. She wasn't expecting him to grab at the purse. Air caught in her throat. She didn't scream until he was three feet away, disappearing into the crowd.

"Stop that boy!" Herbert shouted. "Stop that boy! Thief!" But no one heard him over the thunder, rain, and the crashing waves. If they did, they ignored the man, didn't know what he was shouting about. Their own lives were at stake. There was no boy to be seen. He was gone. Vanished. Lost in the crowd, joyous of the panic and his prize.

The front door of the simple shotgun house batted open and closed, pushing and pulling with the wind, beating the weak frame like an overexerted heart. There was no yard to speak of, only tired, sandy soil dotted with prickly pear and weeds that struggled to stay rooted against the wind. The house's decaying plank siding was weatherworn and gray, lacking any care or whitewash in years. A few of the windows stood halfway open, ragged curtains, punctured with moth holes and rot, fluttered in and out, keeping time with the door. The house looked like it was breathing, trying to stay alive, starting to fear destruction like all of the men and women on the docks. Billy didn't have to go inside to know that the house was empty, to know that his family had already fled.

Sustained gusts of wind and a steady downpour of rain forced Billy to seek shelter inside the house. Sand attacked his eyes, thumbnail-sized drops of rain pelted his skin, threatening to drill all the way down to his bones. Red welts bubbled on his skin like that time Miss Tillie spanked him with a razor strap. He was cold, hungry, and afraid. He didn't want to go inside and see that he was right, that he was alone. Being left on the dock to himself was one thing. He knew what to do there, what was expected of him. There was a job to do. He had to earn his keep. But being inside the house with a hurricane raging, without anyone to tell him what to do, was something different

"Hello," he called as he stepped over the threshold, escaping the slam of the door and its quick return. "It's me, Billy. Is anyone home?"

No one answered. The wind howled and the house groaned. Water dripped from the ceiling, splashing the bare wood floor, giving Billy reason to consider, and fear, that the house might not be safe, that it might collapse on top of him. He didn't know what to do. His whole body felt like it was crawling with a thousand fire ants.

"Hello!" he called out again. The only response was a fearless thunderclap overhead. The house shook so violently that the coin purse in his pocket jangled, adding another desperate note to the hurricane's unwanted chorus.

The house had never been much of a home. Not for Billy, his mother, or his grandmother, Miss Tillie, who ran the house and the business that she conducted inside of it. Billy didn't know much about that, but he understood that his life was different than the other kids he encountered.

There was no man of the house, a father, only Jim Rome, the lumbering black man, a son of an ex-slave who killed his master, or so he said, who worked the door and slept in the toolshed next to the outhouse. Jim bounced rowdy cowboys and ship captains out of the house when they got rough with one of Miss Tillie's girls. He never said much to folks, for the most part, and he talked to Billy out of sight of white folks' eyes. Jim's other job was to keep tabs on Billy as he worked the docks, pickpocketing and running off with anything he could grab. Billy was a fast runner. Jim coached him, taught him to be better, to get a valuable haul, and not get caught. The only time Billy felt safe was when Jim Rome was around.

There were usually four or five girls in the house of a variety of skin color and language. Port cities needed to offer a variety for the well-traveled man, or so Billy had heard, but didn't fully understand. Some girls stayed on for a long time like Teresa the Terrible or Maggie the Nice, but most of the girls didn't stay long at all. They would disappear in the night, never to be seen or heard from again. Billy had learned early on not to get attached to any of the girls. The only consistent people in his life were Miss Tillie, Jim Rome, and his mother, Lady Red to the customers, but Millie Lou to the rest of the household. His mother was strict and tainted with madness. Billy felt like he was climbing a crumbling ladder when she was around. All three of them were gone. The house was empty, except the contents that couldn't be loaded into the wagon and carted off to high ground.

Billy made his way to the back of the house, hoping along the way that he was wrong, that everybody had taken cover in their rooms, under their beds, like they all did when bad storms pushed in from the sea. But no one was to be seen. The beds were stripped of their sheets, and all that was left were stained feather mattresses and bureaus with open drawers, like the occupants had left in a hurry.

"Hello," Billy called, his voice weakening, satisfying itself with the truth.

No one answered.

Billy usually slept in a broom closet off the kitchen. It was the only place he knew to go, the only place he had ever felt safe. He kept his treasures there, things he didn't hand over to Lady Red and Miss Tillie at the end of the day. A lady's handkerchief that still smelled of jasmine, a gold band with a dragon engraved on it, and a tin soldier he'd stole from a blind boy. That one made him feel bad. That's why he kept it.

The closet was empty, too. Everything was gone. Even his bundle of blankets that served as a mattress was gone. Billy was tempted to call out again but he didn't. He pulled the door closed and huddled in the dark corner.

A thin strip of gray light filtered in under the door. At night Billy could listen to the business in the house, watch shadows lurk by, breathe in smoke and incense. Those seemed like good times now. He was afraid. More afraid than he could ever remember.

He shivered, hugging himself. He was wet and cold. His skin felt fragile, like it could shatter any second. He blinked, breathed deep, then looked hopefully to the light under the door. It had dimmed and water pushed into the closet. Lots of water. Billy panicked and screamed for help, but no one heard him.

October 1934

Bedias, Texas

Billy had fastened black cotton sleeves over the two-year-old Chevrolet's headlights. The road ahead of him was difficult to see, which had been the point. The less attention he drew to the car, and himself, the better. Escaping was never easy. He needed to focus, but the woman who sat next to him kept sniffling, crying softly. He gripped the wheel with all of his strength, clenching his teeth tight together so he wouldn't say something he would regret. When he looked over to her, he saw a tear run down her cheek. It did nothing but make him angrier than he already was.

"What's the matter with you?" Billy said.

"I'm scared," the warden's wife, Dolly Rickart, said.

"You should be."

CHAPTER FOUR

October 1934

Wellington, Texas

Jesse Burton stood next to the Model A pickup truck, staring into the barren field across the road, smoking a hand-rolled cigarette. "I hated to ask this of you, Pa."

"You didn't ask nothing of me," Sonny said. "The Rangers did."

"It was my idea. I suggested to the captain that you be the one to go and talk to the warden. I wanted you to know what was going on, that Billy Bunson was on the loose. I wanted you to know that more than anything."

Sonny eased a small, battered suitcase down to the dry ground. A thin puff of dust quickly answered the disturbance, then vanished on a steady breeze. "You don't think the captain would have eventually come out here? He knows my history with Billy as well as you do. Don't matter, I'd be going one way or the other. Has nothing to do with you. It's not a rub with me, if that's what you're worried about."

"It's not that."

"What is it, then?"

"It's a long drive to Huntsville."

"I've been all over this state in the saddle of a good horse. I think I can drive to Huntsville."

"You were young, and had . . ." Jesse stopped mid-sentence, dropped the cigarette, and ground it out with the sharp tip of

37

his black cowboy boot. He was still staring out at the field, and hadn't looked Sonny in the eye since he'd arrived.

"What?" Sonny said. "Since I had two arms and two hands? Is that what you're going to say?"

"Yes. You're not a young man anymore, Pa. I worry about you on the road all by yourself. These are unsettled times. People are desperate."

"And they might see me as weak?"

"You said it."

"I went after Bonnie and Clyde."

"That didn't turn out too well."

Sonny exhaled heavily with agreement, then hoisted the suitcase with his left hand as confidently as he could and let it thump into the truck bed. He settled the small piece of worn luggage between the sideboard and two ten-gallon cans of gasoline. The cans were full. Filling stations were hard to come by on some stretches of the road south of Wellington.

"I ain't dead yet. You want to ride along?" he said.

Sonny understood Jesse's concerns. It wasn't like they weren't something that Sonny hadn't considered himself. But he'd decided that going after Billy Bunson was better than sitting around waiting on him to show up to settle a score. Life after losing an arm wasn't much, but it was better than bein' like a rabbit, scared shitless by the shadow of anything that moved.

"Can't," Jesse answered. "Captain needs me free to chase any other leads. We're tryin' to figure out how close Billy was to this girl he got to help bust him out."

"I can tell you that."

"What then?"

"She'll swoon at the mention of his name, but that's it. She got pulled in, doesn't know him well at all. She thinks he loves her—which he doesn't. He's a real sweet-talker that one. Could probably talk the bloomers right off of Eleanor Roosevelt herself if he had half the chance."

"You could be wrong."

"I'm not."

"I know," Jesse sighed. "You takin' that dog with you?"

"I am, unless you want to look after him." Sonny reached down and patted the top of Blue's head. Like normal, the hound was at Sonny's ankle.

"Nope, I can't do that."

"Wouldn't let you anyway, now that I come to think of it. Dogs don't like you much, do they?"

"I think it's the other way around. Once bitten, twice shy."

"Either way," Sonny said, then reached over to the suitcase and pulled a revolver out of the open side compartment.

"I haven't seen that gun in ages," Jesse said. "It was Grandpa's. I've wanted to fire that gun ever since I can remember."

"It'll be yours one day. Don't get in a hurry." Sonny stared at the gun with admiration. It was an 1873 Colt Army revolver, carried by his father, Jeb Burton, when he'd joined the Frontier Battalion. The revolver was called the Gun that Won the West, and that moniker was most likely true. Sonny could have relied on his government issue .45 that he'd carried in World War I, but he preferred the Colt Army. The Colt felt comfortable in his left hand, still balanced even though Sonny had lost his equilibrium when he'd lost his arm. He knew the Colt better than any other weapon, trusted it with his life. The .45, on the other hand, still smelled of mustard gas and blood. He had barely survived the Great War, had brought it home with him and carried the horrors of the battles with him for years after. The fewer reminders he had of that time in his life the better off he was. The Colt Army was the right gun for this job, he was sure of it. He couldn't afford one ounce of weakness if he was going to face Billy Bunson. That boy smelled fear and doubt as well as any dog.

"You got plenty of ammunition?" Jesse said, looking at the gun with the same admiration as Sonny. "You can stop at the armory and sign out some extra."

"I have plenty, and the Browning Auto-5's in the cab."

"All right then, looks like you're goin' huntin' for bear."

"Wish I was."

"Me, too."

"Well, then, you go do your job and I'll do mine. How's that?" Sonny said, turning his face to meet Jesse's, forcing the boy to look him in the eye. It had been that way between the two of them from the start.

Jesse held Sonny's gaze for a long second, then looked away, turned his attention back to the field, and answered out of the side of his mouth. "We've got no choice."

"You said it yourself," Sonny said. "That woman's done lost a finger. Billy Bunson isn't going to take pity on her 'cause she's pregnant. That might slow him down, make him do something desperate. We need to find them both as soon as we can, and the best thing I can do is go down to Huntsville and figure out the path Billy's gonna take."

"You got any ideas?"

"I'll tell you this. Billy will do anything not to go back to prison. I don't know how he got close enough to the warden's wife to nab her, but it doesn't surprise me none. Billy's slippery as a wet worm, and he's got the charm of that Valentino fella. This escape is a big bet for him. He set the stakes as high as he could by kidnapping that poor woman. He's making a run for it, that's what he's doing. He'll know you've come to me, so he's already trying to outsmart me, leaving breadcrumbs to confuse me."

"You don't think he's coming straight here?"

"Nope. Not right away. He's going to take some time, hide

out, and see if I'm coming for him."

"How will he know?"

"Billy's got a long line of admirers. My guess is there's been eyes on us long before the escape. It'd be part of his plan."

"You're not safe."

"That's not a worry now. The longer we stand here and talk, the closer he gets to Mexico, if he's not already there. That's his end goal. To be free. He can disappear there."

"I think you might be right. We've alerted the authorities on the border."

"You can't go after him."

"No, we can't."

"But I can," Sonny said. "And I will, if I have to."

May 1911

Vinton, Texas

Sonny said his goodbyes to Martha and the boy, then headed for Ysleta to unite with the rest of the Ranger force. The sheriff, his deputies, the captain, and four other Rangers were joining with soldiers from the army. The plan was to ride into El Paso together and make a show of force. Sonny thought it was a bad idea and had wired Captain Hughes his thoughts on the matter. Sonny had argued that they were setting themselves up as sitting ducks to the revolutionaries and the Mexican army.

The captain didn't answer the wire, which meant he disagreed with Sonny's view, or he wasn't about to change his strategy because of a sergeant's concerns. Now, Sonny had no choice but to go where he was told. There were disadvantages when it came to maintaining low ambitions.

He hated to leave his wife and son on their own in a new place, especially after Martha had broken down the night before and told him that she was expecting another child. Neither of them was thrilled at the prospect.

Pregnancy had never been easy for Martha. She'd lost one baby three months into a pregnancy before Jesse had been born, and another, a little girl, was stillborn a year after. That loss had changed Martha in a way that left her crippled in the mind, darker in a way that had left Sonny worried for her welfare. There was little to look forward to if this new birth went bad. Even if it went good, there'd be another mouth to feed on fifty dollars a month. Either way meant a deeper struggle was on the horizon.

It was a pleasant ride to the fort. May in South Texas was temporarily green, offering a mirage of prosperity. The leaves were new and full on the pecan and Osage orange trees. Cedar trees looked renewed, given another chance at life with the onset of much needed rains and the pooling of water over their gangly roots. A riot of sparrows shouted from the top of one of the trees, fighting for a mate and territory like the rest of the living creatures in Texas.

The acacia trees never looked happy regardless of the season, their shape and canopy unmistakably flat and gnarly. Those trees made for a good place to take refuge in a rain if nothing else offered itself as shelter. Blooms were already starting to fade on the honeysuckle, though swarms of insects still fluttered about the small flowers, angling for as much nectar as they could drink. Times of bounty and drunkenness would be gone soon, and the desert would return to its useless brown and decay, succumbing to the heat of summer, leaving it barren, and impossible to believe that anything could grow there.

The well-traveled trail to El Paso was easy to navigate. Sonny's horse, a gelding paint that had most likely come from old Comanche stock, seemed happy to be on a long ride, back to work. The horse was mostly solitary and nipped at Jesse and Martha any time they got too close to it. Such bad behavior was never directed toward Sonny. Him and the horse had an understanding, that neither of them would be mean to each other, take each other for granted, or afford any abuse toward each other. Sonny had a short temper when it came to men mistreating their animals, and had no use for an animal that didn't respect its man. That deal had been sealed a long time ago.

Once they were away from the house, there were few humans to encounter. The land was dotted with struggling ranches and a few leftover homesteads. Cattle wandered freely, enjoying the variety of green leaves to make an easy meal of. Sonny paced the horse as easily as he could, knowing full well when he was expected to arrive at Ysleta. He was in no hurry to ride into another battle. Drawing his weapon had consequences, even if it meant saving his own life, or taking someone else's. Killing had never come easy to Sonny Burton.

May 1911

El Paso, Texas

A small settlement had emerged around Fort Bliss not long after it had been moved to the La Noria Mesa in 1893. In response, El Paso, the border city and hot spot of one conflict after another, pushed all the way to the gate of the fort. A main road led off the trail and Sonny rode into town past shacks, shanties, and small houses. Everyone in town, it seemed, served the army in one capacity or another; launderers, stable boys, general store owners, and the like, rushed about at their businesses. Eking out a living in El Paso forged a dependence on the government's presence, but also resulted in the constant threat of violence. Saloons and houses that served the more primal needs of the soldiers stationed at the fort sat a street behind the proper businesses, out of sight, but most likely not out of mind of the frequent patrons who contributed to their endurance and success. Sonny had no need or desire to stop at such establishments. He was focused on traveling through the city and falling into line with the other Rangers in Ysleta. Celebration, if there was one to be had, would come at the end of the battle with a quick ride home to Martha and Jesse.

A heavy dose of spring sunshine beat down on the road. Traffic was thick in town; a beehive of activity compared to the silence of the trail. Horse-drawn wagons mixed with a small variety of automobiles, odd-looking vehicles called Oldsmobile, Delage, and Franklin, that competed for, and easily won, space on the road. The automobiles had spooked more than one horse since Sonny entered the confines of the city. Luckily, Sonny's horse paid no mind to the clattering machines. He was comforted by that, though the automobiles' presence *did* bother him.

He liked riding a horse. It was the only form of transportation he had ever owned. He had yet to sit behind the steering wheel of an automobile even though Martha had encouraged him to meet the modern times head-on and learn to drive one of the contraptions, instead of resisting it. An automobile couldn't go the places a horse could go, and that was that as far as Sonny was concerned. An Oldsmobile would never entirely replace a horse. Such a thing was an impossible consideration.

Noise filled Sonny's ears, trail dust clung to his face, and all the activity around him made him jittery. Cities made Sonny nervous. The fort was a good mile away. Regardless of his discomfort, Sonny didn't quicken his pace. Instead, he kept the horse at a steady gait, staying as close to the left side of the road as possible, giving leeway to the unpredictable automobiles. More businesses packed the city blocks, one on top of another, and since it was such a fine day, there were plenty of people making their way to and fro—even with an impending battle looming. Perhaps El Paso folk were accustomed to such things, Sonny surmised, pushing off the constant threat of violence with as much normalcy as possible. Maybe that's how they dealt with life on the border.

"Stop! Thief!" a man's voice shouted. The alarming words pierced through all of the other noise, garnering Sonny's attention immediately.

The barrel-chested man was a shop owner with a bald head and wore a red, angry face, which contrasted dramatically against his bleached-white butcher's apron. He pushed through the crowd, yelling the demand repeatedly. "Stop! Thief!"

Sonny looked farther down the road and spied a blond-haired boy, no more than seven or eight, weaving in and out of the crowd, carrying a fully feathered white chicken by the neck. The chicken's feet grazed the ground, but the boy had grace and focus. He didn't look back, didn't consider his pursuer, looked confident in his ability to outrun the butcher and escape with a free bird for dinner.

The horse's ears perked up as Sonny stiffened in the saddle and pulled the reins tighter. Even before a command was given with a quick press with his legs, the horse broke into a run. All Sonny had to do was guide the beast toward the boy and dodge the pedestrians, automobiles, and wagons.

People stopped, their attention drawn by turmoil, by the cry they knew and feared. Women clutched their handbags and men protected their pockets. The butcher might as well have shouted a battle cry.

Sonny made quick gain on the boy, was within twenty yards of him, when the boy came across an alleyway, or a thin gap between buildings, and disappeared. He vanished without a turn or a jump, causing Sonny to rear the horse to a quick stop.

Sonny was spry, in good physical shape, and was able to jump off the horse and break into a run without losing a breath.

But there was nothing to run after. It was like the boy had never existed at all. He was gone; an invisible magician in the middle of the crowd successfully completing an unthinkable magic trick.

The crowd resumed their progress, headed onward since the excitement was over. Some mingled, didn't act concerned. Sonny asked more than one man if he'd seen where the boy had gone. They all said no.

The butcher caught Sonny, out of breath, sweating, anger still plastered across his chubby face. "Where is he?"

Sonny shrugged his shoulders, uncertain of how the boy could have disappeared. "I don't know."

"I knew I shouldn't have taken my eyes off that boy. He's been trouble from the start, that one. I should have knowed better than to trust that Billy Bunson alone in my store."

CHAPTER FIVE

July 1909

Velasco, Texas

Billy Bunson didn't know how to swim. The only time he went into the water was when he saw something shiny. If the waves splashed his face, he retreated to the sandy shore as quickly as he could. The water held mysteries and threats he didn't understand. He saw a man pulled away by the undercurrent one day and knew right then that the water was deadlier than it appeared, that the ocean was something to be feared, not enjoyed. The raging hurricane only confirmed his fears. The sea was coming after him, dead set on drowning him. He was sure of it.

He was soaked to the bone, huddling in the closet, trembling as the water rose against the side of the wall. The water was in a hurry, like it'd been unleashed from a dam after a long wait. Thunder crashed overhead. The house trembled in unison with him, afraid, certain of collapse, unable to withstand the storm for much longer.

The light was dim inside the house; gray shadows punctuated by strong flashes of lightning. Someone screamed in the distance. Panic. Fear. Maybe they were dying. Maybe it was the wind. Or maybe Billy was screaming inside his mind, he wasn't sure. He'd never been so afraid in his life.

The water lapped at his knees, and it wasn't going to retreat any time soon. If he was going to get out of the house alive, now was the time to make a run for it.

Forethought would have told Billy to leave the door open, but he had closed it, sure that he would be safe. He'd made a grave mistake and discovered his error when he tried to open the door, push on it in a foot of water. The wood door felt like it was made of lead. It wouldn't budge. Billy pushed on the door with all of his might, with all of the strength his young arms could muster. He could not move the door at all. It was like it was stuck, held in place by the rising water. It swirled around his knees. He could taste salt on his tongue, and he screamed when something slithered across the back of his calf. It could have been anything, an eel, a shark; his imagination got the best of him. Billy was certain that he was going to die.

"That you, Billy?" a distant voice called out.

It was Jim Rome's voice. Billy tried to answer back but his mouth was caked with salt and fear. The noise he made sounded like a whimper.

"Billy, ya here, boy?" Jim Rome shouted again.

Billy tried to say, "Here!" but only a squeak managed to escape his lips. Desperate, as the water rose to his crotch in a quick wave, he pounded on the door furiously.

"I hear ya, boy. I'm comin' for ya."

When the door pulled open, Jim Rome stood tall and wet before him. Billy had never been so happy to see the black man in his life.

Jim Rome reached down and pulled Billy into his mountain-sized muscular arms, and said, "Your momma's gonna beat the livin' daylights out of you when she sees you. You know that, don't you? You done made her mad as a red crab, causin' me ta backtrack and come rescue you. Then she do what she always do and tell me to finish off beatin' you, but I ain't gonna do no such thing on this day. I sure is happy to see you, Billy. I thought you was dead as my daddy, and gone to hell to boot."

"Me, too," Billy whispered. "Me, too."

May 1911
El Paso, Texas

Billy scurried underneath the First Street Bank, dragging a dead chicken along with him. He stopped at a foundation pier to get his bearings, letting his eyes adjust to the dusky light below the building. The last thing he wanted to do was come face to face with a rattlesnake, scorpion, or something worse. Critters in this part of Texas bit first and didn't bother to let you know they were going to attack. Teresa the Terrible, one of Miss Tillie's longest employed girls, was stung by a tiny scorpion not long after they'd all settled in El Paso and nearly died. Her arm swelled up to the size of her head. Teresa still complained about her arm. It looked funny, too. All red and puffy, like it couldn't decide if it was gonna live or die. Men didn't want to touch her, so Miss Tillie took pity on her and made Teresa the laundry girl, which made her even more surly than she already was. Billy saw the crushed scorpion after it stung her and learned right then that little things had as much power as big things. You had to know what could hurt you or you were gonna be afraid of everything.

Billy Bunson didn't have time to be afraid. Someone on horseback was after him. They probably worked for the sheriff or the army. Some of those army fellas had no use for kids running loose on the street. Especially a thievin' one. They didn't understand that all Billy was trying to do was stay out of trouble. Getting caught was the last thing he needed. The chicken was meant to get him out of hot water for coming home empty-handed. Every pocket he'd tried to pick was empty. People were worried, holding onto their belongings tight. A battle was coming and nobody wanted to lose anything.

Satisfied that underneath the building was free of any spiteful creatures, Billy swiped an empty spiderweb out of his face and made his way to another pier in the middle of the building. A hidey-hole waited for him there. It looked like a shallow grave. *Ollie, Ollie, oxen free.* He'd be safe there.

Billy settled into the hole as quickly as he could, and pulled the chicken as close to his lithe body as possible. He tried to conceal the dead chicken, but in the dim, gray light, the bird still glowed bright white. It'd been killed right before Billy had snatched it out of the butcher's shop. It didn't smell dead yet, but chickens always stank as far as Billy was concerned.

He took a deep breath, regulated his breathing, and melted into the hard dirt of the hidey-hole. There were seven holes scattered around town, safe places for him to flee to when he was in trouble. Jim Rome had insisted Billy dig them right after they'd got the new house settled.

Jim Rome's father had been a thief and a runaway slave. He'd taught Jim all of his survival tricks—for what good it did him. Jim Rome's father was lynched in Waco for talking back to a white woman. Once the man was dead, they set his body afire. The ashes were left to the wind, so said Jim, leaving the Negro to figure out a way to stay alive on his own when he was only twelve. Jim had taught Billy everything he knew, or was in the process of teaching him. Billy wasn't so sure what Jim Rome knew. Some days the Negro seemed dumb as a post, then others, he was the smartest man in the world. The hidey-holes had saved Billy's skin more than once, so he was prone to listen to everything Jim told him whether it sounded like nonsense or not.

Noise from the city sounded normal. Automobiles coughed and puffed along the street. Horses whinnied, or clopped on, in a hurry to go one place or another. And people scurried about, trying to avoid any of the battle that was rumored to be on the way. The army and sheriff's department had beefed up their ranks, and Billy heard someone say the Texas Rangers were coming to town. That didn't worry him none, but all those men meant the house was gonna be busy after everything was all said and done. Miss Tillie and the girls would be ready to relieve them of their tensions. All Billy had to do was get the chicken home without losing it.

He watched the shadows, the boots and women's shoes walk past, listened for his pursuer to call out, but nothing came to his ear. All four sides of the building were visible from where Billy hid, and he checked each side slowly. When he got back to the north side, the place where he'd crawled under, his heart skipped a beat. A single white feather sat on the border between light and dark, at the edge of the building where someone could see.

He'd broken a rule, not checked behind him, left a sign of his existence. That's what Jim Rome insisted of him, that Billy leave no signs that he existed. When time and mood allowed, the two of them practiced, played hide and seek. The way they played, it was more than a kid's game; it was life and death, a lesson that demanded Billy leave no trace of his physical presence for the world to see. Jim would be disappointed. But Billy wasn't gonna tell him. No, sir, nobody was gonna find out about that chicken feather.

He couldn't take his eyes off the feather. He wished for a puff of wind to come along and blow it under the building, but nothing came. The air was still, holding its breath to see what came next. Billy couldn't focus on anything else.

A minute later, he saw a pair of black, dusty boots stop at the feather. A hand reached down and touched it gingerly, like the thing was made of glass, like whoever was touching it was trying to memorize every inch of it. Then the hand appeared below the foundation, grabbed the feather, and disappeared. Billy gasped as a lightning bolt of fear careened from one end of his body to the other.

Maybe it's nothing, he reasoned. Maybe someone had happened along, saw the feather there, and picked it up as a gift for their beloved. Or maybe it was the man on horseback who had chased after him. Maybe he knew Billy was hiding under the building.

He waited to see a face appear where the hand showed itself, but it didn't. The boots walked on, then disappeared at the end of the building, allowing Billy to sigh in relief. His body relaxed, all of the tension from the day draining out into the hole. Before he knew it, Billy fell asleep.

Billy woke with a start. A shock of fear made his skin sizzle. He didn't know how long he'd been asleep, and for a long second, he didn't know where he was. That wasn't unusual. They all moved around a lot, out of one town and into another. In the seven short years of his life, Billy could remember eleven houses, and that didn't count all of the times they'd lived out of a wagon.

He wiped the sleep from his eyes and realized that he was under the First Street Bank, in a hidey-hole, waiting out a pursuer. Light had turned to dark, or at least to a deep, gray gloom. Suppertime was nigh and the chicken would be welcome. Billy reached out for the bird to make sure that it was there. It was. Cold and stiff. He checked the perimeter of the building, watched for anything out of the ordinary, and listened to the sounds of El Paso as it passed from day to night. There was less clatter, less traffic, but no sign of a battle being waged. That was a relief. He could go home safely.

Never go out the same way you went in was another of Jim Rome's rules, so Billy grabbed the chicken and crawled to the back of the building. He stopped in the shadow, watching to make sure he was safe to make a run for home.

As he stood, something told him to look over his shoulder. It felt like he was being stared at. A man dressed in riding clothes was sitting on a stoop, holding a white chicken feather in his left hand.

"Looks like you lost something there, boy," the man said.

Billy's first inclination was to run, but he didn't. The man was holding a gun in his right hand, trained on Billy. The man, who Billy had never seen before, looked serious, like he didn't fool around about anything.

"I didn't lose anything," Billy said.

"You sure about that?" the man said.

"Yup, I'm sure. The chicken lost that feather, I didn't."

A nod of approval and a brief smile was all the man offered to Billy. "Let's me and you take that chicken back to the butcher shop it belongs to."

Billy smiled, and said, "Why that's exactly what I was about to do, kind sir. That's exactly what I was about to do."

"Sure it was," the man said, then grabbed Billy's shoulder with his adult hand and pointed the boy toward the butcher shop. "You're a better thief than you are a liar, boy. You need to work on that part of your schemin'."

"I'll keep that in mind," Billy Bunson said. "But I ain't no thief and no liar. You'll see. I'll show you, mister. You wait and see. I'll show you."

CHAPTER SIX

October 1934
Huntsville, Texas

The weather had remained dry, no rain to muddy the roads. Sonny encountered the occasional dust storm to push through, making the trip to Huntsville long, uneventful, and boring. He had helped a few hitchhikers along the road, men going from one town to the next, in search of work or food, and they'd provided some company. But he didn't really need that. He was only helping a man struggling to find his way. Most of the traffic was heading in the opposite direction, north, or west, leaving the state, fleeing the dust and despair that had settled over all of the country. Sonny was driving straight into pain and ugliness, but he wouldn't move out of Texas if someone paid him to.

Blue was really the only company Sonny had any use for. He'd brought the dog into the cab during the worst of the dust storms and the loneliest stretches of the road. Blue seemed happy to be inside the truck. He slept in the seat, or stuck his head out the window and watched the world go by.

Just when Sonny thought the trip would go on forever, he entered Huntsville proper and drove straight to the prison.

A thin, well-appointed guard stopped Sonny at the gate. A Colt .45 hung confidently in the guard's black leather holster. The man stood like he had an iron rod implanted in his back. "What's your business, sir?"

"I'm here to see the warden. I'm Sonny Burton. He should

be expecting me."

The guard nodded as a flash of recognition passed across his freshly shaven face. "Heard you were comin', Ranger Burton. I still need to see your papers."

Sonny pulled a letter out of his breast pocket with his left hand. "Here you go."

The guard stared at the hook where Sonny's right hand should have been for a second longer than he should have. He looked like a little boy without his mother around to admonish him for staring. Without saying another word, the guard took the letter, glanced at it briefly, and handed it back to Sonny.

Being called a Ranger stung Sonny's ears, caused him to flinch because the title didn't belong to him any longer. There was no use correcting the sentry. Even at home, he was still a Ranger to a lot of folks. There was no escaping the past. He tucked the letter back in his pocket.

"You'll be stopped more than normal, Ranger Burton, so I'd keep that letter of yours handy. We're still on lockdown 'cause of the escape."

Sonny put the truck in gear. "I figured you would be."

"Have a good day, now." The guard stood back and waved Sonny through the gate.

There was no way this was going to be a good day, Sonny thought, but didn't say, as he drove onto prison grounds. "You're gonna have to be a good dog and not cause any trouble, Blue. Can you do that?"

The dog sat in the passenger seat and stared straight ahead. He wagged his tail at the sound of his name. Sonny took the reply as a yes, but he was still worried about leaving the dog in the truck while he spoke to the warden.

The Huntsville Prison was an impressive maze of red brick buildings closed in by tall red brick walls. Sharpshooters patrolled the upper ramparts. All of the roofs were covered in red ceramic tile. Only the blue sky and scorched brown earth, a remnant of the recent unrelenting summer sun, offered any distinction between the fires of hell and the promise of heaven. Sonny wondered if the prison complex looked like a splotch of blood to a soaring bird.

The prison had housed criminals since 1849, offering nearly a century of confinement for the worst offenders to be found in the state of Texas. It was remarkably well kept. The windows sparkled with a clean shine in the waning afternoon light. All of the wood trim looked freshly painted, white as a ball of cotton. Every brick was clean, free of soot and dirt, and every line in sight, walls, peaks, towers, were all straight as a razor's edge. If there had been live grass, Sonny was sure that every blade would have been standing erect, combed and ordered to reach as high as possible. It was hard to imagine that the rules and regulations inside weren't as strict as the exterior maintenance reflected, and even harder to imagine how any man could have escaped from the place. But then again, Billy Bunson was no ordinary criminal. Sonny knew that better than anyone.

He brought the truck to a stop outside of the administration building. He'd been to Huntsville a few times in his life, knew his way around well enough not to get lost. It was a short walk from the warden's office to Old Sparky, the electric chair that had been sending the convicted to their deaths since 1924. He shuddered at the thought of an execution, of the memory of watching two men die from a massive input of harnessed lightning. It was something he never wanted to see again, unless it was Billy. He'd watch Billy Bunson die without regret if he did further harm to that pregnant woman.

Sonny made the familiar trek inside the building, showed the letter to the appropriate people, and in a matter of minutes, found himself in the company of an uptight, distraught warden whose only concern was the safety and whereabouts of his kidnapped wife.

"I'd say it's good to see you, Ranger Burton, if the circumstances were different." Jebidiah Rickart looked like he hadn't had a bit of sleep in a week. His eyes, normally vibrant blue, were as gray as his neatly trimmed hair. He was in his late forties, maybe even his early fifties, aged by his position, and more recently the tragedy he had found himself in—he looked more like a grandparent than a man expecting a child. On his best day, Jeb Rickart presented himself like a general in the army: stiff, upright, and proud. But on this day, he looked like a man on the edge of losing his sanity.

"Sorry for your troubles, Jeb," Sonny said. He hesitated before he spoke again, trying to gauge exactly how lucid the man really was. "I gave up the Ranger business, by the way." Sonny tapped his wooden arm.

"I heard. Force of habit, forgive me, Sonny. I don't mean to cause you to relive a bad memory."

"No offense taken. The world seems to know me as a Ranger. I guess I still think I am, too, or I wouldn't be here, now would I?"

Jeb Rickart forced a smile, then walked over to the window behind his desk and stared out of it. "This is our first child, Dolly's and mine. I thought for a long time I wasn't able. My first wife and I tried to have children, but it didn't happen. Then one day a miracle came into our lives. It was the best day of my life, I tell you, when the thought of having a son or daughter became a reality. I'd made my peace on that ever happening. I thought I'd go through this life without seeing my child's eyes."

"I'll find her, Jeb."

"I know you will, Sonny. I know you will."

"I'm going into town to talk to the girl who we're being told is Billy's girlfriend, to see what I can find out, but before I do that, you need to tell me everything you can about the days before the kidnapping."

"Days?"

"Curious, that's all. If there was anything out of place. Like maybe a bad feeling you couldn't quite put your finger on."

The warden agreed; a bit of perspiration had taken residence on his upper lip. The room was warm, but not that warm. "There was, how'd you know? I just thought it was my own failure, questioning why a girl like Dolly wanted to be with me."

"It's a hunch." Sonny eyed the warden a little closer, then walked over to the desk and looked at a black and white picture of Jeb and Dolly standing in front of a little white clapboard house. A new Chevrolet sat next to the house, and both of them were smiling like they owned the world. First thing Sonny noticed was that Dolly was younger than Jeb by a good ten years, maybe more. "Dolly ever have reason to come into contact with Billy Bunson, Jeb?"

"Yes. She was demanding about teachin' them boys to read. Her mother ran a library for years. I was never real crazy about the idea, but Dolly insisted that if they could learn to read, do something productive while they were inside, they might not come back. She's more hopeful about rehabilitation than I am," the warden said.

It was Sonny's turn to nod. But he didn't say anything. He bit his tongue, trying not to show his discomfort. Billy Bunson knew how to read before they met, and that was when the boy was seven. Sonny was sure of it.

"I'll be needin' a place to stay in town," Sonny said. "I figure I'll be here a few days, and my old back's too rickety to be sleeping on the ground."

Jeb Rickart's face flashed with panic, then he forced it to go away. "We're running out of time, Sonny."

"You heard from Billy?"

"No, but the finger. I can't think about what's next. The finger, Sonny. Can you imagine?"

"Yes, I can, Jeb." Sonny wanted to walk over and put his hand on the warden's shoulder, offer him some comfort. "I can't tell you to relax, but I'm pretty certain you're gonna hear from Billy before he does anything else. He wants something. He'll come to you. I need a place to stay where you know you can get a hold of me when he calls."

"You're sure about this? That we have time?"

"I know Billy Bunson better than anybody alive. That's why I'm here."

"I know, it's Dolly, you see. I can't think straight." A bead of sweat swerved down the side of the warden's face. "You go to Edith Grantley's boardinghouse at the corner of 19th and Avenue M. You tell her I sent you, and to call me if she's got any concerns. Everybody in town's on the lookout for Dolly, so she knows some of what's going on. We haven't told the papers about the finger. I'd be obliged if you wouldn't speak of it to anyone, Sonny. Folks are on edge enough the way it is."

"All right, Jeb, I'll go get settled in, then I'll go over to the jail to talk to that girlfriend. But I'd like to see Billy's cell before I leave, if you don't mind."

"Don't mind at all, but I gotta tell you, there's nothing there to see. Billy was no pack rat."

"Doesn't surprise me none," Sonny said. "It's not things that matter to Billy."

"What does?"

"Freedom."

Both men let the words settle in the office. An oscillating fan worked its way back and forth blowing stale air from one side of the room to the other. A wall clock ticked in unison with Sonny's heart. His mouth went dry as a flash of memory floated across his mind's eye: Billy running, never looking back, sure of where he was going. The boy had morphed in to a man and the thief turned into a killer.

"What do you know about the girl?" Sonny said.

"She's local. A surprise she's involved in all of this, but she isn't talking. I done tried. Begged her is what I did, but that didn't help, either. Says she don't know where Billy's hidin' out."

"Well," Sonny said, "She's probably telling you the truth about that."

Jeb Rickart made his way over to Sonny and offered him his hand. "I sure am relieved you're here, Ranger or not."

Sonny shook the warden's hand awkwardly with his left hand. It was a task he still hadn't got the feel for. He didn't have a tight grip with his remaining hand. He hated to make folks uncomfortable, or imply weakness in any way. "You call me as soon as you hear from Billy."

"I will. We have to save her, Sonny. I don't know what I'll do if anything happens to that baby. I don't know how I'd live with that. This is all my fault."

"You're not to blame."

"I'm the warden."

"You're a man," Sonny said. "A mortal with no special powers except your common sense and the hard work that put you here. We all have weak moments, and men like Billy Bunson know 'em when they see 'em. Billy waits. He makes them happen. Don't be too hard on yourself, Jeb. Only a creature like Billy Bunson could have done this to you. This is not your fault."

"That's kind of you to say, Ranger Burton," the warden said.

Sonny headed for the door. He knew what it was like to lose a child. More than one. He wasn't gonna let that happen to anyone. Especially a good man like Jeb Rickart.

"Tell my secretary, Miss Ziskin, to have Clayton take you over to Billy's cell," the warden said. A quivery sigh escaped from his mouth after he said the last word.

Sonny didn't answer. He hurried out of the office as quickly as he could. The last thing he wanted to see was a man like Jeb Rickart collapse into a mess of sobs. The thought of such a thing made Sonny hunger for Billy Bunson's capture all the more.

CHAPTER SEVEN

May 1911
El Paso, Texas

The street was empty of traffic. Evening had not only brought darkness, but more uncertainty than normal. Warning shots had volleyed back and forth across the border as the sun set. Revolutionaries moved about in the streets, bold in their presence, not afraid to be seen. The Mexican army stood in formation out of range, safe in their own country, while all of Fort Bliss stood on alert, awaiting the first true incursion of violence. The air dripped with dread and fear.

Sonny was late joining the force of Texas Rangers at Ysleta. He knew Captain Hughes would be none too pleased with him. A charge of dereliction of duty, or something worse, was possible, but not likely. He was not late to the fight, only to the final planning.

But first, he had a thief to deal with.

"What's your name?' Sonny said, as he guided the boy toward the butcher's shop. His grip was hard enough to warn the youngster off of running.

"What makes you think I got a name?"

He was a blue-eyed, blond-haired boy, skinny as a sick coyote and dirty as a dried pig, but there was something that shined about him, something that didn't invoke sadness or pity. Sonny wasn't quite sure what that thing was, or why he'd taken upon himself to wait the boy out, to see to it that he returned a stolen chicken, but he had. Truth be told, the boy reminded Sonny of his own son, Jesse, and maybe that's all it was. Imagining a boy left with nothing but his own wits to find a meal for himself, whether it was right or wrong. Sonny knew such a scenario was possible heading into battle. Learning of Martha's pregnancy had given him a deep regret about leaving his family behind, about putting his life at risk. Jesse and Martha needed him to stay alive. The thieving boy had given him an opportunity to stay safe and settle into his remorse. It was a different kind of battle to confront. There was no avoiding duty, but Sonny knew he needed to walk into it with a clear head.

"Everybody's got a name," Sonny said. "What was your father's name?"

"What makes you think I had a father?"

They were half a block from the butcher's shop. All of the businesses they passed were closed for the day; blinds drawn, handwritten closed signs hung in the windows, stoops already dusty. El Paso had gone from vibrant to dead in a matter of hours.

"Everybody's got a father," Sonny answered.

"Doesn't mean nothing," the boy said. "Men come and go is what they do. Ain't never knowed my pa. You?"

"Yes, of course."

"He beat you?"

"If I deserved it."

"We all deserve it. That's what I hear. Everybody I ever knowed gets beat."

"Who gave you your name then?" Sonny said with a flinch, all the while keeping a steady pace down the boardwalk.

"My mother gave me my name. That's the story she tells."

Sonny sucked in a breath of air to consider what the boy said. It could have been the truth by the looks of him. Bein' a city boy that housed soldiers and other travelers, maybe he really didn't know his pa. "I'm sorry to hear that." The boy quickened his pace at the sight of the butcher's shop, but Sonny pulled him back. "Don't think of running off."

"You couldn't catch me. Not this time."

"Probably not."

The boy stopped. "Don't you have some place to be, mister? There's a war a comin'. You look ready to battle. What are you?"

"Nothing more than a simple man."

"You ain't tried nothing with me. Haven't hurt me. What are you?"

"Like I told you, I'm a simple man. I have a job to do, but first you need to return that chicken. You had no right to take it."

"I'm hungry. You ever been so hungry you'd do anything to make that emptiness go away?"

"I've been lucky in life, Billy, but I know hunger, yes, I sure do. I know right from wrong, too. Takin' something from someone without their permission is not the right way to feed yourself. There's a better way."

A white sheet of fear fell across the boy's dirty face. "Why'd you ask me my name if you already knew?"

"I wanted you to tell me is all. Your name's Billy Bunson, right?"

Billy lunged forward, but Sonny was ready, had anticipated the boy's resolve to flee. He had strength and height on the boy, and a little foresight. Sonny would have run, too. He pulled Billy back and surrounded him with both arms, capturing him in a bear hug, a tight but gentle wrap impossible to escape. Tall men had long arms. Sonny was no exception.

To Sonny's surprise, Billy didn't scream or flail about. He relaxed immediately.

"I could stomp your foot, or bite you," Billy said.

"You could, but I'd wrap you in a tighter ball."

"Will you let me go?"

"If you promise not to run off."

"I'm not letting go of the chicken. I'm not giving it back no matter how long you hold me here."

Billy's calmness was convincing, but Sonny didn't loosen his grip. "I'll make you a deal, Billy Bunson."

"What's that?"

"Looks like the butcher's closed and gone home. You need to go home, too. Let's say I'll give you two bits for that chicken so you got something in your pocket."

"Sounds like a fair deal."

"There's a catch."

"What's that?"

"You give me one of the bits back, and I'll make sure the butcher gets it. That way we all get what we need. You got a coin in your pocket, I got a chicken to offer to my captain, and the butcher doesn't have to send the sheriff after you. You can't get into trouble if you pay the man for his chicken, now can you?"

"That's how you knew my name. That butcher . . ."

"It doesn't matter. Do we have a deal?"

Billy hesitated, looked toward the butcher's shop, then said, "Yes."

"Okay, I have to trust you." And with that, he let go of Billy Bunson. Sonny fully expected the boy to run. He was prepared to give chase if necessary.

Billy Bunson stood back and gazed at Sonny. "You're a different kind of man." He held out his hand for his coin.

Sonny complied, dug in his pocket for a coin, fingered two, and produced one bit of silver for Billy's taking. "I'll keep the other one, thank you."

The boy hesitated. "What's your name, mister?"

"Sonny Burton."

"You the law of some kind?"

"A Ranger."

Billy's eyes widened, his breathing quickened, then regulated slowly. He took the coin, and offered Sonny the chicken. "There you go, Ranger Burton. A deal's a deal."

Sonny took the chicken. "I'll get your payment to the butcher, don't you worry about it."

"I have to trust you."

"You do. I'd shy away from that shop if I was you. That butcher's got an eye out for you. I'd assume he keeps a sharp cleaver."

"I'll do that," Billy said. He smiled at Sonny and started to walk away. "Nice doin' business with you, Ranger Burton. I hope you beat the tar out of those Mexicans." And then he took off running, disappearing around a corner, into the shadows, leaving Sonny standing there alone.

Sonny looked at the chicken, smiled to himself, squared his shoulders, and started down the street to retrieve his horse. It only took him a second to stick his hand in his other pocket; a natural habit when he was satisfied with himself. But that satisfaction quickly faded away.

His pocket was empty, and his wallet was gone. Gone like Billy Bunson, vanished into thin air, into the darkness, into the shadows from where he came. The boy didn't fight for a reason. He stole every penny Sonny had on him. Every penny except the one bit of silver left to pay the butcher. That was all the money Sonny had to his name.

"Son of a bitch." Sonny yelled out. "You little son of a bitch. I'll catch you if it's the last thing I do."

May 1911
Ysleta, Texas

Captain John R. Hughes was a serious man of medium height, not skinny or portly, but healthy for his late age. He wore a brushy gray mustache and a thick beard that matched his well-trimmed hair. A life spent exposed to the harsh South Texas sun had left his skin permanently leathered. His hats varied from a ten-gallon to a floppy felt Stetson, depending on the season or the formality of the occasion. The hats were always white. He wore neither as he stood behind his simple desk, his coat off, his suspenders and drop belly exposed. Two hurricane lanterns burned brightly in the small room. The barracks had not been electrified. It looked to have been the end of a long day for the captain.

"You're late, Burton," Hughes said.

"I ran into some trouble in El Paso." Sonny stood stiffly in front of the desk, his spine as straight as possible, shoulders squared, prepared to be taken down a notch.

Hughes gazed at Sonny curiously with deep, experienced eyes. "Really, and what kind of trouble was that? The sheriff is set to wire me at the first round of shooting. I have received no notice of incursion."

"The warning shots died away quickly. More's coming, though, I'm certain of that."

"We all are." Hughes settled down into the chair behind the desk and cleared a few important-looking papers to the side.

"A boy stole a chicken, and I brought him to justice."

"A chicken, you say?"

"Yes."

"A boy?"

"Yes, a street waif, thin as a rail."

"And how exactly was it your duty to bring this child to justice?" Hughes sat back, stroked a wild strand of his beard, and continued to study Sonny as if he were a child himself.

Sonny knew the captain wasn't quick to fly off the handle. He could have been a politician in Austin, but Sonny had heard that Hughes had declined positions of power more than once, which was probably a great loss to the fine people of Texas. Hughes was building his case and would determine whether Sonny's story was worthy of forgiveness or not. Then and only then would judgment be doled out. Sonny had ridden with the captain a long time. He was certain of his ways.

"I saw the boy take the chicken, and I gave the butcher my word that I would catch the thief."

"Your word to return a chicken? On an evening when revolutionaries and soldiers are certain to take up arms against each other? It is our duty as Rangers to protect the citizenship of El Paso, and nothing more. Certainly not wasting time chasing down a petty thief."

"A boy," Sonny said.

"Once a thief, always a thief. You can't change that, Burton." Hughes sat forward in his chair. "You've wasted my time. I need a sergeant I can count on, one that's on time, one that knows his place, and one that doesn't question strategy when he lacks the full scope of knowledge of the situation at hand. I need a sergeant who respects punctuality and order, not one who ignores his place among the men that he commands."

The captain tapped the paper in front of him, drawing Sonny's eyes to it. He recognized it immediately. The paper was the wire that Sonny had sent questioning the captain's plan to have all the men ride into El Paso together. This dressing down was about more than being late.

"I never took you for an ambitious man, Burton," Hughes continued, "but perhaps I was wrong. I've promoted Calbert Dobbs to sergeant. You'll fall in behind him when the time comes. And if that does not suit you, then you can ride north and ignore this skirmish altogether. It's your choice whether to continue as a Ranger or not. As offensive as I find your deeds, your length of valor and service forbids me from sending you packing."

Sonny tried his best not to let the tremble that had traveled all the way through his body show. His face flushed, and he squeezed his hands into loose fists. He hadn't expected such a thing. Insecurity in his position had never been in question, at least, in his mind. Sonny didn't know what to say, or do.

"That'll be all, Burton. Go join the other men if you're riding with us. Otherwise, I'll bid you ado, and thank you for your time as a Ranger."

Sonny's mouth went dry. He'd never considered being anything but a Ranger, had no other skills to fall back on, unless it was being a lawman of some kind. Those positions didn't come easy. He had a pregnant wife and a young boy at home, and would have to take a pay cut of ten dollars a month if he stayed. Either way, Sonny didn't know what he'd say to Martha. There was barely enough money to feed the three of them the way it was. Sonny exhaled, and thought about defending himself, thought about making a case why he was a good sergeant and why what he had done proved that. In the end, he didn't say anything of the like. Captain Hughes was not a man who changed his mind easily. Actions would garner good graces, and the possibility of a promotion, not words.

"I'll join the other men, Captain," Sonny said.

"Good. They're expecting you. Be ready to ride when the call comes for it."

"I am, sir," Sonny said. "I am."

May 1911
El Paso, Texas
Two days later, the front page of the *El Paso Herald* read:
"Soldiers Strip Off Their Uniforms. FIGHT OVER. Hundreds
Killed and Wounded. BLOOD IN THE STREETS. Bedecked
Automobile Sent Out After Madero To Bring Him To Juárez."

All five of the Texas Rangers survived the battle. Sergeant
Calbert Dobbs suffered minor wounds; a bullet graze. They all
remained in Ysleta for several months.

CHAPTER EIGHT

October 1934

Huntsville, Texas

Clayton Randalls had more keys on his belt than any man should have ever had possession of. The jingle-jangle that accompanied his stubby stride was the first thing Sonny noticed about the guard. The second thing Sonny noticed was that the man was not carrying a pistol of any kind. A well-worn baton poked out of a homemade holster on Randalls's left hip. He walked with a slight limp, and a faded scar showed on the right side of his clean-shaven face. His uniform was freshly starched, and his boots shined like they were made of black mirrors. He looked competent and capable, not surprising under Jeb Rickart's command.

Until Billy's escape, Jeb was the most disciplined warden Sonny had ever met. Given that the warden had summoned the guard to escort Sonny was an endorsement of Randalls's status among the ranks. Sonny judged the man appropriately, but with suspicion. Anybody who had come into contact with Billy Bunson was worthy of questioning.

"So you want to see Billy Bunson's cell?" the guard said, as he unconsciously ran a hand over the top of his black, shiny hair. It looked like he'd worked in a fresh dollop of pomade to make himself more presentable than he already was.

"I do." Sonny had to look down to make eye contact with the guard. The top of the man's head came to Sonny's breastbone.

He smelled of mothballs and spearmint.

The guard chewed a stick of gum in even beats, like it was a constant habit. "Ain't much to see," he said in between chews. "Bunson didn't make much of an impact on anything. A model prisoner until he escaped. It's the quiet ones you have to watch out for, I tell you. I figured he was planning something, but I never saw a sign of anything untoward. Slick as an eel, that one."

Sonny was tempted to agree, but decided to keep his opinions to himself. He knew plenty about Billy Bunson. He was more interested in hearing what the guard thought of Billy than sharing his own knowledge.

Without saying another word, the guard turned and headed down the hall, striding away from the warden's office with purpose. "Come on, this way."

The keys clanged and clattered, mixing with the steady beat of the man's shoes as they landed on the highly waxed floor. It was a musical performance that announced Clayton Randalls's presence long before he arrived at his destination. There was something about the guard that troubled Sonny, but he couldn't put his finger on it, at least not yet. Maybe he was a showboater, or purposefully loud to make up for his lack of height. Prison was no place to show any kind of weakness; overcompensating was common. Being a prison guard was a tough job. Sonny knew that, had seen plenty of good ones and bad ones over the years. Brutal men. Gentle men. Honest men. Men on the take. Behind bars day after day, constantly reminded of the worst thing one man could do to another. Huntsville housed the worst of the worst. Old Sparky was a testament to that.

The thought of working inside the prison walls eight hours a day was beyond consideration for Sonny. He would have gone mad. He had more in common with Billy Bunson than he wanted to admit. Sonny valued his own freedom as much as

Billy did. He needed to breathe fresh air and make his own way. Billy told him once that they were kindred spirits, but Sonny didn't believe it, or didn't want to believe such a thing. But now, well, now Sonny was willing to reconsider the thought. Billy Bunson would have done anything to escape from Huntsville.

Maybe the guard felt the same way as Sonny about being inside the prison, only Clayton Randalls was trapped in a job he had to have. Times were hard. There was a Depression on. Jobs were scarce. Being a prison guard put food on the table, was steady work in a time when any kind of respectable work was held by few men. Sonny exhaled at the thought and reminded himself to go easy on Clayton Randalls. His life was hard enough.

Sonny followed along behind the guard, silently memorizing his way back to the warden's office in case he got separated from Randalls. Turn left, turn right at the first hall. Building an escape plan came as naturally to Sonny as it did to Billy Bunson.

Randalls stopped at a green ironclad door at the end of the long hallway, and searched the ring for a specific key.

Sonny stopped next to the cement block wall and waited. It dripped with humidity. The air inside the prison felt tropical, unmoving. Oppression was all around him. He felt like he was trapped inside of a tomb.

"You'll want to keep your distance from the cells," the guard said. "Prisoners would love to get a hold of that hook of yours."

Sonny looked down to the prosthesis and flinched. "I guess they would."

"Heard you got into it with Bonnie and Clyde. They got what was comin' to 'em," Randalls said.

Sonny didn't answer. Bonnie Parker was no more than a girl who got so riddled with bullets that she couldn't be properly embalmed. Nobody deserved that. Not even a criminal like Bonnie. He figured the guard would have found it odd that he felt sorry for Bonnie, but that wasn't it at all. He didn't feel sorry for her. Sonny had seen the effect hate had on a man, on a nation; a seed grows quickly into a monster whether it's Clyde Barrow or Germany retaliating for some kind of offense or another. He had gone to war because of hate and lived to tell about it. Being angry at Bonnie and Clyde wasn't gonna hurt anyone but himself. Sonny knew that. Especially now that Bonnie and Clyde were dead and gone. What he couldn't conceal, or come to terms with, was the hook itself, how it looked to other people, how it made them feel. He wasn't whole. A monster himself. Children stared. Adults looked away from him, treated him as if his deformity was his own fault. Sonny was self-conscious and embarrassed. There wasn't anything he could do about that. Hating Bonnie and Clyde would only make things worse.

Randalls found the key and opened the heavy door. He stepped through it, stopped, then motioned for Sonny to follow.

Sonny did as he was instructed and took his place opposite the guard.

The two-story cellblock was quieter than Sonny had expected it to be. There was a low hum from the overhead fans and some murmurs of distant conversations. No screaming, no yelling. The prison was surprisingly calm.

"Been on lockdown since Billy jumped the fence," Randalls said, as if he could read what Sonny was thinking.

Sonny adjusted to being inside the cellblock as best he could.

A pungent smell immediately accosted his nose. One he'd encountered before. Sweat and anger, piss and fear, the scent of men without regard to women, themselves, or any other living creature who might show discomfort in their presence. The cells were nothing more than a government-run zoo; a collection of caged, wretched men, full of rage and lost manners.

"Come on, don't dillydally," the guard said as he locked the green door behind him. "No time for that. Chow time's comin' and we'll be opening the cells soon."

Randalls led the way. Sonny followed, hugging the outside wall. There was six feet between the exterior wall and the cell bars. He kept his focus on Randalls, and didn't acknowledge the prisoners inside any of the cells. He felt their stares, their hate, their curiosity. A bead of sweat trickled down his forehead while another one formed at the edge of his stump, lubricating the prosthesis. The straps were pulled tight, but he still worried about the wooden arm falling off. It had happened before.

"This is it," Randalls said, coming to a stop. "Like I said, there's nothing to see. That Bunson was neat and clean to a fault. Be nice if the rest of the population took after him."

Sonny tuned the guard out and stared into the cell. It was an eight-by-eight-foot cage with one bunk, a sink with running water, and a hole at the back wall for a prisoner to relieve himself in. The bed was covered with a simple green blanket, tucked in with tight hospital corners. There were no pictures on the walls. No pencil marks or drawings. Nothing personal to be seen. The cell was like Randalls said it was, like Sonny had expected it to be: as clean and empty of any personality as the first day Billy Bunson had stepped into it.

"Doesn't look like he was ever here," the guard continued.

"That's what he wants you to see." Sonny stepped over to the cell door, touched it softly, and ran his left hand over the cold steel, searching for a flaw, a nick, something undetectable at first glance. "I need to get inside and look around."

"Suit yourself. It's been gone over with every eagle-eye boss inside this prison."

Sonny allowed the guard to insert his key into the cell door and open it. He said nothing as he stepped inside. He wished that Clayton Randalls would vanish, but he knew that wasn't going to happen.

Sonny closed his eyes for a long second, recalling the last time he saw Billy Bunson in the flesh. He had delivered the boy—Billy would always be a boy to Sonny—to Huntsville two years ago after a jury in Waco had found him guilty of armed robbery and assault at the First National Bank. Billy was given a twenty-year sentence. He was being led into the prison by a trio of guards, as he said, "See you around, Sonny."

At the time, Sonny had thought that was the end of Billy. It was his first stint in Huntsville, and the prison, under Warden Jeb Rickart, had a reputation for being difficult to break out of.

Sonny had underestimated Billy, who had somehow put together a scheme to trick the warden's wife into teaching him to read all over again. It was a con, a way out. But how?

Sonny took a breath and opened his eyes, focusing on the bed. He knew he had to look at every inch of the cell before he left, not overlook a thing. Billy was a master at covering his tracks, but Sonny had caught a few of his mistakes in the past. Waco being one of them. Billy made you think he was going in one direction, but would double back and go the opposite way. Bait and switch was one of his favorite tactics. Sonny was waiting for Billy as he headed north out of Waco. He had a small army with him big enough to take down Bonnie and Clyde.

"What you lookin' for?" Randalls said as Sonny leaned down to look at the floor.

"Anything that'll tell me where Billy went."

"You don't know?"

Sonny cocked his head to the guard. "No, I don't know anything. Why don't you tell me?"

"Him and the warden's wife were more than teacher and student from what I hear."

"Really. The warden hear that, too?"

76

"I don't know what the warden's heard. Ain't asked me."

"So you're not telling?"

"Would you?"

Sonny ran his hand between the thin mattress on the bunk, then flipped it on its side. "I'd be shouting from the rooftops if I knew something about an escaped convict."

"You don't work here." There was offense taken in the tone Randalls offered Sonny.

"No, I don't. But if what you say is true, then the warden needs to know. He didn't imply any such thing to me."

"He has to know."

"Love is blind."

"Not to a man like Jeb Rickart it's not. He's the most sensible man I've ever known."

Sonny thought back for a minute and considered the conversation he'd had with the warden. The man was thrilled at the prospect of having a child. Maybe that had clouded his judgment, allowed him to close his ears to speculation about his wife that he didn't want to hear. It was worth investigating more, though there was one thing that didn't let Sonny buy into the bit of gossip he'd heard, and that was the finger. Billy had sent a severed finger to let the warden know he was serious. If what Randalls told him was true, Sonny had to wonder if Billy would have cut off Dolly's finger. He had to consider it as a possibility; Billy Bunson's heart was made of ash and ice. But maybe not. Maybe the finger was a ruse to convince the warden he was serious. If that was the case, where did the finger come from?

Sonny didn't say anything else to Randalls. He started running the tips of his fingers over the wood slats that held the mattress in place. They were all where they were supposed to be. Worn from time and use, but nothing seemed out of place. No scratches, no nicks, nothing. Until he touched the third one from the top. It was a little loose.

Randalls stood back and watched, his arms crossed, still put off by Sonny.

Sonny pulled out the slat and examined it for closer inspection. The end had been sawed off. Sonny laid the slat down, and pulled out the next one to it. That slat was two inches longer than the first one Sonny had pulled out. He thought for a second, then looked into the hole where the slat had been. A thick silhouette urged him to investigate closer. After feeling around, he cautiously pulled out a piece of wood with a hole in the center; a template shaped like a key.

"Looks like Billy could come and go as he pleased," Sonny said as he stood.

"How in tarnation do you think he did that?" Randalls said.

Sonny stared at the guard, holding the piece of wood tight like it was a treasure that could be taken away from him. "You're left-handed, aren't you?"

"Yes. So what?"

"Your baton is on your left hip, and you carry your keys on your right hip."

"What's that got to do with anything?"

"Lean against the cell like you would if you were having a chat with a prisoner."

"I don't do that," Randalls said. His entire body tensed and he drew his eyes together like he was suddenly suspicious of Sonny.

"Let's say you might chat with a prisoner late into the shift. Or another guard might."

"Jenkins would. He's lazy like that."

"Okay, Jenkins, then. Let's say Jenkins came along and had a conversation with Billy Bunson, and leaned against the bars while they talked."

"Okay, so what of it?"

"Do prisoners get bread with their meal?"

"Of course they do."

"Billy would have moistened the bread, made it formable, and quietly, softly, made an impression of the key to his cell while the two of them talked. Then he took that impression and used it as a template, carved a key from the slat, and walked out of the cell like he owned it."

"What'd he carve it with? No one has knives in here."

"Could have been a toothbrush. Anything. My guess is whatever he used, he took it with him."

"So, that explains it. We couldn't figure out how he walked out of here."

"He probably had keys carved for every door."

"How'd he get them all?"

"Well, if what you told me is true. One way or another, it might have been the warden's wife who gave him access to those keys—whether she knew it or not."

CHAPTER NINE

May 1911

El Paso, Texas

A hint of gunpowder still hung in the air when the first soldier knocked on the door. He was a thin, spritely man who looked to be about thirty years old. His face was soiled from the battle. Dust, sweat, and blood mixed together, giving him the look of a foreigner even though his skin was white. His shirt was torn at the sleeve and his eyes looked hungry. He was upright and not woefully injured, but that wouldn't have mattered. Miss Tillie would have taken the man's money no matter what condition he was in. Desire was the fuel that lit the lamps in the house.

Jim Rome hulked in the doorway, barring entrance until he knew the man's business for certain. More to the point, it was Jim's job to make sure the soldier had enough money to exercise his needs—or determine if he had other matters to settle. It was possible the man wasn't a customer at all.

Billy stood back in the shadows, atop a trapdoor, told to keep quiet, to hide, to stay put in case the caller was the law of some kind, come to take him away. Billy'd told Jim about his run-in with that Texas Ranger. An alarm had been set. The threat wouldn't pass for days.

There were three trapdoors installed in the house and as many escape routes planned. Everyone in the house had their own way out, knew where to meet if they got separated. Miss Tillie left nothing to chance, no matter what town they were in.

A persistent Ranger could spell trouble for them all.

"What be your business?" Jim said to the man.

"Pleasure."

"You shore about that?"

The man peered around Jim. "Yes. I've been here before. Got a taste for the one called Teresa." He was jittery, had a facial tick like he was coming off a high of some kind.

Jim Rome leaned out the door to get a closer look at the man's face. "I don't recall seein' you b'fore. You shore you been here?"

"As sure as it's daylight. Ask Teresa, she'll remember ol' Roland Flowers. Yes, she will, you ask her. I treat her real nice. She's a pretty girl, that one."

"Well, okay then, I'll do that, but if you be lyin' to me, I'll break you in half if I have to."

"No need for any scufflin' today, friend," the man said. "I done saw enough of that. I got friends comin' this way. They'll vouch for me if need be. I wanted to be first in line, if you know what I mean."

"No need for a scuffle if you got the right coins."

"I said I did. I'd like to see Teresa."

"She ain't a workin' girl no more. You'll have to pick someone else."

"Why's that?"

"Miss Tillie say so, that be why. End of discussion, 'less you want to take it up with the lady of the house yourself."

"No, sir, I do not. I don't have the nerve to face Miss Tillie unless I have to. Well, then, if that's the way it is, I guess I'll have to have a look-see at the other girls. I sure did like that Teresa, though. You sure I can't have her? Can you tell the lady I'll pay extra?"

"I'll ask Miss Tillie," Jim Rome said. "She might like the sound of extra."

"I'll bet she would."

"I'll ask."

Billy hadn't moved. He stood still as a statue watching Jim Rome play gatekeeper and bargainer-in-chief. Miss Tillie trusted Jim Rome to work the door, but she was most likely close by, listening to each word spoken. The walls in the house had holes in them. Lots of holes. Ones for listening and watching. There was no place for cheats in Miss Tillie's world and everyone who was kin or worked for her knew it. Even Billy wasn't immune. He'd taken more than one switch to the bare behind for breaking one rule or another.

Miss Tillie would surely take money for Teresa the Terrible. No man wanted to touch her since Teresa had that confrontation with a scorpion. Her skin looked like she was diseased in some way. That was never good for the flat-on-your-back business.

Jim Rome passed by Billy and pointed his index finger to the floor. That meant stay and keep quiet. Billy didn't move. He did as he was told, and watched Jim Rome disappear.

The soldier stood at the door, flexing his grip, shifting his weight, still jittery, looking over his shoulder every other second. The other soldiers would be there soon. Whiskey would flow, music would play on the piano, and everyone would be happy and merry.

Once Jim disappeared it was as if Billy was the only person left in the world. Everything had gone silent. The calm before the storm. Or the long breath after the battle. Men needed to work off whatever energy they had left in them after the fight. Everyone in the house had scurried around until there was nothing to do but wait.

"I see you back there, boy," the soldier said. "Why don't you come out where I can get a better look at you?"

Billy didn't move. He couldn't believe the man could see him.

"I see your shadow. I sure do," said the man. "What are you afraid of?"

Billy started to breathe quicker. He didn't like being seen. Miss Tillie and Jim Rome wouldn't like it, either.

"Come on, then, step out into the light. I think I got a spare penny to offer." The soldier dug into the front pocket of his trousers and pulled out a small copper coin. "That's to buy you some candy in town."

No it wouldn't, Billy thought. Miss Tillie would know he had it and he'd have to give her the coin. She could smell copper from a mile away. But taking it might've been worth the risk. It had been a long time since he'd been able to walk into the candy store and actually buy something.

"Come on, boy. I ain't gonna hurt you. I want someone to talk with while I wait." The man, Roland Flowers, put his foot on the stoop, but stopped there. If he'd been there before like he said, he knew better than to walk inside the house uninvited.

Billy heard a distant murmur of voices. Miss Tillie telling Jim Rome how much to charge for Teresa the Terrible. He thought they should have given foul women away for free. She'd never been nice to Billy.

"Two pennies, then," Flowers said as he dug for another coin, then produced it like a magician pulling a dove out of his cloak.

The copper twinkled in the sunlight, allowing Billy to see that the coin was real. He couldn't resist any longer and stepped out from his hiding place.

"Well, there you are. I never knowed you was here. You always been here?" Roland Flowers said.

"Yes," Billy answered.

"Well, color me blind." Roland Flowers sucked in a deep

breath and his face flushed red as a cherry.

Billy heard footsteps behind him and scooted back to the shadows.

Jim Rome appeared with a curious look, taking in the change in Roland Flowers's demeanor and expression. "Miss Tillie say two dollars mo' for Teresa. No negotiatin'. Take it or leave it."

The soldier ran his hand through his hair, and jingled the two pennies in the other. "I done changed my mind. How much for that boy there in the shadows?"

Jim Rome answered quick. "He ain't no worker here. He live here, that's all. You get Teresa or nothin'."

Billy understood what was said.

He smelled Miss Tillie before he heard her. She always had a hand-rolled Bugler dangling out of the corner of her mouth, and kept fresh toilet water close at hand. Smoke swirled around her fat face, mixing with fresh jasmine, making her smell unmistakable. Her solid black hair was piled high atop her head. She usually wore a housedress that fell below her knees; purple flowers cut deep at the chest, exposing watermelon cleavage without shame or pride. His grandmother's manner of dress was more for comfort than style.

"How much you gonna pay?" Miss Tillie said, shuffling past Billy. She was a good-sized woman, twice as wide as Roland Flowers. The floorboards groaned under her weight when she walked.

Billy couldn't breathe. He couldn't believe what he was hearing. He knew times were tough, that the battle in El Paso, the start of the Mexican Revolution, had stunted business, but he'd never worried about being farmed out like one of the girls. At least, not until now.

If Billy was tense and soaked in the sweat of disbelief and fear, poor Jim Rome looked like he'd caught a major case of stomach troubles. If it were possible for the Negro to go pale as a bleached sheet, he would have.

Before Roland Flowers could answer, Jim cranked his thumb upward.

It meant run. Run away as fast as you can.

Billy didn't hesitate. But he didn't run. He tapped the trapdoor and fell feet first into the crawl space underneath the house. Scorpions and snakes were the least of his worries. He needed to get away from Roland Flowers and Miss Tillie as quickly as possible.

He scurried away in the darkness, ignoring his grandmother's screams for him to stop and come back. He knew he was going to get a good beating when he returned, but that didn't matter. What *was* going to happen to Billy couldn't compare to what would have happened to him if he had stayed. He knew what the men did to the girls. He couldn't imagine such a thing being done to him.

There were no hidey-holes under the house, and there was plenty of reason not to stop. Billy broke free of the crawl space, stood, and tore into the fastest run he'd ever mustered. He ignored the screams and yells behind him, uncertain of where he was going. All he wanted was to get as far from the house as possible. Then he'd wait it out. See what happened. Once night fell, and the house was full of paying soldiers, he'd tippy-toe back home and act like nothing had ever happened. That was his plan.

The crack of leather against bare skin filled Billy's ears. He jumped every time Miss Tillie swung the belt and slapped it against Jim Rome's back. It took all he had not to scream at her to stop. It wasn't Jim Rome's fault he'd run. He would have done that anyway. There was no way he was going to let Roland Flowers touch him in a dirty way.

Billy was hiding at the corner of the house, too scared to

show his face. Jim was bent over the water trough, not saying a word, grimacing as the belt cut into his skin. Miss Tillie put all the power she had into each lashing.

"Don't you ever send that boy away again without my permission. You understand me, Jim Rome? I say who gets what around here. Not you. Not ever." Miss Tillie swung the belt back, reloaded, and laid the leather against Jim like she was trying to kill the poor Negro.

The crack sounded like thunder. Billy was certain the earth had moved under his feet.

Blood splattered upward, then fell back to the parched ground in thick, red drops. Rain-stained red. The dirt rejected the blood. It sat atop the hard, dry, brown soil in a pool that didn't diminish, didn't soak away.

Billy wasn't sure how much more Jim Rome could take, even though he showed no weakness or trembles.

"Yes, ma'am. I ain't gonna do no such thing ever again. I promise," Jim Rome said.

"You do, and I'll break out the butcher knife. There won't be no next time after that. That boy is my blood and bone. I own him. He's mine. I can sell him anytime I like." Miss Tillie twisted her lip, reared back, and launched into a flurry of slaps. It sounded like she was trying to urge on a lazy horse. She didn't stop until the belt was red and Jim Rome's knees buckled under him.

A tear slid down Billy's cheek, and he looked away. He couldn't watch any longer. He shouldn't have been there. He should have run. By the time he realized he needed to flee, it was too late. As he launched into a run, a hand reached out and grabbed him, then spun him around.

Billy stood face to face with his mother. And by the look on her face, he was sure she wasn't too keen to see him. Before Billy could offer an excuse, defend himself for running, she reared back like Miss Tillie and slapped him so hard all he could hear was ringing in his ears. All he could see was stars, and all he could taste was blood.

"You owe me, boy," his mother said. "Now get over there and take what's comin' to you."

October 1934

Bedias, Texas

Night had fallen around the cabin, covering it in darkness, offering a reprieve from running. There wasn't anyone for a mile or two, stuck back off the main road like they were. Billy knew better than to get comfortable, to be cavalier, to come and go like he pleased. Someone would see him. The radio would have already warned everyone to keep an eye out for an escaped convict. They would say he was armed and dangerous. They'd be right about that. They sure would be.

He slipped out of the cabin and locked the door behind him. It didn't matter much, though. He wasn't going far this time. He had a hidey-hole to dig.

CHAPTER TEN

July 1911
Vinton, Texas

The horse welcomed a slow pace as they made their way toward Vinton. Sonny had a hard time considering the place his home. He'd only spent a few nights there since he'd deposited Martha and Jesse, and left for El Paso. A lot had happened in the short three months since he'd ridden away. A Mexican Revolution. Blood. Battle. Boredom. Loneliness on a dusty trail. Loss of rank. And worry. Lots of worry about the lives he'd left behind. This latest fight had left Sonny without any visible scars, but his shoulders felt as heavy as the horse who pointed its nose north. Death and pain at every turn was starting to wear on him.

A few letters had been exchanged between Sonny and Martha, but nothing else. Martha wasn't much for regular correspondence and neither was Sonny. He hadn't told her that he wasn't a sergeant any longer, and she had remained vague in her letters when it came to her health. A third of her pregnancy, or more, was nearly past, and all she spoke about was the weather and the wind that rolled down off the mountain and rattled the roof at night.

She'd be showing signs of the baby by now.

Sonny urged the horse on at the thought, anxious to get to the house. Regretfully, time spent in Vinton would be a small reprieve. He only had a few weeks' leave.

The trail looked foreign and untraveled even though Sonny

had taken the same route when he'd departed in May. Spring had been in full bloom then; all of the possibility of beauty was on display for as far as the eye could see. The horizon had glowed green. But beauty was as fragile and brief as the bloom on a bluebonnet. Here one day, gone the next, weakened by the persistent sun and starved by the dry earth. Summer had taken a deep hold. All that lay out before Sonny as he rode north was a brown and lifeless vista; only the sapphire blue sky offered the world any color, and it seemed too blue, like it might shatter at any second.

It was a wonder that anything could live on the land at all. Snakes, of course, thrived, as did other creatures; most of them unkind to man and beast alike. Sonny was vigilant for the sight of a rattler on the trail. Deadly snakebites to horses' legs were rare, but it had been known to happen. A startled horse could be as dangerous as an injured horse, rearing back and tossing its rider to the ground. One bang of the head on a rock and that was the end of everything. Sonny had known that to happen, too.

It wasn't long before Sonny entered the valley of his new home. The landscape looked strange and unfamiliar. He had to work at finding his way to the house. *Right at the fork? Or left?* He took the right fork and breathed a sigh of relief once the simple foothills house came into view.

The day had faded into evening, the gloaming as some people called it, that thin amount of time between light and dark, hope and despair; the coming of the unknown. Night unsettled Sonny more than any other time of the day, but he never told anyone that.

He made his way to the house and tied the horse to a hitching post at the water trough, encouraged that it was half full.

No one was about. Quiet and solitude surrounded the small wood-frame house. Sonny wasn't too surprised given the time of day. Martha was a woman prone to silence until she could no longer restrain herself. Once ignited, her German anger raged into a perilous thunderstorm. When that occurred, Sonny knew the best thing to do was keep his mouth shut and take shelter until dangerous weather passed. His boy, Jesse, was like his mother in that way; quiet until someone lit his fuse. Still, everything around the house felt a little too calm, too isolated and untouched.

He stepped onto the porch and discovered it hadn't been swept recently. Martha was a stickler for tidiness no matter where they'd lived. His sense of discomfort, of concern, bloomed into uncertainty and fear.

Sonny hesitated at the door, then knocked, and pushed inside. "Hold your fire. I'm home." He had a deep-barrel voice and used it when need be to announce himself. His voice came in handy in battle and in times when authority was demanded.

The first thing Sonny noticed when he stepped inside was that the house was dark; not a candle or oil lamp burned. Talk of spreading electrification across the country was persistent in Austin, and faraway Washington, D.C., but like the thought of an automobile taking the full place of a horse, Sonny could hardly grasp the idea of every house in South Texas burning electric lights. Magic wires worried him as much as porches littered with three days of dirt.

The second thing he noticed was a foul smell, like someone had brought the contents of the outhouse inside and left it there.

"Is anyone home?" Sonny dug into his pocket for a match. He struck it and brought a small amount of light to the room.

The house was a mess. Blankets covered the windows, the kitchen sink was full of unwashed dishes. It looked like every plate, which were few, sat in the sink untouched by water. More dust covered the floor. Worry transformed into the reality that something was wrong.

He quickly found a lamp, lit it, and hurried to the small bedroom he'd shared with Martha. It was there that he found her and Jesse asleep. Martha was in the bed, and Jesse prone in the trundle at her side.

Sonny wasn't sure if either of them were still alive. Neither had stirred at his entrance. His heart started to race. He was no doctor, had no idea what to do at that second other than to find which way it was: alive or dead.

Jesse was closest. Sonny touched the boy's pale, skinny arm, and found it to be moist and warm. His heart skipped a hopeful beat. "Wake up, boy," Sonny said, as he shook Jesse gently.

Jesse's blue eyes flickered opened. "That you, Pa?"

"It is." Sonny pulled the boy into a sitting position. Sleep caked Jesse's eyes, and he instinctively wiped the crud away to clear his vision.

"I been hopin' you'd come home, Pa. It's Ma. She's been awful sick."

"Why didn't you go to see that man, Hiram Pete, and his wife, Hon. Hi and Hon. They said they'd help out if need be."

"Them folks is sick, too, Pa. A fever's come over the valley. There's a doctor goin' from house to house, but there's not much he can do from what that Mr. Pete said."

Sonny sighed. He knew straight away that he'd walked into an infected house. If he wasn't careful, he'd come down with the fever, too. He pulled his handkerchief over his mouth and nose and fastened it to stay there. He looked like a bandit come to rob the house. Then he turned his attention to Martha. She laid on the bed like a baby, knees to her chest, covered with a thin bedsheet, her back to him.

Jesse coughed as he stood, reinforcing the seriousness of the situation Sonny had found his family in. He was too concerned and panicked to feel guilty for leaving the two of them to fend for themselves. Regret and a deeper emotion, anger at himself, would come later. For now, he had no choice but to make things better.

Sonny put his knee on the bed and touched Martha the same way he'd touched Jesse, unsure if she was alive or dead. "Martha, it's me, Sonny. I've come home."

She moaned and shuddered, moving enough for Sonny to see the blood and a slimy discharge between her legs. The baby was in trouble. Martha was in trouble. He had smelled sickness and death when he'd walked into the house, and now he knew why.

October 1934
Huntsville, Texas

The boardinghouse was easy to find. It sat on the corner of 19th and Avenue M like Jeb Rickart had said it did. The house was oddly structured; a two-story affair painted bright yellow and covered with a flat roof. Most houses of its size were adorned with peaks and spires, but none of those architectural embellishments were evident on this structure. The house looked unfinished in a way, or was more akin to a ship than a house. All that was missing was a bow, a stern, and an ocean.

Sonny parked the Model A truck at the curb, noticed a small X scratched on the street in front of the mailbox, and knew that hobos had deemed the owner, Edith Grantley, generous, willing to give out some food if there was any to be had. It was an assumption, of course. That mark could have been left by anything, or anyone, for any reason. Sonny had seen the mark more than once in his hometown of Wellington, and had come to know its meaning. His home was marked, too, but being so far out on a farm-to-market road like he was, traffic was slim. Only on rare occasions did a man headed to nowhere knock on his door for a handout.

He shrugged off the sight of the X even though its presence made him a little more comfortable. It had been a long time since he'd taken a room in a boardinghouse and he wasn't sure how people would take to the sight of him.

Late afternoon bathed the house in an odd glow, mainly because of its happy color. If there was any comfort to be found, it was here. The warden had sent him to a decent place.

Sonny didn't plan on being in Huntsville too long. Billy's trail would grow cold fast, and that was the last thing he wanted, though from what Sonny knew of Billy, it was entirely possible that the boy was still in town, or close by. If he was trying to gain something, like a ransom, money for some cause or reason, then a full-out run to Mexico wouldn't be the first thing he'd do. Once Dolly Rickart was found that would be another story. Billy Bunson would run as fast as he could and not stop until he was far, far, away.

"What do you think, boy? This do us for a day or two?" Sonny said to Blue.

Blue wagged his tail with a couple of mild twitches. The dog responded in some way or another when Sonny spoke directly to him.

"Well," Sonny said, grabbing his hat and putting it on his head. "I better go see the lady and see how much extra you're gonna cost me to stay here." He'd failed to mention to Jeb that he was traveling with a dog. "You stay here. I won't be gone long this time."

Blue looked at Sonny like he was going to leave forever.

Sonny eased out of the truck and automatically adjusted the straps that held the prosthesis in place. The day had been long and the air was humid. The top strap had nearly slipped off his shoulder when he'd been inside the prison. Once he'd made himself presentable, he walked to the door and buzzed the bell.

There was no sign that announced the place as a boardinghouse. A pot of late-blooming geraniums sat on a white wicker table next to the front door. A settee made in the same fashion as the table looked out over the street. The porch looked freshly painted, the floor free of marring or show of traffic. A thin lace curtain hung at the door window, allowing anyone to see straight into the parlor. A piano sat against the wall with a vase and fresh-cut hydrangeas on top of it.

Sonny heard footsteps padding to the door after a long second. He felt self-conscious all over again, then pushed his vanity away as best he could, stood up straight, and tried not to look too much like an angry old man.

A woman opened the door without any curiosity on her face at all. She stood behind a screen, and said, "How'd do?"

She was a tall woman, about three inches shorter than Sonny. He wasn't used to looking a woman in the eye without having to make some effort. "Fine, thank you, ma'am. I'd like to speak with Edith Grantley if she is available."

"Well, she is, since she's speaking to you." Edith Grantley flashed a quick smile, and her deep brown eyes that matched her hair, the ones that weren't streaked gray, sparkled. Her voice had a smooth Southern drawl flavored with a Baptist Texas accent that immediately put a person at ease. She had manners, too. There wasn't a hint of judgment, or fear, to be seen on her face when it came to the hook. It was in full view. Sonny figured the woman to be in her late forties or early fifties.

"Jeb Rickart sent me over," he said. "Told me I should ask to see if you had a room available to let. I'll be in town for a few days, and he spoke highly of your accommodations. I'm not much for fancy hotels full of people myself and this place being out of the way like it is suits me better."

"Jeb, you say?"

"Yes, ma'am. I came straight from his office to here."

"How's he doing? I can't imagine what he must be going

through with Dolly taken away like that. It's the worst thing that's ever happened around here, and to such a nice man, too. I've known Jeb Rickart and his family nearly all of my life."

"He's a strong man," Sonny said.

"You here to help?"

"I shouldn't say."

Edith studied Sonny's face for a little longer than was polite. "Have we ever met? You sure do look familiar."

"No, I don't think so. I don't get to Huntsville often. It's been a few years since I've been down this way. I escorted a prisoner inside the walls and made a deposit. I thought that was that and left town."

"For what parts?"

"I've lived outside Wellington for the last ten years. I was a . . ." Sonny stopped, restrained himself from telling Edith Grantley too much. He felt foolish. She was a nice woman, easy to talk to. "A room. Do you have a room?"

"Oh, yes, of course I do. I have three boarders and two empty rooms. One on each side of the house on the top floor. Both offer good views and a nice breeze."

"And the cost?"

"For a friend of Jeb's? That would be two dollars a night, and that includes all of your meals and clean towels."

"That's awful generous."

"Well," Edith said, "if you're a friend of Jeb's and here to help, then it's an honor to make you as comfortable as I can."

Sonny looked over his shoulder, then back to Edith. "Well, I'll take it."

"Don't you want to see the room first?"

"I'm sure it's fine, ma'am."

"Edith. Please call me Edith."

"If you insist."

"I do."

"There's one more thing," Sonny said.

"What's that?" Edith's eyes lingered on the hook a few seconds longer than normal. It was the first time Sonny had noticed her paying any real attention to the prosthesis. Still, she didn't seem bothered by it.

"I brought a dog along on this trip and I don't want to leave him to run about. Blue's got a bad leg and other dogs might take advantage of his weakness. He doesn't have a lot of fight left in him. Old boy doesn't know where he's at, and besides, he sticks pretty close to me."

"Well, I can't let you keep him in the room, if that's what you're asking. Word would get out that I had a dog inside the house and that wouldn't be good for future prospects, now would it? Not that there's a steady stream of boarders knocking at the door these days. Times are tough and getting tougher from the way I see it."

"No, ma'am, I wouldn't want to impose, but if you have a garden shed, I sure would appreciate it if you'd let Blue spend the night in it. I'd be happy to pay you extra."

"This dog means a lot to you, then?"

"I 'bout killed him to tell you the truth. Run him over with my truck on a bad day when I wasn't paying attention like I should have been. The animal doctor mended him, and he's been with me ever since. I live alone, and Blue has been good company for me. He sure has. That's why I brought him with me. I didn't want to leave him at home to fend for himself."

"Well, that wouldn't be right, would it?" Edith paused, opened the screen door, and peered out at Blue sitting in the truck, dutifully keeping an eye on Sonny. "He looks harmless."

"As far as I can tell he is. He doesn't bark much, and he doesn't mess inside the house. Either someone taught him some manners before he came to me, or he figured things out on his own. I'll never know."

"I doubt you will. Well, then, my backyard is fenced. I can let him sleep on some blankets in the sleeping porch at the back of the house. Now, if anyone complains, you'll have to figure something else out."

"I'll be happy to pay more."

"Won't be necessary. There won't be too many extra scraps to throw his way, though."

"I'll worry about that." Sonny sighed, relieved. "My name's Sonny, by the way. Sonny Burton." He extended his left hand, and she shook it firmly.

"I knew that," Edith Grantley said with a slight smile, "Clara Ziskin, Jeb's secretary, called and told me you were on your way over."

CHAPTER ELEVEN

It didn't take Sonny long to get himself and Blue settled. His room was on the third floor and looked out over the street. There were no other boarders on the floor, which is why Sonny chose the room. The feather mattress seemed soft and comfortable, and the walls were freshly painted white. Landscape pictures adorned the walls; a cow grazing on a rolling green hill and a waterwheel working on a calm river, gave the room a bucolic feel. Sonny wondered if the paintings were local. He knew little about Huntsville and wouldn't know one place from the other. There was no dust to be seen, and the wood slat floors were freshly mopped. Sonny had stayed in worse places.

Edith Grantley had already put together a bed for Blue on the sleeping porch, and when Sonny found them, they were sitting on the back stoop like old friends catching up after a long absence.

Edith stood as soon as she saw Sonny approaching. Blue remained sitting, but did flick his tail slightly.

"I see you and Blue are going to get along," Sonny said.

"He seems sweet," Edith answered.

Sonny shrugged. He'd never thought of Blue as sweet. The dog was more even-tempered than anything. "I need to leave for a bit."

"You don't need to tell me when you're coming and going, Mr. Burton, unless you won't be here for supper. Then it's nice to know if I need to set you a plate or not."

"You can call me Sonny."

"Of course. I asked you to call me Edith. I should expect the same in return."

"If you don't mind."

"Not at all."

"Well, it looks like Blue is comfortable. That'll be one less worry while I'm out." He turned and started to walk toward the street.

"Sonny?" Edith called out.

He stopped and turned around. It was odd having a woman call after him. "Yes?"

"Should I set you a plate?"

"No, I 'spect not. I don't have a clue how long this will take. I'll grab a bite to eat if need be."

"Okay, then, you make sure and take care of yourself."

"I will." Sonny turned and headed toward his truck. He felt odd, in a good mood, like someone had painted the whole world bright and cheery, in yellow.

The Walker County jail was easy to find. They had been expecting him, too. After Sonny read the arrest report, a trustee short on words led him to the interview room, then quickly returned with Billy Bunson's girlfriend.

Donna Del Rey looked exactly like Sonny expected her to. Blonde, proudly buxom, not quite twenty years old, with stars in her eyes that were starting to fade. She wore a light blue dress with the hem starting to ravel, and no jewelry or any another adornment that Sonny could see. She'd probably never owned a piece of real silver in her life, and if she had, it most likely didn't stay in her possession long.

"I ain't got nothin' to say to you," she said, as Sonny settled across the table from her.

He smiled sadly, dug into his pocket, pulled out a pack of

Wrigley's gum, and offered her a stick.

"I don't want nothin' from you, either."

"I can get you out of here," Sonny said.

"Who says I need to worry about that?"

Sonny shrugged. He felt the strap across his back shift and tighten. The prosthesis tilted on its own, and the girl stared at Sonny's hook.

"How long you been here?" he said.

"I said I wasn't talkin' to you." She looked away from the hook, and into his eyes, summed the age on his face, then looked back to the hook. "What happened to you?"

"I was wondering the same thing about you." Sonny shifted in the chair again, only this time a little more cautiously.

"Your hand," Donna Del Rey said. "What happened to your hand?"

"I was in the wrong place at the wrong time. How about you?" He had never considered that the hook would be useful in any way. He despised its presence, but now he might have to reconsider the idea of it. Maybe it had a purpose.

"I went exactly where Billy told me."

"And you don't think it's odd that you ran straight into a line of policemen searching for you?"

"He said we'd split apart, then meet again." Donna arched her right eyebrow, then broke Sonny's gaze. "I'm not sayin' nothin' else 'til you tell me what happened to your hand."

"All right. I got into a shootout with Bonnie and Clyde outside of Wellington about a year before they were mowed down. I lost my arm after Miss Parker got lucky with a couple of shots. Her luck ran out in the end, though, didn't it?"

"You think mine will, too, don't ya?"

"I think it already did. I think your fate was sealed the second you laid eyes on Billy Bunson. He could sweet-talk the devil and walk away with his pitchfork. You didn't have a chance.

You're his type."

She looked to the floor and let silence fill the room.

Sonny could hear his own heartbeat. He wondered if she could hear hers.

"You don't think he's comin' for me, do you?" she said.

"Nope, and I think you're starting to think the same thing. You feel it deep in your bones. He's going to hang you out to dry, all the while, he's free to run. Why don't you let me tell you what happened?"

"Sure, you're so smart, go right ahead."

"You're a bleeding heart with a soft spot for bad boys," Sonny said, like he was telling a child a bedtime story. "One day, you saw an opportunity to get close to the convicts by helping them learn to read. I don't know how this happened. Maybe you knew the warden's wife somehow, or she was trying to save you, too, I'm not sure, but you came into Billy's orbit. He mesmerized you, made you feel like you were the only girl in the world, promised he'd make you feel real special when he got out. And you could help him do that. All he needed was a nail or two. You could sneak a nail in easy. That's all Billy needed, wasn't it? Nothing more than a simple nail."

Sonny paused, gauged Donna Del Rey's pursed reaction, and figured he was close to being right.

"What you didn't know was that Billy had done this before, conned girls like you into doing things for him that no one else would. He's a genius with emotions as much as he is with mechanical things. You know what he did with that nail? He carved a key out of a bed slat. A replica of a key on a guard's belt. When the guard wasn't looking, Billy pressed a wet piece of bread between the bars and made himself a template, then he set about carving a masterpiece. He made enough keys to walk right out of that prison, jumped into your car, then he dropped you off, and sped straight to the warden's house in the confusion, because who in their right mind is going to look for an escapee at the warden's house? He took the wife hostage, and off he went, leaving you standing there to get caught and used as a swap for a bundle of dough. Sound about right?"

Donna exhaled loudly and looked to the ceiling. "What do you want from me?"

"Not much. Tell me where you were supposed to meet Billy after you got away, that's all."

Her eyes went cold. "He said he'd kill me if I told anyone that."

"Of course, he did. But he's miles away from here by now. He's on his way to his next adventure. He's not waiting for you, and he's not going to make that swap, either." Sonny felt comfortable telling Donna Del Rey what he thought. The warden had seemed a little too nervous, to him. Desperate men do desperate things. Sonny knew he had to put everything together before he could prove what he was thinking, though.

"He's not gonna leave me here! He's gonna trade me for that woman. You wait and see."

"All right. I've got nothing but time and neither do you. Seems to me that the judge won't have any problem seeing that you helped a convict escape from prison. You think you're going to get a slap on the wrist like you did for stealing from the dime store?"

Recognition flashed in Donna's eyes. Sonny had done his research. Knew she'd been in trouble before. "He promised he would get me out," she hissed.

"I'm the only one who can help you now, Donna. I think you know that."

A tear ran down her cheek as she held Sonny's steady gaze. "Did it hurt?"

"What?"

"When they took your arm. Did it hurt?"

"I was asleep. When I came to it was gone. The pain went away, and I've learned to live without it." That was a lie, but she didn't need to know the truth of his feelings. "Where were you supposed to meet Billy, Donna? Tell me, and I'll let the judge know that you cooperated with me."

He had one last piece of information to use that might move her.

"That woman Billy took is pregnant, Donna. She needs our help. What do you think will happen to you if something happens to that woman or that baby? You're an accomplice. Maybe to murder, if it dies before it's born. Think about that, Donna. Do you really want to live with something like that?" Sonny quit talking. He knew if he said another word he would lose her. All the years of interrogating criminals came back to him like riding a bicycle was supposed to.

Silence filled the room for a long minute. It was like the whole world was sleeping, taking a long afternoon siesta.

"Bedias," Donna Del Rey said. "Outside of Bedias in a little place called Cottage Grove."

"And then you were going to make a dash to Mexico and hide out until things cooled off?" Sonny said.

"You sure do seem to know a lot," she said.

"I've heard this story before."

"You can't tell him I told you. He'll come after me. Slip inside in the middle of the night and cut my throat while I'm sleeping. He promised me he'd do that. I need my sleep, ya know. I can't stay awake all of the time waitin' for him to come kill me. I'm already afraid he knows I'm talkin' to you. Billy knows things that nobody else knows."

"Thanks for talking to me. You're a good kid. He doesn't know I'm here." Sonny stood and tossed the whole pack of Wrigley's onto the table. "When we catch him, I won't tell Billy a thing, no matter what. You have my word." He headed to the door, ready to bang on it to be let out.

"You think I'm gonna be in here long?" Donna Del Rey said. "I got a job to go to."

Sonny dropped his hand, and turned around. "A job?" The arrest report hadn't said anything about a job.

"Yes, a job. My Uncle Vern runs the funeral home in town."

"And how long have you worked for your Uncle Vern?"

"Well, on and off since I was sixteen. He has me sit and answer the telephone and answer questions for folks who stop in."

"So a long time, since before you met Billy Bunson."

"Uh-huh, sure, almost four years."

"It's not on your arrest report."

"I didn't want it to look bad for Uncle Vern with me bein' in here. People are funny about doin' business with funeral homes in the first place. I didn't want to cast a bad light on things," Donna said.

Sonny scratched his chin, his mind whirling, piecing together everything he knew, trying to find that one thing he'd obviously overlooked. He walked back to the table, leaned down, and forced Donna Del Rey to look him in the eye.

"You've been real helpful, Donna," Sonny said. "I'll tell the judge that you were cooperative, that you helped us find Billy, I promise you. I'll tell him that and everything I know about Billy and his way of talking people into doing things for him, but I need you to tell me something. That thing you haven't told anybody. Will you tell me that?"

Donna looked away. "Maybe, but I want to go home. Can you get me out of here?"

"If you answer my question, I'll do whatever I can to help you, Donna. I used to be a Texas Ranger. That means something to some folks around here. I'll use every ounce of whatever I got to help you, if you help me. Can you answer my question?"

"If I know the answer."

Sonny sucked in a deep breath. "Billy sent the warden a finger to prove he was serious. I'm thinking maybe it was a trick. That that finger didn't belong to Dolly Rickart at all. He wanted us to think it was Dolly's. Did you get Billy a real finger, Donna? Did you cut off a dead woman's finger and sneak it out before they closed the casket for good? Did you do that for Billy, Donna?"

Donna Del Rey's face had gone pale. Her lip trembled. A tear built in the corner of her right eye, quickly followed by the left, then they both spilled out at the same time. "He said he loved me. That we'd be together forever."

Sonny didn't waver; though he wanted to comfort the girl, he didn't feel like he could. "So you did that? You got a finger for Billy?"

"Yes. Yes, I did that." And then Donna let out a wail, dropped her head onto the table, and gave herself over to a deep, uncontrollable cry. "He said he loved me . . . ," she said in between gasps for air.

Sonny had no choice but to leave her there to herself.

Chapter Twelve

August 1911
El Paso, Texas

The early morning air was sultry, laden with an unusual amount of moisture that sat on Billy's tongue like tiny drops of sugar water. August was usually desert dry, the earth parched and starved for moisture of any kind, but a hurricane had roared through the middle of Texas, scattering untold amounts of fury and rain in every direction. Billy was happy to be a good distance from the storm, from the waves. He still hadn't learned how to swim. But the change in weather was an unusual occurrence. Some days, Billy thought he would dry up from the inside out and burst into a pile of dust, cast out on the street by the wind, and walked on unseen by the good folk of the city. He figured his life wouldn't be so much different if that happened.

El Paso sat at the outer reaches of the worst part of the storm, but had received an unexpected reprieve from dying of thirst. A constant wind accompanied the precipitation, which would have been welcome, except there was a change in the air, an uncertain feeling that had started to rise before the storms came. Miss Tillie, and his mother, Lady Red, had been at each other's throats for weeks. They were barely speaking. Business was down. Money had dwindled away with obvious consequences; more bone broth soup for dinner, instead of meat. Pockets were getting harder to pick because Billy had been made out a thief and the son of a whore. People talked, warned one another of the waifs on the street, especially him. Every time the sheriff, or one of the deputies, collared him, his pockets were empty. They couldn't charge him with a crime if there was no evidence. Billy knew that, and had learned how to get rid of his takings fast—when there were takings to be had. Hidey-holes and loose building siding provided safekeeping, right out in the open. Still, the air had a bad taste to it. His days in El Paso were numbered. Billy could feel the coming of a move as certain as he felt the weak wind of a failed hurricane.

The streets in El Paso were still quiet, the hustle and bustle of the day's business had yet to begin. A lot of folks were still sleeping. A few shopkeepers were already working, restocking their shelves and sweeping off the boardwalks, but Billy steered clear of them. Most of them knew him by sight, and would take a broom to his butt given half the chance. He was no better than a rat to them and he knew it.

It wasn't store shelves he was interested in on this day. What he was after was spark plugs.

The onslaught of automobiles had brought new opportunities that Billy couldn't have imagined only a few years before. Ford Model Ts were the most prolific automobiles on the road, and the ones Billy had focused on. Once he realized that just by looking at a running engine, he understood the basics of its operation. After watching the frustration that most men expressed when the spark plugs fouled, and the engine wouldn't fire, Billy saw a way to make some money. Champion spark plugs sold for a dollar apiece. A whole dollar. There was more than one spark plug in a Model T engine. There were four. No one would pay a dollar for used plugs from a kid, but they sure would pay fifty cents. Especially if the automobile was stalled in the middle of the street and the lady passenger was uncomfortable and embarrassed.

Billy eased down the street to the Darcy Hotel and made his

way behind the building. Most days there were three or four Model Ts parked there. The spots out front were still maintained by hitching posts, and were used mostly by horses and wagons, but Billy had heard tell that the posts were slated to be taken out. Progress was coming to Main Street. One day there would be more automobiles than horses.

The only thing Billy had to be leery about was Clyde Doweller and his mean old dog, Rusty. Rusty was a mangy beast that looked more like a wolf than a dog, and rumor had it that he'd eaten at least one kid, and taken a chunk out of more than one. Anyone who dared to trespass on the Hotel Darcy's lot faced the wrath of Rusty.

Clyde encouraged the dog's bad behavior by not feeding him and being mean to him. Billy had seen Clyde Doweller kick Rusty in the hindquarters more than once when the dog didn't obey a command.

Billy had a plan to win the dog over. He was also counting on Clyde being asleep in his chair on the back porch. Old Clyde's eyes didn't open until the sun hit his pockmarked face, and by Billy's calculation, that meant he had less than an hour to quiet the dog and steal as many spark plugs as he could.

The morning was still quiet when Billy reached the hotel. He had a bone, the marrow intact, still laced with tiny shreds of sinewy beef, a pocket full of meat slivers, and a thin rope that was a little thicker than a horse's lead. He knew he'd taken a risk by taking the bone from his grandmother's larder, but he figured he could replace the bone and offer her some meat with his profits from the sale of the spark plugs. That was his plan: theft and redemption.

As he'd hoped, Clyde Doweller was still asleep on the porch, and Rusty was laying at the man's feet. It was hard to tell if the dog was sleeping, from where Billy was at.

Four Model T Fords sat behind the hotel. All black, all closed as tight as possible, warding off any weather—or thieves.

Billy had shaved as much meat as he could from the bone. It was a small amount of food, but he bet on the dog being as hungry as he was. He tapped his pocket to make sure the meat was still there, then made his way to the opposite side of the hotel, lurking in the shadows as much as possible, not drawing any attention to himself, and fully aware that the rising sun was working against him. Clyde Doweller's natural alarm clock was gaining speed, throwing light on the moist world, making everything it touched glisten in a warm yellow.

The design of the hotel had helped Billy formulate his latest idea. It was three stories tall, and each floor had an outside boardwalk, allowing private entry to the rooms on the back and side of the hotel. The walk passed right over the porch where Clyde was sleeping and Rusty lay guarding the entrance.

Billy crept up the stairs as quietly, and as quickly, as he could. Once he was on the boardwalk, he slowed down, aware that any noise he made could alert the dog, or Clyde, to his presence. He didn't want to be seen, wished he had special powers to make himself invisible. Some days he felt like no one really saw him anyway. People looked at him with sneers, and fear, and disgust. Rarely did he see sadness or caring. He didn't trust either of those things anyway. He ran before they could reach out for him. He didn't want any comfort from strangers. The only thing that interested Billy was the coins in those peoples' pockets.

He arrived at his destination, certain that he had waited too late to get started. The sun was starting to beam with pride, lighting the top of the hotel at first touch with certainty and warmth. Billy took a deep breath, fished his hand into his pocket, and pulled out a handful of meat slivers. He looked over the railing, then dropped a piece of the meat straight down. The ground was wet, but the drop was loud enough to get Rusty's attention.

The dog raised its furry head, squinted its onyx eyes open, and twisted its scarred nose with a healthy snort in the direction of the meat. Judgment crossed the dog's narrow face, but there was no indication that the dog was going to move, that it was going to go after the meat. Rusty turned his head toward the sleeping Clyde, then stared back at the meat.

Billy was starting to get nervous, afraid that he was running out of time. The sun was going to burn Clyde Doweller's eyes wide open, or someone was going to exit the hotel and wake him. Sweat started to bead all over Billy's body. His lungs felt heavy with humidity and fear. There was nothing left for him to do but move down the boardwalk a few feet and drop another piece of meat. Rusty looked at the new piece of meat, and licked his chops. The dog had the scariest teeth Billy had ever seen.

For whatever the reason, the dog had not looked up, was not curious where the meat was coming from. Maybe there was no recognition of such a thing, a gift from the sky, and that was okay with Billy. He was relieved the dog wasn't interested in him—though it had to know he was there. *Couldn't the dog smell him?* Maybe it didn't care. People came and went from the hotel all day. The dog was probably used to people moving about on the second floor.

Rusty still did not move—but Clyde Doweller did. The man let out a wide-mouth, gravelly snore that got both the dog's attention and Billy's. For a second, Billy thought the plot was finished, that he would have to flee to the streets and search for a pocket to pick. There was no way he could go home empty-handed. Not after stealing the best bone from the larder.

Clyde Doweller rolled his head to the other side of the chair, and closed his mouth, but not before a healthy stream of drool flowed out of it. The snore echoed off in the distance and Rusty relaxed. The dog turned his attention back to the gift of the meat that lay untouched, a few feet from its paws.

Billy was desperate. All of the grayness of dawn had been eaten away by the soft light of the coming day. He moved to the end of the boardwalk, dug out all of the meat slivers from his pocket, and dropped them onto the ground.

The small pile was too much for the dog to resist, but it did not lunge at the meat like Billy had figured it would. Instead, Rusty eased himself onto all fours and slowly crept past Clyde Doweller with his head down, being cautious not to make a noise. The dog feared the man more than anything, but it was hungry, and hunger would force any creature to do something it knew better than to do. Billy had taken a gamble that the dog was a kindred spirit, motivated by the same thing he was.

Rusty licked the first piece of meat without stopping. He kept his eyes trained on the pile, while his ears flared erect, pointed to the sky, listening for any sound that Clyde made.

The noisiness of the city had not started yet. Only a few birds sang. They seemed hesitant to enter the day, too.

The dog snatched the second piece of meat as casually as the first, then picked up his pace to the pile of slivers. Once there, Rusty stopped and gobbled the rest of the meat in one bite.

It was now or never for Billy. He dropped the bone to the ground, the final gift from the sky.

The dog's hunger had been ignited by the meat. Rusty attacked the bone without hesitation, then dropped all fours to the ground, going after the marrow like it was the most delectable meal the dog had ever tasted.

Billy's original plan called for him to lead the dog away from Clyde Doweller with the meat and bone, lasso his neck with a slip knot, and tie the dog to a hitching post—out of sight, as far away from the Model Ts as possible. But that plan wasn't going to work. The sun worked against him like an enemy with a persistent grudge. He was almost out of time.

Billy made his way to the opposite side of the boardwalk, insuring that Clyde was still asleep along the way. From there he eased his way to the first automobile. He hid himself on the far side of the vehicle, and set about removing the spark plugs. It was an easy task: pop off the wire and unscrew the plug, then move on to the next one. Four plugs equaled two dollars.

By the time the sun toasted the back of Clyde's eyelids, Billy had lifted sixteen spark plugs and disappeared.

It didn't take long for Billy to cash in on the spark plugs. Once all of the Model Ts started moving down the street, one failed after another. All he had to do was wait, make the offer to the panicked driver, pocket the money, then wait to do it all over again. The risk was that the plugs that he'd stolen were in as bad a shape as the ones he was replacing with each sale. It was a small worry. Once the Model T started and rolled down the street, that worry was gone, and Billy was watching for the next opportunity to show itself. That, and Clyde Doweller and Rusty. The Darcy Hotel guard would be on the lookout for someone like Billy, selling the spark plugs that had come out of his lot. So far, the coast was clear. There'd been no sign of a raging Clyde.

Once all of the speak plugs were sold, Billy beamed with pride as the jingle accompanied the jangle in his pocket. Coins tapping one another was music to his ears. He was heading to a butcher's shop—not the one he'd stolen the chicken from, that butcher had it out for him—but another one, with a mean German man whose wife liked to be sweet-talked. Billy was halfway there when he heard a familiar voice call out his name.

"There you are, Billy boy. I been lookin' all over the place for you." It was Jim Rome in a wagon, pulled by tired Springfield mules.

Billy stopped so quickly it was like he'd run head-on into a wall. Jim Rome never came looking for him unless something was wrong. From the look of the wagon, full of crates and barrels, Billy was pretty certain he knew what was going on. His grandmother was moving the house.

"What are you doin', Jim?" Billy said.

A distant scream called out before the Negro could answer.

"There he is!" Clyde Doweller yelled. "Catch that little thief now! Get 'im, Rusty. Get 'im!"

Billy and Jim Rome locked eyes. "You best get home as soon as you can," Jim said, then raised the whip, readying to slap one of the mule's ass.

Billy didn't have to be told to run twice, either. He sprinted off, doing his best to outrun the dog and the cadre of police that Clyde Doweller had collected to bring him in.

Billy wasn't worried, though. He had plenty of places to hide. But he wanted to get home in time to leave with everyone. The last thing he wanted was to be left behind again.

October 1934
Bedias, Texas

Black cotton sleeves were still fastened over the two-year-old Chevrolet's headlights, making the road difficult to see. Billy had to ditch the car, get rid of it as soon as possible. He was tempted to let it roll into the river, but that was too close, too much of a chance. The car might not sink deep enough. Someone might see it. Put two and two together. Then he'd have to run. He wasn't ready for that yet. Not yet. Running would come soon. But not now. He still had things to do. There was no turning back this time. He had to do whatever it took to stay free. And that meant taking the Chevrolet as far away as possible, dumping it, and stealing another one to return in. All before the rise of dawn. The clock was ticking. There was never as much darkness as Billy needed there to be. Daylight had always made his life more difficult.

CHAPTER THIRTEEN

October 1934

Huntsville, Texas

A pot of coffee sat simmering on the stove, and no one was in the kitchen. Sonny had expected to meet one of the other boarders. Edith Grantley had said there were three, but none had been apparent since his arrival. He hadn't heard one footstep or flush of a toilet through the night, or in the morning. It was like he was the only man in the house and that thought troubled Sonny.

Hesitant to help himself, Sonny eased past the stove and made his way to the porch, where Blue had been confined for the night. The dog had settled down on a fluffy pile of blankets, eyes wide open, staring at the door as if he was waiting for Sonny to return. Blue wagged his tail when he realized the man staring through the screen was his owner.

"Would you like a cup of coffee," Edith said, from behind Sonny.

He startled a little, hadn't heard her enter the kitchen. He turned to face her and couldn't stop a smile from flashing across his face. Edith Grantley looked put together from head to toe. Not a hair was out of place, cut and shaped in the latest style, shoulder-length, curled in the back, and parted on the side. Sonny didn't know what the style was called, all he knew was that it accented the woman's face in a nice way. She looked like a very tall Carole Lombard. Her dress was narrow, store-bought from the looks of it, the front of it covered with a bleached white apron. She wore sensible, black low-heeled shoes, and no jewelry that he could see. Sonny suddenly felt comfortable all over again. "The dog? Has he eaten?" he said.

Edith grabbed the coffeepot and Sonny signaled that he'd take a cup. Then he made his way to the small wood table in the kitchen, and sat down.

"I fed him and put him outside this morning," Edith said.

"You didn't have to do that."

"I was seeing to Mr. Pryor and Mr. Day." Edith poured a cup of steaming coffee. The aroma filled the room and rested under Sonny's nose like an old friend who had been gone for a long time. "I have some oatmeal for you. Would you like some bacon?" She handed Sonny the cup, and made her way to the stove.

"Thank you. I'll pass on the bacon if that's all right with you." He hesitated for a second, then said, "These fellas you spoke of, I haven't seen a sign of them. They're awful quiet."

"Respectful men. Both of them work third-shift at the prison. They come in for a bite to eat, then make their way to bed. You probably won't see much of them until dinnertime."

"Oh, I see. And the third one?"

"Mr. Flynn? He comes and goes. Sells lightning rods. Travels a lot. I keep a room for him on an ongoing basis. He's been here for three years now. Any other questions, Sonny?"

Sonny sipped his coffee and suddenly felt embarrassed. "No, ma'am, I was just curious."

"Well, that's good. There are a few women at the Baptist church who think I'm a wicked woman because I'm unmarried and I allow single men to sleep under my roof. I'm scandalous in some parts of this town."

The embarrassment dissipated, and the coffee warmed Sonny from the inside out. "I'm sorry, I like to know who's about, that's all. It's an old habit."

"I understand." Edith poured herself a cup of coffee. "Mind if I join you since you don't want any bacon?"

"No, I don't mind at all."

"Oatmeal won't be long," she said as she sat down.

Sonny took another cup of coffee, and allowed himself to settle down, for the comfort to continue to come back to him. But the truth was, it had been a very long time since he had sat opposite an attractive woman. He was sure that all of the boarders felt that way about Edith Grantley, but it was an unexpected occurrence for Sonny, one that had slipped from the realm of possibility so far that he didn't know what to say next.

"I never planned on letting out rooms," Edith said. "My husband, Henry, grew up in this house, and we planned on staying here for the rest of our lives. His family has owned the mill in Huntsville as long as anyone can remember. They expected us to have children and carry on the family legacy. But the children never came, and Henry suffered a long fall in the mill some years back. He lingered for a month, and that was the end of that. And then, of course, the Depression hit. I was left with no way to make a living, so I had to let the rooms, or see the house go in a sheriff's sale for back taxes. Henry would have rolled over in his grave if that would have happened. I couldn't bear the thought of such a thing, so I had to do something—regardless of the effect on my reputation."

"I'm sorry for your troubles," Sonny said.

"It's all right. Life can be ruthless and cold-blooded, but I won't let it beat me down. Besides, there's folks that have it a lot worse than me. Jeb Rickart has to be beside himself with Dolly bein' kidnapped by that prisoner. I don't know how he's getting any sleep at all."

"Jeb's got a strong back."

"He does, but plenty of us were worried about him before

the breakout happened."

Sonny sat his coffee cup down, and leaned forward a little bit. "Why do you say that?"

"I shouldn't gossip, especially to you, a stranger in these parts."

"I'm here to help. If there's something I should know, you can tell me. I don't think it would be considered talking out of turn."

"You're sure?"

"As sure as I'm sitting here," Sonny said.

"Well, you know Dolly's not from around here?"

"No, I didn't know that. Where's she from?"

"Can't rightly say. No one knows for sure. She got off the bus one day and stayed. Got a job at the Falco Diner on 8th Street, and before you know it, her and Jeb was courtin' and causing all kinds of tongues to wag because of the difference in their ages."

"How long ago was this?"

"A year at the most."

Sonny drew in a deep breath. Something about this information made him uneasy. He immediately had to wonder if Billy and Dolly had known each other before they met at the prison. A long-term, detailed plan was not out of Billy's wheelhouse. It was definitely something to consider and look into. He needed to find out where Dolly Rickart was from. One more thing to add to his growing list.

Sonny took another slow drink of coffee, then set the cup down. "You don't know what Dolly's name was before she married Jeb, do you?"

"I think it was Cleveland, or something like that. A city name. You'll have to check with Norma down at the diner, she'll know. Or Delouise at the courthouse, she'll know for sure, or be able to look at the marriage records."

"Thank you, I'll talk to them."

Edith stood up from the table. "I almost forgot about your oatmeal."

"It's okay."

"You're not hungry?"

"Yes, but I like talking to you." If Sonny had been thirty years younger, he would have blushed when he'd spoke those words, but he didn't. He smiled. "You made me aware of some things I didn't know. I appreciate that."

Edith stood at the stove, stirring the oatmeal. She plopped a decent helping into a bowl and carried it back to Sonny. "You think it might help?" she said as she set the oatmeal down before him.

"I don't know at this point. Anything could help."

"Well, let's talk about something else. I like Jeb, and I sure hate to think of the mess his life is in right now. What about you? Do you have any children?"

Sonny had taken a big bite of oatmeal and it got stuck about halfway down his throat. Edith was better at making coffee than she was oatmeal. It kind of worried him about supper.

He took a long swig of coffee. "One," he said when he could. "A son, Jesse. He's a Ranger like I was. He has three children of his own. He's lucky that way."

"I don't know what you mean?"

"With children. Martha and I tried for more, but she had trouble carrying them. Lost them in horrible ways, and at the worst times. It was harder on her than it was on me, but I sure would have liked Jesse to of had a brother or sister, or two. He's all by himself, and Martha spoiled him rotten to boot. I figured another brother would have helped put him in his place. Martha watched over that boy with an eagle eye. There was hell to pay if he got his feelings hurt. She was too protective of him."

"I'm sure she felt like she had reason to do what she did,"

119

Edith said. "You have to be proud that your boy's a Ranger."

Sonny took another bite of dry, lumpy oatmeal. "I am," he said, through clenched teeth. He followed the cereal with another swig of coffee. He sat the mug down and nearly tipped it over, caught it with his left hand, and steadied it with the hook. "Sorry, I'm still not used to this contraption." It was a sudden admission, and one that surprised Sonny as soon as he spoke it. He tried not to draw any undue attention to the prosthesis.

"Oh," Edith said, "I assumed it was from the Great War. You're the right age to have gone. I've had other boarders who suffered a loss overseas."

"I was there," Sonny said. "In France mostly." His voice trailed off, and the look on Edith's face was a mix of concern and mortification.

"I'm sorry, I shouldn't have said that. I know the war is difficult to talk about for most men. I won't bring it up again."

"It's all right," Sonny said. "I came back all in one piece, mostly. I had the thousand-yard stare for a few years, but bein' a Ranger helped me get my feet under me. It was Bonnie and Clyde that took my arm. Well, Bonnie actually. She was the shooter. Clyde was the driver. I saw them leave the movie theater in Wellington a few months before I was set to retire, and I gave chase. We got into a shootout in our cars. They crashed off an old bridge embankment and escaped on foot to die another day. I was left with a bad arm that couldn't be saved once the gangrene took hold."

Edith stood at the stove holding her cup of coffee, looking unsure what to say when the phone rang. She answered it without setting the cup down. "Grantley House. This is Edith. How may I help you?"

Sonny watched her, and took a sip of coffee, glad for the interruption.

"Yes, he is," Edith said. "Would you like to speak to him?"

She offered the wall phone receiver to Sonny. "It's the sheriff. He wants to speak to you."

October 1934

Bedias, Texas

Sonny stopped in a parking lot at the corner of Highway 90 and 1636—he'd left Walker County and made his way into Grimes County. The Grimes County sheriff, Merle Loggard, was standing at the front of his car, a 1932 black Ford, waiting on him.

The sheriff was a beanpole of a man with an equine face, a nose as long as Sonny had ever seen, and eyes that didn't look like they could be surprised by anything. His uniform was freshly starched and his shoes bore a military shine. Loggard was a bit younger than Sonny, but he reckoned he could have served in the war, too. Edith's mention of it had brought some thoughts of those days to the forefront. On any other day, Sonny would have noticed the man's pride in his appearance, but he might not have connected the aspiration for perfection directly to service in the war.

"Thanks for coming," Sheriff Loggard said, as he extended his hand for a shake.

Sonny replied with his left hand, as weak as it was. The sheriff had an extremely strong grip for such a skinny man, and gave no leeway to a one-armed man. Sonny liked him right away.

"You said you think this has got something to do with Billy Bunson?"

"I said as much. The Ranger office said you'd be the one to know for sure. That's why I called you." The sheriff headed toward a car sitting under a live oak. It was a late-20s model black Chevrolet coupe. Nothing special about it on first glance. The car didn't look like it had been sitting there for long. "The fella who owns this place found this car parked here this morning. Nobody around. No explanation."

"Not so odd," Sonny said, keeping pace with Loggard. "Somebody could've had trouble on the highway, and pulled off here, at the T. Maybe they went for help."

"Keys were still in it and the engine was running. It was like whoever left it here wanted us to find it pretty quickly."

"You think Billy Bunson did this?"

The sheriff shrugged, and came to a stop in front of the car. "Well, that's for you to figure out, isn't it? It was a black coupe that he was last seen in, wasn't it?"

"It was." Sonny stiffened, and looked away from the car to the nearest road sign. It said: Bedias 1 Mile. "I talked to the girl who helped him bust out of prison at the Hunstville jail. She said they were supposed to meet in Bedias. He knows I've talked to her. He's nowhere near here. Not now." The blood drained from Sonny's face, and the fingers on his left hand trembled.

"What's the matter?"

"That girl, Donna Del Rey. She's not safe."

"She's inside the jail. He can't hurt her in there."

"You don't know what you're dealing with," Sonny said. "I need to get to a phone. Is there one inside this place?"

"I don't know, but we can ask," the sheriff said.

Sonny was almost halfway to the door before Loggard caught him. Something deep inside Sonny told him that he was already too late. He'd fallen for one of Billy's tricks, and in the process, served a death warrant on Donna Del Rey.

CHAPTER FOURTEEN

August 1911

Along the San Andres Spring, North of El Paso

Billy sat in the wagon, facing south, a look of dread on his face, not curious at all about where they were headed. The land had been hilly and sparse for the last two days, until the road, if it could have been called that, curved toward the spring. Desolate mountains and hills were suddenly overtaken by the lush environment a healthy stream offered. Trees stood erect with vibrant green leaves, and the ground was covered with vines and wildflowers that had long since bloomed, but stayed alive, reaching to the sky out of the plentiful shade. Insects hovered over the water in pulsating black clouds, and their collective buzz was loud and annoying. It had been a long time since Billy had spent time around flowing water. He didn't like being so close to water.

"How long before we're where we are going?" he said, swatting away a small swarm of mosquitoes.

Lady Red sat stiffly on the front seat of the wagon, next to Jim Rome, who was driving. There was plenty of daylight between the two of them. They hardly acknowledged each other's presence. But that was nothing new. Lady Red peered down her hooked nose at the help Miss Tillie employed like she had a relentless sty. Jim Rome had been around for as long as Billy could remember, and he'd never heard his mother call the man by his name.

Jim Rome answered Billy with a terse response. "Don't matter much, do it?"

"I liked El Paso," Billy said.

"You say that about every town," Lady Red said. Billy was surprised by her response. She usually ignored him as much as anybody else.

"I'd like to stay somewhere for a little while, that's all," Billy said.

Jim Rome pursed his lips and nickered the two mules that were carting them to their next destination. The mules didn't pay Jim Rome any attention, either. They had a pace that was comfortable for them, and nothing short of a gunshot was going to increase their speed.

"One more day in El Paso and that sheriff was gonna come and drag you out of the house, empty your pockets of them spark plugs, put you behind bars, and throw away the key," Lady Red said.

"At least I'd stay somewhere."

"I can arrange that if you care to push your luck. You wouldn't have lasted a day in that jail. Those men in there would have ripped you apart. That what you want?" Billy's mother said.

"No, ma'am."

Lady Red had not moved since Billy started talking. She faced straight ahead, her thin, stiff body unmoving and unaffected by his protests. Billy didn't look anything like her. Sometimes, he wondered if Lady Red was really his mother when he saw himself in the mirror, but he left it at that. Such things said aloud would have triggered a swat harder than he was willing to take. Questions about his father's origins were forbidden. Worthy of a good beating.

All Billy could see was the back of Lady Red's head, covered with her namesake flaming red hair that fell in curls all the way to her waist. What skin he could see was pale white; her arms were slightly uncovered now that they were out of the direct sun. She'd rather be eaten up with mosquitoes than touched by a sunburn. Billy knew it was best not to argue any further and the answer from both of them was that it didn't matter where they were going, or how long it would take to get there. He needed to stay quiet. He knew that. His opinion or feelings didn't matter. Except when he was needed to work. He dreamed of the day when all he had to do was take care of himself.

Billy laid his head back down on the pile of blankets that topped the bed of the wagon. All of their stuff was there. The other wagon behind them was carrying Miss Tillie, the three girls, and what furniture was deemed necessary to take with them to wherever they were going this time.

The day was getting long and they would be looking for a place to bed down for the night.

Beyond the curve in the road, a voice hollered out, "Stop! You stop there, right now!"

Billy looked between Jim Rome and Lady Red to see two men standing in the middle of the road, both of them brandishing well-worn scatterguns.

"Whoa, there," Jim Rome said, pulling back on the mules' reins, bringing the wagon to a stop.

The men didn't move. Billy wasn't worried at all. Jim had a scattergun of his own, out of sight, at his feet, along with a long knife under the seat, well within reach. Lady Red had her weapons stashed for traveling, too. A derringer strapped to her ankle, and another in her small carrying case that sat next to Jim's shotgun. Along with that, Miss Tillie wasn't that far behind, and her and the girls had their own armory of weapons. This wasn't the first time they'd been jumped on the road and it probably wouldn't be the last.

Billy looked over his shoulder and couldn't see Miss Tillie's wagon around the curve. They were all alone. The birds had stopped singing and the insects had stopped buzzing. The air felt still and rancid; a dead smell drifted from the running spring.

"Well, what do we have here?" the taller of the two men said. He had a dirty face, shaggy hair, and britches as thin as lace. He looked like he didn't have anything to lose, and his beady black eyes made Billy nervous.

The other man was portly, dressed in similar shabby clothes held up by a pair of worn suspenders, and he had tobacco-stained teeth. He wore a perpetual, uncomfortable smile on his face, and his eyes seemed to shoot out in opposite directions.

Billy had confidence in Jim Rome's ability to look after him and Lady Red, but these two men looked unpredictable.

"Passin' through," Jim Rome said.

"Wasn't talkin' to you, boy. I was talkin' to the lady," Tall Man said.

Lady Red didn't flinch. "We're heading to Austin. There's another wagon behind us, so you won't catch us by surprise."

Fat Man licked his lips, then glanced over to his partner. "We know all about that other wagon. Don't you worry none about them. They will be a little preoccupied for a while."

"You best not hurt them," Lady Red said.

"Ain't got no control about what happens to them now, do I, ma'am?" Tall Man said.

"What you want?" Jim Rome said.

Fat Man raised his scattergun a little higher so it was aimed directly at Jim's head. "You don't speak unless you're spoke to, boy. Do you understand what I'm sayin'?"

"Yes, sir. Yes, sir, I do," Jim said.

Billy focused on Jim's hands, watching for a signal of some kind. The black man held steady on the reins. Billy didn't like road robbers calling Jim a boy. That was a strike against them, for sure.

"Now," Tall Man said, like he was the one in charge, "all

three of you need to raise your hands in the air and climb down off that wagon."

"We don't have any money, if that's what you're after," Lady Red said.

"Everybody's got money of one kind or another, pretty girl. I said, get down. That's what I meant." Tall Man matched Fat Man's aim, only he trained his gun at Lady Red's head. "I don't want to have to prove to you how serious I am, but I'll take your head off right in front of the boy, if I have to."

Lady Red raised her arms in the air. "That's not necessary."

Jim Rome followed, and so did Billy. He didn't like it none, but he didn't figure he had any other choice.

"Now," Tall Man said, "I want you all to get off that wagon one at a time, and walk straight over to my partner there. Ladies first, of course."

Both men had been cautious not to use each other's name. Billy figured them for longtime thieves, been gettin' away with it without gettin' caught. Neither one of them looked like they had a whole lot of brains, though. Anybody could hide in the brush along a spring and jump out at travelers. Now it was a matter of who was more prepared, them or Jim and Lady Red. Billy was betting on his side, but the fact that he couldn't see Miss Tillie's wagon worried him. Maybe the brains of the operation had her held up—or maybe the two men before him were smarter than Billy thought they were.

Lady Red stepped off the wagon and walked confidently to Fat Man. He gazed at her like a hungry wolf. The man had no idea what he was messing with.

Jim Rome waited for Billy to climb off the wagon, then followed him.

Fat Man stood back from the trio a few feet, then Tall Man walked straight toward Jim with his scattergun lowered to gut level. "You need to get down on your knees, boy," he said.

"Is any of this really necessary?" Lady Red said. "Tell us what you want, and I will see if we can come to some sort of agreement."

Jim Rome didn't move. He stared at the Tall Man as if he weren't there.

"What we want," Tall Man said, "is for Negroes not to be alone with white women in this county. That is an offense to our laws. I said down on your knees, boy."

Lady Red stiffened her shoulders, and said, "He is my driver and nothing more. He is a hired hand. Is that against your laws, too, sir?"

"Don't get sassy with me woman, you hear? I ain't got no patience for any woman who cohabitates with the likes of this here heathen."

Fat Man said nothing, stood back, and watched. Billy was starting to feel afraid, that something bad was going to happen to Jim. He knew how folks felt about men like Jim, hated him because of the color of his skin, but they didn't know Jim like Billy did. He had saved Billy's hide more than once, took a beating for him from Miss Tillie. There was no way Billy was going to stand back and let Jim be hurt by these two numbskulls.

Tall Man pulled both hammers back on the scattergun. "I said down on your knees. And either one of you make a move, my partner here will take your knees out, you understand? This is between us and the heathen here. It's been a long time since we showed Negroes around here their place. Those people have been gettin' uppity. Need to see what happens to them if they step out of line and associate with a white woman all alone."

"We have nothing to do with that," Lady Red said. "We're not from around here."

"And you're not staying here, either," Tall Man answered with a spit to the ground. "I ain't tellin' you again, you hear?"

Jim Rome shrugged like he was denser than he looked. A

bead of sweat showed at the corner of his forehead and short-cropped hair. "Yes, sir, I understand." He knelt down, put his hands behind his head, and lowered his chin toward the ground. The act looked familiar to Billy, like Jim had done it before.

Tall Man moved around to the back of Jim. "Lower your hands to the ground."

Jim did as he was told.

The air went out of Billy's lungs.

Lady Red looked pale, more helpless than Billy had ever seen her.

The birds and the insects held their breath. Not even a breeze bothered to move.

Tall Man jammed the double-barrels at the crook of Jim's head and neck. "This might hurt a little bit."

"Please, sir . . ." Lady Red said. "We'll be on our way and won't stop until we leave your county. He can walk behind the wagon."

"One more word out of you, woman, and I'll shoot the boy instead of the Negro. There's no deal to be had here. After I blow his head off, we'll hang him from the tree and set him afire, you hear?"

Jim trembled a tiny bit. Billy saw it, he wasn't sure if either man did. He'd never heard his mother beg before. She was worried. There was no plan to save Jim. Not if they wanted to stay alive.

Tall Man drew in a breath, and stepped forward a few inches, pushing Jim's head farther down.

"You move another muscle, mister, and it'll be your head that gets blown off, not that man there." The voice came from behind them. It was a man's voice. A voice Billy had heard before. He glanced over his shoulder and saw two men sitting on proud horses. One of them he recognized, the other he did not. It was that man from El Paso, that Ranger who had laid in wait for him when he'd stolen that chicken.

Billy didn't know who the other man was, but he assumed he was a Ranger, too. Both of them had their guns drawn, pistols, six-shooters, and aimed at Tall Man and Fat Man. A wave of relief flowed through Billy like he'd never felt before.

"Now," the Ranger continued, "both of you need to drop your weapons, or you'll be the ones to lose your heads, you understand me?"

Both of the scatterguns fell to the ground.

"We were trying to scare them is all," Tall Man said. "We weren't going to hurt them."

"Whatever you say, mister. Right now, you need to put your hands in the air," the Ranger said, as he climbed down off his horse.

The other Ranger stayed mounted, not wavering one bit. The man looked serious, like he would not hesitate to shoot if one of the men made a run for it.

The Ranger that Billy knew walked by him, stuck his free hand out, and let it graze against his shoulder as he passed. "You all right, boy?"

"Yes, sir. I am now. I sure am glad to see you."

CHAPTER FIFTEEN

October 1934

Huntsville, Texas

The Grimes County sheriff, Merle Loggard, escorted Sonny back to the jail in Huntsville as quickly as he could—but they were too late. A host of automobiles were parked around the entrance; a collection of black and white Fords, bubbles on top, adding a rotation of blue distress to the dusky sky like Sonny had never seen before. Sonny's heart dropped as soon as he set the truck's brakes.

He followed the sheriff inside only to be met by the Walker County sheriff, Lee Howard. Howard was a known associate, had been the sheriff in Huntsville, and the surrounding area, for twenty years. His face was as weathered as the saddle of an old trail horse, and his eyes had seen more tragedies than any man should have ever had to have seen. The sheriff had served in the Great War, too, adding more weight to his broad shoulders. Howard and Sonny'd had a few dealings in the past, small-time crooks, but nothing to do with Billy Bunson.

"It's pretty bad, Sonny," Sheriff Howard said, dropping his head in failure.

"I was afraid it would be," Sonny said. "She's dead then?"

"Afraid so," Howard said. "Had to have happened since dawn. Her breakfast is there untouched."

Sonny took off his hat with his left hand. Howard's gaze lingered a little longer than normal on the prosthesis. Sonny was used to that, to people staring at the hook. He probably would have, too. He hadn't seen Sheriff Howard since he'd had the run-in with Bonnie and Clyde. There was reason to stare, to be a little shocked by the fake arm—but Howard didn't say anything. He looked away to Sheriff Loggard.

"Merle," Howard said, acknowledging the Grimes County sheriff. "We're gonna need more help on this if you got the men to spare."

"We'll do what we can to help catch this maniac, Lee. The whole region's gonna be up in arms over this. First the warden's wife, and now this. Nobody's gonna feel safe. Can't say I blame them. Not until we catch this Bunson fella."

"You want to see this, Sonny?" Howard said.

"I do," he said. "I should have known she was at risk after I talked to her. I feel pretty bad about not being able to keep her safe."

"This is a jail for God's sake," Sheriff Howard said. "It's my job to keep the prisoners safe, not yours. You interviewed her. Did your job. She died on my watch. You can't blame yourself."

"Billy Bunson walked straight out of the Huntsville Prison. Why wouldn't you think he could walk right in here and do whatever he wanted to? I should've thought of that. I didn't give her safety a second thought."

"Why would you?" the sheriff countered.

Sonny exhaled, and let his shoulders drop to match Sheriff Howard's. "Where is she?"

"In her cell. The second one on the left. Coroner is on his way. Nobody's touched a thing."

"You got pictures?" Sonny said.

"Only because I have to."

The other sheriff stood back, offering nothing, but observing everything. Sonny figured Merle Loggard was happy that this was Lee Howard's jail and not his.

It was a slow walk back to the cell. Halfway there, the first hint of death touched Sonny's nose. The smell nearly stopped him in his tracks, but he kept going. He'd smelled death before. His life had been long, most of it spent as a Texas Ranger, allowing him to witness the worst things one man could do to another, but there was war, too, and living with Martha, walking in the door and finding her in misery, in the middle of losing another baby. Only that smell was worse than this one. This one, distant and metallic, had its own weight to it. He owned this death even before he saw it, felt ruined and inept in ways he'd never considered before. Donna Del Rey's death was his fault, no question about it no matter what Lee Howard said, and Sonny knew right then and there that he'd carry this death with him until he drew his own last breath. Even if he brought Billy Bunson to justice, there would be no redemption to be found for him. Not from this. His failure had cost a misdirected young girl her life.

Sonny drew in another deep breath as he walked around the corner, unprepared for what he saw: Donna Del Rey hanging from the light fixture, her neck broken, tossed oddly to the left side, a chair kicked over, and a pool of blood and piss completely formed underneath her. Her death could have been confused with a suicide at first glance were it not for the butcher knife that was stuck squarely in the center of her back.

The stabbing looked like an afterthought, but Billy wanted Sonny to know exactly who had committed the murder. It was a message. It was a dare. There would be no coming back from this. Billy Bunson would do anything not to go back to prison. He'd die before he'd do that. Sonny understood that completely now. He'd thought it, said it, but now he had no choice but to believe it.

He stopped at the open cell door and focused on the girl's face. She had been pretty in life, but in death she looked afraid, troubled, lost. Donna Del Rey had most likely been all of those things in life. We all are, Sonny thought, but the sad thing was she would spend eternity with her face expressing her innermost fears. Sonny didn't think Billy could have planned that, arranged her face the way he wanted it to look, but then again, maybe he did. Billy had talents that Sonny knew nothing of.

The cell door stood open, just like it had been found. The bare light burned dimly and nearly touched Donna's face. The light gave her complexion a pure white look to it, like all of her blood had been drained out of her. A single fly bounced off of the light bulb, then dove to the floor. Its buzz was the only sound above his own heartbeat that Sonny could hear.

Footsteps approached Sonny from behind. He glanced over his shoulder to see Lee Howard joining him. Howard's face was gray and ashen in the muted light, and his eyes were tinged with concern, and something else Sonny couldn't identify.

"You can't blame yourself for this, Burton," the sheriff said.

"The hell I can't. I led that boy right to her."

"Now, we can't say for sure, one hundred percent that Billy Bunson killed this girl, can we?"

"You might question that, but I don't."

"Anything's possible. He could have another helper, someone working the inside. It could have been more than him. Otherwise, I have to accept that Billy Bunson walked right into this jail, right under our noses, unlocked this cell, walked in, and murdered this girl. Who does that? I've been a law officer for all of my life and I've never come across anything like that. It's almost beyond belief."

"You've never come across Billy Bunson."

"He ain't the devil."

"He might be." Sonny twisted his head like he had a bug in his ear. He didn't. He was trying to get rid of the idea that Billy was the devil. "Billy Bunson is all about signals and signs. He's marked his way through life as he went so he would know where he was and where to run. Him and his old Negro friend spoke in a silent language only they knew. Thumbs up, thumbs down. I've seen a knife stuck in the back of a man who betrayed his momma. She was a good teacher that one. Billy had something to say to me. No, he did this all right. I wanted to help him. I had hope for him."

"You thought you could save him?"

"I did, but there was no saving him. Trust me, Billy Bunson did this. He did it exactly the way you said he did. You wait and see."

"I'm not going to argue with you."

"Wouldn't do you any good."

"It wouldn't, but I hope you're wrong. I hope no one can walk in and out of my jail and commit a murder any time they want." Sheriff Howard paused, raised his brow, and chomped on his lip in a hard way. "You seem to know this character pretty well."

"Something's happened. Something inside that prison that set off a rage in Billy like neither of us have ever seen."

"What do you think that is?"

"Not sure. But I aim to find out."

"We need to find him is what we need to do. We need to find Billy Bunson before he kills again, before we find the warden's wife dead on the side of the road."

"I don't think that's going to happen," Sonny said.

"Why's that?"

"I think she knew Billy before he went into prison. I think she's more to him than a hostage."

Lee Howard did a double take on Sonny's face, like he needed to check and see if he really believed what he'd said. He did. "That's quite an accusation, Burton. If what you're sayin' is true, then Jeb Rickart took some powerful bait. Married a girl, and got her pregnant. So, what?"

"So Billy could escape from prison. He needed help. He needed somebody on the inside. Bein' the warden's wife is as inside as you can get."

"So Dolly was his accomplice?"

"That's what I'm thinking."

"Have you shared this with Jeb?"

"No."

"Good." Howard broke his gaze with Sonny, and returned it to Donna. "Why'd he kill her?"

"Because she probably knew where he was at, or where he was going. Or maybe he did it to raise the stakes. When he asks Jeb for a ransom, then Jeb, and the rest of us, for that matter, will take him more serious. Dolly's not safe either is the message. He'll do anything to get what he wants. This will scare the shit out of Jeb Rickart. That's exactly what he wants."

"And what's that, Burton? What does the vile man really want?"

"His freedom. He wants to be free."

Sheriff Howard stuffed his hands in his pockets. "I wish I could cut her down. I can hardly bear to look at her like that."

"Her family know?"

"I'm going down to the funeral home to tell her uncle, Vern Del Rey, here in a minute. It'd be easier to tell him this was a suicide, but it's not. There's no way that girl could have stabbed herself in the back."

"You want me to go with you?"

"No, not necessary. Besides, there's a fella waitin' for you in the front office."

Sonny stiffened. "Really, who's that?"

"Didn't give me a name. Didn't have to. One look at him told me he was a Ranger, too."

CHAPTER SIXTEEN

"I didn't expect to see you here," Sonny said to his son, Jesse.

Jesse Burton stood with a steely gaze fixed on his face. He was dressed to work, was at the jail on business; shined black boots, khaki trousers with a shirt to match, and a white Stetson on his head. He wore a Cinco badge, but the show of authority wasn't required. Sonny never wore a badge. Never felt the need to. Most Rangers of his generation didn't. They didn't wear uniforms, either. But times were changing. Texas Rangers were starting to look and act more like everyday law enforcement officers, and less like Rangers, as far as Sonny was concerned.

Jesse doffed his hat for a quick second. "Good to see you, too, Pa. Captain sent me down. Sheriff Howard and Jeb Rickart asked for an official presence and some more help with this Billy Bunson case. He figured since you were already here, we could work together."

Jeb Rickart is getting nervous and impatient, Sonny thought, but didn't say aloud. "Why would the captain think that?"

"Maybe because we put the halts to that fella in Wellington. We've worked together before."

Sonny agreed, though it was a stiff acceptance, and a memory he was not fond of revisiting. Not long after he'd lost his arm, unknown young girls started turning up dead in the fields around Wellington. Sonny and Jesse figured out what was going on before the killer was about to claim another girl. Afterwards, you'd have thought he'd saved the world from complete destruction. It wasn't the kind of notoriety that Sonny sought out. Any kind of talk of him being a hero unsettled him more than it made him feel proud. Jesse's career, however, had benefited from solving that case, and good for him. He was young, still making a name for himself. Sonny didn't need any of that. He was glad to go home and while away the days in the company of Blue, leaving the rest of the world to itself—until Jesse and Jonesy had interfered with his solace and told him that Billy Bunson was on the loose.

"We did. That was awful quick. Were you close by?" Sonny said.

Jesse shook his head. "On my way. I didn't know about the murdered girl in the cell until I arrived. We can have more men down here in an instant if we need them."

"We?"

"You're not going home, are you?"

"It's a thought, now that you're here."

"But you won't leave without a conclusion, will you? It's not like you to leave something undone."

"You need to go in and take a look at that young girl hanging in the cell. Her death's on me. I'm no good to you, or anybody else. You can't count on me. No one can. I should have never come down here to begin with."

Jesse stared at the top of his boots, listening to every word his father said and didn't say. "He would have come for you if you wouldn't have come for him."

"And Donna Del Rey would still be alive."

"In jail."

"Still alive. And as for me, maybe it was time to face Billy one on one, on my own territory. He could have put me out of my misery."

They stood in a hallway that led directly into offices housed in the sheriff's department building. They weren't out of earshot of the dispatcher or the secretary that sat in front of Lee Howard's office. There was a quietness in the air.

"We need to work together," Jesse said, ignoring the confession of doubt. "I need your help, and you need mine. This is too big for one man."

"One Ranger . . ."

"Yes, I know how that goes. Believe me, I know how that goes. I've lived it all my life." Jesse looked Sonny directly in the eye. "I'm sorry, I shouldn't have said that. This is business, Pa. Serious business. There's still lives at stake. What have you got?"

"You're right. I don't have much, especially now, considering this murder. I haven't been here that long. I was getting settled. I didn't expect Billy to do this. I expected him to ransom the warden's wife, make a deal for her, then flee to Mexico, but then I got the feeling that she might have been working with Billy all along."

"Why do you say that?" Jesse said.

Sonny glanced over to the dispatcher who looked like he was trying too hard not to listen to their conversation. "I think we should go outside." He didn't wait for Jesse to agree. Sonny made his way to the front door without saying another word.

Jesse followed after his father dutifully. But he might as well have been chasing after a senior officer. Jesse's reaction would have been the same either way.

Sonny walked outside and had to readjust to the bright sun and fresh air. The smell of death was replaced by the familiar aroma of Texas dirt and dust. A low breeze blew from the south, pushing against Sonny. If it had been any stronger, the wind would have pushed him back inside the building. He stopped at the rear of the truck and looked for Blue. The dog was under Edith Grantley's care. Sonny worried about Blue, in his new environment, in a way that he wasn't accustomed to.

"So, you really think the warden's wife is an accomplice?" Jesse said.

"I can't prove it, not yet, and now with the murder of his known accomplice, that idea might have to be put to the wayside, but you need to consider Dolly Rickart as a potential suspect."

"That's why I'm here. The sheriff needs more resources, and none of us needs this thing to turn into another Lindberg story."

"Or Bonnie and Clyde."

"I hadn't considered that." Jesse leaned against the truck bed, fished out a bag of Bugler tobacco, and started to roll a cigarette. Sonny had never smoked and found the habit uninteresting and vile, but he didn't offer his opinion to Jesse. At least vocally. He was sure his disapproval was obvious on his face.

"So, here's what I'm thinking," Sonny said. "Dolly shows up a year ago, takes a job at the local diner that Jeb Rickart frequents, and not long after they started dating, then they get married real quick-like. As soon as she was installed as the warden's wife, she started a bleeding-heart reading program for the inmates, which Billy joined, even though he already knew how to read. Then not long after that, Dolly got pregnant, a blessed occasion for sure, since Jeb never had kids, or thought he could never have kids. And then Billy walks right out of prison, takes Dolly hostage, all with the help of Donna Del Rey, a local girl who was sure Billy loved her. Now Donna's dead, not able to rat him out, and Billy and Dolly are on the run together. He should have asked for a ransom by now. Nobody's heard a word from him."

"That's something, Pa. But don't you think it's a stretch to think Billy would plan something this detailed so far in advance."

"Billy always had a plan."

"I know. You've said that."

"I'm right about it, too. I've known that fella since he was a boy. He was smart, cunning, forever on the lookout for a way to make an escape. Nothing's changed. Imagine the life he could have had if he had been born into a different circumstance. He was expected to become a thief before he was weaned. It's in his blood."

"And you've outthought him at every turn." Jesse stuffed the bag of tobacco back into his pocket, stuck the cigarette in his mouth, and lit it.

"Not this time. I'm old and tired. I didn't see this coming, and I have no idea where Billy is, or what he's going to do next. This is a new bag of shenanigans. He wants something else. He's up to something else, and I honestly don't know what that is. I won't until I see him and talk to him. If, and when, that happens, it will be too late—for one of us."

"We need to find that woman, one way or the other. There's an unborn child to be concerned about." Jesse let the words trail off. They had a hard tinge to them, were laced with an old memory, an old grudge. Jesse and Martha had both blamed Sonny for the loss of the last child Martha had tried to bear. According to them, it was Sonny's fault for leaving them, for doing his duty in El Paso. Martha never forgave Sonny, and Jesse most likely hadn't, either. The grudge was as old as Sonny's hat, and nearly as worn. There was nothing he could do about what had happened years back.

"You know," Sonny said, "you might have hit on something that I hadn't thought of."

"What's that?" Jesse said, his attention pulled away from Sonny as a long black Cadillac hearse pulled into the parking lot.

Sonny ignored the coroner's arrival. "That baby. If it's not Jeb's like I'm thinking, and it is Billy's, then he's going through a change of some kind."

"A scoundrel like him? Giving half a crap about a baby, about anything but himself? I know a child can change a man. I've got three of my own, and I worry day and night about them when I'm away from home, but I can't see a man like Billy Bunson being moved from murderer to caring father. Doesn't make sense to me, Pa."

"Consider it. Consider that Billy has run off with the woman who's going to be the mother of his child. We need to find out as much about her as possible, because right now we don't know anything about her. Who her people are, where she's from, or who she really is. We find out those things, we might get an idea where her and Billy are heading next."

Jesse was still focused on the coroner's wagon. "It's as good a place to start as any. Where are you staying?"

"At the Grantley boardinghouse. I think all of the rooms are full if you're looking for a place."

"Nope. Got a room in the downtown hotel. You think we ought to go out and talk to Jeb?" Jesse said, pulling his attention away from the hearse.

"Sounds like a good idea to me. I'll let Sheriff Howard know we're leaving, see if he needs me for anything else."

"I'll wait here. I like to avoid coroners as often as I can."

"Me, too," Sonny said. "Me, too."

August 1911
Along the San Andres Spring, North of El Paso
"You move another muscle, mister, and it'll be your head that gets blown off, not that man there," Sonny said, aiming his Winchester rifle at a tall man, who looked like he was getting ready to execute a black man on the side of the road. A shorter, stouter man, stood off to the side of the road, holding a wagon at bay with a redheaded woman as captive, and a boy, a boy

that Sonny knew. A thief from El Paso named Billy Bunson.

He was riding back to Fort Bliss with Calbert Dobbs, the man who the captain had made sergeant when Sonny had shown up late to the Mexican Revolution. Sonny bore no ill will to Dobbs, who, as it had turned out, was a better sergeant than he had ever been.

"Now," Sonny continued, "both of you need to drop your weapons, or you'll be the ones to lose your heads, you understand me?"

Both of the scatterguns fell to the ground.

"We were trying to scare them is all," the tall man said. "We weren't going to hurt them."

"Whatever you say, mister. Right now, you need to put your hands in the air," Sonny said, as he climbed down off his horse, a reliable chestnut gelding that was under threat of being replaced by an automobile.

Sergeant Dobbs stayed mounted, not wavering one bit. He looked serious, and wouldn't hesitate to shoot if one of the men made a run for it.

Sonny dismounted, walked by the boy, and stuck his free hand out and let it graze against his shoulder as he passed. "You all right, boy?"

"Yes, sir. I am now," Billy Bunson said. "I sure am happy to see you, Ranger Burton."

CHAPTER SEVENTEEN

October 1934

Bedias, Texas

"Wake up," Billy said. "We have to go."

The cabin was completely dark. Blankets were tacked over the windows, allowing no light or suspicious eyes inside. It was still night, teetering toward dawn, toward daylight when it would be harder to flee unseen.

Dolly Rickart jumped with a start, opening her eyes wide, pulling away from Billy like a frightened animal trying to escape the grasp of a predator.

"It's me." Billy's voice was low, a whisper. She recognized him almost immediately. "We have to go," he repeated.

Dolly sat up in the bed, dressed only in a shift. Her belly had started to bulge into a ball shape, and her breasts, ample on a normal day, threatened to flow out of her nightclothes if she moved the wrong way. "Where's Donna?"

Billy offered Dolly his hand. "Don't you worry about that."

Dolly drew back. "What happened to Donna, Billy? You promised her she'd join us, that she wouldn't be left behind to take all the heat."

"Sonny Burton showed up."

"So? You expected he would."

"I did. I wanted him to show up," Billy said. "He has to be dealt with. We're not free as long as he still breathes."

"I don't like that part of this, Billy."

"It has to be that way. Burton knows me better than anyone else on this earth."

"He was your friend."

"I could never be like him or his kind."

"The good ones?"

"That's what you think? Because someone wears a badge, it don't make them good. You ought to know that. You saw how those guards in prison treated me and the other convicts. Like dirt. Burton looked at me like I was less than him, not as good, and never would be."

"He couldn't help you."

"I didn't want help," Billy said. He shifted his weight, changing the subject. "He got to Donna first. He didn't waste any time getting down here. I thought I had more time."

"What'd you do, Billy?"

"They'll have all of the roads blocked. They'll go house to house looking for us. I know what they'll do. They won't stop until we're caught, or dead. You're gonna have to drive us out of here. They're lookin' for me."

"Me, too."

"They won't expect you to be drivin'. We'll hide your hair in a cap, make you look like a boy from the distance."

"A fat boy," Dolly said, rubbing her belly. "You didn't answer my question," Dolly said as she pulled herself from the bed, and pushed by Billy. "What'd you do?"

"I did what I had to do. Where are you going?"

"I have to use the outhouse. Is that all right?"

Billy rushed to the door, blocking it with his entire body. "You can't waltz outside like you're the warden's wife."

"I am the warden's wife." Dolly stopped about a foot from Billy.

"As far as everyone knows."

"I have to pee, Billy."

"All right. Take it slow, like we talked about."

"I know, crouch down and edge along the cabin. Do my best not to be seen. I'm not a child. You don't have to repeat things to me. I don't want to get caught any more than you do."

"They'll take you away."

"Is that what you're afraid of?"

"Don't you worry about what I'm afraid of. Wait," Billy said, holding up his index finger. He hurried across the room, peered behind the blanket on the window, then went to the other window. There were only two. He looked out of it, then made his way back to the door and cracked it open slowly. "Okay, it looks clear."

"You're sure?"

"As sure as I can be. We're not going to be safe until we're miles away from here. We have to go, Dolly."

"I understand."

Billy opened the door enough to let Dolly out, but she didn't move. Enough light pushed inside for her to get a clear look at Billy. "Why is there blood on your shirt, Billy? What'd you do?"

Billy sighed, and looked away from Dolly. "I had to kill her."

"What do you mean you had to kill her?" Dolly's voice cracked as the realization set in.

"She told Burton we were supposed to meet in Bedias. She told him we were here. We have to go, Dolly. Do you understand now? They're coming for us."

"And you killed her for that?"

"I don't know what else she told him."

Dolly trembled. "Nobody was supposed to get hurt, Billy. You promised me no one would get hurt. She was a sweet girl."

"It was her or us."

"There's no going back now, is there?"

"No," Billy said. "There never has been."

A healthy flow of tears trailed down Dolly's cheeks. She

pushed by Billy, but he grabbed her by the arm. "Don't touch me," she said as she pulled out of his grasp. "Don't you ever touch me again."

"You're mad?"

Dolly stopped. "You killed a girl. What'd you expect, a gold star?"

"I expected you to understand."

"Leave me alone." Dolly crouched down and hurried along the side of the cabin as quickly as she could.

Billy watched every step she took, making sure she didn't try and make a run for it. He didn't think she would. But he wasn't sure. Not now that she realized how things were gonna be.

August 1911

Vinton, Texas

Billy and Jim Rome sat in the wagon outside of the marshal's office, waiting for whatever was going to happen next to happen. Miss Tillie's wagon, held up by a felled tree, sat next to them. Miss Tillie was inside the small building along with Lady Red, the two Rangers, and the two highwaymen. Billy secretly hoped for a quick hanging, but he knew better. Both men would probably get a slap on the wrist, then be set free. Billy was relieved that Jim Rome didn't get killed.

"Were you scared, Jim?" Billy said.

"Nah, I knowed someone would show up. Miss Tillie or someone else."

"I feel bad that I couldn't save you."

"You're only a boy. How you gonna save a man like me?"

"I could have ran at that fella, and you could have taken his gun. We'd done that before."

"That man woulda kilt you is what he woulda done. Nah, you done the right thing. Don't you worry about nothin', boy.

We here. That's all that matters."

Billy settled back on the wagon's bench. He didn't believe Jim Rome's words. Something in the Negro's voice had changed. There was a fluttery canter to it, a shake of disappointment left over from the feeling of fear. Tall Man was gonna kill Jim, Billy was sure of it and so was Jim. The incident scared him in a way Billy had never seen before.

"What do you think's gonna happen now?" Billy said.

Jim shrugged his shoulders and looked down the road. "We be movin' on, I 'spect. Nothin' worth staying here for. Not many peoples live 'round here that I can see. This has been a stopping place, not a stayin' place. Miss Tillie like busy places, you knows that."

"We goin' to Austin, Jim? Is that where we're goin'?"

"Don't know. I drive until I get told to stop. I do what I'm told. I'm jus' like you, boy. Don't have no place to go but with these folks, so what's it matter?"

"I don't know. I wanna know, that's all."

"Quiet now, boy." Jim looked to the door. It opened with Miss Tillie leading the way, her chin struck to the sky in victory, with Lady Red behind her, and Ranger Burton bringing up the rear. The Ranger closed the door behind him, and Billy assumed the matter was over, that the robbers had been dealt with. He wondered if there was a jail cell in the tiny building that housed the post office and the marshal's office.

Jim climbed down off the wagon and hurried to the driver's side of the other wagon to offer aid to Miss Tillie. She made no attempt to move. Lady Red stood at her mother's side.

"Well, we thank you, Ranger. This might have got bloody if you and your partner hadn't of showed up when you did," Miss Tillie said. She had her traveling clothes on, her girth stuffed into riding pants, with the rest of her body covered with a long coat, buttoned to the throat. She made Billy hot and uncomfortable looking at her, but Miss Tillie had a bad itch when it came to green things, so she had to protect herself no matter the weather.

"We were heading home," the Ranger said. "It was a matter of luck, that's all. Those fellas are a little dense, pulling a stunt like that along the road. Anyone could have motored along and stopped the encounter."

"You live around here?" Miss Tillie said, looking around, surprised it seemed, that someone could live in such a place.

"I do. Not far from here."

"Not much here, from what I can see."

No one else said a word. Rangers made everyone nervous. They were usually on the other end of the chase, not the cause of it. The girls in the other wagon listened to every word spoken with tight-jawed expressions of suspicion plastered on their faces. Billy had dealt with this Ranger and knew him to be smart and persistent. Miss Tillie didn't know who she was talking with. Billy thought she might be playing a dummy hand, which was a mistake. She'd come up on the short end of the stick if she underestimated the Ranger.

"That's what I like about it," Ranger Burton said. "The people that live in the valley look out for each other, are welcoming from what I know. We haven't been here long."

"It's a nice place to raise a family then?" Miss Tillie said.

"I think it might be."

"You don't think anyone would object if we stayed on for a little while then, do you? We've lived in a city for so long, I've long forgotten the quietness of a place like this. I was findin' it hard to breathe in El Paso," Miss Tillie said.

Billy's heart skipped a beat. There was nothing around. Not one automobile in sight. Only a scattering of houses and one general store to supply all of the goods to all the people around. There was no place to take from without drawing attention to himself. It would take a good shopkeeper a time or two to figure what Billy was planning. He sighed and figured Miss Tillie was up to something, too. Surely there was no way any of them could make a living in a place like Vinton. From the looks of things, it was a wonder anyone could.

"I don't think anyone will mind if you take a spot down by the spring for a few days," the Ranger said. "But, I'll tell you this. I know that boy there. The first chicken that goes missing, well, I'll be on you to leave. You'll be on the other side of my kindness, ma'am, if you understand what I mean."

"Oh, I understand, Ranger. Billy'll behave while we're here, won't you, Billy?"

"Yes, ma'am."

"Well," Miss Tillie said, "that settles it then. We'll take our place down by the spring. If there's anything you or your partner think you need, you come down and pay us a visit, you hear?"

Billy drew back a little bit. If he wasn't mistaken, it looked like Miss Tillie was a little smitten with the Ranger. Or like he originally thought, she was gaming something.

Lady Red didn't look none too pleased with the announcement that they were staying in Vinton. Her displeasure would come later. Billy was sure of it. His mother wasn't going to make a scene in front of the Ranger.

"That's kind of you, ma'am, but I best be getting on home. I'm sure Martha's got supper waiting," the Ranger said.

"I'm sure she does. If you change your mind, you know where to find us."

"I do," Ranger Burton said, then turned his attention directly to Billy. "You mind what I said, boy. One feather goes missing, I'm coming for you, you understand?"

"Yes, sir," Billy said. "I understand. I surely do."

CHAPTER EIGHTEEN

October 1934
Huntsville, Texas

Miss Ziskin eyed Sonny and Jesse warily. "He's not seeing anyone right now."

"You tell him I'm here. He'll see me." Sonny said.

The woman pursed her lips, recently freshened with bright red lipstick, then patted the left side of her brittle gray hair. The pencil stuffed behind her ear slid down a little bit, but she didn't care to catch it. Tension held fast on her administrative face; Miss Ziskin obviously didn't approve of being challenged by a stranger like Sonny. "I'll buzz him and let him decide."

"That's a good idea." Sonny stiffened and felt the strap to the prosthesis pull tight across his back. There'd be an indentation in his skin at the end of the day. His back would be rubbed raw if he didn't take the time to readjust the bindings. One more thing to make him uncomfortable. He wasn't looking forward to asking Jeb Rickart some hard questions.

Jesse stood at Sonny's side, quiet, not uncomfortable at all, taking everything in.

"Ranger Burton and his partner are here to see you," Miss Ziskin said into the telephone receiver. She had a nasally voice, like she was getting over a bad cold. "Yes, I told him you weren't seeing anyone, but he insisted." She listened for a couple of long seconds, then said. "Do you have any information about Dolly?"

151

"I have some questions," Sonny said.

"I'm not his partner," Jesse interjected, leaning forward, forcing a smile that no one could believe.

Sonny glared at him, bit his tongue, and wanted to lash out, *Not now, junior,* but he didn't. He rolled his eyes and wondered how long he was going to be stuck with Jesse getting in his way. Sonny wasn't used to working with anyone, not even Jesse.

"Okay, I'll send them in." Miss Ziskin set the receiver in the cradle, and said, "Go on in."

"Thank you," Sonny said as he headed to the door, leaving Jesse to follow along. He needed the boy to hold his tongue once they were inside the office.

They walked in to see Jeb Rickart standing behind his desk, looking out the window, his back to them. Jesse closed the door, and rejoined Sonny. Both men stopped in front of the desk, an impenetrable wall that separated them, and the rest of the world, from the warden.

"You think she's part of this, don't you, Sonny?" Jeb said, not turning around. "I heard the rumors before this happened. I know what people thought of her. But they didn't know her like I did—or like I thought I did."

"You're thinking the same thing," Sonny said softly.

Jeb turned around. He looked like he hadn't slept in a week. Bulbous dark circles floated under his bloodshot eyes. He wore a thick five o'clock shadow; the stubble on his face was dark, more like a midnight shadow promising to bloom into a full beard if he didn't take a razor to his face before long. His white shirt was wrinkled and his armpits were stained brown. A fan whirled overhead, but it didn't help dissipate the humidity in the room. Sonny wondered why the warden didn't open the windows, until he realized they bore bars on the outside and were nailed shut from the inside. The only way to open the windows was to break them. Escape was prevented in every inch of the place, except when it came to Billy Bunson and his recent antics.

"How could I not question why Dolly was with me?" Jeb said. "What did she see in a man like me? She made me feel like a king is what she did. Cooked me nice meals, made me feel like I was the only man in the world. I swear, until this happened, I thought I'd hit the Irish Sweepstakes."

"Where'd she come from, Jeb?"

The warden leaned on the desk. "She said she was raised in an orphanage in Little Rock, then got a job as a seamstress in Dallas. She didn't like living in the city and lit out for some place smaller. She liked the look of this town when she got off the bus, so she decided to stay."

"And you believed her?"

Jesse shifted his weight uncomfortably. His forehead bore a sheet of sweat, and it had started to drip down the side of his face, but he remained silent.

"Why wouldn't I?" Jeb said. "Times are tough. People are leaving one place to start over in another. Everyone is looking for a better life. The prison isn't going out of business any time soon, is it? We gotta pay wages. She was lucky to find a job at the diner. There's work to be had around here. Word gets out. Jobs draw people like porch lights draw moths."

"She had no past that you could find?"

"I didn't look real hard. I took her word for it. I believed the story she told me."

Sonny exhaled, and looked to the ceiling. "I'm sorry to ask such a thing, Jeb, but is it possible that Dolly knew Billy before he was sent here, that he knew her before you met her?"

Jeb leaned farther across the desk. "Are you suggesting that this escape was the plan all along? That's the craziest thing I've heard so far."

"Yes, I am thinking it might be. I can't prove it."

"Why in the hell did you come in here? To make me feel worse about what's happened? Especially now that there's been a girl murdered? What exactly are you doing, Burton? Making me second-guess the entire last year of my life? The last happy year of my life? Dolly has a kind heart. She wouldn't do this to anyone. I know people, Burton. I've been behind these walls for a lot of years, and I know a con when I see it. Dolly didn't con me, do you understand? I would have seen it, known she wasn't truthful and honest. I know a liar when I see one."

"I'm sorry," Sonny said as calmly as he could. "I was hoping you could tell me something, anything, that might help us find Billy. Donna Del Rey told me she was supposed to meet Billy in Bedias. Sheriff Loggard's got every road going in and out of that town blocked, and they're canvassing every nook and cranny of the place, but my guess is that Billy and Dolly are long gone, or making their way out, one way or another. He won't run. He has a plan. Some place to go. Some place to hide. You haven't heard from Dolly, have you Jeb? She hasn't reached out to you in any way, asked for help?"

"Not a word." The warden's face was red, the sadness in his eyes replaced with a growing rage. "I haven't heard one single word from my wife, Burton. Not one. Do you know how painful this is? How worried I am about her and our baby? How could you question such a thing?"

"I believe you, Warden," Jesse said, stepping forward to the desk. "I think what we need to know is, did Dolly have any other friends or family around that might hide her and Billy until things calm down?"

Jeb Rickart stared at Jesse like he had asked the stupidest question he had ever heard. "I have no clue what either of you are talking about. Do you understand? My wife is pregnant, and she's been kidnapped by a cold-blooded killer. She's not part of this scheme. She's a victim, and she's in danger. Now, I'd like it very much if you would both leave. If I hear a word from Dolly, I'll alert everyone involved. Do I make myself clear?"

Jesse started to say something else, to persist, but Sonny grabbed his arm. "We're leaving, Jeb. Sorry to bother you. My apologies for upsetting you." He moved toward the door, pulling Jesse with him.

"Would you let go of me," Jesse said under his breath.

"No," Sonny answered.

They exited the office, closed the door, and came toe to toe with Miss Ziskin. Her face was white as a bleached handkerchief, and she had an envelope in her trembling hand.

"Are you all right, ma'am?" Sonny said.

"I got another letter for the warden. It's a ransom note, and there's something else in it, too." Her voice quivered, and her knees buckled. Her eyes rolled back into her head as she fainted. Jesse caught her before she hit the floor.

The envelope dropped from her hand. A fleshy looking object rolled across the floor and stopped just shy of Jeb's door. Certain that Jesse had Miss Ziskin in a secure hold, Sonny picked up the object. It was a small toe, gray and severed with no sign of blood on it at all. He figured it came from the funeral home like the finger had; another of Billy's cons to pull on Jeb's heartstrings and confuse his mind.

"Are you going to tell him, or am I?" Jesse said, fanning Miss Ziskin's face with the palm of his hand.

"I will," Sonny said. He grabbed the envelope but hesitated before he dropped the cold toe back into it. He thought about telling Jeb that he didn't think the finger, and now the toe, belonged to Dolly, but something told him not to. Sonny liked to keep things close to the vest, and he didn't trust that Billy wasn't somehow manipulating Jeb in a way that he didn't know about. He pulled the paper back and read enough of the letter to see that Miss Ziskin was right; it was a ransom note. The kidnapper was demanding fifty thousand dollars for the return of Dolly. Another letter would come with drop instructions. That meant there was still time to find the two of them, Sonny thought. *There's still time.* Once Billy had the money, if the drop was successful, he'd be gone like the wind. There'd be no finding him then.

Sonny sat in the passenger seat of Jesse's car. The last of the evening light filtered through the windshield of the car. Night approached, and most of the houses past the building that housed the sheriff's department had their porch lights on, and their front screen doors open. The engine was off, and Jesse had the driver's side window rolled down. He smoked a cigarette slowly. Both men looked worn out from the day, but Sonny showed the strain more than Jesse. His face looked haggard, skin loose, eyes tired, like he was on the other side of a fever of some kind.

"This day didn't go like I thought it would," Jesse said.

"I'm worried Jeb's going to go off the deep end," Sonny answered.

"Wouldn't you?"

"He didn't take too kindly to my questions, but they had to be asked. What did you hope for?"

"That the two county sheriffs would put an end to this, find Billy in Bedias, lock him up, and return Dolly to her home. I was hoping this would be over for you, too, so you could go home. It doesn't look like this work agrees with you like it once did."

"I'm fine."

"If you say so."

"I do."

Jesse took a long drag off the hand-rolled cigarette, and studied Sonny's face closer than he usually did. "Maybe it was a mistake asking you come down here."

"I had no choice."

"I know, but I'm concerned."

Sonny reached across his waist with his left hand, and grabbed hold of the door handle. "I'll be fine. I need some sleep. I was hoping the roadblocks would catch Billy, too, but I didn't really think they would. You know that. I think he's going to have to slip up, do something out of character for us to catch him. He's got something in mind. A long-term plan. I wish I knew what that was other than being free. Mexico is most likely his landing place, but I could be wrong about that. Could be Canada for all I know. But he's got to get out of the States. That won't be so hard, but either way is a long journey. He's hovering around Huntsville, biding his time for some money. I still think this has more to do with that woman than Jeb Rickart thinks it does."

"Me, too." Jesse took a final drag off the cigarette, then flipped it into the distance. Sonny watched the red-hot tip spiral away, leaving a thin trail of smoke and sparks as it went. The cigarette reminded Sonny of fireworks, of a happier time, when there was something to celebrate, even if it was a holiday, the Fourth of July, instead of a sad moment when there were lives at stake.

"I'll be gettin' along, then." He glanced over to the Model A truck, ready to flee, ready to leave behind the day as much as Jesse was. "You've got the boardinghouse phone number if you need to get ahold of me."

"I do. You want me to pick you up in the morning?"

"Call first. Let's see what's going on."

"Okay."

Sonny pushed out of the car, closed the door, and started his solitary walk toward his truck.

"Pa," Jesse said.

Sonny stopped, and looked over his shoulder. "Yes?"

"I'm glad to be here with you."

Sonny didn't know what to say.

Edith Grantley was sitting in the parlor playing the piano when Sonny walked in the door. He didn't know the title of the song, but knew that it was an old one, written by a long since dead composer a hundred or more years back. There was little he knew about fancy music, but he liked the sound of what Edith was playing. It was slow, sweet, and clear. No fuzz on the notes like there was on the radio. He stood there watching and listening, not moving, leaving the violent world that he'd come from behind; a dead girl hanging in a cell, a calcified toe rolling across the floor, with a certainty that there would be more blood to witness—until Billy was caught, or killed.

As if she could feel his presence, Edith ended the music and looked over her shoulder. "I thought I heard you come in."

"I didn't want to disturb you." Sonny stepped all the way into the foyer. It was then that he saw Blue lying to the left of the piano. A smile flickered across his face. Blue saw Sonny at about the same time. The dog stood, and started wagging his tail.

"Everyone's gone to work," Edith said, standing. "Blue's good company. Alert and loyal. Nice to have around with all that's going on around Huntsville."

"You've come to know him like I do."

"We're fast friends. I saved you a plate for dinner. I can warm it if you'd like?"

"Sure," Sonny said, "that'd be nice." If he were at home, he would have warmed himself a can of Van Camp's, ate it in his chair, and fallen asleep there with Blue at his feet. But he wasn't home. Hardly. It had been a long time since he'd been in a house run by a woman.

Edith straightened the hem of her dress so it fell below her knee, then made her way past Sonny. She smelled like a perfect summer day; lilacs and honeybees all mixed together on a slight breeze.

Sonny and Blue followed Edith into the kitchen.

"You go on now, Blue." Edith opened the door to the back porch and shooed the dog from the kitchen in a gentle way, then turned her attention back to Sonny. "Sit down. Take the weariness off your feet."

"It shows that bad?"

"It shows," she said, as she pulled a bowl of stew out of the icebox and emptied it into a sauce pan.

"Long day."

"I'll ask, but I take it there's still no word on Dolly?"

Sonny really didn't want to talk about anything related to Billy and his deeds. He looked away from Edith, down to the floor. She must have understood, or felt, his reluctance. In a fluid, quick move, she lit the gas stove and stirred the stew. The smell of beef, vegetables, and gravy filled the room. It smelled better than breakfast. Sitting in the kitchen was the kind of comfort he needed. Food, silence, and someone to talk to. The last thing he wanted was to be alone.

CHAPTER NINETEEN

August 1911

Vinton, Texas

Billy stood at the side of the wagon, regulating the air in and out of his lungs as best he could. He imagined himself invisible, even though he knew such a thing was impossible. Still, if he believed in magic powers deep enough, maybe they would come true. His aim was to sneak up on Jim Rome, who sat dozing ten yards away, and lift his knife out of the sheath without getting caught. If he couldn't steal anything for real—an act that had been strictly forbidden by Miss Tillie—then he could at least practice.

The camp had been struck along the banks of the spring. Three white ten-by-ten tents arched at the bend of the road behind them. They sat high enough to avoid a sudden flood if the cloudless sky changed and unleashed a downpour on them. The mules were unhitched from the wagons and tethered to a stay line in an open field across the road. They grazed leisurely on what green grass they could find. The wagons still held most of the belongings they'd been packed with, but a few kitchen chairs had been situated around a fire that smoldered in the center of the arch. It was rare that someone passed on the road, either on horseback or in an automobile, and they paid the camp little attention. Automobiles never failed to draw Billy's attention. They meant opportunity and riches to be had—somewhere down the road.

The wagon that Jim Rome sat on was next to the other one, idle and awaiting the order from Miss Tillie to be hitched up. Billy had no idea how long she planned on detaining them in Vinton. The stop made no sense to him. He saw no reason or any gain to be had by staying in a place where there was nothing, no cause or draw for business. They could only eat fish and rabbit for so long.

Billy drew in another deep breath and held still so nothing in his body moved. No twitch of the finger, no blink of the eye was allowed. The air tasted faintly of woodsmoke. The invisible residue coated his tongue, but he didn't swallow. Instead, he took an easy, calculated step, making sure not to make a sound. Then he stopped and examined Jim Rome again. No movement, no clue that he had been heard. The Negro was sound asleep, and the knife on his side gleamed like a distant treasure, attainable with caution, dangerous to hold, impossible to keep, but that was not the point. Billy would never steal a thing from Jim Rome. Even thieves had rules.

Billy took another step, then another and another, until he was within reach of the knife. Through it all, Jim did not move, and if anyone, his mother, Teresa the Terrible, or Miss Tillie, noticed his game, they ignored it. Everyone looked bored, like they were waiting for something to drop from the sky to rescue them from their plight.

Inch by inch, Billy slowly raised his hand upward, aiming toward the hilt of the long knife. It was an old Bowie knife honed so sharp that it could cut through a turtle shell. Jim Rome had carried the knife ever since Billy had known him, and had never let anyone touch it. The knife was special to Jim, and that was reason enough for Billy to want to hold it, to feel it in his grasp.

Billy regulated his breathing slower, and put one finger after the other on the knife, watching for any sign of movement from

Jim. A rouse. A snore. A sudden realization of the threat Billy represented. But none came. Jim Rome slept like it was midnight after a hard day's work.

Billy had a full grasp on the hilt. Now came the hard part: lifting the long blade out of the sheath. His ploy was to take a breath, pull upward a hair, then stop. Repeat until the knife was safely in his possession. His heart beat more rapidly than he was accustomed to, threatening to betray him. A heavy breath would follow if he did not get hold of himself. Jim would hear him and wake up.

One more pull and the knife was his—but he would not run away with it if he was successful. He would ease into the shadows and leave Jim Rome sleeping. But that was not to be. Jim Rome's index finger flinched as a fly lit on it. Then he snored and blustered his lips, spewing a thin stream of spittle forward. He coughed. Then his eyes flicked open and he saw Billy; he immediately understood his intent, but Jim wasn't fast enough. Billy already had the advantage of weight and momentum. There was no stopping him. He grabbed the last remaining bit of the polished steel and tore into a run, straight for the woods that skirted the spring.

"You come back here, boy!" Jim Rome hollered as he stood. "I'll skin your hide you let anything happen to that knife."

Billy paid him no mind. Jim Rome had skinned his hide before, taking three lazy swings with a belt to his butt before the punishment was too much for the Negro to bear. No one else interfered. They looked away from what they were doing, then right back to whatever that was, leaving Jim and Billy to work out their differences. Only Miss Tillie stared after Billy, but she said nothing, leaving it be.

Billy carried the knife upward like a valiant sword. But it was more than a victory stance. It was a matter of safety. If he tripped or was tackled, the knife would fly away, not toward him, saving himself from the chance of injury, or something worse.

Jim Rome gave chase, but he was no match for Billy's speed and knowledge of the deer paths that crisscrossed in and out of the spring. He had started plotting his escape as soon as he birthed the idea of stealing Jim's knife. Now it was time to see if he had made any mistakes.

He didn't need to look over his shoulder to see how close Jim was getting to him. He could hear the Negro struggling through the brush, pushing by the trees in a rage, shouting, falling farther and farther behind; all the while, Billy powered forward with his destination and hiding place already determined.

Billy felt victorious, and wore a wide smile across his face. His feet hit the dirt with no worry of being heard or seen. It was as if he was flying through the woods, every sense heightened, with a dash of invincibility. Any time he had been successful in completing a plan, his body and brain tingled. He liked how that felt—but this, this was special. Taking Jim Rome's knife was like stealing gold from a bank. No one could sneak up on Jim. No one but Billy. He almost laughed out loud at the thought, but powered his legs to run even harder. Somewhere Jim was still shouting, but his voice was getting more distant. Jim sounded out of breath, lost. Billy kept running.

The deer trail curved right, then ended at the bank of the spring. Billy didn't stop, didn't slow. He hopscotched across the lazy flow of water on four rocks that he had placed there when he was planning his escape. He almost yelled, "Ollie, Ollie, oxen free!" but he didn't. Not yet. He wasn't safe. He had to go down a steep ravine, then to the other side, before he would be at his hiding place.

The run down the ravine was much easier than going back up. Billy was covered in sweat, and somewhere along the trail he had alerted a swarm of biting flies that were attracted to his skin like a bear to honey. He struggled upward, but his goal was in sight. His legs burned and his lungs and heart pumped like they were about to explode. Through it all, he held on to Jim Rome's knife as tight as he could, fearing he would drop it, nick the steel, damage it or lose it. Then Jim really would tan his hide.

Billy reached the top of the ravine, itching, fighting off the flies the best that he could. He almost jumped and twirled, but he didn't. He came to a complete and sudden stop.

"Well, well, what do we have here, Lucius?" It was Fat Man. Tall Man stood next to him. They looked like they had been waiting on Billy.

The blood drained from Billy's head to his feet in a matter of seconds. He flinched; instinct told him to turn and run. But he was out of breath, beat from the run out of the camp.

"You thinkin' about runnin', boy? Go right ahead, and I'll shoot you in the back of the head. You'll be dead, quick-like." Tall Man—Lucius—produced a revolver and pulled the hammer back, chambering a round.

"I ain't afraid of you," Billy said in between pants. He jabbed the knife in their direction.

"Well, lookie there, Benny, the boy's got him a knife," Lucius said. Fat Man's name was Benny. At least Billy knew what their names were now. "You best put that knife down, boy, before you get yourself hurt."

Billy stood still and tried to figure out his options. If he ran, the two men would most likely shoot him. It was then that Billy realized that he'd failed to plot an escape plan from his safe place. He'd fully believed that he could outrun Jim Rome, and he'd been right about that, but he hadn't considered the need to escape once he'd arrived. It was an oversight that looked to have grave consequences. He could either do what the man said, or he could do something else. *Think quick, Billy. Think quick.*

Lucius—Tall Man—took a step forward. "I ain't gonna tell you again, boy. Drop the knife."

"No," Billy said. "I'm not gonna do it. Shoot me. Go ahead. Shoot me." It scared him to say such a thing, but he really didn't believe the two men were killers. They were bumbling thieves and nothing more. "Besides, what are you doin' here?"

"What's it to you?" Lucius said.

It was as Billy thought. If they were going to shoot him, they would have already done it. "Why aren't you in jail?"

"Marshal let us go is why," Benny said.

"You got a bone to pick with me, that why you're here?"

"Could be," Lucius answered, still holding the gun on Billy. "You and your ilk."

"Ilk? What's that word mean?" Billy said.

"You stupid, boy?" Lucius lowered the gun to his side, leaving his finger on the trigger.

"Maybe," Billy said. "Ilk's a fancy word comin' from someone like you. You sure that's what you mean?"

Benny smiled, and looked to Lucius, who wasn't smiling. He dropped the look on his face as soon as he realized his partner wasn't having fun. "You best be nice, boy, Lucius got himself a mean streak. He'll shoot you sure as it's daylight. Don't test him."

"Really," Billy said, "how many men you killed in your life, Lucius?"

Lucius stared at him like he didn't know what to say. "More'n you," he said.

"If you say so."

"I do. You ain't killed no man. You're jus' a boy."

"Yeah, you're only a boy," Benny said, imitating Lucius's tone the best he could.

Lucius nudged Benny with his elbow. "Be quiet, the both of you. Now, the way I see it, you need to take us back to your camp, boy, and we can finish what we started."

"You gonna rob us again? That don't seem so bright," Billy said. He gripped the knife a little harder, and considered throwing it at Lucius, but he didn't. He wasn't real confident in his knife-throwing skills, and he'd never practiced with Jim Rome's knife before. If he missed his target, then the two bumblers would have a gun and the knife. Billy didn't like the odds of letting go of the knife. Besides, he'd worked too hard to get it out of Jim Rome's sheath. He wasn't going to throw it away.

"You don't worry about what we're gonna do," Lucius said. "Now I ain't gonna tell you again. Drop the knife."

Billy heard a twig snap behind him. He thought it might be Jim coming to tan his hide. "I can't do that," he said. "It's my friend's knife, and I promised him that I wouldn't let anything happen to it. Where'd you get that gun? It sure is a nice one." He was biding his time now that he'd heard the twig break.

Lucius looked at the revolver, then back to Billy. "Don't you worry none about my gun other than it fires. That's what you should be worried about."

"Oh, I'm worried about it. But what's the marshal gonna do when he finds out you held me up, again. A gun on a boy?"

"Marshal ain't gonna find out," Lucius sneered. "You ain't gonna tell him."

"If you say so."

"I do."

Billy took a breath. He was going to take a run at Lucius to try and knock the gun from his hand, then grab it and take off into the woods. He might get lucky and know the deer trails better than they did. But he didn't chance it. A rock came flying from behind him. The fist-sized piece of granite struck Lucius square in the chest. Neither he, nor Benny, were expecting an attack. Lucius staggered back, and grabbed his chest. The gun fell to the ground with a thud, and the air was filled with a man gasping for breath, fighting pain and fear. Benny looked like he had been hit, too. His face twisted into a stupor, then to uncertainty, looking to Lucius for direction, for a command. He looked like a lost little boy.

Lucius screamed in agony, then fell backward, falling into the brush.

Billy saw his chance even before Jim Rome shouted at him. "Get the gun!"

There was no time to hesitate. Billy gripped the knife, hustled to the gun, grabbed it, and pointed it at Benny. "You makin' a big mistake, boy," the man said.

"Don't stand there," Jim Rome ordered. "Run. Run now back to the womens. Tell 'em we got more troubles with these two. Go. Run!"

This time Billy did hesitate, but only for a second. He knew Jim was right. But they both needed to run. Jim obviously had other plans. Payback. Or stopping the two men from bothering them once and for all. Whatever it was, it didn't include Billy. After Billy handed off the gun to Jim, the Negro swatted Billy gently, moving him down the ravine. Billy didn't look back, though he was worried there was only one gun between Lucius and Benny. Billy kept the knife and ran with all of his might toward camp to alert the women.

October 1934

Iola, Texas

The small market sat at the intersection of a country road, gravel and mud, and a lonely paved road that led north. Night had fallen, covering the world in darkness and safety. Dolly still sat behind the steering wheel, her hair piled under a hat, no trace of lipstick or makeup on her face, with a man's wool coat pulled across her belly to ensure no one could see the bulge. The ploy had worked. They'd driven straight out of Bedias with Billy secured on the floor with a sawed-off scattergun clutched in his hand.

Dolly pulled the car, a late 1920s Plymouth, off the road and into the parking lot of the business. The lights were still on, and there was only one car parked next to the building. A single gas pump stood erect, not far from the door.

"Get as close to the door as you can," Billy said.

"We need to get gas." Dolly gripped the steering wheel tight as she turned toward the door.

"You don't worry about what we need."

She glanced into the rearview mirror to see his face. He looked away.

The Plymouth came to a stop outside the door, announcing to whoever was inside that a customer had arrived. Billy pulled his coat, a long black duster, to his neck, grabbed the shotgun, and pushed out of the door like he was on a mission.

"Don't do anything . . ." Dolly said as he slammed the door closed. He cut her plea off unheard and unnoticed. He didn't care what she'd said. All he cared about was getting what they needed and not getting caught.

Billy pushed the door open, and came to a stop. He scanned the little market, looking for anything that moved, listening for any sound that would let him know that there was someone inside other than the clerk who stood behind the counter. Not even a fly buzzed.

"Can I help you, there, mister?" It was the clerk. He looked pale and tired.

Billy didn't answer. He flipped the duster back, drew out the scattergun, leveled it, and pulled both triggers without saying a word.

The clerk had no warning, no time to dodge or flee. The buckshot slapped him back against the wall, leaving him there, stunned for a couple of heartbeats. Then he slid down the wall, leaving a trail of blood as he went.

Billy moved forward toward the cash register, ejecting the spent shells and reloading as he went. The clerk didn't move. His eyes were fixed, his head tilted to the left side, the rest of him crumbled lifelessly to the floor.

There was no stopping Billy now. He helped himself to the money in the cash register; then he casually walked into the closest aisle, grabbed an apple, took a bite from it, and started filling his pockets with crackers, pears, a few cans of potted meat, and some cans of milk. Once his pockets were full, he headed out the door, and dumped the haul in the back seat of the Plymouth. After topping off the gas tank, they were back on the road. Only this time, Billy was driving.

CHAPTER TWENTY

October 1934

Hunstville, Texas

Sonny slowly unbuttoned his shirt. Like starting and stopping the Model A truck, taking his shirt off was a process, a once mindless task that took forethought, patience, and a steadiness that he lacked at the end of any day, but especially this day. His left hand trembled as he pinched the fabric of his shirt and pulled the button forward, doing his best to slide it through the hole one-handed. It took an extra ten seconds to accomplish something he had done for himself since he'd been a child, something that now took him a silent marathon to do. He attacked each button one by one, until the last one was free. That did not end the struggle. He had to tilt his body to the right and use gravity and his hand to pull the shirt off his body. There had been countless times when the cotton had stuck on his hook, ripped or snagged it, rendering the shirt useless. Any mending skills had been lost with the amputation of his arm, but unlike a lot of people, Sonny had the means to buy another shirt. Still, he hated to spend money if he didn't have to, and this time he was lucky. The shirt fell to the floor and crumbled into a small pile at his feet. The next challenge came with removing his pants. Every part of living had been affected by the loss of his arm. Most days he didn't think about it, didn't spend time ruminating on the loss, but on this day, after witnessing a death, and eating a bite of dinner with a nice woman, he felt more incomplete than he had in a long time.

After stepping out of his pants, the next task he faced was removing the prosthesis. That entailed opening a series of buckles and unleashing the straps, until he was free of it, too. Unlike his shirt and pants, Sonny didn't let the fake arm fall to the floor. It wasn't that it was fragile, hardly, it was made of solid wood and steel, but it would raise a clatter, and there was the slight possibility that the prosthesis could be damaged. As much as he hated to admit it, he had come to rely on the contraption. It steadied him, gave him a little bit of balance back. With the last buckle undone, he gently guided the prosthesis to the top of the bureau, where it would remain until morning.

The strap had rubbed the skin across his back raw. It had happened before, and he had a salve in his suitcase that would take away the immediate burn. Pete Jorgenson, the veterinarian from Wellington, had given him the salve, which he used to treat dry and overused cow udders. The rawness would be quick to disappear. If he was at home he would have gone on about his business without the prosthesis for as long as it took the irritation to heal. He didn't feel like he could do that in Huntsville. He needed his balance, his confidence. The hook drew less stares and questions than an armless man would.

He could have fallen straight into bed as exhausted as he was, but he didn't. After changing into his pajamas, he sat at the edge of the bed and stared out the window.

It was dark beyond the house, and most everyone who lived on Edith's street had turned off all of their lights and gone to bed. The moon and stars were covered by a ceiling of thick clouds, offering little to see beyond the window. A thin strip of yellowish light seeped under the door, a nightlight left on at the top of the stairs so the boarders could see where they were as they came and went. A few crickets chirped, and a slight breeze pushed through the open window, causing the thin cotton curtains to pulse in and out, like they were lungs, breathing the sweet, night air. There was no sound from inside the house. Quietness reigned. Blue slept on the porch, providing Sonny with an aloneness that he had not felt in a long time. He hadn't realized how much he had come to rely on Blue for his own safety and security. Blue was a good guard dog, alerting Sonny to any sounds or trespassers that he might not have heard otherwise. He missed having the dog at his feet, with his hunting dog ears alert, especially with Billy Bunson free in the world. There was no telling what that boy would try next. For all Sonny knew, he could be standing across the street, casing the house, planning his next bit of madness.

Sonny's eyes had adjusted to the darkness, and he had relaxed the best he could—considering his thoughts about Billy. His gun, the 1873 Colt Army revolver that he carried all of his working life, lay on top of the bureau next to the prosthesis. It was cocked and loaded. Without Blue in the room, the Colt was all he had to defend himself. He could fire it left-handed. His aim was not as steady as it had been with his right hand, but he was confident that he could ward off an intruder, Billy, if he had to.

The air was cool, tinged with a moisture; humidity, not the promise of rain. A fan sat idle next to the Colt, and the only thing keeping Sonny from turning it on was the effort itself. Nighttime paralyzed him. Not since the shootout with Bonnie and Clyde, but before, after he had come home from the war. His nightmares seemed real. His dreams felt like a punishment, forcing him to relive the horrors he witnessed in France, over and over again. The visions had seeped away slowly, but he knew for the most part that the memories of war were never far away. He was haunted by screams, by suffering, by the sight of blood and death that no man should have to witness. As stoically as he had tried to take in Donna Del Rey's death, Sonny knew that he had been traumatized by the sight of the girl, dangling lifeless in the cell, her death caused by his presence. Witnessing a murder was a match thrown on a pile of wood soaked in the petrol of violence and despair. He thought he had seen enough death in his lifetime to have an immunity to such a thing, but maybe that wasn't possible. Maybe no human being could become immune to murder and rage, to blood and sadness.

Sonny clinched his left hand into a tight fist and cursed himself. The young Sonny. The Sonny who'd had more than one chance to put a stop to Billy Bunson. The Sonny who could have killed the boy once he grew into a man, rightfully, more than once, but gave him a pass, opted for rehabilitation. When that wasn't possible, Billy should have spent his life in prison, where he belonged, in solitary confinement with no way to escape. Killing had never come easy to Sonny Burton. But he wished it had.

"What would be the difference between you and him?" Sonny said aloud, softly; then he lowered his head as the words drifted out the window and into the cool, still night air. "You would have been a cold-blooded killer, too."

August 1911
Vinton, Texas
Calbert Dobbs stood at the door. "There's trouble down by the spring," he said in his best sergeant's voice.

Sonny stiffened, then looked over his shoulder to Martha, who hovered over the stove, acting like she wasn't listening. "That didn't take long," he said.

"We best get down there," Dobbs said, then turned and hurried off for his horse.

Sonny grabbed his hat and gun belt off the rack by the door and followed. Dobbs was halfway down the lane before Sonny mounted his own horse. He gave the horse its head once he was settled and let the animal run full out, certain that he was going to find bad news for someone.

It was a short ride. Before the road curved Sonny smelled the first hint of smoke. He glanced forward and saw a thin black stream spiraling upward. It wasn't a campfire. The aroma was unusual. New, mineral-like, tar or oil, he couldn't be sure. He feared an automobile accident, a turn taken too fast, the driver too inexperienced for the power of the motor. He had already seen a few of those wrecks and the outcomes had not been pleasant. He'd rather be thrown from a horse than drive one of those vehicles straight into a tree.

Dobbs got to the camp first, and was already off his horse by the time Sonny could see the entire camp.

There was no one around. The camp was as deserted as a ghost town. With the exception of one thing. The source of the smoke. It was unmistakably a man, hung from a tall live oak tree, tarred and set on fire. Death had already come to visit. His arms were limp, covered in a fire that promised to burn until all of the flesh and bone was gone. There was no struggle, no screams of agony, only the putrid, horrible smell of burning skin mixed with tar and smoke. It was one of the most horrible things Sonny had ever seen. He coughed, then gagged once he realized what he was breathing in, tasting on his tongue. If he had eaten recently, his stomach would have protested. A hard test. Sonny had a strong stomach, but this was beyond his strength to endure. This tested his basic senses, to comprehend and react to what he was seeing. He looked away, gathered himself the best he could, coughed again, then spit the bile that had rushed up his throat to the ground.

Calbert Dobbs stood back twenty feet from the man, staring

at him like he could hardly believe what he was seeing. His face was white, his stomach obviously fighting the same unfathomable war as Sonny's.

Sonny had joined Dobbs, standing shoulder to shoulder with the man, forging a bond and union that allowed them to hold each other up. "Nothing we can do for him now," he said.

"Maybe not before. Poor soul. No one deserves to die like that."

"No, they don't. They most certainly don't."

Dobbs took off his Stetson and rubbed his forehead. "Looks like that big black fella."

"I imagine you're right."

"I don't know what to do." Dobbs's voice trembled as he looked to the ground.

"We have to let the fire burn out."

Dobbs looked past the man in the tree. "You hear that?"

"I did. There's more trouble out there." Sonny cocked his ear, listened closer, and heard something scream. It could have been an owl. On any other day, he would have written the sound off as an animal in distress or claiming victory, but not now, seeing the man lynched and burning. Billy Bunson and his kind always attracted trouble.

"There were three or four women and that boy," Dobbs said.

"We're going to need the marshal."

"We best see what we can do to help first."

"How'd you know there was trouble here?" Sonny said.

"Fella was driving by, saw this, and came into the general store asking if anyone had seen the marshal. I was there. Marshal wasn't."

They hurried to their horses. Once mounted, Dobbs headed toward the woods, spied a trail, and followed it. Sonny rode directly behind him.

Both of them seemed relieved to be away from the fire, as

they pushed into the undergrowth. "Where's the marshal?" Sonny said.

"Beats me. Probably home asleep."

"Not much to do around here, but still . . . he had to know these folks would draw trouble."

"He let those two highwaymen go."

"I'm not surprised, even after we asked him not to."

"Judge won't be through for weeks. Nothing to charge them with when you get right down to it. This is a small place . . ."

"You're telling me."

Another scream came. This time it was closer, and definitely not an owl. It was a woman, more angry than scared. They slowed, conscious of not alerting anyone to their presence. "I got a bad feeling about this," Sonny whispered.

October 1934

Hunstville, Texas

Sonny woke in the middle of the night with a start. He was covered in sweat. His left hand was full of the sheet, grasped like he feared falling from a mountain cliff. He wasn't sure what he was afraid of, couldn't recall a dream or nightmare, but his heart raced like he had been running, or facing something that caused him to panic, to be afraid. He exhaled deeply, and sat up on the side of the bed. He rested his hand on his knee, tilted in the same direction. A stiff wind would have toppled him over. Sonny felt weak, disoriented. For a minute he didn't know where he was. He thought he was home, in Wellington, life as normal as it had been. But a breeze pushing in the window, the curtains drawing his attention, and his eyes adjusting to being awake allowed him to see that he was in a boarder's room. He remembered then, that he was in Hunstville. Donna Del Rey's limp body hanging in the jail cell flashed in his memory, pulling him directly back into the present.

An alarm clock set on the nightstand next to the bed ticking away the seconds. It was a little after three o'clock in the morning.

The house, modern by most standards, had one indoor bathroom, and an outhouse in the backyard. Sonny had no intention of making much noise, but he had a need to attend to now that he was awake. He made his way downstairs as quietly as possible.

The house was as silent as a church after services. Vacant and museum-like, a monument to the life Edith Grantley had lived in the house. Silhouettes of unknown people populated the walls, next to portraits and pictures of places that meant nothing to Sonny.

Blue stirred as Sonny entered the porch, wagged his tail, but stayed in the bed Edith had built for him. "You stay, boy," Sonny said as he made his way outside. The dog obeyed, but watched Sonny as he passed by.

The night air was a little cooler outside of the house than it was inside. Sonny stopped to listen to the sleeping world. Nothing stirred. Even the crickets had taken leave of the night. There was nothing to be heard except the constant presence of the slight breeze slipping past his eardrums. Not even an owl hooted. Sonny wondered if this was what death was like; lonely, dark, void of life of any kind.

He quickly did his business and made his way back into the house. He was surprised to find Edith standing in the kitchen, pouring some milk into a saucepan. She was dressed in her nightclothes, presentable to strangers, a housecoat buttoned all the way to the top, the sleeves long, no undue skin exposed anywhere, comfortable slippers on her feet, her hair pulled upward and wrapped in a cotton scarf.

"Did I wake you?" Sonny said.

"I'm a light sleeper. Have been ever since caring for my husband during his illness. I was awake on and off all night thinking about Jeb and Dolly and all that's been happening around here."

"You don't have to be afraid." Sonny stood at the door. A single light that hung from the ceiling lit the room. They both spoke in hushed tones, even though Sonny was pretty certain that no one else was in the house.

"I'm more sad than anything else. I'm warming up some milk. Would you like some?" Edith said.

For some reason, Sonny didn't hesitate to answer yes. Any other time he would have demurred, but Edith's presence in the middle of the night was a nice surprise. He sat down at the table, not taking his eyes off her.

"Good," she said as she stirred the milk with a wooden spoon. "Do you think you can catch him?"

"There's a lot of good people on the hunt for him. He'll make a mistake sooner or later. It's what happens in the meantime that worries me."

"Me, too."

"I fear for that unborn child."

"Of course you do." Edith turned around and made eye contact with Sonny, then looked to his empty sleeve. She let her eyes settle there longer than she normally would have.

Sonny had failed to realize that he didn't have the prosthesis on, that she hadn't seen him without the fake arm. He felt self-conscious, then moved to the edge of the chair, considering fleeing to his room.

"I'm sorry, I shouldn't stare," Edith said, stopping Sonny from leaving the kitchen. "Were you right-handed, if you don't mind me asking?"

Sonny grabbed as much air as possible in his lungs and tried to relax. The tone in Edith's voice brought him comfort. He couldn't blame her for curiosity. Most people didn't ask. "Yes, I had to learn how to do everything all over again. I'm still slow, still trying to figure out how to live everyday life with my left hand."

"It's been difficult."

"It has been. I thought for a while I might wither away and die, but I couldn't bring myself to do that."

"That's why you're here?"

"I'm still alive. I may not be whole, but I still have my mind. If I can help stop Billy Bunson, then it will all be worth it."

Edith poured warm milk into a mug, and carried it over to Sonny. "Seems to me you're all here, Sonny Burton. Not having an arm doesn't make you less. The fact that you drove down here to help says more to me than what it might to someone else."

"Not everyone sees things the way you do."

"No," Edith said, "I don't think they do."

CHAPTER TWENTY-ONE

October 1934

A country road south of Huntsville

Billy drove with the headlights turned off. The sky was overcast, covered by clouds, and the night was deep, angling toward dawn. Darkness still won the war over light, a temporary victory that would leave the night with nothing to show for the battle.

The car, another '32 Ford filched from the sparse streets of Iola. This car had meat on its bones, roaring along the road like an angry lion chasing down a gazelle. Not that Billy had ever seen such a thing. But he'd seen his fair share of Hollywood flickers on Saturday night in prison. Most recently, *Tarzan the Ape Man,* starring that swimmer Johnny Weissmuller. Tarzan looked soft to Billy, but he liked the idea of swinging from vine to vine, escaping his prey or going after it. Tarzan couldn't face down a lion, and hardly any car on the road could overtake a '32 Ford. He wished there were more of them to steal.

"You're gonna get us killed, Billy. Slow down, please," Dolly said, gripping the side of the car's bench seat with all of her might.

"I know what I'm doin'. You don't want to get stopped, do you? Cops have an eye out for us like a mouse has for a cat."

"I didn't ask to be a mouse. I didn't ask for this."

"Look," he said, turning to her, grinding his jaw teeth, "if that's the way you're gonna be, we'll get that last set of instructions to Jeb, and I'll swap you for the money like the letter says

I will. Then you can explain to him why Junior there doesn't look a thing like ol' Jeb, and resembles me. You can deal with that even though you said you didn't want to." He kept one eye on the dark road, edging the berm as close as he could, using it as a guide.

"I don't think he'd care who the baby looks like."

Billy flexed his fingers over the steering wheel, making a fist the best he could. He was tempted to lash out, to smack Dolly and put her in her place, but even he wouldn't hit a pregnant woman. "Is that what you want? To go back to Jeb?"

"I didn't know people were gonna get hurt. You promised."

"Things change."

"I still don't like it. We're gonna be on the run for the rest of our lives."

"No one will find us. If this plan works, then we'll have all of the money we will ever need. You remember the dream. You helped build it."

"I remember."

"Our life in a little shack, a place of our own—something we've never had before—with our kids playin' in the house, growing up a million miles from here. There won't be need for killin' there. Peace and quiet for the rest of our lives. I'll fish and hunt, and you won't have to work. Maybe teach the natives to read like you were tryin' to do on the inside. It'll be paradise. I never had a life like that. I never dreamed I could, until I met you. Everything I do is for the dream."

"You promise?"

Billy relaxed his fist and looked straight ahead, deeper into the dark. Not far ahead, he could see a bright spot in the road. It looked like two cars blocking the road. He slowed down and considered his options. The bad thing was, he was running low on shotgun shells.

"I promise," he said. "As sure as it's past midnight, I promise."

August 1911
Vinton, Texas

Like Billy had feared, Benny had had a gun of his own, and had somehow used it to overpower Jim. Billy had no idea how that had happened, or how Lucius and Benny had rounded up the women like they were loose cows. Miss Tillie and Lady Red were dirty fighters, but they were dealing with vicious men who were a lot smarter than Billy gave them credit for. Billy feared more than anything that he was going to end up alone.

Miss Tillie, Lady Red, Teresa the Terrible, and a frail, young blond girl called Matilda, stood next to the trunk of a giant live oak. The tree offered a healthy dose of shade to the ground with its mass of leaves. Like the oak in the clearing, this one looked like a good hanging tree.

Billy rounded back and hunkered behind a smaller tree about twenty yards away. He clutched Jim Rome's knife in his right hand, while his left hand and the rest of his body, trembled with an equal amount of fear and rage. He had watched the two men lynch Jim, then cover him in tar and set his body on fire. It was the worst thing Billy had ever seen in his life. The thought of it made him want to vomit. But that would've alerted the bumblers—well, they weren't bumblers now, they were kill-ers—to his presence. It was up to him to save the women. Jim was gone and would never be of any help again. There was no one to save them. Billy had to.

"You going to hang all four of us like you did that Negro?" Miss Tillie said, her voice loud and booming.

Lucius stepped forward and aimed the long barrel of his scat-tergun at Miss Tillie's head. "I done told you once to shut up, woman. If I have to make an example out of you, then I will. You ought to believe I do what I say I'll do. I done showed you with that Negro. You'll go get you another if I let you go, then we'd have to do this all over again, won't we? White women left alone with a Negro leads to trouble every time."

"Won't be stayin', I can tell you that," Miss Tillie said.

"Well, that's progress."

Benny was wide-eyed, looking all around, responding to every sound the forest had to offer. "We need to go, Lucius. Smoke's gonna draw the marshal, or worse, them Rangers. I didn't like the looks of them, I'll tell you. They'll hang us for sure if'n they catch us."

"We need to tie these women up is what we need to do. Have us some fun for free is what we need to do, Benny, then we'll get, leave this shithole once and for all. We shoulda done that a long time ago."

"We gotta run is what we gotta do."

"You in charge now, Benny? You tellin' me what to do now? When did you grow a set big enough to do that? Huh?"

"I'm sayin' we gotta run is all," Benny said.

"Tie 'em up, then we'll see what comes next," Lucius said.

Billy watched the two men closely, trying to hatch a plan, trying to figure out how to get both guns drawn away from the women, and himself, all the while exacting revenge on the two men. He owed Jim Rome that. Revenge for his death. Jim didn't do nothin' to them. They had no good cause to kill him. They done it out of meanness, out of ignorance, out of some kind of hate that Billy understood all too well, but sure didn't like. He didn't know what he was going to do, so he didn't do anything. He watched and waited for the opportunity to save the women to show itself. He sure hoped that would happen soon, before something else bad happened. He didn't think he could live with himself if he let something happen to Miss Tillie or Lady

Red. He would have even been sad to see Teresa the Terrible die unnecessarily.

Benny lowered his rifle to the ground and went after the rope that he intended to use to tie the women up with.

"Don't even think about making a move," Lucius said. "Any of you move a hair and I'll pull the trigger first and ask questions later, you understand?"

Not one of the women said a word. They all glared at Lucius like angry hens plotting their own revenge. Billy didn't think that Lucius knew what he was dealing with. If he made one mistake, one of the women would pounce, make him pay for what he had done to Jim Rome, and to them for that matter, holding them like slaves. Billy wouldn't have to worry about saving them then. But that hadn't happened. Rescuing them was still on him. If he pulled it off, saved them from the killers, then maybe all of them would be a little nicer to him. That was something to hope for, a reason to put himself in harm's way.

Benny tied up Matilda first. She submitted easily, didn't offer a fight, or even attempt to bite him. Lucius remained focused and beady-eyed, his finger heavy on the trigger of the scattergun. No one, it seemed, doubted that he would kill again if he was given a reason. All of the women most likely would have preferred to die than to be touched by a man like him. None of them ever showed affection to Jim Rome, but Billy could tell they were all upset about losing the Negro.

Benny was still working on binding Matilda's feet when something caught Lucius's attention.

Lucius turned away from the women for a brief second. The noise could have been anything. A squirrel dropping a nut, a man searching the woods, a Ranger on the hunt for a killer. Or it could have been nothing. Lucius's own imagination playing tricks on him, playing his own fear and nervousness about the deed he'd committed. Either way, Teresa the Terrible saw it as a chance to act. She was the closest to Benny's scattergun that lay on the ground.

Teresa dove forward, hands and head first like she was diving into a pool of water to escape. But that was not the plan. She landed five feet from the barrel of the gun, tucked herself into a roll, and came up on her knees within inches of the butt end. It was an impressive display of athleticism, one Billy had never seen before. All he knew was that men had favored Teresa in the past, regardless of her harsh demeanor.

The dive did not go unnoticed. Motion and noise drew both men's attention as well as Billy's. He knew he had to help. He knew it was now or never. He couldn't leave the women there to fend for themselves.

Billy rushed out of his hiding place, with Jim Rome's knife raised in the air, screaming like a mad Indian attacking unsuspecting settlers.

Lucius didn't know which way to turn—to Teresa or to Billy. His head went back and forth, not focusing on anything, the barrel following the lead of his grip.

Thankfully, Matilda was not as meek as she appeared. She pulled her free leg back and kicked Benny under the jaw, snapping his head backward, eliciting a cry of agony loud enough to tell anyone within a mile where they were. Red rain exploded from his mouth, mixing with a few brown-stained teeth, pebbles tinkling to ground, forever lost in the leaf litter.

Teresa grabbed a hold of the scattergun, evening their odds. Miss Tillie and Lady Red wisely dropped to the ground, making themselves smaller, less of a target.

Billy continued rushing forward at an all-out run. He was so completely focused on Lucius that the rest of the world all but disappeared. All he could hear was the chorus of revenge in his mind, playing over and over again: *I'm going to kill you. I'm going to kill you. I'm going to kill you.* All he could see was Lucius coming closer and closer.

Lucius decided that Billy was the most immediate threat and pulled one trigger. The scattergun shot out an orange blast, followed by the peppering of shot.

Billy had watched closely, anticipated Lucius taking a shot at him, though he'd assumed that he would have used both barrels instead of one. He dove to the right, allowing the knife to fly from his hand. He didn't want to land on it. Scattershot pinged all around him. A few of the shots caught him in the side. They stung like he had stepped into a hornet's nest and riled the occupants, but he wasn't seriously hurt. Once he landed on the ground, he rolled to the right, taking shelter behind another live oak.

The knife lay three feet from his grasp, in between him and Lucius.

Lucius realized he missed Billy, and turned the barrel toward Teresa.

She was leveling her aim at him.

He fired first.

Teresa took the shot squarely in the chest, sending her flying backward. Her finger caught the trigger, but the gun was pointed straight in the air when it went off.

The air smelled of gunpowder and blood. The gunshot echoed off in the distance and the slight scream that came from Teresa's mouth faded away quickly.

Billy jumped from behind the tree, scooped the knife off the ground, and ran straight toward Lucius—screaming. "I'm going to kill you. I'm going to kill you. I'm going to kill you."

Lucius knew he had to reload, but there wasn't time. Billy was too close, too fast, coming at him with a large knife. Fear filled in his eyes. The whites of them shined in the dark shady dark forest like beacons on an ocean, leading ships into port.

Lucius dropped the scattergun and turned to run.

Lady Red saw what was happening, was white with panic and fear, too, seeing Teresa's body motionless on the ground. She rushed after Lucius, coming up behind Billy, screaming at him to go, to run faster, to kill the man. "Kill him, kill him, kill him."

And that's what Billy did.

He gained on Lucius and dove straight at him with the knife cutting the air before him. The knife punctured Lucius's skin at the nape of the neck. The blade, sharp and recently honed, went all the way through, exiting through the man's throat.

Lucius fell forward, and as he fell, Billy pulled back and tumbled off to the side. The knife laid on the ground next to him.

Lady Red stopped. Billy saw her look over her shoulder, and followed her gaze.

The two Rangers came into view, riding hard, hoping to save the day like they had before. But they were too late.

Lady Red looked to Billy, and said in between pants, "Get up and run. Don't look back. Don't come back. You hear? Don't ever come back, or they'll know you killed him." Then she picked up the knife, swung upward as high as she could, and drove it as deep as she could into Lucius's back.

Lady Red staggered backward, making sure the Rangers had seen what she had done. Her eyes demanding that Billy obey her command.

He had no choice. He knew what he had done. He got to his feet and ran straight away, unsure if he would ever see Lady Red or Miss Tillie again.

CHAPTER TWENTY-TWO

October 1934
Hunstville, Texas

Sonny sipped a cup of coffee, ignoring the newspaper on the table. He knew what the lead story was. The last thing he wanted to see was Donna Del Rey's face plastered on the front page of the paper, local girl gone bad, her mug shot staring back at him, accusing him of allowing Billy Bunson to roam free, sneak into the jail, and kill her. The paper, and the whole town as far as that went, would want to know how that happened. How an escaped convict could slip into a jail, under the noses of all of the policemen there, and kill a sweet, young girl like Donna Del Rey. They would demand answers. Everyone would demand answers. But there were none to be had. No one knew what they were dealing with. No one knew what Billy was capable of. No one but Sonny. He didn't need to see the front page of the newspaper. He knew the story that had been written all too well.

The night had dragged after he had gone back to bed; even though he'd been warmed and comforted by the milk and Edith's company, he had struggled to sleep. There were no nightmares to recollect because there was little sleep to be had. His feet hit the floor at first light. If he had slept an hour, he was lucky. He wanted nothing more than to get on with it. Not that he was looking forward to the day, but he was hopeful, given the sun was shining, the weather was calm, that something would break, that Billy would slip up, and today would be the day that justice was served, and the fine people of Texas had one less criminal to worry about.

But that feeling of hope was slipping away with every ticking second. Sonny knew better than to fantasize about capturing Billy. He'd done that before and wound up on the wrong end of the stick. Exactly where he was now. He wondered how long it would be before the sheriff placed the blame of Donna's death on him. It was coming. He could feel it. Dread ate his hope like it was nothing more than a snack in a bag, discarded without thought, digesting it like it wasn't worthy of being remembered—or felt at all.

Edith had appeared in the kitchen not long after he'd come down from his room, poured Sonny a cup of coffee, then disappeared, off on a chore, doing one thing or another. He didn't mind being alone. Blue was out on the porch. Not long after, footsteps overhead told Sonny he wasn't the only person in the house. One of the other boarders was there.

A man walked into the kitchen and stopped at the door. "You must be the Ranger that's staying here." He was tall, late thirties, slender with well-defined muscles. He wore a pair of blue prison guard pants, a glossy black belt, and a ribbed white undershirt. Edith had told him that two of the men who boarded with her worked third shift at the prison. The man's face was pointed, accented by a thin mustache and tired gray eyes. He looked hardened by his days spent behind walls. He looked like a prison guard.

"Ex-Ranger," Sonny said as he stood, extending his left hand. "Sonny Burton. Nice to meet you."

The man hesitated and stared at the silver hook where Sonny's right hand should have been, then reached in and shook his left hand. "Nice to meet you. I'm Marcel Pryor. The Great War?" he said as he pulled his hand away.

"No, it'd be easier, though, to say yes and let it be that. Everybody asks if it was the war that took my arm."

"Most folks know someone who lost an arm or a leg, or they see them around town. A few fellas from Huntsville came back that way. Hard not to notice. You're about the right age, so I made an assumption. Sorry about that."

Sonny sat back down, and Pryor made his way to the icebox. He opened it and pulled out a glass bottle of milk.

"I got into a shootout with Bonnie and Clyde," Sonny said. "I got into a chase with them in Wellington. Bonnie poked a rifle out the window and I took a couple of bullets. Gangrene set in on the arm, then they had no choice but to take it," Sonny said.

"Boy, howdy, that's a better story than what I was expecting."

"It is to everyone but me."

"I'm sorry."

"No need."

"What happened to Bonnie? I mean, I know what happened to her and Clyde, everybody knows that, but that day? What happened to her that day? How'd they get away?"

"They ran off an old bridge and wrecked their car. The battery went flying into the air and crashed through the windshield. It landed on Bonnie's leg. The battery acid burned her, nearly left her lame. Clyde carried her away. I was dealing with my own injury. I ran my car off the road, too. Didn't have a radio in it like some fellas have now. I was lucky a farmer came along and found me when he did, or I would have lost more than my arm."

"You must have been happy when Frank Hamer ambushed them and sent them to face their maker."

"As much as any man can be happy when two people are riddled with bullets."

Pryor poured himself a glass of milk. "Mind if I join you?"

"Not at all. I'm about to leave, though."

"Figured you might be. You're here because of the Billy Bunson breakout, aren't you?"

"Doing a favor for the Rangers. I've known Billy on and off since he was a boy."

"Really, how's that?"

"Our paths crossed more than once is all. Fate. Spite. Call it what you want. I tried to save that boy from himself once, but it was no use. Whatever evil he had drank in his life soaked into his bones and blood. There was no changing him. No saving him. He had skills, smart skills, the kind that any successful man would envy. He could have had anything he wanted, but I was too late, if it was ever possible at all to show someone like Billy how to turn a corner."

"He's a sly one, that Billy."

Sonny stiffened, and took a drink of his coffee. He didn't take his eyes off of Pryor as he sipped, then said, "You knew him on the inside?"

"Sure, it would have been hard not to."

"How's that?"

"Things changed as soon as he came in, or at least not long after. The warden's wife started teaching those boys to read. Seemed more like her idea than his, but none of us thought too much about it—at least, at first."

"And then?"

"Well, it seemed pretty obvious to a few of us that there was some chemistry between the two of them. A warmness that made us uncomfortable. Sometimes it was just her teaching him."

"Without supervision?"

"There was always someone outside the door as far as I know."

"I heard that from Clayton Randalls, too. One of the other guards. You ever work with him?"

"Sure, thing. Clayton's a lifer, you know? Ain't never gonna be nothing other than what he is. Loves being a guard, he does. Ate up. You probably don't know what that means. Uptight. Strict. Follows all the rules to a T. He didn't like what he saw happening between Billy and the warden's wife, but he stayed tight-lipped about it."

"To the warden."

"We all talk, I guess."

"And that's it? You suspected something was going on between the two of them, and that's it? You didn't see Billy get into anything else?"

"Anything else? Billy Bunson was into everything. Making and selling hooch on the side, angling to stay in the good graces of the right people. He got along real well with the Negro inmates. Too well as far as I'm concerned, but it don't matter much what I thought. Billy had protection from all corners. Nobody ever laid a hand on him, and if they did, there was a price to pay. He even softened ol' Clayton, took to his ear in the middle of the night, confessing his sins. I never saw Clayton fall for anything like that."

"Billy was conning him."

"I tried to tell Clayton but he wouldn't hear of such a thing until it was too late."

"The road behind Billy Bunson is littered with men like Clayton Randalls."

"Well, Billy sure did walk into the prison like the cock of the walk, and he was, no mistake about that. He sure was," Pryor said.

Sonny tapped his finger on the table, digesting everything he'd heard. "That doesn't surprise me. That doesn't surprise me one bit."

"You gonna catch him?"

"I hope so. But it doesn't matter much if it's me or not. I want to see him put back behind bars where he belongs."

Blue barked from outside, drawing both men's attention. Then a knock came at the back door. Sonny was closer, so he stood, only to see Jesse standing on the side of the door, wearing a grim face.

"Can I come in, Pa?" Jesse said.

"Sure, something the matter?"

Jesse opened the door to the porch and walked in, eyeing Blue, who was focused on him like he was an unwelcome intruder. "I'm surprised your boarding woman lets that dog in the house."

"He likes her," Sonny said.

"Lucky her."

Once Jesse was inside, Sonny took his spot at the kitchen table. "This is Marcel Pryor. Works over at the prison. This is my son, Jesse. He's a Ranger working the official angle."

"Can we talk privately, Pa?" Jesse said, standing stiffly by the door.

"I was just leaving," Pryor interjected. "Nice to meet you, Sonny. Good luck. We're all rooting for you."

"Thanks. Nice to meet you, too." Sonny watched Pryor leave the room, then turned his attention back to Jesse. "You going to tell me what this is all about?"

Jesse stayed where he was. "Billy robbed a gas station north of Bedias last night at a little spot in the road."

"Got through the roadblock, did he? I'm not surprised."

"He killed the clerk. Nearly cut him in half with a shotgun."

"He's getting desperate. Something's getting under his skin."

"Did you hear what I said? He killed a man. That's two victims in a matter of two days," Jesse said. "Every agency within a hundred miles is up in arms, and they're looking to us to settle this mess."

"Took a little heat this morning from the captain, did you?"

"You could say that."

"What are you going to do about it?"

"I don't know. I was hoping you would know what he's going to do next."

"He's going to collect his ransom. Get his money, give up this charade of caring about the warden's wife, and set off for somewhere to be free. My guess is it's Mexico or Canada, but I could be wrong about that. He'll be going alone. I can tell you that. Billy Bunson rides alone. And there's going to be more dead bodies along the way. He'll kill anybody who gets in the way of what he wants." Sonny stood, and adjusted himself, including the prosthesis. "Let me get my hat and my gun, and we'll go take a look at this place he robbed and see what we can see."

"Ain't much to see."

"I'll let you know if I agree with you once we're there."

August 1911

Vinton, Texas

The fire burned itself out, leaving little to be recognized of the man in the tree. He was nothing but a charred figure, void of fingers or a face, black from head to toe, smoldering like a lump of coal tossed to the side of a fire.

Sonny and Dobbs had the three camp women in custody, only one on criminal charges. The red-haired woman had killed Lucius. Sonny was convinced that she had acted in self-defense, but that wasn't his call. That was up to the judge.

Benny, Lucius's sidekick, was in custody, too, and Sonny hoped the judge and the local law would go harder on him than they had before. There'd been no saving Lucius, stabbed like he was in the back.

The boy, Billy Bunson, was missing. Gone. And his mother, the redhead, along with the other two, wasn't saying where he was. All the women were silent, wouldn't say a word, looking after Teresa's gunshot wound the best they could—she looked dead. It was like the boy had never existed at all—but Sonny knew better.

They were hiding something, and Sonny aimed to find out what that something was.

CHAPTER TWENTY-THREE

October 1934
Point Blank, Texas

The narrow road wound on for what seemed like miles in the darkness. Gravel had been used to fill in holes in some parts, but the road was mostly dirt, dry in the late fall. Spring must have been a muddy mess, making the road impossible to travel, to get in and out of. Help from the seasons would have been a plus for Billy, but he was okay with the way things were. He already had an escape plan. He'd been to this place before.

The road skirted the river. Water ran slow and tired after a hot summer, ankle-deep in some places, making the river better suited for a flatboat than a canoe. Billy wasn't interested in a boat at the moment. All he was interested in was getting to the cottage without being caught. It would be their hiding place, where they could lay low until it was time to get the ransom money from Jeb Rickart.

"How'd you know about this place?" Dolly said, sitting as close to Billy as she could.

"Was here a long time ago. When I was a kid. I stumbled on it and was safe here for a good while. I hope it's as secluded as it was then. I figure it is with the Depression on, though some river folks might've stayed here, making a livin' off the water."

"You know how to fish?"

"I stay out of the water if I can." Billy could hardly see the road in the dark. He had the headlights off, concerned about attracting undue attention. He drove slowly, and tried to keep to the edge of the road, feeling his way as much as seeing his way forward. Dolly was distracting him. He didn't like that. "You need to shut up 'til we get where we're going. I can hardly see."

"I was making conversation, trying not to think about everything's that happened."

"Leave everything to me. Don't worry. There's plenty of food from the store I took to last us until we need to get more. We'll have everything we need."

"I'm worried about the baby."

"Why?"

"It's not moving."

"Maybe it's sleeping."

"I don't think so."

"How do you know?"

"I've been spotting blood, and there's been a little bit of pain in my left side."

Billy let off the gas, and slowed the car down to a crawl. "What do you need to do about it?"

"I might need to see a doctor."

"We can't do that right now. Not until we get farther away from Huntsville. Every copper and their brother is looking for us."

"I know, but I'm scared."

"You'll have to get by until we get the money. Once we get on the road for good, we'll find a doctor."

"Promise?"

"Yes."

The road curved one last time, and the structure that Billy had been looking for came into view. It was a dark, shadowy cottage that cantilevered over the riverbank, two sides of it guarded by towering cottonwood trees. Nothing looked like it had changed, but it was hard to tell in the dark.

He turned off the engine and coasted to the parking spot alongside the cottage for a quick unloading. After that, he'd ditch the Ford as soon as he could. If he could find a deep enough spot in the river, he'd sink the car and be done with it.

"You stay here until I know if it's safe or not."

"It's dark, no lights on."

"That don't mean nobody's here. Stay put until I tell you it's okay, you hear?"

"You're as bad as Jeb, always telling me what to do."

Billy ignored her and eased out of the car as quietly as he could. The smell of dead fish greeted his nose; pungent, sour, rotten. He could taste death on his tongue. It would take a little while to adjust to being so close to water. He didn't like the thought, but the river offered an alternative escape route, a quick getaway if he needed it.

He stood still, listening to the world as it slept, as closely as he could. The river ran slow, so there was only a trickle of water to be heard. Distant and weak; dripping water over settled rock. Insects were sparse as well. A buzz here and there, but no summer chorus to be heard. October had quieted everything down. Some leaves had started to fall, littering the ground with a blanket of brittleness that could serve as an alarm if someone was worried about intruders. Not even an owl hooted.

Billy looked back to the car to make sure Dolly was following orders, sitting still until he came back. She was. He moved forward, doing his best to remain silent and unseen.

It didn't take long for him to get to the porch that hung out over the river. He wondered how such a thing survived spring floods, but it seemed sturdy under his feet. Nothing to worry about anytime soon. Leaves covered the wood structure all the way to the front door. There was no sign of bait boxes or any human existence to be found. Before he pushed open the door, he drew his handgun, a six-shooter that Dolly had stolen from Jeb's closet. The gun looked fifty years old, but fired like it was brand-new. Billy had tried it out in Bedias.

Armed and ready to shoot if he had to, Billy pushed inside the door of the cottage. The smell of dead fish was replaced with a musty, displaced odor that most empty houses held. Billy was encouraged, but not sure he was alone. He lit a match, happy to see a messy place that looked unlived in. He wondered if the former occupants had set out for California, or some other paradise, leaving a vacancy for someone else.

As he turned, he scanned the room slowly. Billy started to relax, happy that his plan worked out. And then he stopped. A young black man stood next to the kitchen sink, a shotgun in his hands, staring right at him.

"Well, looka here. I'd say you best blow out that match and raise your hands straight into the air." The man had a flashlight resting on top of the gun. He lit it, blinding Billy almost immediately. "You move an inch and I'll blow your fool head off, you hear?"

July 1917
Houston, Texas
Billy stood back and watched the black soldier walk over to the spigot and take a drink. He knew what was coming, had seen it too many times since he'd come to Houston not to.

"Hey there, boy. You can't drink from that." a sturdy white man known as Flannigan said to the soldier.

The soldier was a sergeant in the Twenty-fourth infantry, called to Houston from New Mexico to help guard Camp Logan while it was being built as quickly as possible. War on the Germans had been declared in April, and every man in the country was needed, put forth into service in the best way possible. Bad thing was, the Twenty-fourth infantry was a black regiment, and Texas remained segregated, causing conflicts for men who were not accustomed to such laws in New Mexico. Skirmishes had started almost immediately between the white members of the city police and the regiment. Simple things such as drinking water out of the same water tank, especially when it was clearly marked "Whites Only," was enough to start a conflict.

"I don't see no sign," the black sergeant said.

Billy didn't know the soldier's name, had never seen him around the camp or the businesses that had sprung up, some of them in tents, around the construction site.

Flannigan was a crew boss at Camp Logan. He was a mean, redheaded Irishman that liked whiskey, women, and a good fist-fight. But he was also a hard worker, demanding of his men, but gained their respect by working alongside them, swinging hammers, digging holes, whatever it took to get the job done. He was short, strong as an ox, and muscled like a young man, even though he was older, middle-aged. Billy gave Flannigan as much leeway as he could, staying in his good graces by being a fetcher.

"Don't need to be no sign, boy. This is Texas. You see a white man drink out of a spigot, you best find one that your own kind takes to and drink out of that one."

The soldier stiffened. His uniform was crisp and clean, boots and belt shined a glossy black. A sidearm hung holstered on his hip. "I don't think I like your attitude, sir."

Flannigan's ears tinged red. "I don't give a damn what you like and don't like. I run this pit, and my rules are the rules. You got a problem with that, then you best take your darky ass to the captain and find out who's in charge here. Now, I'll tell you one more time, you can't drink from that spigot. You understand?"

Billy stood silently. He knew better than to say a word, to

move, to involve himself in any way. He didn't question that Flannigan would get his way, but there'd been an uncomfortable feeling in the air, building like a storm, for a while. He didn't know what the soldier would do. The New Mexico regiment didn't like how they were being treated in Texas. They had to ride separate streetcars in Houston, weren't allowed to eat in a restaurant if whites ate there or speak unless they were spoken to. Some soldiers had never encountered segregation before and didn't know how to deal with it. Billy figured the sergeant was one of those kind of men.

The sergeant glared at Flannigan, then leaned down, turned the water on, and took a sip, never taking his eyes off the Irish boss.

Flannigan's ears erupted red, the seed set, and anger spread across his face like a wildfire lit on dry kindling. He didn't say a word. Instead he grunted loudly, almost akin to a bull, and launched into a run straight at the sergeant.

There was no hint of fear on the soldier's face. He kept drinking the water, his body loose, certain of the outcome of his action before he had ever started it. At the last second, he dropped to the ground, throwing Flannigan's aim off as he launched into the air.

Flannigan bounced off the wall, knocking the air from his lungs, the pain and failure only fueling his rage even more. In response, the soldier had rolled straight to the wall, avoiding being touched by Flannigan. He levered himself on his knees, then jumped to his feet, his weapon drawn and pointing straight at Flannigan's head, all before the boss came to a full stop. Billy admired the sergeant's catlike reactions, had never seen anything like it, but he feared what was to come next. Men had started to gather, workers attuned to fights and conflict. They held shovels and sledgehammers, and had no use for a black man standing over a white man with a gun on him.

"You move an inch toward me, and I'll kill you," the sergeant said to Flannigan.

Flannigan gasped, caught his breath, blinked his eyes, and realized what had happened, what was happening. "You best put that weapon down, boy, or you'll meet your maker by sundown."

"I will do no such thing. Not until you call these men off."

Flannigan stared at the soldier. "I'm going to stand up."

"You best not come toward me."

More men gathered behind Billy. They offered grunts and groans. Softly, from a distance, Billy heard, "Kill him, kill him." A shiver ran down Billy's back; a memory flashed in his mind. A bad day long ago when he was a boy materialized in front of his eyes as if it were real. He had no desire to see the outcome of the fight before him. The sergeant was outnumbered, overwhelmed, his fate certain if he didn't back down and show the crowd that he knew his place. Billy stepped back, then turned, and threaded his way through the crowd, happy to see a cadre of black soldiers, along with the captain, heading toward the sergeant and Flannigan.

This wasn't Billy's fight, and he was going to make sure and get as far away from it as he could.

The sun beat down unmercifully on the construction site, adding to the discomfort of the humidity that hung thickly, promising to infect all who breathed the air with a heavy spell of consumption. By the time Billy escaped the ring of men that had formed around Flannigan and the sergeant, he could hardly breathe. But it was more than the weather, than the fight. It was the memory of Jim Rome's death come back to haunt him six years later. Billy hadn't been able to outrun the loss of his friend, his one and only friend, if he was being honest. He was nearly a man now and fending for himself for more years than he cared to admit. Houston had been a good place for him, giving him a place to work, to sleep, to live without stealing—any more than he had to. But losing Jim, and Lady Red and Miss Tillie, too, was more than he thought he could bear, even now.

He broke into a full run, fleeing Camp Logan like it was on fire. Sweat cascaded down his face, stinging his eyes, clouding his vision. The street was crowded with people walking on the boardwalks, and automobiles driving up and down the road. There were only a few horses tied to hitching posts. Billy paid little notice to any of them. Didn't care. All he wanted to do was get away from the camp as quickly as he could.

"Hey," a man shouted. "What's going on down there?"

Billy froze. The voice sounded familiar. He turned to face the man who had shouted at him. Sure enough, it was Sonny Burton. Only he wasn't dressed like a Texas Ranger. He was wearing an army uniform, standing with a platoon of men who looked like they were about to leave for the fight overseas.

CHAPTER TWENTY-FOUR

October 1934
Iola, Texas

The blood on the wood floor had already dried. It looked like a black mirror with overhead light glinting off the thick pool, reflecting the open eyes of a dead man. The body had not been moved. The clerk, Myron Falstall, had been a young man doing his best to make a living for his small family. They were gathered outside, waiting to collect his mortal remains, all huddled in a black mass of sobs, fear, and anger. Sonny had tipped his hat as he'd passed by the family, offering no words because there was nothing he could say that would ease their pain. He had silently vowed to stop Billy Bunson as soon as he could. Rage boiled under his skin as soon as he smelled the spilled blood, but there was nothing he could do to force the emotion away. Billy had fled into the night, off again on one of his escapes. Regret left a bad taste in Sonny's mouth, and he knew the only way to be rid of it was to hunt Billy Bunson down and kill him the first chance he got.

Grimes County Sheriff Merle Loggard stood next to the counter and open cash register, a chaw of Red Man comfortably poking out the side of his check. He looked like he was sucking on a rock. A tarnished spittoon sat next to Loggard's right boot. "Seein' a lot of you lately, Burton," he said. "Every time you show up there's somebody else dead. I don't know 'bout you, but that's not the kind of reputation I'd want if'n it was me."

"You know my son, Jesse. He's official on this, I'm not." He wasn't taking the bait. Lashing out at the sheriff would do him no good in the long run.

Jesse stood rigidly to the left of Sonny, eyeing everything in sight, as if he were cataloging the contents of the entire store.

Loggard offered his hand to Jesse, who took it and shook it firmly. "You got any eyewitnesses sure that this was Bunson?"

"Wish I did," Loggard said. "All we got is speculation."

"It was him." Sonny leaned down and examined the pattern of buckshot that had killed the clerk. "He walked in with his sawed-off, didn't give this fella a fleeting chance to figure out what was coming his way, and then started blasting away. He doesn't stalk like a cat, or play with his prey. This was no game. He was after money and food. A quick hit, then he was on down the road. I've seen this before. More times than I'd like to admit." He stood back up and walked down the middle aisle of the store. The floor was littered with toppled cans of peas and corn.

Sonny stared at the shelf, and took in its contents, then said, "He took all of the condensed milk except one can. He must of dropped it or knocked it off."

Jesse moved away from Loggard. "Why would he take milk?"

"He's holing up with that woman. She needs the milk to keep her strength. He cares about that. I'm a little surprised. Billy doesn't usually care about anything but himself. I could be wrong, but I don't think I am," Sonny said.

"You still think that baby is his, don't you?" Loggard said.

"Makes sense to me. Even more now. But Dolly, she's the wild card. Does she tolerate things like this? Killing, robbing, being on the run while she's pregnant? You got anything on her?"

Loggard shifted his weight. "Nothing yet. Called Arkansas and came up empty-handed. You know how it is, folks leave no trace of themselves. Not folks who think killin' and stealin' is a right. She materialized out of thin air, then found herself in the clutches of that Bunson fella."

"Love is blind."

Loggard joined Sonny. "Bad seeds is what they are. The both of 'em are animals, killin' an innocent like that clerk. Don't deserve no consideration. A bullet between the eyes, even if she is pregnant, is good enough. That one's a bad seed, too, unborn, brought into the world by the likes of them. That spawn will grow into a killer, too. We'd be savin' a life or two in the future by endin' that one now."

Sonny recoiled. He felt his mouth go dry. "A judge will have that say."

Loggard stiffened and glared at Sonny. "If you say so. They'll get no second chance from me, I can tell you that."

Jesse slid in between the two men. "Anything else here we need to see?"

"All the evidence has been filed. Photographer's been here and gone. Coroner's jus' waitin' for my nod to take the body away."

"Well," Sonny said, "let's let the man do his job, and give those poor people waiting out there the body of their boy. No need to keep him from them any longer."

"You fellas gonna be 'round if I need you?" Loggard said.

Jesse answered before Sonny could. "You can call Sheriff Howard in Walker County and leave a message if something comes up. I check with him a few times a day."

"We need to catch this beast before he kills again," Loggard said.

Sonny fidgeted, then looked to the exit. "He's going quiet. Got a ransom to lift. Then he runs. If we miss him then, it might be our last chance. He'll be ready to fly."

"Even with a baby on the way?" Jesse said.

"Well," Sonny answered, "that might change things, but I'll believe it when I see it."

Jesse parked the car on a desolate lane five miles from the murder scene. He lit a stubby cigarette and rolled down the window. "You need to go easy on Sheriff Loggard."

"I suppose I do."

"A man like that from around here has probably never dealt with a murder spree like this before. Criminals like Billy Bunson come along once in a lifetime. He sleeps at his desk most days waiting on something to happen, or figuring out how to get reelected so he can keep doing what he's doing."

"Not much different than Jonesy at home except Jonesy's one of the best cops I've ever known. This fella Loggard trips over his own shoestrings."

"You should go easy on him. Makes us look bad." Jesse took a long drag off the cigarette and exhaled slowly.

"Us?"

"The Rangers."

"I knew what you meant. That's not me anymore."

"Then quit acting like you're in charge."

"I figured this would come up sooner or later. You best speak to that captain of yours. If I remember right, it was his bright idea that I drive down here and ferret out Billy Bunson, not yours."

"I'm here now. Have been since Billy snuck into the jail and murdered that poor girl."

"You're blaming me for that?"

"I didn't say that. What's the matter with you? You've always been contrary and contentious, but I swear, I've never seen you like this."

"It's Billy is what it is. I should have killed him a long time ago. Loggard's right that he's an animal and should be put out of his misery. I've known that for years."

"This isn't your fault."

"If you say so."

Jesse took another drag off his cigarette. "So, what do we do now?"

"We need to head back to the Walker County jail. I need to look at that map in the sheriff's office. We need to figure out where Billy's hiding. He's close. I know he is. He isn't running yet."

"You really think he's playing cat and mouse with us?"

"With me."

"You?"

"Yes."

"Why do you think that?"

"Because he wants to kill me as much as I want to kill him. He lost his chance with me, too. It's a two-way street. We have our regrets for letting each other live. The time has come for one of us to walk away victorious. I'm not the man I used to be. He's counting on that, thinks it gives him an edge, and he might be right about that. But I'm not going to surrender to him, sit and wait for a bullet to blow out my brains. I'm going after him, and I swear, I'll stop him if it's the last thing I do."

"I won't let him get to you," Jesse said.

"I'd feel better about this if you'd stay out of it."

"I can't."

"I know."

Jesse tossed the remaining cigarette out the window, started the car, and drove down the lane. "Let's go get the son of a bitch."

Sonny didn't answer. He stared out the window, at the passing fields, lost in regret. Jesse had never faced a battle like the one with Billy, the one he was about to face. There was no way to stop what was coming, no way to save his son from the fight. He had put on the uniform and badge and welcomed the future, whatever it may be.

May 1918

Cantigny, France

Sonny stood on the banks of the Somme River, his face freshly washed, the hope of victory present, but not certain in his mind or in the minds of his fellow soldiers. General Pershing had demanded that no inch of Cantigny be surrendered, and with the help of the French army, that's what had to happen. The Germans were not taking the fight lying down. They counterattacked, used their gas attacks at every turn. Sonny's eyes burned, even freshly washed out. But it was more than the gas. It was the smoke from the flamethrowers, the powder smoke from the guns, the tanks, all of the weapons firing at once and the residue they left behind. And it was only the start of the battle.

Sonny didn't know what he was thinking, joining like he did, a middle-aged man joining a fight that he didn't understand. All he knew was that his way of life was under threat. The Germans meant to conquer the world, strip away the freedoms of every American man, woman, and child. He couldn't sit back and watch from afar, even if Martha had forbidden him from joining the army. She had hardly spoken to him in the days before he left.

And now, in France, he faced the first test of battle. Not only for him, for all the army. The French were weary, and the Germans, too. They had fought a long war already. The Americans were fresh. More than ten thousand a day hit the French dirt with their new boots to face the spring offensive by the Germans.

There was reason to be uncertain. News of a French defeat two hours away on the Aisne River had spread through the camp like wildfire. There would be no easy victory against the Germans. Now it was the Americans' turn in Cantigny.

Sonny wasn't sure if he'd live to see midnight, and truth be told, he had never been so scared in his life. But he knew he had no choice but to stand and fight with the rest of the platoon. Fighting the Germans was what they had signed up for, no matter what.

October 1934
Hunstville, Texas

Sheriff Walker sat behind his desk, weary, like he hadn't had a good night's sleep in all of his life. His skin looked gray and his eyes clouded. He moved like a leper fearing his fingers were about to fall off. "I didn't expect to see you two any time soon," he said to Sonny and Jesse.

Sonny stood at the edge of the doorway, waiting for an invitation into the office. "Loggard's got the scene over in Grimes County under control. We figured we'd be better off trying to find Billy. Any word?"

"Merle's a good man. Slow as a turtle, thick as a post sometimes, but I pity the moron who underestimates him."

Jesse cast a glance to Sonny but didn't say anything.

"He's doing his best," Sonny said.

"I haven't seen hide nor tail of Billy," Walker answered. "It's like he's got a contract with darkness to not let him be seen."

"It's not that," Sonny said. "He knows how we think is all, and then he outthinks us."

"How's he know cops so well?" Walker said.

"He studied us. Has a score to settle. Me and another Ranger

210

slipped up once, let two men go free who shouldn't have. They killed a friend of Billy's. He swore vengeance on us all then— even though he was only a boy."

"Hard to believe a monster like him was ever a child. Shame someone couldn't have saved him."

"There was no saving Billy Bunson," Sonny said. "He had the deck stacked against him from his first breath."

Chapter Twenty-Five

October 1934
Point Blank, Texas

Billy did as he was told and blew out the match, then stood frozen with his hands over his head, staring at the black man holding the shotgun on him. His heart didn't race. He remained calm. There was no fear to hide, only surprise. A strong beam of light encased him as if he were no more than a raccoon, transfixed and uncertain whether to move or not.

"I didn't know anyone was here," Billy said.

"You alone?"

Billy hesitated. He thought about Dolly out in the car waiting for him. One sound from her and he was made. She'd be in danger. He wasn't used to thinking for two people. He didn't like it. "Yeah, I'm alone. You?"

"Whatcha doin' here?"

"I stayed here before. Looking for a place to sleep, that's all. This your place? I'll go if it is. I don't aim to take nothing but my leave."

"Don't you move an inch," the black man said. Billy's eyes had adjusted to the bright light as well as they could, and he could see a little clearer. The man was hardly a man, a little north of a boy by a few years, maybe twenty, if that. He looked tattered and dirty, like he was on the run himself from some unspeakable place, some unspeakable event.

"I ain't going anywhere," Billy said. "Offering to leave is all.

You don't look like you need no trouble. I know I sure don't."

"Everybody's got trouble these days. 'Specially us folk in certain parts of this godforsaken place."

Billy silently agreed; let his shoulders relax. "I ain't one of them fellas. I need to lay low for a few days is all."

"You got the law after you?"

"Ain't saying. Might give you reason to march me out the door and find out for yourself."

"No law 'round here cares a whit what I say. I could hand 'em Tex Lucas or John Dillinger and they'd still find a reason to spit on me. You got problems with the law, you ain't got problems from me."

"I'm glad to hear that, friend," Billy said.

"Ain't your friend, you understand?"

"What's your name?"

"What's it matter to you?"

"We're standing here in a dark cabin in the middle of nowhere. Now the way I figure it, if you was gonna shoot me, you woulda already done that, wouldn't you?"

"Maybe."

"Then we should know each other's name. Maybe we can work out a deal."

"Ain't gonna be no deal. I tend to come up on the short end of such things. But my name's Moses. Moses Calley. Not that it matters to you."

"It does, Moses, it sure does matter to me," Billy said, stiffening. He heard a noise come from outside. A footstep on gravel. One. No more. He hoped he was wrong. He hoped it was that raccoon he was imagining, not Dolly.

Moses heard the sound, too. "You said you was alone."

"I didn't say there wasn't no one coming for me."

"I don't hear nothin' else."

"Mighta been a deer."

"Sure, if'n you say so."

Before Billy could take another breath, before he could form another word to come out of his mouth, Dolly pushed open the door with Billy's sawed-off shotgun leveled at Moses. "You move an inch and I'll shoot you," Dolly said to Moses. She sounded mean, like a canine bitch who'd had her puppies stolen.

Moses swung the barrel of his shotgun from Billy to Dolly. He was lucky that Dolly didn't mean what she'd said.

Dolly didn't budge. And she didn't pull the triggers, either. The flashlight glare blinded her and kept her from seeing her target clearly.

Billy saw a chance to jump Moses, but he didn't move, either. He saw an opportunity, not an escape. "Now, now, both of you relax and don't go pullin' no triggers. Ain't no need for anyone to get hurt the way I see it. Now, why don't you both lay your guns down, and let's see if we can't work this out like calm, normal adults."

"You lied to me," Moses said.

"Take a look at her, Moses. She's pregnant. I was protecting her."

"Don't look like she needs no protectin' to me."

Billy couldn't argue with that. "I told her to stay in the car."

"You needed help," Dolly said.

Billy stood firm. "Both of you relax and put down the guns. You gonna shoot a pregnant woman, Moses?"

Moses still held the flashlight on Dolly, bathing her in a bright whiteness that made her shadow look huge on the wall behind her. There was no mistaking the bulge in her belly, that she was carrying a child. "No," he said. "I guess I can't do that. But I ain't lowerin' my gun 'til she does."

"It's okay, Dolly. Ease the gun to the floor slowly," Billy said. He meant it, too. He didn't want anything to happen to either of them. He needed Dolly for the ransom money, and the way he saw it, Moses might have some use, too.

Dolly glared at Billy, trying to see through the light. He overexaggerated a nod, telling her he meant what he'd said. She leaned down, but didn't drop the shotgun from her grasp. Moses hadn't moved.

"What are you waiting on, Moses?" Billy said.

"Jus' tryin' to decide whether to trust you or not."

"Look," Billy said. "I might have some work for you. I ain't gonna lie, it'll be dangerous, and it'll take some foolin' the law, a switch if you want to call it that. But there's some money to be made shortly, and I could use an extra set of hands. Especially an extra set of black hands."

"Why's that?"

"Most of 'em won't be expecting me to work with someone else, to divvy up what they'll be bringing me. They think I'm selfish, that I'll want to keep it all to myself, but they're wrong about that. I need to be free, not rich."

"What you two got yourself messed up in?" Moses said.

Billy smiled. He knew he had him. "Don't you worry about that. Put that gun down and we'll talk business. I think you'll like what I have to say."

Moses exhaled loudly, then dropped his shoulders in agreement. "We each drop on three," he said to Dolly.

"All right," Dolly said, eyeing Billy.

He gave her the okay with a light nod.

"One, two, three," Moses, said, then laid the shotgun down as gently as he could. Dolly did the same.

"Good," Billy said. "Both of you stand up, and let's talk business."

"Well, I'll be darned if it isn't Billy Bunson," Sonny Burton said, breaking ranks with the soldiers, taking a long stride toward Billy. "That is you, isn't it? Don't lie, now. I've looked high and low for you, boy, since that day in Vinton. What was it, six, seven years ago?"

Billy felt like he had a mouthful of cotton. He couldn't bring himself to speak, to move. He'd spent every day of his life looking over his shoulder, at least until he'd come to Houston, until he'd taken up with Flannigan and his crew. He'd gotten sloppy, felt safe, and then out of nowhere, he found himself standing in front of the likes of Sonny Burton.

"You're not a Ranger anymore?" Billy said.

Burton stopped short of him. "On my way to war with the rest of these fellas. What are you doing here?"

"Trying to avoid trouble. Negro went an' got uppity with one of the crew bosses at the camp. A fight's brewin' as sure as it's gonna rain. Negroes aren't takin' kindly to the lack of hospitality here in Houston."

"I don't imagine they are," Sonny said, studying Billy like he was a specimen of some kind. "You've growed up a bit, but your face is the same. I'd recognize you anywhere."

Billy looked past Sonny, and didn't say anything.

"Don't go thinking about running, boy. Those fellas got all kinds of mean energy right now, waiting to spend it. Chasing you would give them something to do," Sonny said.

"Fight's coming. They'll have plenty to let go on," Billy answered.

The city noise around them sounded distant even though it was close. Billy was fully focused on Sonny Burton. It felt like he was encased in glass, cut off from life, imprisoned in an invisible cell. Burton could hold Billy with his gaze. He didn't like that.

"You vanished from Vinton," Sonny said. "Left your ma there, and her ma, too, to face the music. Your ma killed that man, at least that's the way I saw it and the way she said it happened, but you know, Miss Tillie, well, her face told me otherwise. I wasn't so sure what happened once I looked her in the eye. Now, why don't you tell me what happened that day for old time's sake."

"I don't know what you're talkin' about, mister." Billy stood stiff as a board. His ears rang and his tongue tasted like pig sweat.

Sonny reached to take Billy's shoulder with his right hand. "Why don't we go sit down on that bench over there?" He pointed to the boardwalk, to a bench under an overhang in front of the barbershop.

A rise from a crowd roared in the distance, and two soldiers ran down the street as fast as they could. Cars and trucks came to a stop, filling the air with the smell of gas and oil. There were no horses in sight. The beasts had been forced from the roads to paddocks. Made pets instead of modes of transportation. Billy felt sorry for the horses. Nobody had any use for them anymore.

Rain clouds built over the sea, boosting the humidity to almost unbearable limits. A riot was about to ignite, a battle between whites and blacks over mistreatment, a tale that was as old as the hills, and maybe older. None of that, the weather or the threat of violence, worried Billy as much as the man standing before him. He had no desire to relive the day he'd killed the man who had killed Jim Rome. He'd tried his best to forget what had happened, but he couldn't.

"What happened to them?" Billy said, pulling his shoulder back, but doing nothing else to escape.

"Who?" Burton said.

"Miss Tillie. Lady Red."

"Your ma?"

"Yeah, what happened to her?"

"She's in prison. She murdered a man."

Billy sucked in a deep breath. Lady Red had never done much for him, hadn't showed him love or put a stable roof over his head, but she'd kept the secret, taken a fall for him. He didn't expect that. The thought of it made him warm from the waist down, like he'd pissed himself in disbelief. "And Miss Tillie?" he said.

"Tipped over dead the day they carted your ma off to prison. Mad as a rattlesnake she was, screaming and hollering that your ma was innocent. Then she grabbed her chest, heaved forward, and fell facedown on the ground. There was no saving her. Took eight men to put her in a coffin is what it did."

"Losin' Lady Red killed her. They fought like mad cats, then licked each other's wounds clean afterward. I never seen them too far apart except when they were working," Billy said. He was tempted to keep on talking, tempted to tell Sonny Burton that it was him that had killed Miss Tillie. It was his fault that Lady Red got taken away, that it should be him in prison, not his ma, but he didn't say a word. He wasn't about to confess straight out of the gate.

"That was a bad situation," Sonny said. "Those two fellas should have never been let loose. At least until you all was gone. Me and my sergeant argued with the sheriff for that, but it wasn't to be. I'm sorry we couldn't stop what happened. Now, why don't you tell me the truth. It's you and me right here. I ain't no judge and jury. I'd like to know so I don't have to carry the wonder with me wherever I go."

"Ain't nothin' to tell," Billy said. "You saw it, you said so yourself."

"I came upon it is what happened. There was deception in the air from the start. Your ma didn't look like a mad killer to me. She looked panicked. And then you ran. Why's that? Why'd you run if she did the stabbing?"

"She told me to. She said run. So I did. I knowed better than to do anything else. I'd had her lickin's before and I wasn't about to take another. Besides, did you see what they did to Jim Rome? I wanted as far away from that as possible. I could smell him burning. I still can."

"Me, too. I'm sorry that happened to your friend."

"He was my friend, and it was my fault he died." Billy's lip quivered. He looked away, to the ground. He'd held the truth in for so long—and now he'd learned that Lady Red was in prison because of him. It was too much to take.

"Why was it your fault?" Sonny Burton's voice was calm, even-toned.

"I stole Jim's knife. It was a prank. Jim didn't let nobody touch that knife. I was bored, practicing my thievin' because Miss Tillie'd ordered me to keep my sticky hands in my pockets. He chased after me, and we ran straight into the woods. Those fellas was waitin' for us, or comin' after us, I don't know which."

"Your ma didn't kill that man, did she?"

Billy couldn't answer. His lips felt glued together.

Screams and yells thundered into the air, garnering everyone's attention. Everyone ran toward the melee. Everyone except Sonny Burton. He raised his arm to stop Billy from escaping, but he was too late. Billy dodged to the left, and hustled into the running crowd as quickly as he could.

Sonny Burton gave chase, but he was no match for Billy. He ran like the wind, crying like a fool of a child as he went. He had never wanted his mother so much as at that moment, and he swore to himself that no mattered what it took, he was going to get her out of that prison. One way or another, he was going to set his mother free.

Chapter Twenty-Six

October 1934

Hunstville, Texas

Sonny and Jesse stared at the map on Sheriff Howard's office wall. It was a map, all of Texas, with the counties and towns noted, as much as possible. The sheriff stood at the door, distancing himself from the two men, watching and listening closely. He didn't look enthused or encouraged that they would make any progress.

Walker twisted a toothpick in his mouth, and said, "The newspapers from Austin and Dallas are circling Jeb Rickart out at the prison. They think he's dead meat. Story's gettin' bigger than a boil on a bull's ass if you ask me. Civilians are gonna start a rage if we don't put an end to Billy Bunson's shenanigans soon."

Sonny didn't flinch, didn't take his eyes away from the map. They'd already pinned Huntsville, Bedias, and Iola. "He wants us to think he's heading west, but I think that's all it is. A ploy to drive us farther out. He probably thinks we are going to assume he's going to make a stop in Kurten or Wixon Valley. We need to put some men out there, put the locals on alert if they're not already, but I'd guess he's north in Madisonville or east in Dodge. Typical, Billy. He doubles back and hides in plain sight."

"State police are on all the arteries out of Hunstville, and widening out as we go. All the adjacent counties, including Merle Loggard from Grimes, are out kicking up dust on the roads, looking for anything out of the ordinary. We need to find the little son of a bitch before he kills again."

Sonny agreed but didn't say so. "I think he's laying low. Making a play for the ransom money. He can't be on the run and collect that, too. He's got a plan, and we need to figure out what that plan is."

The sheriff shuffled into the office and sat down behind his desk. "And your advice is not to put too much effort into looking west since he done made a landing in Bedias and Iola?"

"Yes," Sonny said.

"Well, that leaves a lot of ground to cover, doesn't it?"

Jesse stood studying the map along with Sonny, seemingly ignoring the conversation. "He could be in Arkansas as far as we know. Or New Mexico. He can mail a letter from anywhere."

Walker rubbed his temples. "You fellas don't have a clue, do you?"

Sonny turned to face the sheriff. "If I did, I wouldn't be standing here. I want him caught as much as you do. Maybe more. But for now, we need to keep looking and wait for him to tell Jeb Rickart where to drop the ransom money. That'll give us something."

"You think so?" Walker said.

"I hope so," Sonny answered. "Come on, Jesse, let's hit the road, see if we can't kick something up."

"I think that's a good idea," Jesse said. "Where do you want to go?"

"East. Due east toward Dodge." Sonny headed out the door. There might as well have been a fire in the office. He nearly broke into a trot to escape the room.

The day grew long, and Sonny tired pretty quickly of sitting in the passenger's seat. It felt like they had driven every square mile of Walker County. "The answer is on the map," Sonny said.

Jesse stared straight ahead. A cigarette dangled from his lips, and his right hand rested on the gearshift. His window was rolled down, and a plume of dust a quarter mile long trailed after them. "You might as well throw a dart at it. Same thing we're doing here."

Sonny stiffened in the seat, wishing he could stretch his long legs, but he didn't say so. He liked being on the move. "No, I really think the answer's right in front of us. Billy's a creature of habit. He believes in patterns, in processes. Once he figured out he was good at taking things apart and putting them back together, he saw a way to outwit nearly everyone he came into contact with."

"How'd he figure that out?"

"I don't know. Maybe he always knew. I ran across him in Houston before I shipped out to France and he was apprenticing with a man named Flannigan. I had hopes for him then. I thought he was lost before that. I looked up and there he was. I figured if he had a builder's trade, he'd leave the thieving and crime life behind, but it didn't take. I don't know what set him off, but the next time I saw him he was on a holy terror and he hasn't stopped since."

Jesse took a drag off the cigarette, and exhaled. "That was after you came back."

"Yes, after the war . . ." Sonny let the words trail off and stared out over a desolate field, all brown and tattered from the long summer and the searing sun. Everything in his field of vision looked dead, like there was no hope of anything prospering, of good from anything. Even the crows looked ragged and tired. The landscape didn't help fight off memories of the war, of the life he lived in France. It was over ten years past, but it still felt like yesterday, like a gas attack was coming at any second.

Sonny cleared his throat, then said, "There's a pattern with Billy. He knows I'm on to him, so he's trying to muddle things up, but he can't help himself. You wait and see, his methods will show themselves."

"I sure hope you're right," Jesse said, as he tossed the cigarette out the window. It was luck or lack of effort that a spark from the butt didn't set the world on fire.

Dog-tired and beat from traveling more miles than he could count, Sonny was happier than he should have been to see Edith Grantley's boardinghouse come into view.

"As long as nothing happens, I'll pick you up in the morning," Jesse said.

"I think we need to talk to Jeb Rickart again, then coordinate with Sheriff Walker and Sheriff Loggard to see if they've got any leads we don't know about on the two murders they're covering."

"Sounds like a plan," Jesse said, as he piloted his car to the curb and brought it to a stop. "You sure you're up to all of this?"

"I'm fine."

"You look tired."

"Old people look tired all of the time. We've seen enough of the world to know it's not going to get any better. It's going to get worse."

"Then why do we do what we do?"

"Because we respect the law. Not human law, but moral law. We don't allow our reactions to control us. We're not Billy Bunson. We only kill a man if we have to, and then it haunts us for the rest of our days, tires us out. The grayness you see is nothing more than the weariness brought on by living too long."

"You believe that?"

"I should have died in France."

"But you didn't."

Sonny lowered his head, exhaled, then reached over to open the car door. "I'll see you tomorrow."

"Sleep well."

"If only that were possible." Sonny stepped out of the car and headed toward the front door of Edith's house. He stopped to watch Jesse pull away, and didn't move until the taillights vanished into the darkness, then he walked inside the house, feeling empty and hopeless.

There was no music playing, no one in sight, not a smell of dinner lingering. All Sonny heard was the regulator clock on the mantel ticking away like a metronome. Nothing looked amiss, and nothing felt wrong, but Sonny wasn't propelled to move forward. He stood there waiting until he heard a set of footsteps descending the stairs.

"I thought I heard a car," Edith said, stopping at the landing. She wore a green flower print dress, cut a few inches below the knee, and she didn't have a hair out of place. She looked put together, ready to welcome a new guest into her house. Discipline showed in every inch of the house.

"You look like somebody tied you to the bumper of their car and dragged you all over Walker County," she said.

"That's exactly what happened today."

"It's not over, is it? I can tell by looking at you that man hasn't been put behind bars. Your shoulders are dipped lower than Jeb's, and you're about as pale as a ghost. Let me guess, you haven't eaten a decent meal all day."

"Never gave it a thought."

"I can make you an egg sandwich."

"That'd be fine." Sonny hadn't budged and neither had Edith. "I take it the other fellas have already had their supper."

"Everyone but you. Now, don't worry a stitch about that. I don't mind cookin' for you, you know that."

"I don't like to be any trouble."

"You pay rent."

Sonny forced a smile. "Speaking of trouble, you're not getting tired of looking after Blue, are you?"

"I don't know why you think that, that dog's the best dog I've ever met. I'm hopin' you'll leave him behind when this mess is over."

"No chance of that."

"I know. He's out on the porch. Probably listenin' to every word we say. Come on, let's get you some supper before you fall over."

Sonny followed Edith into the kitchen, made his way past her as she set about making him something to eat, and went out on the porch to see Blue. The dog stood from his makeshift bed, wagged his tail, and headed straight for a pet. "Good to see you're still living like a king. Don't get used to it," he said, scratching Blue behind the ears. Both were happy to be in each other's company.

Edith turned on the radio. Music filled the house. The announcer said the musician was Count Basie and His Orchestra. Happy piano music. Ivories tinkling, an air of happiness latched onto every note. Sonny wanted to ask Edith to turn the radio off, but he didn't, couldn't bring himself to. It was her house, and it was obvious that she loved music. He knew she was trying to lighten the mood, make him forget about the day he'd had. He appreciated it as much as it made him uncomfortable.

The music was followed by the smell of bacon grease warming to meet some eggs. Sonny hadn't realized how hungry he was. He patted Blue on the head. "You remember what I said about that king stuff." He squared his shoulders. He was talking as much to himself as he was to the dog.

He walked into the kitchen. Edith stood in front of the stove, swaying back and forth, keeping time with the music. For a brief second, Sonny wished he were a younger man, wished that he was whole, at the very least. Seeing Edith happy at the stove lifted him to places he had thought were unattainable. With all that was going on, the feeling was odd, out of place for him to feel desire. Acknowledging the feeling dropped a curtain of shame over his face, and he looked away from Edith. He couldn't ignore the music, the smell of the food, and the change of air in the room and under his skin. No amount of shame could make his feelings go away.

Edith looked over her shoulder, and smiled. "Blue was happy to see you, I bet."

"And me him," Sonny said.

"You're a good pair."

"We are."

"Well, go on, sit down. What are you waiting for?"

One part of Sonny wanted to do nothing else but rush upstairs, pack his suitcase, run straight out of the house, and get as far away from Huntsville as he could. But his feet were frozen, and any words that might come out of his mouth were stuck in his throat. The other part of Sonny, the one he had not confronted in years, the man that he was, the man who needed food, who needed comfort and safety, wanted nothing more than to stay right there forever and do exactly what Edith told him to do.

"You are one of the quietest men I have ever met," Edith said, turning her attention back to the stove. "Who knows what's going on in that mind of yours."

He'd be ashamed if she knew.

Sonny sat down at the table and tried to ignore the music, and the growing pangs of hunger in his stomach.

"I love Count Basie, don't you?" Edith said, salting the eggs.

"I couldn't tell one band from the next to be honest with you."

"Well, that's a shame."

"I never listen to music closely. It's background noise to me. I like to hear the news, or a baseball game in the summer. Music never meant much to me."

"That's even more of a shame."

"I suppose it is."

Edith moved over to the counter and pulled out two pieces of white bread from the breadbox, then put the hard-cooked eggs on the bread, and offered the sandwich to Sonny. He took the plate and stared at it for a second.

"Glass of milk?" Edith said.

"Sure." Sonny sat the plate down and waited to take a bite of the food. The immediacy of his hunger disappeared, and he realized what had been missing from his life. Even though Martha had been gruff and distant, she took care of him, washed his clothes, and kept a clean house. It had been ten years since she'd died. He lowered his head and tried to breathe normally.

Edith set a chilled glass of milk in front of Sonny. "Are you all right?"

"I'm fine. It's been a long day."

Edith sat down in the chair next to Sonny.

"Aren't you going to eat?"

"Already have. You go on, now. We can sit here and talk, unless you'd rather not, of course. I'd surely understand it if you want some time to yourself." Edith placed the palms of her hands on the table, readying herself to propel upward.

"No, stay. Please, stay," Sonny said.

Edith relaxed back into the chair. She didn't say anything, and smiled. The radio played on, switching from one band to the next. The windows were open a quarter, and the white cotton kitchen curtains puffed in and out on a soft breeze. All of the air in the small room had been touched by the heaviness of bacon grease. It dissipated as quickly as it had appeared, replaced with the clean smell of night air. A cricket sawed its legs outside the window, adding to the calm orchestra that played.

Sonny ate slowly, enjoying the sandwich, the feeling in the kitchen. Edith said nothing until he was finished eating. She sat and watched his every move.

"Would you like another sandwich?" Edith said.

"No." Sonny took a long drink of milk, wiped his mouth with a blue cloth napkin, then laid it down on the plate. "That was very good, thank you very much."

Edith stood, collected the glass and plate, and headed toward the sink. Sonny watched her go.

The music on the radio shifted gears to a slower pace, a waltz or a ballad, Sonny wasn't sure which. Edith deposited the dirty dish in the sink, then turned around to face Sonny. She swayed a bit with the music, subtly, curiously. "Do you dance, Mr. Burton?"

The question startled Sonny. He wasn't expecting it. "No. No, I don't."

"Have you ever?"

"Not much. Martha wasn't much for music, either. She was, well, she took care of things. Having a good time wasn't in her nature."

"Well, that's a shame."

"It is."

"So you've never danced?"

"Not much. Not in years."

"Would you like to?"

Sonny stared at her, and felt his pulse quicken, his mouth go dry. "What would the other boarders think?"

"They're gone. It's just you and me." Edith walked to the

middle of the room and stopped. "Would you like to dance?"

All of the blood drained out of Sonny's face. He raised the prosthesis. "With this?"

"Of course," Edith said. "You still have two feet, don't you?"

"I do."

"Well?"

Sonny didn't move. The music played on. The Regulator clock ticked away. Edith Grantley stood waiting, looking very much like a woman who wasn't about to be told no. He walked straight to her and stopped within inches of her face. He could smell her perfume, or maybe it was soap. It didn't matter. She smelled like the night, only in a garden of flowers; lilacs and lilies, gardenias and roses. A full bouquet.

She took hold of his hook. "Do you mind?"

"No." It was a whisper. He helped hoist the arm up as she melted into position with him.

"Put your other hand at my waist. You know what to do," Edith said. "Dancing is a bit like riding a horse, isn't it? There's a rhythm."

Sonny did as he was told. Every cell in his body suddenly felt as if they were alive for the first time. Edith swayed and stepped and Sonny followed, but only for a minute, only until he caught on to the beat, then he stepped into the lead. Edith surrendered and all that was left was the music, the open window, the empty house, and the two of them left alone to dance the night away.

CHAPTER TWENTY-SEVEN

July 1917
Houston, Texas

Billy ran straight past the riot, straight past the burning barrels and the hordes of white men fighting hand to hand against a smaller number of Negroes. Madness and screams rose into the air, creating a horrible thunder. The men used whatever they could find to fight with; a shovel, a pitchfork, a hammer. There hadn't been any gunshots yet, but it was coming. Someone would pull a knife or a gun. Someone was going to die. Billy knew the smell of death all too well.

Tears streamed down his face as he ran away from Sonny Burton. Fear pushed his feet as sadness and hope filled his lungs. He didn't care if he ever saw Burton again. But the chance encounter had given him something he had searched for for years: the location of his mother, of Lady Red. She was in prison for a crime that he'd committed.

Dodging the fighting was easy since Billy was smaller than most of the men. He was rib-thin. Food was scarce, but his small size could be attributed to more than that. He worked hard every day for Flannigan building the new camp. There wasn't an ounce of fat on his body. By the time he reached the shed where he kept his belongings, where he slept and lived when he wasn't working, he was out of breath, nearly exhausted. The battle was behind him, but he feared it would catch up to him. He feared all of Houston would burn to the ground before nightfall.

"Where you been, boy?" It was Flannigan's voice, from behind him.

"Outside the camp. They's fighting," Billy said.

"Why do you think I'm here." Flannigan was as short and stout as a teapot, his fair skin burned red by the sun to match his unruly hair. He was probably fifty years old, bloated and scarred by life. His shirt was sweat-soaked from a hard day's work. Flannigan was no slacker.

"You started this," Billy said with a hiss. He stood at the door, not daring to go in the shed and retrieve his traveling bag. Flannigan's motive for seeking him out was unclear to Billy.

"That Negro had no right to drink out of that spigot," Flannigan said.

"Not my place to say one way or the other about such things."

Flannigan stepped forward and stopped, leaving a good foot between him and Billy. "You like them darkies, don't you, boy?"

Billy knew better than to tell the truth. Flannigan had never had a Negro as a friend in his life. Billy had. "I stay away from 'em if I can. They're all liars and thieves."

"You say so."

"I do. How come you're not fightin'?"

"Not my day to die."

"If you say so."

"I do. Where you going?"

"Hiding out until the smoke clears. Not my day to die, either," Billy said.

"You say so."

"I do."

"There's gonna be cleanup to be done after this mess is over. Don't get lazy," Flannigan said, then walked away.

Billy did nothing to tell Flannigan what his next move was.

He felt like a slave around the man, like Flannigan would do something to stop him from running away if he got wind of it.

Billy waited until Flannigan was out of sight before he started packing his travel bag. Sneaking away while a riot raged on was a good cover. No one would miss him for a while. And when they did, he'd be long gone. Houston would be behind him. It was a place he didn't want to ever see again.

July 1917
Huntsville, Texas

Billy stopped outside of the prison. It was an imposing place, all surrounded by red brick walls with guard towers. Armed men looked down on him, watching every move he made. He felt like a mouse with an owl sitting in a tree above him, ready to pounce, ready to rip him to shreds. He was starting to think that visiting his mother was a bad idea, but he'd come a long way. He wasn't going to turn around and go back to Houston.

Billy tried to stand as tall as he could, walked straight to the entrance shack, and stopped. He told himself that he had every right to be there, to not be afraid.

A clean-shaven guard with steely blue eyes and a hooked nose looked down at him. "What can I do for you, kid?"

"I'm here to see my ma."

"You don't say?"

"That's what I said. I'm here to see my ma. Can I do that?"

"Well, you probably can. What's your ma's name?"

"Lady Red." Billy stuttered, then realized that Lady Red wasn't his mother's real name. "Millie Lou Bernhardt. I mean Millie Lou Bernhardt."

"Okay. Good thing, I don't think there's no Lady Red in there. Let me call and check to see if she can take visitors."

"What do you mean, 'if she can?' "

233

"Some can, some can't. I don't make the rules, kid. I work the gate. Let me call in to see. It'll only take a second."

"Okay." Billy watched every move the guard made. He wore a sidearm. A government-issue .45. Most men who worked in jobs that demanded a gun had favored the .45 since its creation in 1911. Farther inside the guard shack, Billy saw three rifles hanging on the wall. He didn't know the caliber or make. They looked like serious killing machines. It was no surprise to him that the shack was loaded with weapons.

A ring of keys jangled on the guard's hip as he tapped his foot, waiting for a response from whoever he was talking to. Another weapon, a short hickory club, rested opposite the .45 on the man's hip. The guard looked like he was a master of all the weapons within his reach. Billy figured all of the guards were skilled, had a greater knowledge of weapons than he did. He envied the man in the guardhouse.

"How old are you, boy?" the guard said.

Billy didn't hesitate to lie. "Eighteen."

The guard scrunched his forehead in disbelief. "Are you sure?"

"I had the fever when I was a baby. Doctors told my ma that I'd be small for my age all my life. You can ask her yourself if you don't believe me. She's right inside there."

The guard stared at Billy, judging him, calculating, looking into his eyes to see if he could tell whether he was lying or not. "He says he's eighteen," he said into the phone. The guard didn't take his eyes off of Billy. "I think he's tellin' the truth." He leaned back, and hung up the receiver. "All right, kid, you're cleared to go in, but I have to take you."

Billy scrunched his shoulders. "Okay by me."

"Good thing." The guard grabbed Billy gently by the shoulder and guided him toward the entrance. "If it turns out you lied to me and I get in trouble, I'll come lookin' for you and tan your hide, you hear me?"

"I'm eighteen."

"I guess I have to believe you."

"I guess you do." Billy let the man push him forward. He had no other place to go.

He sat in a small room that was empty except for a simple wood table and two chairs. Three of the walls were painted a stark white. No pictures hung on any of the walls. The other wall was made of iron bars. It had a door with a lock on it. No one could get in or out unless they had a key.

The guard had left him there. It had been twenty minutes, maybe longer. It felt like he had been sitting in the room forever. There was no sound, at least that was definable, and there was no movement to the air. Everything was stale and stiff.

A bare light bulb burned over the table, and more lights lit the hallway outside of the cell. The hallway was like a tunnel full of twists and turns. Billy wasn't sure he could find his way if he got free. The thought brought on a sudden burst of panic to his whole body like he had never felt before.

A pair of footsteps approached, drawing Billy's attention away from his fears. He looked over his shoulder as Lady Red and a stubby, gray-haired prison matron rounded the corner.

The guard was nowhere to be seen, replaced by a woman. She wore no gun on her hip, only a billy club and a ring full of keys. Both of them stopped outside the door. Billy stood slowly as the matron unlocked the door.

Time had been unkind to Lady Red. She hardly looked like herself, or the self that Billy remembered. She had stood tall, her hair vibrant red, glossy and shiny in the sun, and she'd had a curvy shape, accenting her beauty with tight skirts and blouses. Now she looked haggard, worn down, a shell of her former self. She was hunched over and it looked like it hurt to move. Her hair was faded; red had turned to orange, mixed with gray. The skin on her arms and face was wrinkled, and she was plump, her body covered by a simple dress that looked like it was a potato sack.

Lady Red walked into the cell without any change of expression on her face. She didn't look happy or sad to see Billy. She looked asleep, only her eyes were wide open.

"Fifteen minutes," the matron said, then closed the door and locked it.

"Sit down, Billy," Lady Red said. "You don't expect me to give you a hug, do you?"

Billy stood motionless, and watched as the matron went back to the corner in the hall and took her perch.

"No, I guess I don't," Billy said.

They both sat down at the same time. Lady Red had her back to the cell door. "How'd you find me?"

"I ran into Sonny Burton in Houston. He told me you were here."

"Figures. That Ranger never did us any favors."

Billy leaned in, and whispered. "I can get you out of here."

Lady Red didn't move, or moderate her voice. "Why would I want that?"

"What do you mean? It's my fault you're here. You didn't kill that man." It was still a whisper.

Billy's mother twisted her lips, then rolled her tongue with more effort than it should have taken. It was a trick she had when she was trying to restrain herself. "Don't you ever say that again."

"But it's the truth."

She leaned in and matched his whisper. "Look, you little shit, I don't want out of here. For the first time in my life I can count on the same roof stayin' over my head, and three squares a day hittin' the bottom of my stomach. I don't have to lay on my back to make a livin' and I don't have to worry about what's happened to you. You look like you can take of yourself. You don't need me. Besides, what are you thinking, that you could trade me places?"

"I'll bust you out."

Lady Red leaned back and laughed, drawing the matron's attention. "Quiet down in there," she said.

Lady Red ignored her. "You're joking."

"No, I can do it. I need time to figure it out."

"There's more men here with guns than you've ever seen. Besides, like I said, I don't want to leave. Don't you understand that?"

"No. Why wouldn't you want to be free with me?"

"Didn't you hear a word I said?"

"Yes. It's easy here. But you're locked up."

"I don't have to be a whore here. You wouldn't understand that. How much a relief that is. You don't know what it's like for your own mother to sell you out to strangers for their pleasure. No. And let me tell you why, because I wouldn't let her. Miss Tillie would have sold you for a dollar if she could have got away with it. I had no choice, but you do. You need to get out of here, and leave me alone."

"You can't mean that," Billy said.

Lady Red leaned in again. "Listen to me. I don't want you here. I don't want to ever see you again. You're free of me. You understand? Free. I killed that man. I'll swear to it until the day I die. You need to leave." Lady Red stood, walked to the door, and yelled to the matron. "I need to go."

Billy didn't know what to do. He knew if he ran to his mother, she would most likely knock him to the floor. There was no arguing with her. There never had been. She'd made up her mind. She didn't want to be free. She didn't want to be with him. All she wanted was to be left alone. He didn't matter to her.

His body quaked and before he could do anything to stop them, tears rolled down his cheeks.

"Get me out of here, now," Lady Red yelled. "Now!"

The matron hurried to the lock and opened the door. Lady Red fled like the place was on fire.

Billy turned to watch her leave, her back to him, running away like he didn't exist. Like he had never existed.

October 1934
Huntsville, Texas

Billy coasted the stolen Ford coupe to a silent stop. He looked over to Moses Calley, and said, "You need to do exactly as I tell you."

"This best pay off like you say it will. I done been inside a jail cell before, and I ain't got no desire to go back any time soon."

"You any good with a gun?"

"I been eatin' squirrel and rabbit for the best part of my life. What you think?"

Billy reached under the seat, pulled out a .45, and handed it to Moses. "You any good with that one?"

Moses took the gun, examining it like he was familiar with it. "If I have to be."

Billy leaned down and pulled out another gun like the one he'd handed Moses.

"Where'd you get these guns?" Moses said.

"You don't need to worry about that. I need you as backup. Anything happens to me you need to hightail it back to Dolly, and get her as far away from here as you can."

Moses looked around, out into the darkness. "There ain't nothin' here. No bank, no gas station. Jus' houses on this street."

"I told you that you don't need to worry about why we're here. The less you know, the better off you are."

"Something tells me you're right about that. What do you need me to do?" Moses loaded a round into the chamber, then looked to Billy to tell him what to do next.

CHAPTER TWENTY-EIGHT

May 1918

Cantigny, France

The sky was black with smoke, and the ground was covered with more blood than Sonny had ever seen. Rain fell from low clouds in a dreary mist that hung a few feet off the ground. Mud sucked at the heels of his boots, pulling him back, holding him in place for longer than it should have, either in warning or curse. All of the color had been drained from the world. Every direction you looked it was the same, tainted with gray and white like out-of-focus newspaper print. Even the streams of blood looked like they'd been made of glass, reflecting the black sky.

Blurry vision made the remains of the battlefield look otherworldly from inside Sonny's gas mask. The interior stank, too, of the bitterness of Sonny's own breath, filtering the latest German attack, the latest battle he had somehow survived. He could hardly stand, hardly put one foot in front of the other. His knees were weak and his stomach was empty. Only fear and duty kept him from collapsing.

His platoon had been separated, caught in a cross fire, then pinned down and gassed relentlessly until both German sectors of the attack had been wiped out by Allied Forces. The battle had lasted through the night, twelve hours from sunset to sunrise. If a new day was present, it was hard to tell. Day and night were no different. Time was measured in breaths, not seconds or minutes. Both armies had created a darkness that the sun could not penetrate and the wind could not blow away. Black skies seemed to be a permanent tattoo on Sonny's eyes.

He followed the thin line of men, less than twenty soldiers, all with their tin-pan hats securely on their heads, and their gas masks properly strapped across their faces. The mask amplified breathing and made it almost impossible to hear clearly. Orders were distributed by hand signal, from one soldier to the next. No one had issued a halt command. He feared getting stranded in the valley of death, the black and gray world battered and bruised, cordoned off by barbed wire and cross boards to deter tanks and the rush of a brigade, screaming for a fight. Just because one battle had been won, didn't mean another wasn't waiting over the horizon.

To his left, Sonny could see the smoldering village, and to his right, the remainder of what was once an Allied camp. Shredded canvas tents flapped in the wind. Once white, now covered in soot and ash, not one tent stood fully erect. Most leaned with the threat of immediate collapse, like everything else in sight. Beyond the tents was one of the most heartbreaking things Sonny had seen since arriving in the war zone: A corral of horses, shot where they stood, tied to the hitch ropes with no way to escape. The ones that survived the gunfire had suffered a worse death. They had endured the burning asphyxiation of repeated gas attacks. There was no burying the beasts. They would be left to the elements of nature; flies, foxes, or whatever predator would venture into the field once the humans had made their way past. Square in the middle of the field among at least a hundred dead horses, Sonny spied a soldier kneeling over the body of a dead horse. It might've been a roan mare, or a black gelding, it was impossible to tell. But there was no mistaking the posture of mourning. The soldier had lost more than his mount. He had lost a friend.

Sonny breathed in and out in a deep hiss and looked away, leaving the man to his grief, while Sonny marched away from his own, or toward it, he wasn't sure. If he'd never been aware that death could come before joining the army, he knew it now. He took nothing for granted. Not even the ground he stood on.

October 1934
Huntsville, Texas

A dim light cast soft shadows across the wallpapered staircase. The radio played in the kitchen; distant, soft notes that floated effortlessly through the house. Night had turned toward midnight; darkness blanketed the boardinghouse. Windows were still open to let the October air circulate inside the house. Crickets chirped back and forth, adding to the natural rhythm of the night, joining the orchestra with the courage to belong. Sonny and Edith stood at the bottom of the stairs, both hesitant to make their way upward.

"You've made me forget a long, horrible day. I thank you for that," Sonny said.

"I'm happy I could do that for you." Edith's voice was low. She stood so close to Sonny that he could smell her skin and hear her breathe in and out of her nose. He didn't want to move. "You needed to relax a little," she added.

"That's never been easy for me."

"I can tell."

Sonny looked away from her, up the stairs. The house was put together for the coming of night, with the exception of the radio playing.

Edith reached out and took Sonny's hand into hers. "The night doesn't have to end. At least if you don't want it to."

Sonny flushed, tempted to pull his hand away but he didn't. The warmth of her touch was a salve to a wound he didn't know was still open. He couldn't comprehend what she was saying, what she was implying. Words and thoughts jumbled into a stew of emotions that had no name; the recipe long forgotten. Sonny thought the human part of his life was over with, dead, cut off with his arm. He'd lived a solitary life since Martha had died.

When Sonny didn't reply, Edith let her hand slip from his. "Unless, you'd rather not. I understand," she said.

"It's not about want. It's been so long that I wouldn't know how to make this night go on."

"You danced with me, Sonny Burton. We can leave the radio on and keep dancing. There are some nights in a man's life that he shouldn't spend alone. I think this is one of those nights for you. And, to be honest, it's not like I'm a regular dancer myself. Regardless of living in a house full of men, I want you to know I've never allowed the company of myself to any of my boarders. Never considered it, not once. Not until now. Not until you walked in the door and I looked into those soft blue eyes of yours, and watched you with your dog. I knew you were different. I knew you were a whole man, no matter what my eyes saw, no matter what you thought about yourself."

Sonny stood looking at Edith and he knew she'd meant every word she'd said. He exhaled again, took her hand into his, then turned and headed up the stairs, slowly, one at a time, making sure she was still in his tow, that she hadn't changed her mind.

He stopped at the door to his room, and looked at her questioningly. Edith's face remained soft and expressionless. She had made up her mind long before the trip up the stairs had been made. That's what the determination in her eyes said to Sonny. He didn't say anything, else. He opened the door, stood back, and let her in his room—if that's what she wanted.

Edith walked into the middle of the room, and stopped. She looked around with a pleased smile on her face. Sonny was neat about his life. The bed was made. His clothes were hung in the closet and put away in the single dresser. The room looked like it had when Sonny first walked in the door.

"Are you just going to stand there?" Edith said.

Sonny stood at the door with his entire focus on her. "For a minute. Maybe longer."

"Working up your nerve?" She said in jest, sweetly. Sonny understood what she meant right away.

"Listening to the song that's playing, trying to catch the beat."

"You are." Edith grinned, then looked away. The light from the hall caught her strong jawbone, the reflection of diamonds flickered in her eyes.

Sonny walked into the room and closed the door behind him. His whole body tingled. He thought he could feel his right arm, his hand, but it was wishful thinking, phantom pains. All of his nerves were on fire and his body remembered that it had been whole once upon a time.

The music seemed farther away, softened by the closed door, but Sonny could still hear it; the steady beat competed with the sound of his racing heart.

"Would you like to dance a little more?" he said.

"I thought you'd never ask."

There was nothing but fear to hold him back. Desire and curiosity pushed him forward into Edith's waiting arms. They picked up where they had left off, only there was no invisible wall of decency between their bodies. Sonny allowed himself to press against Edith, and she in turn, did not pull away. She swayed with him, matched his moves so they meshed into one. It had been a long time since Sonny had held a woman close, but he had not forgotten everything, had not lost the need to want and feel wanted—but he was still uncomfortable with the aim of his hook, fearing it would nick or scratch Edith.

Sonny dared to look into Edith's eyes. She was staring at him, her face comfortably angled toward his, waiting. She had done enough. The next move was his. He didn't hesitate any longer. It was now or never. Stop and ask her to leave his room, or move forward, and take whatever risk lay before him. He leaned in and kissed Edith, tentatively at first, the taste of her lips as unknown to him as a fine meal at an expensive hotel. She responded by kissing him back as slowly, matching the uptick of desire with Sonny's.

Only the lamppost outside offered any light into the bedroom, but that didn't matter. Sonny's eyes were closed, and all he saw were the heavens full of stars and moons. When he parted from Edith and opened his eyes, he was shocked that she was still standing before him, that what had happened was real instead of a dream.

She pulled away from him—gently, with the promise that she wasn't going far. Sonny didn't take his eyes off her. The smell of her soap, sweet and clean, lingered between them. In a move that looked more like a dance than anything else, Edith loosened her dress, wiggled slightly, and willed the garment to drop to the floor. All that was left between her and nakedness was a thin shift that cut across her knee.

Sonny froze, his eyes glued to Edith's, as she stepped forward. She said nothing as she reached out to the top button of his shirt. He reached for her hand. "No," he said.

Edith did as she was asked to and stopped. "You've changed your mind?"

"No one other than you has ever seen me without my arm, without this," he said, raising the prosthesis to his right, piloting the hook as far away from Edith as possible.

She didn't move. His hand still dominated hers. "I'm standing here because of the kind of man that you are. Not the man that you were, or the man that *you* think you are. I don't know how to make that any clearer to you, Sonny Burton. Do you want me to leave?"

He sighed deeply. "No, I want you to stay." His eyes were glassy, filled with an emotion he didn't know how to name.

Before she did anything else, Edith leaned in and kissed Sonny with more passion than before. He responded in kind, but he remained aware of everything that was happening; he was now sitting on the edge of the bed and Edith stood over him. He could smell her, taste her, see all of her through the shift when he opened his eyes. The beauty of her body did not betray her age. She looked twenty years younger than she was.

Edith pulled away slowly, then resumed unbuttoning Sonny's shirt. He assisted the best he could, sitting back, moving his left arm to make it easier for her to fully remove the garment. With the skill of a nurse, Edith eased the shirt from Sonny's skin, leaving him bare, the straps and mechanics of the prosthesis fully exposed. The expression on her face did not change. There was no sign of disgust, no repulsion, no emotion at all. She studied the fake arm and hook, then moved forward, easing the top buckle apart, the puzzle of its operation quickly solved.

Sonny's first instinct was to stop her again, to put his hand on hers. But he knew better, sure that the act would send her packing. He didn't want that. "I can do that," he whispered.

"I'd like to do it, if you don't mind." She was on to the second buckle, easing her way through the contraption with as much gentleness and lack of prejudice as was humanly possible. "These straps have rubbed your skin raw. Does it hurt?" Edith said, loosening the last one.

"I'm used to it. I have a salve the vet in Wellington gave me to use."

"You should see a proper doctor."

"I'm fine."

The prosthesis was completely in Edith's grasp. She said

nothing else as she eased it off of Sonny's body. She placed the arm on the dresser like it was nothing more than a plate being put where it belonged.

A puff of cool night air pushed in the open second-floor window. The thin cotton curtains reached out, then fell back again with little effort. Sonny shivered. He felt cold, exposed, vulnerable. He didn't dare look at his stump. He wanted to pretend the ugly thing wasn't there.

Edith glided back to Sonny and stopped before him. Without saying another word, she lifted the shift over her head and let it fall to the floor.

Sonny gasped at the sight of her, forgot that he was naked from the waist up, but felt a stir of life from within his body that was ancient and foreign to him. He stood, following an unknown demand, then slid his left arm under Edith's, palmed her waist, and pulled her forward to him. "I didn't know I was looking for you, but I sure am happy I found you." Then they kissed deeply, both on a journey together that promised to last all through the night.

CHAPTER TWENTY-NINE

October 1934
Huntsville, Texas

Billy edged alongside the house, easing each step to the ground, trying his best not to make any noise at all. The sky was cloudy, blotting out the moon and stars. A steady breeze pushed in from the west, bringing with it the promise of rain. Luckily, the ground was dry, not pliable. Leaves still held onto their limbs, death and decay certain in their future. The long summer drought, partnered with Billy's desire not to be heard, not to be seen, allowed him the silence of a thief, even though that was not his intent. He wore dark clothes, along with a black skull cap and gloves. One hand held a .45, cocked and loaded, while the other was empty, used to feel his way against the house. In case the gun wasn't enough, he had strapped a knife to his ankle, hidden by his thick work boot. He always carried at least two weapons. His fists counted as a third, but they had always been his weakest weapon. Fast legs had saved him far more times than his fists had.

Moses Calley trailed behind Billy by ten feet. He carried the .45 that Billy had given him in the car, the barrel pointed upward, his finger comfortably on the trigger. There was a comfort in the way Moses carried the gun that gave Billy some much needed confidence. This was an information collecting expedition. He wasn't going to blind-test any man in anything more than that. He needed to know how Moses handled himself first.

Billy stopped every few feet to make sure Moses was all right, and that he wasn't making any noticeable noise. Billy envied Moses's black skin, the ability to fade into the darkness. Only the whites of his eyes shone. Moses was dressed like Billy, in clothes that favored the night.

They had gone over a few hand signals, up was go, down was stop, the same ones that Jim Rome had taught Billy. There was no way to tell Moses where they were or why they were there. The less Moses knew, the better off he was. That way he wouldn't have to lie if they got caught. Billy wasn't sure how good a liar Moses was. Billy liked Moses. He liked having a partner, someone to ride with him, to help him plan. The more pregnant Dolly got, the less she was interested in Billy's plans. The drop was coming soon. He'd need Moses then. Fortune had smiled on him by putting Moses in that cabin. It was the kind of luck Billy had needed to smile on him when it did.

Billy stopped at the corner of a window, then motioned for Moses to do the same. They both froze, letting their feet settle on the hard ground. The breeze pushed past Billy, fluttering the curtains of the window, allowing a dim ray of light to pierce the darkness. Soft music murmured inside. Low voices. A man and woman. Billy peered inside cautiously, and caught a glimpse of the prey he was after: Sonny Burton. He almost let his gaze linger too long. Burton glanced out the window, looking away from the woman he was standing with, dancing with. Billy couldn't look away. The sight of the two of them together, holding each other in a proper waltz, her with her fingers wrapped into Burton's hook, was an unexpected find. Another bit of luck.

Billy came away from the window, then motioned for Moses to go back to the car. Slowly. Quietly. Moses motioned that he understood, then turned and made his way along the opposite side of the house. Billy didn't follow right away. He wanted one last look.

A quick glance was all he needed. If he stayed longer there was a chance Burton would detect his presence, and that's the last thing he wanted. He wasn't there for a confrontation. Not now. Not yet.

He made his way back to the car, and eased inside it as slowly as he had sneaked alongside the house.

Moses was waiting for him, sitting in the passenger's seat. "What was that all about?"

Billy didn't answer. He started the car, put it in reverse, and backed up into the closest alley. He headed out of town, eyeing the rearview every other second to make sure he wasn't being followed, that they hadn't been seen.

"You gonna answer me, or not?" Moses said.

"Making sure everything is where it's supposed to be."

"What's that mean?"

"The cops brought in the Rangers to find me. One of them is staying in that house."

"Jesus Christ, man, are you crazy? What you thinkin' messin' around with a Ranger like that?"

"We got a history. Besides, he's not a Ranger anymore."

"Is he a Ranger or ain't he?"

"Once a Ranger, always a Ranger." Billy kept his eyes forward, except when he was looking at the rearview mirror.

"Okay, then, what you mean you got a history?"

"Our paths have crossed on and off since I was a kid. They brought him in because he knows me. They think he can help them figure out what I'm going to do next. He's put me behind bars more than once."

"You knows him, too."

Billy chuckled. "I thought I did."

"So?"

"I don't know, something's changed. Burton put me in Huntsville. He missed seein' Dolly by a minute when he caught me. Then he went and got himself shot by Bonnie Parker."

"Bonnie and Clyde? That Bonnie Parker?"

"One and the same. She got a shot off that took his right arm from him. I thought that was the end of him. The Rangers put him out to pasture, replaced him with his son, whose head is thick as a brick. He's here, too, by the way. The son. He's fully abled, at least physically, helping his pa keep the locals calm."

"So they is two Rangers here? Christ, why didn't you tell me that 'fore now? I woulda gone the other way."

"You still can." Billy took his eyes off the road and glared at Moses with as much hate and anger as he could muster. "I mean now. You ain't on this ride with me, Rangers or not, you can get out now, you hear?"

"I ain't jumpin' out of no movin' car. 'Sides, I ain't got no other place to go but where I'm at. I jus' wished you'd a told me about two Rangers is all. They put the fear of Jesus in me."

Billy relaxed and turned his attention back to the road. "I told you, there's nothing to worry about. I needed to make sure Burton was where he was supposed to be."

"How'd you know he was there?"

"A guard, Clayton Randalls, told me a few guards stayed at this boardinghouse, and it's the place the warden sends visitors to when they come in from out of town. Randalls was right. Burton was there, but I sure didn't expect to see him dancing with the woman who runs the place."

December 1918
Austin, Texas
A burst of cold air had pushed down out of the north. Most of

the businesses in Austin were closed, and the majority of the citizenship had retreated inside their houses, doing their best to keep warm. Billy, on the other hand, had other plans.

The skies were gray, overcast, as daylight tilted toward darkness. The night would be thicker, almost impenetrable if there weren't moontowers to contend with. Electricity had come to Austin in the 1890s when the Colorado River had been dammed up to power the cotton mills. Moontowers stood a little over two hundred feet tall and were decked out with twenty arc lights that burned all night, casting a swath of bright light down onto the ground. Thirty-one towers stood tall, peppered throughout Austin, and unfortunately, a moontower stood adjacent to the building that Billy wanted to gain entry into. It didn't matter if the night was overcast or not; the moontower stood sentry.

Luckily the weather cooperated with Billy's plans by driving people inside. Cold weather was unusual this far south in Texas; there were times when a freezing rain would deposit a sheet of ice on everything in its path, or an inch of snow would fall every ten years, giving hope to the children of the city for a white Christmas. This push of cold air couldn't have come at a better time. Billy was getting desperate. Pickpocketing and shoplifting in Austin hadn't been near as profitable as he had needed it to be.

Billy stood on the corner of Congress Avenue, shivering, his coat thin as a newly sheared sheep, his hands stuffed inside his pockets, biding his time. He was perched inside an alleyway, within running distance to one of his hidey-holes—which he would have rather been waiting in, but then he wouldn't have been able to see the Wells Fargo lights go dim.

A few men braved the renovated boardwalk. Hitching posts were a thing of the past. Parking places were defined by marks where the horses once stood in waiting; mechanical beasts named Ford and Chevrolet that were less reliable in the cold weather than the warm-blooded beasts they'd replaced. The wind blew out every man's long coat like it was untethered to anything of strength. Hats rolled down the street like tumbleweeds, and an air of loneliness hung over the city, like some kind of epidemic had befallen the weak and the vulnerable.

Billy's migration north had been slow and methodical. A boy of sixteen on his own drew little attention, wasn't too uncommon, but Billy's curse was that he looked younger than he really was. He was thin, boyish in his looks, and lacked facial hair of any kind. His skin was as smooth as a baby's. He had learned not to draw attention to himself and could survive long stretches at a time by stealing one thing or another. When that strategy became too difficult or risky, Billy often found work in a mechanic's shop. His aptitude for engines, power systems, and locks allowed him to talk in a language, and show a skill, that very few boys, or men, possessed. But staying in one place too long became a hindrance to any long-term security. Something set him on the path to flee; a raised eye from a shopkeeper, a sheriff closing in, that bad feeling in his stomach that had predicted hurricanes and hangings. He had been in Austin for six months.

One man walked out of the Wells Fargo office not long before another walked in. The sky turned grayer, and time ticked off another hour, leaving Billy nearly frozen. His teeth chattered as the lights in the office dimmed. It was the sign he'd been waiting for: The guard was settling in for a long night. Almost in unison, black smoke started to stream steadily from the red brick chimney above the back room. The guard had refreshed the coal furnace.

Billy stalked the shadows that fell over the building, doing his best not to look like anything was the matter. He made his way across the street, fished a hairpin out of the inside of his coat, then proceeded to poke and roll the tumblers inside the simple lock on the front door of the Wells Fargo office. It never ceased to amaze him that a place that maintained a trove of valuables would leave themselves open to thoughtless intrusion. At least it was for him.

The lock popped and Billy eased the door open as silently as possible. His bet was the guard was comfortable in front of the fire, warming himself from his hourly rounds. The man, a thin, mustached man who wore a look of perpetual boredom on his face, worked the evening shift, and was as predictable as a clock—which had been his downfall, or would be his downfall. Routines and patterns were easy to spot for someone with an eye like Billy's.

Three teller cages greeted Billy. But he knew what to expect. He had posed as a customer more than once, standing in line, then changing his mind at the last minute about a nonexistent transaction, leaving the building without issue—or notice.

This was as big a job as he had ever pulled off. One, to be honest, that begged for another hand or two, but there hadn't been anyone who had presented themselves that looked up to the task. He hadn't been in Austin long enough to find anyone else of his sort.

Billy walked softly, as stealthily as possible, to the back of the office. A door led to more unseen offices, along with another door that led down into the basement where the furnace burned and the guard passed most of his time. One floor creak would alert the guard to his presence. Being thin in build had its advantages.

He made it to the basement door without being detected. It was locked. Something unexpected, but not something that would turn him back. Billy saw the obstacle as a challenge, not something that would stop him. He examined the lock, all the while listening for any sound that would send him fleeing. There was nothing but the silence of an empty building. It was almost a certainty that the guard was sleeping.

He took out the hairpin and wiggled it in the lock.

"You need to stop right there," a man's voice said from behind him.

Billy started, hadn't heard anything, hadn't been concerned about someone being upstairs. He was convinced the guard was in the basement.

"Now," the man said, "you need to drop that pin on the floor and stand up as slow as you can. In case you're wondering, I got a barrel trained on the back of your head, so don't go getting any bright ideas about running."

Billy exhaled in defeat. He had no idea how to escape the situation he found himself in. He hadn't planned for being caught from behind. He wouldn't make that mistake again.

He did as he was told, dropped the pin, and stood slowly.

"Turn around," the man said.

Billy did, moving slowly, looking for an escape as he went. Once he was completely turned, Billy found himself face to face with a man he had never seen before. It wasn't the guard. This man wore a sheriff's badge.

Defeat and capture became more definite. Billy lowered his head.

"You want to tell me why you're in here, boy?"

"I was lookin' for a place to stay warm."

"Ain't no one ever told you that it is stupid to lie to a man who has a gun trained on you?"

"No, I can't say they have."

"Well, take my advice."

"I will."

"Do I have to ask you again?"

"I got locked in and I was tryin' to find my way out."

The sheriff, a medium-sized man with a bushy black goatee,

shook his head. "I know who you are, Billy Bunson, had my eye on you for weeks. More than one shopkeeper has brought your existence to my attention. You've been skirting the law for a while, but it looks like your luck has run out."

"Looks like." Billy heard footsteps climbing the stairs from the basement. The commotion and voices had obviously provoked the guard to come and investigate.

"You are lucky, though," the sheriff said.

"How's that?"

"Well, if I would have caught you in possession of stolen goods you would have been in a lot more trouble than you are right now. As it stands, it looks like you're gonna face a charge for breaking and entering. About six months behind bars by my count, depending on the judge's mood and discretion, considering your age. Let me guess, you're an orphan. Your folks aren't around?"

"You could say that."

"That might present you with some luck, too," the sheriff said, as the guard opened the door, wearing a curious look on his face.

No matter which way Billy turned, there was no way out. His heart sunk. He was caught, was going to jail. The one place he feared more than anything else. Even water.

October 1934
Huntsville, Texas

Billy stopped the car once he was outside of Huntsville and covered the headlights with burlap bags. He attached two smaller bags on the taillights. Leaving his fate to chance was a calculation he didn't care for. There were only a few more things to put in place before the payoff came, and he could hit the road again, leave Huntsville, and Texas for that matter, behind him once and for all.

Once he settled into the driver's seat and drove off, Moses said, "So the first time you went to jail was in Austin."

"I was a kid."

"Me, too. I didn't do nothin', though, the first time I got throwed in. I was walkin' down the street and a man ran out of a shop and says I stole money from the till. 'Fore I knew it, I was surrounded by white folk jeering at me like I was a dog. Sheriff comes along, frisks me, and pulls a wad of money out of my pocket—or acts like it—and shows it to the crowd. Three years later I walked out from behind the bars. I was fifteen then, with nowheres to go, and no one to take me in."

"What did you do?"

"Same thing you did. What I had to."

Billy exhaled heavily. "I was only supposed to be in for six months for the theft, but I was there for seven years. Only reason I got out then was 'cause of my age when I was sentenced. They could only keep me for so many months for the theft."

"What in tarnation did you do?"

"Killed a man. Don't say I regret it, either." Billy focused his eyes straight ahead, eyeing the edge of the road the best he could with the dimmed light he had to use, then glanced over to Moses. "You were a kid like me, even younger. I wasn't lettin' anyone take me. You understand?"

"More than I'd like to admit."

Billy returned his attention to the road. "No one messed with me after that. Man had it comin' to him. He had it comin' to him."

"He did, boss, he sure did," Moses said, then let his words drop off. He stared out into the darkness, watching the world go by as Billy drove, and didn't say another word until they were back at the cabin.

CHAPTER THIRTY

October 1934
Huntsville, Texas

"Where are we heading?" Jesse said.

Sonny didn't answer. He sat staring at the house with a wistful look on his face. Jesse's question sounded like a short mumble. Even though Sonny's body was in the car, his heart and mind were somewhere else; lost in wonder. Was the night real or a fantasy?

Jesse had his hands resting on the steering wheel of the new model Plymouth. He wore a curious look on his face. "You all right, Pa?"

Sonny stirred toward him, like he had been woken from a dream. "Yes, what did you say?"

"You all right?"

"I'm fine," Sonny said. He didn't want to leave the house. He didn't want to face the bright sunshine of the day, and the uncertainty of what lay before him. All he wanted to do was go back inside, grab Edith, and climbed back inside her arms. He had forgotten the comforts of being with a woman, of laying with someone who cared about you. He feared if he drove off with Jesse he would die, never to return.

"You don't seem like it."

"I'm fine. Now, what did you say before you asked me how I was?"

"Where are we headed?"

Sonny cocked his head sideways. "I'm in charge?"

"Not officially. But if I say we're going left, you're gonna say go right. I'm not stupid. I know how this works. We've been in this car together more in the last few days than we have in the last few years. More than that if I was being honest. You walk into a room, and I'm there, you're in charge, Pa. Doesn't matter how old I am, or what I've done on my own, that's the way it's been and the way it will always be."

Sonny didn't respond. He studied Jesse's face for a long second. "Your mother held her jaw like that when she was standing her ground with me. Happened a lot, you know."

"I know. Standing between the two of you was like playing dodgeball."

"It was." Sonny sighed, turned his attention back to the house for a long second, then faced Jesse again. "You got any fresh ideas today?"

"If I was here by myself, I'd put a tail on Jeb Rickart, stay far enough away that he doesn't see 'im. If we can't figure out where Billy Bunson is, I think Jeb will lead us to him if we stay out of the way. He wants his wife back in the worst way, and he's the kind of man that's in charge of everything around him. He won't let us work that ransom drop. He'll want to do it himself."

"You're right. That's why the drop hasn't happened yet, at least Jeb hasn't let anyone know when and where. We've been too close. The sheriff, too. You're right, Jesse. I think Jeb will lead us to Billy. I've thought that all along, which is why I never told him more than I had to. We should tail him."

Jesse grabbed the steering wheel a little tighter. It would have taken a magnifying glass to see the smile roll across his face, but it was there. Sonny saw it, knew to look for it.

"I brought a map in case we need it. It's in the glove box," Jesse said.

"Okay, then."

Jesse started the car, put it in gear, and pulled away from the curb. Sonny watched the boardinghouse fall from sight, craning his neck to catch one last glimpse of it before it completely disappeared.

"You sure you're all right?" Jesse said.

"I'm fine. More than fine, really."

"That's a surprise."

"It is to me, too, Jesse. It is to me, too."

They parked outside the prison entrance, shoveled in between two black Fords. There was no reason to believe that Jeb would recognize Jesse's car. The warden hadn't seen it as far as Sonny knew. The Plymouth had no markings on it to announce that it belonged to a Texas Ranger. It wasn't a normal police car. No bubble on top, no spotlight anchored on the driver-side door. The car was a normal, everyday car, like the clothes Jesse wore. Rangers didn't wear uniforms or badges unless they wanted to, though most of them wore white Stetsons. Sonny had traded his Ranger hat for a brown felt Stetson. The new hat didn't wear right, but he had worn a white Stetson for more years than he could count. It needed to be broken in.

They both rolled down the windows at the same time, and Jesse dug into his breast pocket for a hand-rolled Bugler. Sonny watched him orchestrate lighting the cigarette, felt a tinge of envy that a mindless task was so easy for his son, then stopped the emotion dead in its tracks. He wouldn't wish losing an arm on anyone, or harbor jealousy toward those that were whole in body. It wasn't right. But he knew why the feeling existed, why it showed itself. Sonny suddenly held a strong desire to be normal, regardless of what Edith had said, of the kindness she had showed him. If only . . .

He took his attention away from Jesse and focused on the

entrance to the prison. "It'd be easier if we had someone on the inside. Someone to let us know what Jeb's up to."

"His secretary seems pretty loyal. What about that guard that showed you around?" Jesse drew in on the cigarette, then exhaled out the window.

"Randalls? He makes me uneasy. He's a talker. My guess is, we approach him in any way, it'll work its way back to Jeb, at least if it would put Randalls in a good light."

"Those are the only two I can think of."

"We'll wait it out for a while."

Jesse tapped the ash off the end of the cigarette onto the street. "And hope that Billy lays low."

"If the drop is next, then he will."

"And if it's not?"

"Then I hate to think what he might do. No telling, to be honest. Billy Bunson doesn't respect the sanctity of any life. Not even his own."

"You sure about that?"

Sonny turned his attention back to Jesse. At first, he was annoyed, but he let that feeling slip away. He was curious what Jesse was thinking. "Why do you ask?"

"Seems to me that Billy has gone to a lot of trouble to stay close. If he was concerned about his own hide, he would have sped out of Texas faster than a twister in spring. Jeb's payoff might be big, but Billy's had bigger payoffs that sent him on the run."

"I can see that."

"Think of the risk he took silencing that Donna Del Rey girl. He sneaked into the sheriff's department, murdered her, hung her like a piece of meat, then waltzed out of there without alerting one person to his presence. Now, granted," Jesse said, aiming the Bugler to his mouth, "he's got the skills and know-how to pull off such a thing, but he didn't have to take that risk to get the payoff from Jeb." Jesse took a drag then, and waited for Sonny to respond.

Sonny considered Jesse's point, and found it valid. "If that girl would have lived, she would have told us where Billy's hideouts were. She would have confessed to giving him the finger from the funeral home, that she participated in that ruse. He couldn't afford that."

"He could have survived her telling the world her story," Jesse said. "He felt like he had to silence her. He had something to protect."

"Dolly?"

"Maybe more than that."

"The baby?"

"Could be that the idea of a child never occurred to Billy, that he never thought he could have one. Maybe there's a side of Billy Bunson nobody knows."

"We're still speculating that Billy's the father of Dolly's baby."

"If I'm a bettin' man, I'd slide all of my chips to that side of the table. Randalls said the two of them had alone time when she was teaching him to read, and there's Billy's ability to come and go with the keys he made."

"That could be part of it."

"You're not convinced?"

"No, I guess I'm not." Sonny turned away from Jesse and looked back to the entrance as a car pulled out. Jeb Rickart was driving. It looked like he was alone. "There's our man. You ready?"

Jesse tossed the cigarette out the window. "Yeah, I'm ready." He started the car in the same orchestrated move as he had when he lit the Bugler.

"Give him some space, but keep him in sight."

"I got this, Pa. It's not the first time I've tailed somebody."

"I guess I can't help myself," Sonny said.

"I guess you can't," Jesse answered as he eased the Plymouth out of the parking spot and crept down the street, keeping a couple of car lengths between them and Jeb Rickart.

Late July 1918
In transit to Amiens, France

The Allied forces had started to push toward the German border. Sonny and his battalion had been freed from the trenches and were on the move north. There were rumors that Turkey and Austria-Hungary were about to fall, that an armistice with each of them was near, that the alliance between the Central Powers was about to collapse. A win felt close, but no one said anything. It had been nearly a year of fighting hard battles; push forward, fall back. The toll of war could be seen on every man's face as they marched forward, including Sonny's. He had lost over forty pounds. His uniform was loose, and his skin felt the same. Rations were sparse, and a bowl of decent food was a dream. A pot of Martha's sauerkraut, even as he endured warfare with the Germans, would have been a welcome meal.

They had marched all morning. One foot in front of the other. It was hard to ignore the silence all around him. The soldier next to him, a fella named Darren Beechler from Delaware, wore a pasty look on his face; his blue eyes were faded and his skin, pushed up by his skinny jowl, was loose like Sonny's. They all looked like skeletons walking above ground, carrying rifles, unsure that the life before them was real.

There was no one to the right of Sonny. He anchored the corner of the squad due to his height and ability to keep step—even when his feet felt like they weighed a hundred pounds apiece. Beechler was a hair shorter and faced the same struggle lifting his boots. Same with the two men on the other side of

Beechler, men named Morton and Smith. One was from out east somewhere, the other from California. Deep in the night, all the men had to talk about was where they were from, their girls back home, and how much they missed their old lives. During the day, they marched forward, leading fifty men from one battle into another. Lieutenant Joe Mason headed up the squad, set ten feet ahead. His march was no Virginia Military Institute march. It was tired and haggard like the rest of the men.

The gray fog of the morning had lifted, and the way to the Amiens Front was starting to clear. Summer in Northern France felt a lot like life in the panhandle of Texas to Sonny; muggy, oppressive, the heat unrelenting. He felt like he had bathed in sweat.

"This feels like Texas," Sonny muttered, breaking the silence of voices. The cadence of boots was about to drive him mad.

Beechler's head snapped back like he had been woken up from a nap. "You ain't never been east in the summer have you, Burton?"

"No, I cannot say I have." Sonny looked away from the man, and took in the landscape around them. They were in a treeless section of the road, and the openness made him nervous. There were times he disagreed with Lieutenant Mason's decisions, but had learned not to confront the man's authority publicly or in private. Mason wore his VMI training like a royal wore a title, held it above everyone's head like a medallion forged of privileged gold. It didn't matter that Sonny had been riding with the Texas Rangers while Mason was still in diapers; he was only a sergeant. The frustrations of his lack of ambition, of never taking the lead, being fully in charge, came to roost in the worst possible moments; life and death moments that offered the opportunity to rebel—or not.

"You all right, Burton?" Beechler said.

"Worried about our route, that's all." The words were slightly above a whisper.

Beechler agreed silently. They both focused on Mason, who was leading the squad completely unaware of what was going on behind him. The lieutenant often wore a look that bordered between dazed and confused.

The road eased to the crest of a mild hill. Two fallow fields occupied both sides of the road. A farmhouse sat off to the right, the sun beating down on its white cladding, exposing open windows and broken rafters. Not much else remained of the roof. Black swaths arched upward out of the windows, marring the house with the scar of fire and smoke. A barn had stood behind the house, but it was nothing more than a crumbled heap of charred timbers. There was no smell of ash in the air, so the fire must have burned some time ago. No humans or animals were to be seen around the farm.

The left side of the road was more desolate than the right. A wide vista disappeared at the flat horizon. The closest trees looked to be two miles away, maybe farther. Sonny relaxed a little bit, calculated the possibility of ambush as low—but he still didn't like where they were; how exposed they were.

Mosquitoes and no-see-ums swarmed in and around the squad, shifting head-sized clouds, dotted black like flying grains of pepper; a murmuration of small, distant starlings. Beechler swatted the swarm away, sending it spiraling. "Worse than sand flies. You got sand flies in Texas, Burton?"

"Down on the coast. I never spent much time there. I've been in El Paso, Austin, and north in the panhandle for a time. Others places, passing through. I 'spect I've ridden across half of Texas. Probably seen more rattlesnakes than sand flies."

"I'll take the sand flies. I guess I was lucky to live close to the shore, spent many a day as a boy fishing on the beach, then along the Indian River. What I'd give for a taste of my mother's chowder. I'd sure take some of that weather back, too, the cool breeze off the ocean, the salt in the air. I didn't know how much it meant to me until I came here."

One foot in front of the other. They marched up the hill. Men behind Sonny struggled. He could hear their breathing change, become heavier. The packs on their backs were full and replenished for the move north.

"We all feel that way. I'm sure Mason misses his mother, too," Sonny said.

Beechler chuckled under his breath. "I'm sure he does. If he has one."

Sonny was about to laugh, but a sudden sound caught his attention: a faraway crack that could not be mistaken as anything other than gunfire. He looked to Beechler in time to see his cheek wobble with the physics of motion and force. A bullet pierced Beechler's flesh, disappeared, then exploded out the other side before Sonny could blink. A wide-eyed recognition of pain crossed Beechler's face, then he collapsed to the ground. The rest of the men followed. All of them, except Lieutenant Mason. He stopped and turned around to see what had happened.

Sonny screamed, "Get down!" But it was too late. Another crack, followed by another, cut through the air.

Mason's head exploded under his helmet; a mass of flesh and blood, falling to the ground in a surprise collapse, like Beechler.

Sonny didn't attempt to save either man. That was too risky. He had to save himself, and the rest of the men. "Take cover," he yelled, scurrying to the opposite side of the road. He rolled into a shallow ditch, deep enough to give him cover from the sniper—who he speculated was in the burned-out house. "Take cover!"

I'm not a praying man, he thought to himself, *but a time like this might force a man to reconsider praying to a god, the God, whoever, to end this damned war.*

Sonny had seen enough death to last him a lifetime.

CHAPTER THIRTY-ONE

October 1934

Point Blank, Texas

Billy untied a boat from the pier that stood behind the house, holding onto the rope tighter than a man normally would. He feared falling into the water, being pulled under by the river's current. Over the years, he had still never learned how to swim.

The boat was a typical riverboat; flat-bottomed, squared bow, two bench seats, with a three horsepower, two-stroke outboard Evinrude motor bolted onto the stern. Billy knew more about automobiles than boat motors, but the contraption was simple in its construction and operation. It had only taken him a few hours to get the motor in tip-top running shape.

He eased into the boat, stepping carefully so he didn't rock it too much. Once his footing was steady—the water was smooth, not wavy—he crawled to the back bench, and sat down. The boat slipped away from the shore without any effort and caught the current right away. He drifted out into the middle of the Trinity River before starting the motor. The river ran slow in the autumn, but it was fast enough to put Billy fifty feet from shore before he knew it. And he was heading south, instead of north, the direction he intended to go.

This was a test run. One last check to make sure he had everything in place before the drop was made. Moses and Dolly were in the cabin with chores of their own. Time was running out. They all had to be ready for what was next.

Billy tilted the propeller shaft into the water, squeezed the primer bulb, advanced the throttle, released the choke, then gave the starter cord a good yank. The perfectly tuned motor caught right away and purred to life, spitting out a puff of blue smoke as it revved. Relieved, he took control of the tiller, gunned the motor, and spun the bow of the boat around to face north. He sped off without looking back, certain of his destination.

He hugged the shoreline as close as he could. The water was clear because of the lack of rain, which had offered Billy another piece of luck. He could see rocks and logs well enough to avoid them, but he had to be careful not to get too close to the shallows. If he got stuck or hit something hard, the propeller would be in danger of breaking—and without that Billy would be left to float, or use the oars in the boat, to get to shore. He would be a sitting duck for anyone with good aim if he lost control of the motor during a chase.

He had learned this part of the river as well as he could, but rivers changed constantly. One day a log was there, then gone the next. Still he was getting more comfortable with the escape route he'd chosen—if he needed to use it. He hoped using the boat would be his last choice. But Sonny Burton knew his fear of water, and the river would be the least of the Ranger's concerns. That was Billy's hope anyway.

He motored along the shore, getting farther and farther away from the cabin. He carried the .45 with him in case he needed it. He'd learned a long time ago to carry a gun wherever he went. Once everything else was in its place, he planned on arming the boat with a couple of shotguns, a rifle, and enough ammunition to see him out of any confrontation.

It didn't take long to reach his destination. He pulled the boat into a cove south of Onalaska, another small river town. He had already stolen a car, a '29 Model A Ford sedan, and hidden it in a blackberry thicket. The leaves had yet to fall to the ground, and the vines covered the Ford completely, like a garage built by Mother Nature herself.

Billy wanted to make sure the Ford hadn't been discovered, then he'd load it with some more supplies; food, medicine, bandages, simple things him and Dolly might need after they got away. The plan was for Moses to head in the opposite direction if they got separated. They would split up and meet in Austin. At least, that's what Billy had told Moses, but in truth, he had no intention of meeting Moses again. Moses was on his own. Billy knew it was a risk double-crossing the man, but it was a chance he was willing to take. If Moses got caught and ratted out their plans, then Billy and Dolly could walk right into a trap. That wasn't going to happen. They weren't going anywhere near Austin.

Billy clambered onto the shore with a gunny sack full of supplies over his back, climbed through a weedy patch, and found the Model A right where he'd left it. It looked undisturbed. He quickly loaded the supplies in the back seat, recovered the car with the vines he'd disturbed, and turned to head back to the boat.

"Well, well, what do we have here?"

Billy found himself face to face with a portly man who held a shotgun, aimed squarely at his head. He stopped, and froze in place. The .45 was stuffed in the small of his back. He raised his hands into the air slowly without being told. The empty gunny sack flittered to the ground like an autumn leaf. "Ain't no concern of yours, mister. You always go around pointing guns at people?"

The white man's eyes narrowed. His clothes looked like he wore them every day, his face was unshaven, and his feet were bare of any shoes. "I do if they's someone on my land who ain't supposed to be there."

"I didn't see no signs."

"Best not get too lippy with me, boy. Ain't no one ever told you to be nice to a man with a gun?"

"Truth is I have been told that, so I guess you could call me a slow learner."

"You ain't from around here, are you, boy?"

"Does that matter?"

"Folks don't like strangers lurkin' about."

Billy stepped forward. "I won't be here long."

The man flicked the barrel end of the shotgun. "You best stop right there."

Billy did as he was told. "I don't mean no one any harm. If you let me gather my things, I'll be on my way."

"You ain't goin' anywheres." The man squinted again, examining Billy's face closer. "You look familiar. Kind of like that new picture the sheriff hung at the post office. You ain't got any trouble with the law, do you, boy?"

A shiver ran down Billy's spine. Anger and fear woke deep inside of his being. He had to contain himself, look for a way out. He took a deep breath, and spied the ground at the man's feet for something, anything he could use to defend himself.

"You better answer me, boy." The man moved his thick finger toward the trigger.

Time was slipping away. This wasn't supposed to happen. He wasn't supposed to get caught like this. An image of Dolly waiting on him as the police surrounded the cabin flashed through Billy's mind. He couldn't stand the thought of her getting caught, of her going to jail, any more than he could ever consider going back inside himself. The image and the fear urged him on. Billy lunged at the man, covering six feet in one swoop, fully prepared to be sawed in half by close-range buckshot.

The move surprised the man. He didn't react, didn't pull the trigger. By the time he would have got to it, both men were a bundle of flesh, wrestling to the ground. The shotgun went flying. It landed out of both men's reach.

As the attacker, Billy had the upper hand. It didn't hurt that he was younger, more spry than the portly man. Billy also had more motivation. Survival was life or death for him. In the scramble and twist of arms and legs, Billy fought off an attempt by the man to bite him, and sought out something to end the struggle once and for all.

He had spied a fist-sized rock before he jumped, and reached for it with some struggle. It only took a second to grip the rock, to get a hold of it, but once it was fully in his grasp, Billy smashed the rock against the side of the man's head. It sounded like he had kicked a pumpkin. Blood exploded immediately. The man was stunned, eyes wide open, garbling his words, groaning. His hairy arms went limp.

Billy hit him in the head again. And again. And then again. Until the man stopped moving, until the life left him, and the world all around Billy was covered in blood. It looked like the entire thicket had turned red with anger and rage.

December 1925
Austin, Texas
Billy walked out of the jail with two dollars in his pocket and nowhere to go. The world had changed a lot in seven years. The automobiles were different. There were streetlights everywhere. Buildings looked taller. Even the sun appeared to be brighter than it ever had been.

There was no point in being an aimless stargazer. Billy had one thing on his mind, and that was getting out of Austin as soon as he could. The only way he knew how to do that was to hop a train.

He made his way to the stockyards as quickly as possible. He took in everything around him like it was the first time he had been free in the world. Being locked up had changed him, made him skittish. Loud noises made him jump. He was suspicious of every person who walked toward him on the street. No one was to be trusted. He had no friends. Nowhere to flop. Not that he would have anyway. He feared falling into a trap, of making a mistake that would get him thrown back in jail on the day he got out. He couldn't stand the thought of it. Life behind bars wasn't for him. He swore to all that was right in his world that he would never go back. Never ever. No matter what.

It didn't take him long to find the stockyards, and even a shorter time to find a train with an open boxcar, heading north. He jumped inside as the train started to move, certain to avoid any bulls on the lookout for hobos.

Billy steadied himself once he was inside, and was surprised and disappointed that he wasn't alone. Another man sat on a hay bale, leaning back on the far wall, chewing on what looked to be a piece of dried wheat. The man paid Billy no mind. He was older, ragged, but fit. He wore a blue short-sleeved work shirt, denim pants, and heavy black boots. His arms were muscular, veins riding on top of the skin, pushed upward from the muscle because they had nowhere else to go. His hair was black, streaked with gray, and his equine face was a field of stubble.

Billy made his way to the other end of the boxcar. The noise of metal wheels against metal rails intensified as the train gained speed. It was a constant thunder that threatened to drown out every thought in Billy's mind. He was busy looking for an escape route if the bulls came after him on a stop. Or if the stranger across the way threatened him. The loud sound of motion unnerved him.

He sat down directly across from the other rider.

"Next stop is Waco. Best hide in the bales, when we slow,"

the man hollered out. "Cops got a bad sense of themselves. Easy ridin' after that, but the same kind of men patrol in Dallas."

Billy didn't acknowledge the instructions. He stared at the man, trying his best to look like a mad dog, even though he really looked younger than he was, like a kid lost in the world with nowhere to go.

April 1932
Little Rock, Arkansas

Billy had bounced around from one place to another before landing in Little Rock. He liked cities. Knew them the best. Could fade into the shadows easier than out on a sharecropper's farm. Pickpocketing was easier work than hoeing a cotton field for pennies on the day, if that. A drought had taken hold, along with all of the other woes in the world, and there was little to farm the way it was.

Some days Billy wandered the sidewalks, planning a heist that never materialized. He still feared being caught and sent back to jail. Small jobs, petty theft, was his choice these days.

The coming of spring did offer him some hope. Leaves had burst onto the trees, offering a healthy dose of shade on sunny days. But more importantly, people were outside, moving around more. Opportunity waited in traffic of all kinds.

Billy was following after a man wearing a new black bowler. When he passed the library a ray of sunshine caught his eye. The light beamed through a copse of tall oak trees, spotlighting the front steps of the newly built Carnegie-funded building. It was not the architecture of carved stone lions that caught his eye. It was the woman standing at the top of the steps that brought him to a stop.

She was dressed in a yellow dress that hugged her body, and fell below the knees. The dress didn't look new, but like the woman, it looked cared for. A closer look might reveal some mending, but Billy could not see any from where he stood. Her shoes were the same, worn, but cared for. No one these days could afford much of anything that was store-bought, and took care of what they had. She wore her chestnut brown hair, long. It flowed over her shoulders and matched her eyes. As the woman placed a placard in its holder, she looked and saw Billy staring at her. She smiled.

"Come on," she said, motioning him to join her.

He looked away from her, to the sign. It said: LEARN TO READ.

Of course, he already knew how to read. Had learned early, as a boy, at the feet of Jim Rome. The Negro was proud of his reading skill, and insisted on passing it on to Billy so he wouldn't ever be on the receiving end of a bad deal. "If you can read anythings," Jim had said, "then you can spot a thief and a liar long befores any man that can't read. Harder to swindle you if you can read the writing on the wall."

The woman mistook Billy's lack of interest for fear. "There's nothing to be afraid of," she said. "Why don't you come and talk to me?"

Billy couldn't resist. A quick look down the sidewalk told him that the man in the bowler was long gone anyway. He made his way up the stairs and stopped before the woman. She smiled at him again. He couldn't remember the last time he'd seen anything so pretty. He blushed and looked away.

"You know how to read?" the woman said.

"No," Billy lied.

"We're giving lessons at night. Seven to be exact."

"You the teacher?"

"No, I help, though."

"How long does it take?"

"To learn?"

"The time. At night?"

"Oh, an hour, once a week."

"And you'll be here every week?"

"I will be as long as the creek doesn't rise."

"Not much chance of that lately."

"I suppose not."

Billy looked to the ground, then back to the woman. "Well, I guess it wouldn't hurt to learn something new."

The woman smiled again. "Good. Reading opens up the world."

"I've heard that." He turned to go, then stopped. "What's your name?"

The question seemed to surprise the woman. "Dolly. Dolly Smith. And yours?"

"Billy."

"Billy?"

"For now. Just Billy."

"Okay, Just Billy, I'll look forward to seeing you this evening."

"I can't wait, Dolly Smith. I can't wait."

CHAPTER THIRTY-TWO

June 1919

Vinton, Texas

An unexpected knock at the door startled Sonny out of a shallow sleep. For a second, he didn't know where he was. That had happened a lot since he'd come back from France. Real or imagined noises startled him awake. Some nights he hardly slept a wink, and some days he could barely stay awake. He gripped the chair with both hands, sizing up what was what. Was the knock a bomb in his memory, or a knock at the door?

Martha stood at the kitchen sink, a paring knife in one hand, a potato in the other. "You gonna sit there all day?"

Sonny pushed the sound of a gunshot from his mind as best he could. The lighting in the house was dim. Curtains were pulled tight; a gathering of blankets hung over the windows to keep the sun and heat at bay. The sun had been conquered, but there was no escaping the heat. The house was sweltering. Even the walls sweated.

He stood, and hitched his pants. He hadn't put on much weight since his return from the war, even though Martha had taken it as her sole duty to put some meat back on his bones. He couldn't tell her that the taste and smell of German food sickened him. It reminded him of the men he'd killed, and the men who had killed his friends. Everything reminded him of the war. It was as pervasive as the summer heat in South Texas.

The knock came again. He should have expected it, but he

didn't. Sonny startled again. He glanced to the shotgun that stood sentry next to the door, making sure it was still there, that it was handy if he needed it. He had no idea where Jesse was.

"Who is it?" Sonny said through the door.

A garbled answer came back. "Calbert Dobbs. Captain Hughes wants to see you."

Sonny opened the door slowly. He could have kept quiet, acted like he wasn't there, but he wouldn't do that to Dobbs. "I see you made it back alive." He stepped outside, closed the door behind him, and offered Dobbs his hand.

Dobbs shook Sonny's hand like an old friend would. The two of them had ridden a lot of miles together, covered each other's backs more than once. Dobbs was the closest friend Sonny had in the Rangers. He was a good sergeant, too.

"You look like hell, Burton," Dobbs said.

Dobbs was a little shorter than Sonny and wore his seriousness on his shoulders. He stood erect, straight as an arrow. A good wind would have snapped him in half. The man had no give in his stance or attitude at all.

"I do. What's Hughes want?" Sonny said.

"You know what he wants."

"I'm not ready to ride again."

"From the looks of you that's exactly what you need to do. Get outside, breathe some good air, and break that thousand-yard stare."

"Says you."

"I was there. I know what you saw. Not every man came back shell-shocked, but a good amount of them did. I was there to see the slaughter," Dobbs said. His voice was calm and steady. Both of his hands were jammed in his pockets, and he wore an understanding look on his normally tense face. "I can't tell you what to do, Burton, but if you don't ride into the future with me, you're gonna die sooner rather than later. What good is it to your wife, to your boy, if you sit here and wither away?"

Sonny stiffened, didn't like being told what to do, but he respected Dobbs, hadn't held one bit of a grudge against the man when the captain had demoted him from sergeant in El Paso, and given the job to Dobbs. Besides, Dobbs was better in the lead than he was. No one ever said so, but Dobbs held an ambition to be captain one day. It was obvious to everyone, even Sonny—who had no interest in climbing the ranks.

"That your car?" Sonny said, nodding to the black Model T parked in front of the house.

"Our horse-riding days are over with."

"They are. I was gone a little over a year and the whole world seems to have changed overnight."

"What are you going to do if you don't go back to bein' a Ranger again, Burton? It's the only thing you know. And, you're good at it. You got a legacy to protect. Now, I can't force you to clean yourself up and take yourself in to see the captain first thing in the morning, but I'll be happy to come drive you in."

"And if I don't?"

"I don't expect the captain will ask again. There's only so many spots he can hold, and yours is one of them. This ain't the first time he's called you in."

"But it'll be the last."

"I believe so," Dobbs said.

"All right, I'll think about it."

"I'd urge you to do more than that. Should I come by in the morning or not? I don't want to waste my time, either."

Sonny sighed, looking past Dobbs to the Model T again. "You know I prefer horses."

"We all do, but that's not the world we live in anymore, is it?"

"No," Sonny said, "it's not."

October 1934
Huntsville, Texas

Jesse parked the car half a block from the First National Bank. Sonny didn't take his eyes off of Jeb Rickart's car, a beige Chevrolet, the same one, it looked like, that sat in the picture of Jeb and Dolly that Sonny had spied in the warden's office.

Neither man said a word. Both of them watched Jeb get out of his car, cross the street carefully, then disappear into the bank. Nobody else would have questioned why a man of Jeb's stature would be visiting a bank first thing in the morning, but Sonny did, and Jesse, too.

"Looks like you were right," Sonny said.

"I was hoping I wasn't. We need to stay on him. He's going alone on this one, hasn't called the sheriff, or us, to give us the details of the drop."

"My guess is Billy told him not to in the drop instructions. We didn't see that note. And, Jeb still thinks the finger belongs to Dolly, still thinks she's a hostage."

"I don't know how he can believe that," Jesse said.

"Love makes you see things differently, especially when you've given up on it."

Jesse turned his attention from the bank. "You really think that's what this is about? That Jeb is so blind that he can't see he's being duped?"

"Man like him doesn't want to see that. He loves Dolly. He's sure of it, like he was sure that it was her finger that Billy sent him. He can't believe she would betray him. He would lose everything he believes in, everything he's worked for."

"But you believe she has betrayed him."

"I do. You know I do. I've questioned her from the start."

Jesse was about to pull a rolled Bugler from his pocket, but restrained himself. He nodded toward the bank, and grabbed the steering wheel with both hands. "That didn't take long."

Sonny followed Jesse's gaze, and carefully surveyed Jeb as he made his way back to the Chevrolet. The warden didn't carry anything, and nothing looked to be tucked in his pockets; no envelopes sticking out, nothing to see that would suggest he was carrying a large amount of money. Jeb got into the car like he normally would.

Sonny cocked his eye, and furrowed his brow.

"What's the matter?" Jesse said as he started the engine.

"Something's not right. Why would he leave the bank with no money?"

"Because he's betting on being watched?"

The engine started running and Jesse brought it to a steady idle. He had his eye on Jeb's car, which still hadn't moved.

Sonny scratched his head. "You might be right. Don't follow him."

"What? Are you crazy? We'll lose him."

"Maybe. Maybe not. You said you brought a map, where's it at?"

"He's pulling away, Pa."

"If you follow him, he'll spook. He needs to go where he's going."

"And get there without us."

"Where'd you say the map was?"

Jesse exhaled, frustrated. The tips of his ears burned red. "In the glove box."

Sonny opened the door to the small compartment, grabbed the map, and tossed it to Jesse. "Open it."

Jesse looked at Sonny, incredulous.

"You got two hands," Sonny said. "Maps aren't made for one-armed men."

Before Jesse opened the map, he looked down the street. Sonny did, too. Jeb Rickart was long gone.

"Now what?" Jesse said, with the map open.

"Look at Huntsville, then over to Bedias."

"Okay, it's pretty much a straight line."

"Show me."

Jesse angled the paper map so Sonny could see what he saw. He took his finger, calculating the distance from Huntsville to Bedias. "Billy's plans were never too complicated. He thought he was being smart, but there was a pattern." His finger stopped on Point Blank. "It's a simple pattern. If he ran south, he'd double back, and escape north. Same with east, he'd end up hiding in a hole somewhere west. I think he wanted us to look in Bedias, but he's really hiding out in a place called Point Blank. We haven't been there, have we?"

"Why would we? It's a little spot in the road along the Trinity River."

"Well," Sonny said, "How hard do you think it'll be to spot a Chevrolet like Jeb Rickart's?"

"Might stick out."

"That's what I'm thinking," Sonny said. "If we hurry, we might make it in time to stop ol' Jeb from making the biggest mistake he's ever made."

The Trinity River sat on the eastern edge of Point Blank. Along with the expected shacks and lean-tos occupied by people who depended on the waterway to sustain them, a beige 1934 Chevrolet sedan sat idling in the middle of the dry dirt road. Jeb Rickart was a long way from home, a long way from his routine and expectations.

Jesse pulled his car off the road as soon as he saw Jeb and angled it behind a grove of cottonwoods. There was enough cover for them to keep an eye on the Chevrolet.

"We got lucky," Jesse said.

"We did." He looked over his shoulder to the guns in the back seat, then pulled out his Colt Army and made sure it was fully loaded with cartridges.

Jesse followed suit, then said, "What do you think he's waiting on?"

A beat-up Model T truck passed behind them on the same road Jeb sat on. The truck was going too fast to get a look at the driver, but Sonny was pretty sure it was a black man behind the steering wheel.

"A ride," Sonny said.

They both watched as the truck stopped behind the Chevrolet.

Sonny's stump itched. It seemed to do that at the worst possible time, when there was trouble about. He ignored the itch the best he could, and kept an eye on Jeb's car.

It didn't take long for Jeb to get out of the Chevrolet. He looked around, surveying everything in sight. Sonny and Jesse instinctively ducked down, then inched upward to keep watch.

Satisfied, Jeb walked to the trunk of the car, opened it, grabbed a brown satchel, then hurried to the truck and got in.

"Looks like he stopped at another bank after we let him get away," Sonny said.

"The first one was a decoy."

"Part of Billy's plan to make sure Jeb wasn't being followed."

"It was a good plan."

The truck pulled away and headed down the road. Jesse looked to Sonny. "What now?"

"You best follow him. That truck's going to disappear real quick, and he's going to take away any hope we got of catching Billy Bunson along with it."

CHAPTER THIRTY-THREE

October 1934

Huntsville, Texas

Jeb Rickart got out of the truck, looked over his shoulder, and hurried to the porch of a dilapidated river shack. He carried a small brown satchel close to his chest, cradling it like it held a king's ransom. The ransom was most likely for a queen; his queen, Dolly.

The truck sat idling until Jeb reached the door, then drove off slowly, leaving the warden alone to face whatever waited behind the door of the shack. Sonny assumed it was Billy and Dolly waiting on the drop, but when it came to Billy Bunson, Sonny had learned a long time ago not to assume anything. There could be no one inside. Billy could be anywhere, watching, looking out for cops—which if that were the case, then Sonny and Jesse had been spotted as soon as they'd driven up. There was no way to know, but to make sure, Sonny did a slow scan of the area. He didn't see a thing out of place. Billy was patient as a snake—he wouldn't show himself until he had the full advantage of his plan.

Jeb knocked on the door three times and waited, tapping his right foot to the beat of some unseen drummer. The door opened straight away, and Jeb disappeared inside. He was out of sight, out of the line of fire, with no way to protect himself, which is the last thing Sonny had been hoping for. Jeb Rickart had no idea what he was walking into, making a deal with the devil, without any backup, but Sonny did. He feared for Jeb's life.

Seeing the warden make his move, Jesse put the Plymouth in gear, but Sonny put his left hand on his son's forearm. A Remington 12-gauge shotgun, loaded and ready to go, sat across his lap. "Wait. Don't go yet. They need to make the handoff, then Billy's going to try and escape out the back door, there." He pointed to the shack. Jesse looked to where Sonny was pointing. "Once that happens, we'll go after him. At this point, waiting is the only option we have. If we go in shooting, we all could die. Besides, Billy's got a plan for that."

"It'd be easier if the sheriff was in on this."

"There wasn't time. Jeb struck out on his own. He doesn't know the risk he's taking."

"I could have stopped at a phone booth along the way."

"Too late for coulda, woulda, shouldas. Besides, we got this handled, Jesse," Sonny said. "You and me. That's the way you wanted it, right?"

Jesse looked dumbfounded, like he didn't know what to say. "I've wanted to ride with you since I was old enough to understand that when you left, you wouldn't be coming back home for a long time."

Sonny didn't take his eyes off the cabin. "It was my job, the only job I was ever good at."

"I know that now, but I didn't know it then. I wanted to be with you even though you seemed annoyed by my presence when you were around. I thought you were leaving because of me."

Sonny lowered his head for a second, then looked back to the cabin, afraid he was going to miss something. Maybe this wasn't the best time to rehash the past, but he'd opened the can. There was no closing it now. Jesse had things to say, so he might as well say them. "How could you think such a thing?"

"You never seemed to like me much."

"I figured you liked being with your mother more than me," Sonny said.

Jesse shifted in his seat, easing his grip off the steering wheel. "Why in the hell would you think something like that? I was a kid. I had no choice."

"Neither did I."

"How was I to understand that bein' a Ranger was a life, not a job? I had to have two daughters of my own before it hit me square between the eyes that you were doing what you had to do. That didn't mean you liked it all of the time."

"I loved it," Sonny said. "That was the problem. I got itchy if I was home too long. I was in your mother's way. I dirtied too many things that needed to be cleaned. I was extra work for her."

"I knew your marriage was difficult. I wish it wouldn't have been that way."

Sonny closed his eyes. Memories of Martha flashed in his mind, playing on the dark side of his eyelids like a newsreel he didn't care to see; her standing at the sink cleaning, sweeping the floor, grumbling about the work she had to do. And then the image switched to the present, to dancing with Edith. That sight forced his eyes open. "Me and your mother liked each other once upon a time, Jesse. I don't ever want you to think otherwise. We were oil and water is all. Life didn't work out for her the way she wanted it to. She would have been thrilled if I aimed to take the captain's seat."

"But you never wanted that."

"No, I didn't. I guess I liked someone else to take the heat when the shit hit the fan. I don't play politics well."

Jesse turned his attention back to the shack. "Jeb's been in there a little while."

"Starting to make me a little nervous, too. We might have let him walk into a trap he might not be able to walk out of on his own. Let's give it another minute or so. If Billy doesn't show his cards, then we need to go in after the warden."

"I agree."

Nothing looked out of place. The sky was calm, trees didn't sway or flutter, and birds went about their business without the fear of human presence. A blue jay perched on top of a tall pine across from the shack, while a small flock of sparrows pecked at the gravel alongside the road. If anything would have been out of place, the birds would have lit into the air or showed nervousness of some kind.

"I'm glad you decided to be a Ranger, Jesse," Sonny said. "It's not an easy life. Well, maybe a little easier these days sitting in this comfortable Plymouth instead of on the back of a horse. It's a job you can be proud of."

"The mode of travel might of changed," Jesse answered, "but there are still plenty of bad people out in the world. Maybe more so now, than before."

"You might be right about that." Sonny stopped, took in what he was seeing in the distance, then said. "Our wait's over."

Billy Bunson eased out of the back door of the shack. The sight of him nearly stopped Sonny's heart. The boy was a man now, starting to show wear and tear from the hard life he'd lived. His jaw was hard-set, and even from where Sonny sat, he could see Billy's eyes were as black as a crow's wing. He was almost unrecognizable. Almost. But there was no mistaking his gait, his cocky step, his arrogant lips, his skilled and battered hands.

Twenty-five years of memories of his own life made Sonny look briefly away. He had arrested Billy Bunson more times than he could count with the hope that it would be the last, but it never was. When Sonny'd lost his arm, he thought he'd never have to deal with Billy again, but now he was nearly face to face with the one black mark left on his name. Sonny hadn't realized how bad he'd wanted redemption until he saw Billy creep out of the shack, and make a run for freedom—one more time.

"Let's go," Sonny said. "Let's go, before he gets away. He's probably got a boat on the river, but he won't go there. It's a decoy. There's a getaway car somewhere else. The one thing Billy's afraid of is the water. Let's go!"

Jesse did as he was told, punched the accelerator of the car, and headed straight for the shack.

Billy was left with no option but to run behind the shack. Sonny smiled at the sight, proud of himself for outwitting his foil one more time. He felt a tingle of excitement that he hadn't felt in a long time. He nearly forgot that his right hand and arm were made out of a dead tree. He felt alive, almost like time hadn't passed at all. He felt like he was in El Paso, in Austin, in all of the places he'd chased Billy Bunson down. It was like time had given him a second chance to do something right that he'd failed at so many times before.

There was nowhere for Billy Bunson to run to. No woods to hide in, the river was no longer an option, and the rest of the shacks along the river looked to be occupied by people who wouldn't take too kindly to a visitor of Billy's kind, especially if he brought the law with him.

Jesse was gaining on Billy, was within twenty-five yards of him. Sonny lifted the shotgun with his left hand and the hook, then jabbed it out the open passenger window, resting the barrel forward on the sill to steady the sight. The car bounced so hard it was difficult to get a good aim on Billy once he put his finger on the trigger.

Fifteen yards out, a black car jumped out from alongside one of the river shacks. The appearance of the Ford caught Jesse by surprise, but not Sonny. Jesse slammed on the brakes and spun the wheel hard to the left to avoid a collision, but they were too close. Jesse's car slid sideways and clipped the fender of the black Model A, sending it spinning in the opposite direction.

Jesse did his best to keep the Plymouth under control. The crash happened so fast that it had caught them both unprepared for the impact, but not so unprepared that Sonny didn't see who was driving the car. It was a blond woman. The same woman he'd seen in the happy black and white picture in the warden's office. It was Dolly Rickart, the warden's wife, set on running off with Billy, set on making the biggest mistake of her life. There was no sign of Jeb, and that worried Sonny—but there was nothing he could do to save Jeb.

Dolly's car spun wildly from the collision and slid into a boulder, causing it to bounce off the road. The car careened down the riverbank, and plowed into the water. Sounds of metal against metal, a racing heartbeat, and splashing water competed for Sonny's attention. Fear of the unknown swept across him; even though he should have feared for his own safety, he didn't. He feared for Dolly's life more than his own.

After spinning around, Jesse was able to bring his Plymouth to a stop, facing the opposite direction. "You all right, Pa?"

"I'm fine," Sonny said. "You better go get her out of that car. She'll drown. There's a baby to consider. Now go."

Jesse was halfway out of the car before Sonny's words vanished into the air. It took Sonny longer to move. The collision had jostled his insides and loosened his prosthesis. He had to get his breath and swallow his pride. The tingle of victory had vanished into a familiar pile of doubt and regret.

He watched Jesse jump into the water, open the car door, and pull the woman out as gently as he could. Dolly was limp, unconscious. Blood ran down the side of her forehead, but her right hand quivered with life. She wasn't dead, hopefully stunned, knocked out from the impact.

Sonny looked away, down the road, all around him. Billy

Bunson was fifty yards down the road, running as fast as he could, sprinting like an Olympian runner. In the time it took Sonny to shake off being stunned, the truck that had picked up Jeb Rickart appeared from a lane ahead of Billy.

The truck stopped and Billy jumped in it as Sonny scooted behind the steering wheel, jammed the Plymouth in gear, turned the car around, and punched the accelerator. Gravel jumped into the air and fell to the ground in the shape of a rooster tail.

Obviously fearing for his life, Billy ran faster than Sonny thought a man should be able to.

Sonny grabbed the shotgun, stuck the butt under his left arm for leverage, leaned as far as he could out the window, and steered the Plymouth the best he could with his hook and left knee. When he got within range, he pulled one of the two triggers. The glass in the back of the truck's cab exploded; the truck Billy and his getaway driver were in swerved to the right, back to the left, and back to the right again, slowing as it moved forward. Sonny was sure he'd hit the driver, but he couldn't see Billy.

The older Model A truck was no match for Jesse's Plymouth. It was an eight cylinder against a four, David against Goliath when it came to motors; Sonny had the advantage, but he needed to finish the job. He pulled the other trigger of the double barrel, hitting his target straight on.

Confidence pulsed through Sonny's good arm as he guided the car toward the rear of the truck. He planned on ramming it since the shotgun was of no use to him at the moment. Until Billy popped up, leveled a 30/30 rifle on the tailgate, and shot straight at Sonny.

Sonny ducked to the side as the glass shattered into a spiderweb of cracks. A hole punched through the center of the windshield, three inches from Sonny's head. Wind from the car's speed pushed at the weakened glass, causing it to collapse inside the Plymouth. Another shot came as Sonny swerved, doing his best to make himself less of a target. He couldn't stop and reload, so Billy had the upper hand now. At least when Bonnie Parker had shot at Sonny, he'd been able to return fire, but it wasn't that that brought an end to their chase—it was a bridge that was out, a stroke of bad luck that Clyde Barrow had not counted on. Sonny suspected he'd meet no such luck this time around. Besides, the encounter with Bonnie and Clyde had left Sonny without a right arm. He hadn't been that lucky.

With no other choice, Sonny slammed on the brakes of the Plymouth, aimed it to the right, and brought the car to a screeching stop behind one of the massive live oaks that lined the road. The sudden stop jerked the shotgun from under his arm, and it went tumbling to the ground.

The Model A truck sped off down the road with Billy still settled in the bed, firing off one round after another as they went.

CHAPTER THIRTY-FOUR

October 1934

Point Blank, Texas

Once Billy saw Sonny Burton's car slam on the brakes, he dropped down into the truck bed, crawled to the front, and shouted to Moses, "Get us out of here!"

"I'm going as fast as I can."

Dust kicked up behind the truck, obscuring Billy's vision as they sped away. He couldn't see what happened to Dolly. All he knew was that she rammed Burton's car, and landed in the river. The thought of her being hurt enraged him. He had to know what happened to her. This was the part of the plan that he didn't like, being separated from Dolly. Anything could happen . . . but if it worked out, then the two of them would be free as birds for the rest of their lives. That had been the plan from the beginning, from the second he'd entered the Hunstville Prison. Trick Jeb. Fake a kidnapping. Ransom the money. Kill Jeb, then make a run for Canada. It had sounded simple, and the truth was, busting out of prison had been easier than he thought it would be. Dolly had played Jeb Rickart like a violin. Deceiving the desperate old man took a lot less effort than Billy thought it would. He had to turn his head, force the thought out of his mind about Dolly climbing into the warden's bed. That was the price of freedom, and all of it was worth the risk—at least it was when the words had come out of his mouth. Things had gotten off track. If there was one thing worse than one Ranger, it was two.

"Go left at the fork," Billy yelled. "You go right, and we'll end up in Onalaska." He didn't have to say anything else. Moses knew what had happened in Onalaska. Billy had returned to the shack covered in blood after resupplying gas and food in the car. He had no choice but to tell Moses and Dolly what he'd done, that he'd had no choice but to put the dead man in the boat and set it adrift. He'd driven the car back to the shack then, and reconfigured his plan for Dolly to escape. With two vehicles, Billy knew Sonny Burton would chase after the truck if he was in it.

Jeb had sworn that he hadn't gone to the sheriff, that he hadn't been followed, that he'd done everything that Billy had asked. But Billy knew Burton wouldn't give up, especially after Jeb had told him that Burton had tailed him to the first bank. Billy knew then that time was short. That Burton was close by. *Poor Jeb,* he thought as he looked down at his bloody hands. *Poor Jeb.* That part of the plan was over, had gone like he knew it would. Desperate men die easy.

"Where we going?" Moses yelled out the cab of the truck.

"Don't you worry about it. Drive." Billy crawled back to the tailgate, and peered through the roiling dust. Like he'd suspected, Burton had put himself back on the road, and was speeding toward the truck. There was no way the truck was going to outrun the newer model Plymouth Burton was driving. Billy was amazed the man could drive so well with his wood arm. One thing was for sure, the man still had the same stubborn streak he'd always had. Sonny Burton didn't give up, that was for sure.

Billy reloaded the rifle, checked his .45, and made sure two other shotguns were close by. He was going to need every cartridge and shell he could get ahold of to put the final touch on Burton. He needed to kill the Ranger, put an end to him and his meddling so he could be free of him once and for all.

The plan was to meet Dolly in Little Rock if they got separated. From there, they were going to find their way across the border somewhere in Minnesota, somewhere where the forest was thick. Billy didn't know exactly how he was going to do that, but he was confident he'd figure it out once he had Canada in his sights.

The Plymouth gained on the truck, was easily in range of the rifle, but Billy held back, didn't fire. He wanted to see what Burton's plan was. The Ranger had to know Billy was armed to go to war, that he was driving straight into a firing squad.

It was a moment of hesitation that Billy would come to regret.

Somehow, Sonny Burton had managed to steady a shotgun, pull the trigger, and drive at the same time, all with one good hand and one metal hook.

The glass in the back of the truck's cab shattered, sending pointed shards flying everywhere, but mostly forward. Moses yelped, then the truck slid to the right, back to the left, and back to the right again, losing speed as it went.

Burton didn't stop with one shot. He let loose with another one, peppering the truck with bullet holes as he gained on it. The shot barely missed Billy. He was afraid to move, but he knew he had to do something. He couldn't lay there and wait to die. In addition to being shot at, the truck was slowing, still weaving out of control, and Billy feared they would hit something any second.

He grabbed the .45. It held six cartridges in the magazine, and one in the chamber. He tossed the 30/30 rifle to the side, and grabbed one of the shotguns. It was a double-barrel, giving him nine chances in all to take out Sonny Burton. Without another thought, Billy sucked in a deep breath, peered over the tailgate, eyed his target, and started shooting the .45.

The car that Burton was driving was too far away for the

shotgun to be effective, but spraying birdshot might be helpful if the car got close enough. The car swerved, then regained control, but Billy's plan was working. He smiled, then let out a maniacal laugh that got lost in the thunder of engines, gunshot echoes, and his beating heart.

The shots stopped coming from Burton's car and the Plymouth swerved, then slid in the gravel sideways. Burton was losing control. It was the break Billy needed and to his delight, he saw the Ranger's shotgun tumble to the ground from the driver's side window. That didn't mean Burton was hit, he might have lost his grip on the shotgun. Billy wasn't counting on the shotgun being the only weapon the Ranger had. "Hey, are you all right in there?" Billy yelled to Moses.

Only the wind answered him back.

The truck had straightened out, losing momentum quickly. Billy looked to Burton's car and watched it careen off the road in a cloud of dust. If he was going to make a move, now was the time.

Billy dropped the .45, held onto the shotgun, and made his way to the cab.

Like he feared, Moses was slumped over to the right with blood pouring from a wound in the back of his head. Burton's shot had been dead-on. One out of five did the trick. Moses was dead before he knew what hit him.

Billy reached over the bed, opened the driver's side door, then jumped inside. He nearly lost the shotgun, making it a one on one with Burton. Moses had another .45 in the cab, so at least there was that. He wouldn't be without a gun. It was all he could do to push Moses out of the way, close the door, and regain control of the truck.

He immediately punched the accelerator and rejoined the road. A quick glance to the rearview mirror told him that he was free of Burton. He needed to get down the road as fast as he could and disappear into one of the side lanes. He knew right where he was going. Had found another place after he'd killed the man in Onalaska. Billy knew he'd need another escape route. He couldn't very well leave the Model A hidden in the thickets when people would be out looking for the man. The river escape was null and void, then. He needed another place to gather himself, and pick up another car. They'd be looking for the truck. Every damn cop in Texas would be looking for the truck. Billy saw his marker ahead, looked in the mirror again to make sure Burton hadn't caught him, then turned down a lane that had barely been used over the summer. It was like driving into a tunnel. One Billy could completely disappear into.

He couldn't get Dolly out of his mind. Billy felt hobbled, unable to move, to leave his safe spot, his hidey-hole, next to the river. Anger and fear pulsed through his veins at the same time. He was angry with himself for letting Dolly go off on her own, and it was worse now that he didn't know what had happened to her. There were only two possibilities. Dolly was either dead or in custody. Dead might be better than in custody, the more Billy thought about it. He knew the cops and their tricks, knew they'd put the screws to Dolly to get her to talk. It was hard telling how she would stand up under that kind of pressure. He hated to think it, but the more he thought of her being questioned by the likes of Sonny Burton, the more he really didn't want Dolly to make it out of the river.

Burton, on the other hand, was still alive as far as Billy knew. Because the Plymouth spun out didn't mean that one of Billy's shots had taken the Ranger out. He needed confirmation of that, but the last thing he wanted to do was backtrack and run headlong into a trap. Cops were crawling everywhere. If they weren't, they would be soon.

Billy hadn't got out of the truck. He looked over to Moses,

collapsed in the seat, dead as dead could be. There was no choice but to dump the body, which he did, without remorse or regret. Billy pulled the Negro out of the seat through the passenger door, took the .45, dragged the body to the river, and got back in the truck. The longer he stayed there, the easier it would be for Burton to find him.

If Sonny Burton wasn't dead, then he would stop at nothing to find Billy. Billy knew that like he knew it was dark at night and light during the day. He had a backup plan for Burton in case. Billy was going to put an end to the Ranger once and for all.

Billy knew that Sonny Burton had a weakness now that he'd never had before. A weakness that he'd danced with under the moon.

Night fell on the streets of Huntsville. Sirens waffled in the distance. Clouds covered the moon and stars. The street the boardinghouse sat on didn't garner a whole lot of traffic, especially once the day came to an end and everyone was home from work. Billy sat in a black, 1932 Chevrolet, watching the house, dodging any headlights that lit the interior of the car as they drove by. So far, there'd been no sign of Sonny Burton— which helped, but was not a deal breaker for the plan. Burton would show up sooner or later. Hopefully after the deed was done.

Billy was waiting on the two guards who boarded at the house to leave for their shift. He wanted the woman in the house to be there alone. Other than the dog. He could handle the dog. He had outwitted dogs more than once in his life.

Everything he needed sat next to him in the seat. Moses's .45 chambered and loaded, a knife a little short of a full Bowie, and a fresh steak he'd bought at the butcher shop before they closed. There wasn't a dog alive that could resist a fresh piece of meat like the one sitting next to Billy's leg.

A murmur of voices drew Billy's attention. He had the window rolled down for that purpose.

Two men walked out of the front door of the boardinghouse. He recognized them both, recognized their uniforms. They were prison guards. As far as Billy knew, they were the only two boarders in the house, other than Sonny Burton.

He watched the men walk together, get into a car parked in front of the house, then drive off. Then he waited, watching the house, and keeping a close eye on the rearview mirror.

Satisfied that the woman was in the house alone, Billy made sure the bag of Jeb's money was hidden under a blanket, then left the car, carrying his tools of the trade with him. First thing he had to do was get rid of the dog—which, as it was, turned out to be easier than Billy thought it would be. He trailed meat halfway around the block, then snuck back, unlatched the gate, and made his way into the dark. Again, he waited, but not for long. The dog eased out of the yard, eating one piece of the steak after the other. Once it was out of sight, Billy eased into the yard, closed the gate, and made his way to the back door of the boardinghouse. To his delight, the door was unlocked.

Billy made his way inside the house, stopping at the back door of the porch that led into the kitchen. He could smell food and realized that he was hungry, hadn't eaten a decent meal all day. But that didn't matter now. All he wanted to do was finish the job he'd come to do.

The kitchen was empty. There was no sign of the woman. Billy didn't want to go looking for her. He wanted her in the kitchen. He could have waited, but that added to the risk of getting caught. The dog would have come in handy. A bark would have drawn the woman to him. Something he didn't think all the way through.

Don't get sloppy, Billy, you're almost there, he said to himself.

To his relief, the woman walked into the kitchen. She went to the icebox and opened it, allowing Billy the opportunity to step in from the porch unseen and unheard.

The woman stood back from the icebox, and closed it.

Billy cocked the .45, drawing her attention to him. She was holding a bottle of milk. It slipped from her hands and shattered on the floor, sending white liquid everywhere. The woman's black shoes were wet and white. Her face, paralyzed with fear, looked like a mirror of the floor.

"Don't move an inch," Billy said. "Don't say a word, or scream. If you do, I'll pull the trigger, you understand?"

The woman nodded her head. Her eyes were as wide as the Texas sky and her fingers trembled.

"Good," Billy said, walking over to the woman. He stopped, and put the gun to her temple. "We have some business to take care of."

CHAPTER THIRTY-FIVE

October 1934
Oakhurst, Texas

Sonny lost sight of the truck Billy Bunson was driving. "Damn it, damn it," he yelled as he smacked the steering wheel with his good hand. The thought of Billy slipping out of his grasp one more time was more than Sonny could take. He was angry, frustrated, and left without any kind of plan. That realization made him even angrier. He slammed his body back in the seat, and exhaled loudly. "Damn it," he yelled again.

After closing his eyes for a second, trying to get his bearings, forcing himself to focus, Sonny returned to the steering wheel. If Dolly Rickart was still alive, could talk, then she held the key to what Billy was up to. Dolly would know where he was going to go next.

Sonny put the Plymouth in gear and hightailed it back to the shack. He heard sirens as he sped along the river. Someone had called the police. He could only hope it was Merle Loggard from the Grimes County sheriff's department, come to help out. Bad thing was, the sirens would spook Billy if he was close by. There was no way to get in contact with Loggard to tell him to come in silent.

Sonny arrived back at the shack in Point Blank in a cloud of dust. The black Model A was tire-first in the river. The driver's side door stood open. Dolly Rickart sat on the ground, her knees pulled to her chest, holding her right hand to her head, putting pressure on it with a white towel. The towel was dotted red with blood. It looked more like a pinpoint map than a blood-soaked rag. Jesse stood to the right of Dolly, his .45 in hand, staring at the woman. She didn't look like she was hurt too bad to Sonny.

The sirens grew closer as Sonny got out of the car. He looked over his shoulder. There was nothing to see but open road. "Everything all right?"

"Not really," Jesse said.

Dolly's face was framed in anger. She didn't acknowledge Sonny's presence. Her face was as pale as a piece of chalk.

"How so?" Sonny said.

Jesse cocked his head to the shack. "Jeb's inside."

"Not good, uh?" Sonny interpreted Jesse's downbeat tone and stance quickly.

"Seems Jeb met a quick end once he passed off the drop to Billy. Took a knife to his chest."

Sonny wasn't surprised, but saddened by the news. Still no response from Dolly. She looked catatonic, eyes glazed to the distance, not reacting to anything that was being said at all. "Jeb already had a broken heart. He knew he'd been snookered. He couldn't face it that he was so desperate to fall for such a thin ploy. The promise of a baby tipped him over the rational edge he normally stood on."

Dolly flinched. "You don't know anything about me and Jeb," she said to Sonny, making eye contact with him for the first time.

"I know Jeb was fool enough to love the likes of you," Sonny said. "I'd tell you that you ought to be ashamed of yourself, but that admonishment would fall on deaf ears."

"I have nothing to be ashamed of."

Sonny ignored Dolly, turning his attention back to Jesse. "You sure there's nothing we can do for Jeb?"

"Wait for the pine box is all."

The first police car came into view, rounding the curve at high speed. Another followed it. They were both black and white, locals, not the county sheriff.

"You call them?" Sonny said to Jesse.

"Nope. No phone in the shack. I don't know what that's about." Jesse looked to Dolly. "What about you? You know anything about that?"

"I don't know anything," she answered.

The first car passed by, not slowing a bit. A large plume of dust followed the black and white, and the scream of the siren hurt Sonny's ears. He waited until both cars were past before he said anything. "That's your line, isn't it?"

"What?" Dolly said.

"You don't know anything."

"That's right. Those two men didn't tell me anything."

Jesse stood stiffly and didn't interfere.

Sonny took a few steps closer to Dolly, towering over her with a hard-set jaw and his hand jammed in his pocket. The hook dangled stiffly, only moving when Sonny moved. "Seems a little odd to me that he left you on your own. Don't tell me that you don't have a meet-up spot picked out."

"I don't know anything."

"You can say that for all I care, but I know it's a lie."

Dolly dropped the towel from her head, looked at it, then tossed it aside. "I had nothing to do with this. I was captive. Those two men killed Jeb. I escaped. That's what happened." She sniffled and her eyes grew wet with tears.

"So, this is the way you're going to play it," Sonny said.

"I watched the murder of my husband. I am with child. Can't you see that?"

"Why'd you run?"

Dolly wiped her eyes. "I was trying to get away."

Sonny exhaled and stood back. He looked to Jesse, who wore a blank stare on his face. He didn't indicate one way or the other whether he believed Dolly. "That's quite a story."

"It's the truth."

"And my job is to prove otherwise."

"They said you wouldn't believe me."

"Time will tell," Sonny said. "I'm a patient man. The law's a patient entity, but it will be interesting to see who your baby resembles, Billy Bunson or Jeb Rickart. Nature will bear out your story if you won't. Wait and see."

A look flickered across Dolly's face that Sonny couldn't quite identify. He wasn't sure if it was recognition, fear, or something else, but he was sure he'd hit a nerve, given Dolly something to think about that she hadn't considered. He didn't believe a word she said. She was in on everything . . . including Jeb's murder, as far as he was concerned.

Dolly stiffened, but remained sitting with her knees pulled to her chest. Her pregnancy was nearly hidden. "I knew Billy Bunson in the prison literacy class, and that's all. I'm offended by your implications, sir."

"I imagine you are."

The sirens faded in the distance, then stopped.

Sonny looked over his shoulder. "I wonder what they found?"

Dolly looked away from him, back out to the river.

He turned his attention away from the sudden silence. "Billy Bunson knew how to read long before he showed up in your class, Mrs. Rickart. You know that as well as I do."

"You don't know anything."

"I've known Billy Bunson nearly all of his life, arrested him more times than I care to admit. I think I know a little more about Billy than you think I do."

"He said you'd say that, said you wouldn't believe me, but I can't help that. You're not a judge. You're not even a lawman from what he told me. You're all used up and not a threat to anyone. He said I shouldn't pay you any mind. I'll have my say in court."

"You and Billy sure did talk a lot."

"I've been tied up for days in his company."

"Captive?"

"Of course."

Sonny flexed his left hand, and somewhere deep in his body's memory, his right hand flexed into a fist, too. "You're a liar. A lowlife liar, Mrs. Rickart, and I aim to prove it if it's the last thing I do."

Jesse stepped in between Dolly and Sonny. "That's enough, Pa. I think it's time we take her in and let Sheriff Loggard figure all of this out. This isn't helping at all."

Sonny held Jesse's gaze, and tried his best to regulate his breathing. "All right, but I'd handcuff her if I was you. I'll stay here until the sheriff's people, and the coroner, show up."

"I'll make the call from that market at the crossroads we saw," Jesse said.

"I'd be careful of her. She thinks she's a snake charmer."

Jesse helped Dolly to her feet. "You all right?" he said.

"I'm fine," Dolly said.

Jesse shook his head and walked to his car. Sonny watched him as he went, then looked to Dolly. "You should go sit on the steps and wait."

"There are chairs inside," she said.

"I don't you want you out of my sight, you understand?" He was fully aware that Jeb's body was inside the cabin, but he didn't want to see it, or her to try something. Hard telling if the cabin was booby-trapped in one way or the other. He didn't trust her or Billy.

"If you say so." Dolly made her way to the steps with Sonny close behind her. She sat down like a sullen toddler who had been told no. Sonny offered her no sympathy.

It was just him and her, waiting. There was no sign of anyone, but Sonny thought Billy might double-back to rescue Dolly. He didn't let on to Dolly that he was concerned. He barely said a word to her. He was too busy listening for a stick to crack under a foot; Billy trying to sneak up on him. Every pore of his skin was on alert.

Jesse returned about forty-five minutes later, and it wasn't long before a couple of county police cars and an ambulance swarmed around the cabin. Sheriff Loggard was in the first car, and made his way to Sonny.

"You keep an eye on her," Sonny said to Jesse, then met Loggard halfway. Three deputies and the men from the ambulance trailed after the sheriff and stopped a respectable distance behind, waiting for instructions.

"Jeb's inside?" Loggard asked.

Sonny nodded. "Billy got away."

"That's what Jesse told us. We've got roadblocks on every road leading out of here."

"Good. I think he might be close, might try and rescue her." A glint caught Sonny's eye and he looked to the west as the sun sunk below the horizon.

Loggard looked over to Dolly. "She's in on it, isn't she?"

"Playing dumb. Like she's the victim. I don't trust it."

"Neither do I." Loggard squared his shoulders, and looked to the cabin. "I guess we'd better get on with this."

Sonny nodded. "I'll wait in the car if you don't mind."

"Take her with you."

"All right, but be careful. Billy's a smart one. He might have the place booby-trapped."

"Good thinking. We'll keep an eye out." Loggard, the deputies, and the men from the ambulance made their way into the cabin as Sonny herded Dolly into Jesse's Plymouth. He put her in the back seat, then climbed in the other side.

Once he got settled, she started to say something, but Sonny put his hand up. "Save it for the sheriff. He's going to have a lot of questions for you."

Dolly gritted her teeth and looked out the window as evening fell into night. "How long will that be?"

"As long as it takes the sheriff to do his job, and figure out what you and your boyfriend did here."

"I didn't do anything."

"If you say so."

Dolly didn't say anything else. Silence settled between them, and Sonny watched the sad event—investigating Jeb Rickart's murder—playing out before him. He was glad to be in the car instead of in the thick of things for once. He wasn't sure how much time had passed when Dolly spoke up again, unprovoked, maybe tired of the silence—or her own fears. Sonny wasn't sure which.

"You're a mean, bitter man, Sonny Burton, just like Billy Bunson said you were. You sure don't seem like the kind of man who dances at midnight to me."

The words echoed inside Sonny's head, and he suddenly felt like the earth stopped spinning. Fear and realization ran up his back at the same time as he realized what Dolly had said. *Billy knew about Edith* . . . and there was great potential that she was in danger. That hurting Edith was part of Billy's plan.

He rushed out of the car, and found Jesse. "I have to go. I have to go. You need to get her out of the car, because I need it. I have to get to the boardinghouse I'm staying at. Have the sheriff send me some backup. I can't stay here for another minute. I have to go."

October 1934

Huntsville, Texas

It was late by the time Sonny made it back to Huntsville. Sonny parked a block from Edith's house. If Billy was there, the last thing he wanted to do was skid to the curb, and let him know that he'd been made. The house was in plain sight. There were no lights in the top floor, but the entire bottom floor was lit like a party was about to happen. No cars lined the street in front of the house, causing Sonny to look at his watch. Marcel Pryor and the other boarder who was a prison guard had already left the house for their shift. Sonny worried that Edith was in the house alone. If he was right and Billy did make his way back to Huntsville with the intention of doing Edith harm, then he would have made sure that there wasn't anyone else around. Edith had no idea what she was in store for. She wouldn't suspect a thing if Billy knocked on her door. She would think he was a potential boarder. There was one empty room to let. Billy could easily see himself inside, then unleash his madness upon Edith. She couldn't handle a maniac like Billy. Sonny shivered at the thought.

He grabbed his .45, and exited the car. There was no sign of the backup he'd asked Jesse to send. He was on his own with only darkness as his friend.

The October night was cool like all of the others, but the clouds of recent nights had passed on, allowing the stars to twinkle overhead and the man in the moon to gaze down on him. All things considered, he would have preferred cloud cover, and a little more darkness. Being tall made it difficult to conceal himself, but Sonny lurched forward, finding his way quickly to the shadow that the nearest house offered him.

He could hear the radio on inside, playing, ironically, an episode of *The Lone Ranger*. Sonny liked the serial, but he held no interest in listening to it this evening. He eased alongside of the house, doing his best to not be seen. His aim was to get to the alley in the back, then make his way down to Edith's that way. There was no way to know if Billy had a lookout, or had set a booby trap of some kind. He'd employed both tactics in the past.

Once he was past the house, the sound of the radio diminished until it sounded like static. There were no other sounds to be heard. No owls, no cats fighting, no dogs barking. He could hardly hear any cars. Traffic on the roads had died down with the onset of darkness. Everyone was settling in for a restful night. That thought pushed Sonny faster. Gravel crunched under his feet, and he would have slowed down, but if he knew anything about Billy Bunson, it was what he was capable of. Edith was in danger. Sonny knew it deep in his bones.

He made it to the back of Edith's house. Even though it was chilly outside, his gun hand was warm with sweat. He could see the light shining from the kitchen through the back porch. Sonny eased into the yard, then made his way to the door that led inside. There was no sound coming from inside the house. Nothing looked out of place from where Sonny stood. He hesitated to go inside, especially when he considered the obvious. Normally after a long day, he was greeted happily by Blue—but there was no sign of the dog at all. He wasn't in his bed on the porch, or anywhere to be seen. All Sonny could hope for was that Blue was inside with Edith, and everything was all right, that he wasn't overreacting.

The feeling in his gut told him that it was a false hope.

CHAPTER THIRTY-SIX

October 1934
Huntsville, Texas

Billy stood with the gun pointed at the woman's head. "Is there anyone else here?" he said.

"No," she said. Perspiration beaded on her lip and a tremble ticked her fingers like they were about to separate from her hands on their own.

"Are you expecting anyone?"

"What do you want?" she whispered. "I have food in the larder. A little pin money in the breadbox."

Billy glanced over to the counter next to the stove, eyeing the breadbox. "Good to know."

"Please don't hurt me."

"You didn't answer my question. Are you expecting anyone?"

"No. I don't know. I have three boarders. Two are at work. They left. The other one could return any time."

The woman flinched when she spoke, then looked away for a second. Billy wasn't sure if she was lying or not. It felt like she was, so he wouldn't trust her words or her actions. Anybody could come walking in the boardinghouse door at any time, and Billy knew it. "I know about one of them. The Ranger," he said.

The woman jerked a little bit, and looked him in the eye. "He's not a Ranger."

"Sure he is. Sonny Burton will always be a Ranger. He don't know how to be anything else." Billy hesitated, staring the

309

woman up and down. She would have been a looker in her day. Kind of reminded him of Dolly, plain and innocent on the outside, but suggestive, like there was a tiger lurking in the shadows waiting to be lured out. Too bad he wasn't here for that purpose. Could have been fun. "You like him, don't you?"

"He's a nice man," the woman said.

Billy smirked. " 'A nice man.' You don't know him very well is all. I've seen him do some really bad things."

The woman didn't respond. The look on her face told Billy that she didn't believe him. "So no one's here?" he said.

"No one's here."

"If you're lying, I will kill you."

The woman trembled a little more noticeably. Billy wondered if she was one of them shakers, touched by the fear of the spirit. A group of them had tried to save him once. He stole their pulpit money and ran away as soon as he could.

"What's your name?" Billy said.

"Edith Grantley."

"Where's Mr. Grantley?"

"Dead. He died. I'm here alone, I swear."

"You're sure?"

"Yes. I am absolutely positive."

"Okay, here's what we're going to do, Edith Grantley. You're going to get your pin money, then take me to the rest of the money you keep in the house, and then we're going to leave. If you make one peep that's out of line, try to alert anyone you're in trouble, I'll kill you. You understand me? I'll kill you."

"You're him, aren't you? You're that Billy Bunson? The man who broke out of prison, and took that poor woman with you."

Billy smirked again, only he let the smirk linger this time. His story had worked. Edith believed Dolly was a hostage. The whole town needed to believe that, especially if Dolly had been taken into custody. "He told you about me, didn't he?"

"Who?" Edith said.

"Sonny. Sonny Burton. The Ranger. He likes you, too. I can tell. Something about him has changed. What did he tell you about me?"

"I saw your picture in the newspaper, at the post office. You're famous here. Everybody knows what you look like."

"That's why we have to leave. Me and you. I need a driver. Now, what did Sonny Burton tell you about me?"

"I don't know. I mean I don't remember."

Billy jammed the barrel of the gun harder into Edith's skin. "Don't lie to me."

Edith had to catch her breath. When she spoke, her voice trembled as much as her fingers; every word sounded like a violin in an earthquake. "He said he'd known you since you were a boy. He regretted that he couldn't save you. That's all, really. He didn't say much else. Sonny's not much of a talker. You should know that."

"Don't tell me what I should know. Okay, go on, get your pin money." Billy pushed Edith forward, releasing her.

She stumbled, then made her way to the breadbox, opened it, took out a thin wad of bills, and handed it to Billy. She gasped a little bit when his fingers grazed hers.

Billy took the money, looked at it, flipped through it, then stuffed it into his pocket. "What's the matter?"

"You're young. You have a kind face. Your mother must of loved you."

A hard iciness flashed into Billy's eyes and stayed there. An unexpected rush of anger flowed through his veins. Without any hesitation at all, he raised the gun and aimed it at the woman's head. "You mention my mother again and I will empty the chamber on you, lady. Now, where's the rest of your money? I know you have some rent money here. You look too smart to trust a bank. Go on, we need to get out of here before someone walks in and finds us in a compromising position. You wouldn't like that, would you?"

"No." If Edith was pale before, now she was white as a sheet. "I'm sorry," she whispered. "There's a piano in the parlor. I keep the rent money there."

"Lead the way." Billy directed her with the swoop of the weapon, then followed after her as she made her way out of the kitchen.

The house was quiet with the exception of the tick of a mantel clock somewhere. The drip of a faucet joined the lonely orchestra of the empty house. The floors creaked under each of Billy's steps. Normally, he would have been concerned that the sounds would alert someone, but his only concern was Sonny Burton coming back to the house unexpectedly, or a potential boarder ringing the bell. There were situations that couldn't be controlled—and he knew he had been inside too long the way it was.

Billy figured Sonny had his hands full with the investigation. He was counting on the cops finding Moses's body, and the other man thrown into the river, by now. The fact that Dolly was either in custody, hurt, or dead, was never far from his mind. All that mattered to him was executing the plan to get some money and some insurance, in the form of Edith Grantley, and getting on the road. He never wanted out of a town so much. He hated Huntsville. It was a prison town, a reminder that he had to look over his shoulder to stay free.

There was also payback to consider, too. Once Sonny Burton figured out that Edith was gone, Billy was certain that would send the old man over the edge—taking away any advantage Sonny might have. It's hard to think straight when your heart is more concerned about a woman than your head is.

Edith stopped inside the parlor and turned on the overhead light. She made her way to the piano bench, opened it, and pulled out a small gray metal box. Billy didn't take his eyes off of her, but kept his ears open.

"There's not much here," Edith said, as she opened the box, and dug out another wad of bills. This one was a little larger than the pin money wad, neatly bound by a rubber band. "Fifty-seven dollars to be exact."

Billy walked to Edith, took the money with his left hand—the .45 remained in his right—and said, "That'll get us down the road a piece. Now, let's go. I know you have a car parked out back."

"I can't leave the house empty. I can't leave it like that."

Billy stuffed the money in his pocket, and aimed the gun at Edith's head again. "What do I have to do to convince you that I am serious? You have no choice, lady. Let's go." He flicked the gun toward the door as he turned sideways, motioning to her to usher them out of the room.

Edith headed for the door. Her fingers still quaked, and she looked like she was going to throw up.

As they entered the entryway between the parlor and the kitchen, the front door swung open and a short, portly man wearing a wrinkled tan overcoat and tatty black fedora pushed his way inside. He was struggling with a large Samsonite suitcase. His head was down, focused on the load, perspiration obvious on his cheeks, totally entranced with getting the heavy suitcase inside the house.

Billy and Edith stopped dead in their tracks. Billy had enough time to stash the .45 behind his back before the man looked back at him.

"Oh," he said, "Mrs. Grantley. I'm sorry to barge in so late and make so much noise. I picked up a new parcel of lightning rods from the bus depot. Business has been brisk, I tell you. Brisk." He stood then, and let go of the suitcase handle since it was completely inside the doorframe. He wore thick glasses, and his eyes looked like bulging carp eyes. It was a wonder he could see two feet in front of him. "You must be a new boarder," he said to Billy.

Billy stared at the little man, then to Edith. "I thought you said there were only three boarders in the house."

Edith stiffened. Panic held in her jaw like a curtain dropped from the ceiling. "This is Mr. Flynn. Walter Flynn. He's a lightning rod salesman. Comes and goes for weeks at a time. I never know when he's going to be here. No offense, Mr. Flynn, but sometimes I forget that he keeps a residence in the house." Her voice warbled like a nervous redstart.

Mr. Flynn stepped forward and extended his hand to Billy. "That's me, Walter P. Flynn, lightning rod sales extraordinaire. I've been the top salesman for the Warren & Warren Lightning Rod Company for the last three years running. Of course, I've got the best territory in the country, from here to central Oklahoma. Lord knows there's plenty of thunderstorms in these parts to keep ten salesmen busy. I'm a lucky man, I tell you, a lucky man." Mr. Flynn looked at Billy, then to his extended hand, which Billy didn't look too interested in taking hold of.

"Anybody ever told you that you have bad timing, Mr. Flynn?" Billy said, staring at the man as coldly as he could.

"Oh, I've been told that a million times. I sure have. Thing about that is you can't take it personal is all. You gotta pick up your case and waltz on down to the next farm. Won't be long before you encounter a bare roof and a heart inside that knows of someone who watched their own house burn down to the ground because of a lightning strike. It's a numbers game, I tell you. You can't give up, that's all. You can't ever take no for an answer."

Billy stared at the man, a little perplexed, but more annoyed than anything else. His presence complicated things, put a wringer in his plan. He didn't like it when that happened.

314

"You have bad timing right now. I'm not buyin' what you're sellin'," Billy said. He pulled the .45 from behind his back in a swift motion, and didn't think about what to do next. The gun leveled out with the barrel aimed straight at Mr. Flynn's forehead.

Edith shivered.

Mr. Flynn gasped at the sight of the gun, and started to say something, started to protest, started to back up to the door, but it was too late.

Billy pulled the trigger.

CHAPTER THIRTY-SEVEN

October 1934

Huntsville, Texas

The gunshot echoed through the house, garnering Sonny's immediate attention. He froze at the back door, making sure he was positive about what he had heard. A woman's scream, distant, from inside followed, touching Sonny's ears before the gunshot faded away. Then silence followed. No more screams. No hurrying footsteps. Nothing.

Fear and the age-old instinct to run into a dire situation propelled Sonny inside the house. He wasn't concerned about making noise, about announcing his presence. His only concern was Edith's safety. He had his trusted Single Action Army Colt barrel-up, and his finger sat ready on the trigger. He had practiced shooting left-handed for hours, but the truth was, he hadn't found himself in a position where his aim and ability mattered as much as it did at that moment.

The kitchen was empty. Sonny quickly made his way to the far wall, hugging the shadows the best he could. He heard a scuffle of footsteps as he reached safety. He didn't hesitate to peer into the entryway.

Billy restrained Edith from behind, his left hand over her mouth, his right hand with a .45 to her head; all the while he pushed her toward the door. A short man lay dead on the floor. Blood ran from his head at a steady pace. The only consolation for the poor sap was that death had come quick to him.

Billy had his back to the kitchen, had left himself vulnerable from behind. If he were alone, without a hold on Edith, Sonny would have shot him then and there—in the back, no question, no worry about the repercussions. Billy Bunson needed put down like the wild, rabid animal that he was.

Sonny stepped into the doorway, and hollered, "Stop right there, Billy. You move another inch and I'll make Swiss cheese out of your back."

Billy froze in place, but he didn't let go of Edith. Neither of them could see Sonny unless they turned around. They were about three feet from exiting out the front door. "Sonny Burton, why am I not surprised. It's good to hear your voice, old friend."

"That's stretching things, isn't it, Billy? We were never friends."

"If you say so."

"Here's what I say, Billy. First thing you need to do is remove the barrel of that gun from that poor woman's head. Slowly. Very slowly."

"And what if I don't?"

"Then you'll give me no choice but to shoot you, right here and now."

Billy laughed. It was a little boy's laugh, mocking, direct, one that didn't hold an ounce of belief in what Sonny said. "Okay, shoot me. The bullets go through me and takes your lady here out of the game. Or the first rustle of your metal hook I hear, I pull the trigger and blow the back of her head off, you understand? Either way, she goes with me, and you're left here all alone. One more time. Every time I see you, you're alone. Why is that, Burton? You make a lot more noise than you used to. I guess I should thank Bonnie Parker for that."

"You're slipping, Billy. You didn't hear me come up behind you."

"Maybe I did. Maybe I know you won't shoot me."

"There's a dead man at your feet, and you're holding a woman hostage, Billy, and that's for starters. I've got plenty of cause to shoot you and be done with this spree of yours once and for all."

"You think I can be reformed, don't you? That I should be locked up for the rest of my life."

"You're wrong. I think you'll figure out how to get out of any prison you get put in. You're a danger to society. You can con any man in any situation to get what you want. I think you and Old Sparky will have a date in the future, is what I think," Sonny said. "And I'll be happy to pull the switch. It's the only way I'll believe the world is rid of you."

Billy twisted his lip in hate. Sonny hit a nerve. "And what do you think that is, Burton? What do you think I want?"

"Same as the rest of us, to do anything you want to."

"That's pretty good. I'm surprised at your answer." Billy hadn't moved, and neither had Edith. Both of them acted like a deer caught in the headlights. Edith was terrified. Billy looked like he was frozen, waiting for the chance to break out of conversation and go in another rampage. Blood and rage had found a welcoming home on his face once he let the hate fade away.

"Bad thing is, Billy," Sonny said, "you never had no one teach you restraint. That's not your fault. Not really. You never stayed in one place long enough to get any dirt under your fingernails or roots attached to your toes. No one taught you right from wrong."

"A boy has to eat."

"I don't disagree with that."

"But you believe in justice. That I should face justice for all the bad things you think I've done. That's what you said. Old Sparky should have his way with me. Who are you to say what's bad? Have you ever killed a man, Burton? You don't have to answer me because I know the answer. Of course, you have. You went to war, you've been a lawman for a lot of years. I know what lawmen do. They hang innocent men because of the color of their skin, then cover them in tar, and set them on fire. You didn't do that, but you might as well have. You set those men free when you should have locked them up. If my family would have been uppity white folks, you would have. But we was whores and thieves. We weren't worth your protection. I blamed you for Jim Rome's death. I want you to know that. Anything I've done since has been in his name, to pay you back, to pay all of you back for taking him and my family away from me. They weren't much, but they were all I had. Now, you've gone and done it again."

Sonny mumbled something garbled. He hadn't thought about the dead Negro in Vinton in a long time. He'd considered that man's murder one of his great failures. Billy was right. He could have stopped it from happening, but he didn't. Like he hadn't stopped Billy all these years. Doubt started to erode his confidence when he needed it the most. That was the problem with someone like Billy, with knowing someone for so long. They know how to get under your skin.

"You let the idea of justice keep you awake at night," Billy continued. "That's the difference between you and me. I do what I have to do to survive."

"To stay free," Sonny said. "That's what you want more than anything. If you don't let her go, Billy, I'm going to have to kill you, you know that, don't you? There's no freedom in death."

"It's now or later, is that what you're saying?"

"We all have to die, Billy, and we all have to face justice no matter who we are," Sonny said. "There's no escaping it. Now, do as I told you. Remove the barrel from the woman's head slowly, then place the gun on the floor gently, and slide it to me. You've got five seconds. Then I pull the trigger." There was no hesitation or quiver in Sonny's voice. He was serious, rigid, ready to follow through with what he'd said. Billy Bunson wasn't getting away this time. Nothing mattered now other than that. This was the end of the road. Billy Bunson's last chance.

Surprisingly, Billy did exactly what Sonny told him to. No more digs, no more words, only the simple action Sonny had laid out. With Billy crouched down, with the gun on the floor, Sonny wanted to tell Edith to run, but he didn't. She was still too close to Billy. He could grab her, and there was the possibility that Billy had at least one more weapon on him. Sonny was betting on one, at least two guns in his possession.

Billy slid the .45 to Sonny with surprising accuracy. It came to a stop at the toe of his right boot. Then, Billy stood, facing Sonny for the first time. "Don't you even think about going out that door, lady," he said to Edith, all the while staring into Sonny's eyes.

Edith stood as still as humanly possible, focused forward. She hadn't said a word, hadn't indicated any recognition of Sonny's presence at all.

"Now what, Burton?" Billy said.

"You got a gun in your boot? A knife strapped to your calf? Remove 'em. Do the same thing you did with the .45."

"What if I tell you that I don't have anything else on me?"

"I'm not going to believe you. You move a muscle this way, and I'll do what I have to do."

"I don't have anything else on me." Billy's stare was ice cold.

"Take off your boots, then your pants."

"In front of a lady?"

"She can leave the room."

"I don't like that idea."

"Why's that?" Sonny said.

"You know why."

"I do. Now, do what I told you. Edith, I want you to walk forward slowly, then I want you to go over, pick up the phone, and have the operator call the police. You hear me?"

Edith didn't move. "The phone line's been cut," she said.

"I should have figured," Sonny said.

Billy smirked again. "Looks like a Mexican standoff, huh, Burton. What are you going to do now? You're on your own. Me and you. You got a plan? I don't think you do."

Sonny knew Billy was right, but he didn't say so, didn't imply that anything he'd said mattered. "You weren't expecting to see me, were you, Billy?"

"Seriously? Why do you think I'm here? I knew you'd come here, riding high, ready to save this damsel in distress. Where's your white hat?"

"I gave it up."

"That's a shame."

Sonny felt like he'd been had. He had no choice but to pull the trigger. But when he did, he dropped the barrel down to the right. The bullet grazed Billy's arm.

The smell of gunpowder invaded the entryway. Unfortunately, it was a smell that Sonny knew all too well. He'd never liked to fire a gun. And, he'd broken a cardinal rule: Never aim a gun at a man unless you intend to kill him. He didn't want to kill Billy. If killing were easy for him, Billy would have been dead a long time ago.

Billy grabbed his arm and spun around, knocking himself into Edith. She was surprised, sent stumbling forward. She banged into the door face-first, and stood stunned as a bird that had flown into a window. A yelp escaped her lips and terror stuck in her eyes—but she wasn't seriously hurt.

It looked like Billy was going to fall to the floor, but, somehow, he managed to stay on his feet. Then he bounced up and down on his feet like he'd walked barefoot through a raging fire. "Sonofabitch, Burton, what the hell are you trying to do?" He pulled his hand off the wound and looked at it. The shirt he was wearing had a thin screeching bullet-inflicted tear that immediately turned bright red with rushing blood.

"You're not going to die, Billy. I'm trying to get your attention and prove to you that my left-handed aim is as good as it has ever been. Are you okay, Edith?"

Before she could utter a word, Billy spun around again. His quick movement caught Sonny by surprise. Billy grabbed Edith again, got her from behind, and produced a knife from somewhere and pressed it across Edith's throat.

Edith faced Sonny with a look of terror plastered across her pale white face. Billy wore a smile on his. He looked like a child who had one-upped a smarter grown-up. "Now, you drop your gun, Burton." To prove he was serious, he pressed the knife a little harder on Edith's throat, drawing a thin drip of blood.

Billy's head was situated directly behind Edith's, disallowing a kill shot. He sighed.

"Are you going to make me prove my aim is true, too, Burton? Do you want to watch your lady die?" Billy said.

"No," Sonny whispered. He had no choice but to lay the gun on the floor, like Billy had said.

"Now," Billy said, "kick it to me. Then we'll be on our way."

Sonny didn't hesitate. But he didn't kick the gun to Billy. He kicked it to the left, where it went flying, and disappeared into the parlor, out of reach, out of sight.

Billy had shifted his weight, had anticipated Sonny doing what he was told to do. The disappearing gun drew Billy's attention away from Sonny, like he had intended. The knife dropped away from Edith's throat, giving her enough room to wither to the floor in a faint. Poor woman couldn't take it anymore. Her timing was perfect. Between the fall and the distraction, Sonny had a split second to react, to attack. He didn't have any hidden weapons; he had a hook attached to the prosthesis, and it was all that he needed.

Billy turned his attention back to Sonny; a look of surprise, maybe shock, fell across his face as the old man rushed him.

Billy gripped the knife, reaching back like he was going to throw it, but he didn't have time. Sonny had done the same thing, raised his right arm into the air, by forcing it upward with his left hand.

Billy's eyes were drawn to the hook. Realization registered on his face. He had overlooked the obvious weapon that Sonny carried with him, had miscalculated its use.

Sonny skirted the body of the dead man, came within striking range, and swung the hook down across Billy's wrist, sending the knife flying to the ground. Metal slammed against metal. A thunderclap of sharpness clanged inside the entryway. But Sonny wasn't done. His blood was racing though his veins faster than it ever had. Sweat ran down the back of his neck. His lungs were full of air while the rest of his body was numb. He knew what he had to do. He knew that if Billy Bunson had the chance, he would either run, or kill Sonny and Edith. That wasn't going to happen.

Sonny's bold act had disarmed Billy's confidence long enough for Sonny to readjust the hook. They both spun around in a dance of death; an old lion facing down a young interloper for the sake of the pride. It was a fight for life, with each man readying the next parcel of attack.

Sonny didn't hesitate. He swung the hook with all of his might, sending the sharp edge directly into Billy's chest. The aim was for the heart. And by the sound of Billy's gasp, by the suddenness of his weakness, Sonny was almost certain that he had hit his target directly.

Blood spurted from Billy's chest, but his rage, anger, and fear propelled him forward. He took a swing at Sonny, catching the man's jaw with his fist.

The force of the hit caused Sonny to stumble backwards, pulling the hook out of Billy's chest as he went. He fell over Edith, went sprawling across the floor.

Billy still stood over them all. The dead man. Edith. Sonny. His eyes searched the room while the color drained from his face. He coughed and blood erupted from his mouth. He put his hand over his mouth, then pulled it away, examining the bright red as it fell to his side. Billy's knees buckled, then, and he fell face-first to the floor.

Sonny scampered to his feet and hurried to Billy's side. There was no saving him. That's not what Sonny wanted to do. "Go on, now," he said, leaning down. "Go be free. You're not alone, boy. I won't leave until you're gone. There won't be any more pain, no resentment, no reason to hate. Go on, now, be free of all of that."

Billy's eyes were wide open, focused on Sonny. He took a last gasp, then turned his head away, and died.

To Sonny's surprise, a tear escaped his eye. He'd felt sorry for the boy, had always wished Billy Bunson would come to a good end instead of a bad one. But that didn't happen. Sonny had hoped that he wouldn't be the one who killed the boy.

He hoped the nightmare was over.

CHAPTER THIRTY-EIGHT

November 1934

Huntsville, Texas

Sonny's truck sat in front of the boardinghouse with his suitcase strapped into the bed, and Blue settled in the front seat. Edith stood at the end of the walk, a bandage on her throat, and a look of concern on her face. A strong autumn wind was determined to blow the last remaining leaves off the surrounding trees, and the gray skies were growing darker in the west, threatening rain and even more wind. Edith stood stiffly with her hands at her sides, pinning down her dress from blowing upward.

Sonny and Jesse stood face to face next to the driver's door of the truck, one the reflection of the other in an odd way. They looked different from each other, with Jesse favoring his mother, but their attitudes were similar. Too similar sometimes.

"I don't think it's a good thing for you to be driving off to Wellington on your own, Pa," Jesse said.

"I can't stay here forever," Sonny answered. "I need to get back home."

"To do what?"

"To live, I 'spect."

"Seems to me that there's someone here who wouldn't mind you staying." Jesse flicked his head toward Edith.

"That will work itself out in time," Sonny said. "Besides, I'll be back for Dolly's trial."

"That won't be too much longer," Jesse said.

"I've been here long enough. I've nearly forgotten what my days are supposed to be like."

"Maybe that's a good thing. The work seemed to agree with you. Maybe Jonesy could take you on as a deputy."

"It wasn't the work that I was here for. No, I think you're a man more suited in age for this kind of thing than I am. Me and Blue need to sit on the porch and watch the world go by for a little while."

"Well," Jesse said, "You won't have to worry about Billy Bunson anymore."

"You're right about that."

"You don't seem to be happy about that. By the way, what happened to the ransom money?"

"It's the bank's to decide, or Jeb's estate, but I sure hope Dolly doesn't get a cent of it."

"That'll end that," Jesse said.

"Killing a man is never easy, Jesse. Billy was a gifted boy. He had a mechanic's mind and charisma that shone like the sun. Somehow, life decided that he didn't deserve the rightful things that most of us had, like a father and mother who loved us, saw to it that we were educated, and knew right from wrong. Billy got cheated. He could have been a king at anything he set his mind to."

"The world's better off without him."

"You didn't have to look him in the eye when he died."

"I didn't." Jesse looked over his shoulder to Edith, then to the clouds. A gust of wind nearly knocked his hat off his head, and he had to put his hand atop it to keep it settled on his head.

"That white hat looks good on you, Jesse. I was proud to ride along with another Ranger."

"Me, too." A smile washed across Jesse's face. "I best let you say goodbye so you can outrun the storm."

"Storms have a way of catching up with me."

Jesse stuck his hand out for a shake. Sonny looked at it, offered his, then pulled Jesse in for a hug, when he took it. "I'm proud of you, boy. I mean it."

"Thanks, Pa," Jesse said as he released him from the hug. "You be careful on your way home."

Sonny watched Jesse walk to his car, then turned his attention to Edith as she made her way to him.

"So, this is it?" she said.

"Yes. Jesse tried to talk me into staying."

"And you can't."

"No, I don't think so. I need to go home for a little while. But I'll be back." Sonny was staring straight into Edith's eyes, and her into his. "I hope you'll be here."

Edith sighed. "I'm not going anywhere. It'll be hard knowing Mr. Flynn died in the house for no reason, and the memory of all that happened will haunt me for the rest of my life. But you saved me, Sonny Burton. I'll never forget that. When you come back, I'll be right here waiting on you."

"I hope so." Sonny said, stepping in to embrace Edith. They kissed as the gray clouds and heavy wind swirled around them. A small tornado of red, crispy leaves whipped up and down the street, causing Sonny to pull away, and consider the weather. "I won't be gone long."

"Okay," Edith whispered. "Okay."

Sonny tipped his hat, then turned, and headed for the truck. He hesitated for a second before opening the door. He looked at the sky, then to Edith, and reconsidered his plans. But only for a second. He knew if he didn't leave now, he never would, and he wasn't sure if that was the right thing to do or not.

He climbed in the truck, orchestrated his prosthesis to start the Model A, put it in gear, and pulled away from the curb slowly. Blue hung his head out the window, looking back, as if to say goodbye, too, then settled back inside for the long ride home.

ABOUT THE AUTHOR

Larry D. Sweazy is a multiple-award author of fourteen western and mystery novels, and over eighty nonfiction articles and short stories. He is also a freelance indexer and has written indexes for over nine hundred and fifty books in twenty years. Larry lives in Indiana with his wife, Rose, where he is hard at work on his next novel. More information can be found at www.larrydsweazy.com.

The employees of Five Star Publishing hope you have enjoyed this book.

Our Five Star novels explore little-known chapters from America's history, stories told from unique perspectives that will entertain a broad range of readers.

Other Five Star books are available at your local library, bookstore, all major book distributors, and directly from Five Star/Gale.

Connect with Five Star Publishing

Visit us on Facebook:
https://www.facebook.com/FiveStarCengage

Email:
FiveStar@cengage.com

For information about titles and placing orders:
(800) 223-1244
gale.orders@cengage.com

To share your comments, write to us:
Five Star Publishing
Attn: Publisher
10 Water St., Suite 310
Waterville, ME 04901